Starseeker

Starseeker is a thriller with a big heart and a real glimpse of the human soul, full of plot and passion, music and mystery. It's very rare to find a book that moves the heart, touches the spirit and yet remains so well grounded in everyday life. It'll stick to your fingers, this one—don't miss it.' *Melvin Burgess*

'A lovely, sure-footed novel. Bowler . . . is lyrical and emotionally charged—on full throttle, revving up our sense of what it is like to be a young person in the world today.' *Observer*

'One of the truly individual voices in British teenage fiction.' *Independent*

'An intensely moving and powerful story.' *Mail on Sunday*

'Compelling and suspenseful.' *Sunday Times*

'A tremendously moving novel from this Carnegie Medal winner.' *Financial Times*

'Powerful and mysterious . . . a sensitive, self-affirming novel. This is Tim Bowler's best book yet.' *Wendy Cooling*

'Absolutely magnificent, one of the best books I've read this year.' *Angie Simpson, Children's Core-Stock Coordinator, Waterstones*

'A thundering read, full of challenging ideas, strong emotions and layers of plotting. Bowler is a fearless writer with complex, demanding ideas . . . utterly compelling.' *Lindsey Fraser, Guardian*

'A fantastic book.' *Sunday Express*

'A memorable book. Tim Bowler's best yet.' *David Almond*

Starseeker

Other books by Tim Bowler

Midget
Dragon's Rock
River Boy
Shadows
Storm Catchers

Starseeker

Tim Bowler

OXFORD
UNIVERSITY PRESS

OXFORD
UNIVERSITY PRESS

Great Clarendon Street, Oxford OX2 6DP

Oxford University Press is a department of the University of Oxford.
It furthers the University's objective of excellence in research, scholarship,
and education by publishing worldwide in

Oxford New York
Auckland Bangkok Buenos Aires
Cape Town Chennai Dar es Salaam Delhi Hong Kong Istanbul
Karachi Kolkata Kuala Lumpur Madrid Melbourne Mexico City Mumbai
Nairobi São Paulo Shanghai Taipei Tokyo Toronto

Oxford is a registered trade mark of Oxford University Press
in the UK and in certain other countries

British Library Cataloguing in Publication Data available

ISBN 0 19 275305 3

7 9 10 8

Typeset by AFS Image Setters Ltd, Glasgow

Printed in Great Britain by
Cox & Wyman Ltd, Reading, Berkshire

To the Memory of Nan

'The universe is composed not of matter but of music'

Dr Donald Hatch

1

He didn't see her; but he heard her voice. It came whispering on the dusk like a dark, dreamy echo: a young girl's voice, so light it was like hearing the voice of a spirit in the trees of Buckland Forest behind him; yet it was coming from the direction of The Grange. He stared at the old house and listened again; then realized with a start that it was the sound of weeping.

He looked at the others. Skin and Daz were still staring over the wall towards the house. Speed was slumped on the ground, eating a doughnut, his fat stubby fingers covered in sugar and jam; but he looked up. 'Luke? You OK? You look kind of funny.'

'I'm fine.'

It was obvious none of the other boys had heard the voice. Speed had turned straight back to his doughnut and the other two hadn't even glanced round. Their eyes were fixed, as they had been for the last hour, on the front door of the house, Daz's ferrety features twitching but Skin's dangerously still and his face as fierce as fire. Luke hesitated, then spoke again.

'Can anybody hear anything?'

'Speedy burping,' said Daz, not looking round. 'But that's nothing new.'

Luke frowned. The girl's voice seemed so clear now. Why couldn't the others hear it? He inched closer to the wall and peered over. Before him the garden of The Grange stretched away with its great untended lawn and flowerbeds and broken-down sheds, and beyond that, over

1

to the left, the house itself, tall and gaunt in the failing light.

'Any sign of Mrs Little?' called Speed from below the wall.

'Not yet,' said Skin.

'Maybe she won't come out tonight.'

'She will.'

'You can't be certain she's going to come out. I mean, she hardly ever leaves the place.' Speed took another bite from the doughnut. Skin flashed an angry glance at him, then turned back to the house.

'She'll come.' He narrowed his eyes to slits. 'She always goes to the village shop on Friday evenings and she'll do the same tonight. Just watch.'

'Well, she'll have to hurry up,' said Speed. 'Or it'll be closed.'

'It's late-night opening. She's got time.' Skin stiffened suddenly. 'There she is. Keep still and get ready to duck if she looks this way.'

Luke held himself rigid and watched as Mrs Little emerged from the house with her shopping bags, closed the front door behind her and made her way towards the gate. Daz shook his head. 'That is one seriously ugly old woman.'

It was true. She had to be the most repulsive-looking woman Luke had ever seen. She was certainly the most unpopular person in Upper Dinton. It was hard to believe there could ever have been a Mr Little, not that anyone in the village knew anything about him. They didn't know much about her either, except that she'd lived at The Grange for about two years, all by herself, and that if anyone came near the house, she snapped at them and told them to get lost. It was as though she hated everybody in the world, especially fourteen-year-old louts, as she clearly saw them.

2

But now it was payback time. Now they were going to get their own back for the times she'd mouthed them off. Because Mrs Little was rich. No one knew exactly how rich but it was obvious she was loaded. The Grange was the most expensive property in Upper Dinton, a beautiful old house, set apart from the rest of the village and with a great walled garden stretching right up to the edge of Buckland Forest—you had to have plenty of money to buy a place like this. But it wasn't money Skin was after.

It was the box. Money would do, too, of course, if there was some lying around, but what Skin wanted—to the point of obsession—was the box he'd seen the old woman holding that time he peered through the window to check the place out. There had to be something really valuable inside it, jewels probably. Not that he'd seen any; but that didn't matter. Whatever was inside, it was worth going for. The way she'd cradled the box and looked about her as she checked the contents, like a miser guarding her hoard—even if it wasn't jewels inside, it had to be something pretty important to Mrs Little, so it was worth nicking for that reason alone.

'She's going,' murmured Daz.

Luke watched the old woman's figure disappear up the track towards Nut Bush Lane, then turn down it in the direction of the village. He felt Skin's eyes upon him.

'Right, Luke. Over to you.'

'I don't know if I want to do this any more.'

'Sure you do.' Skin looked him over. 'We've been through this. You want to be part of the gang. And we want you to be part of the gang. But we need to know we can trust you. We need to know you've got the bottle.' His eyes hardened. 'Because if you haven't, we don't want you and you can clear off back to your piano playing and your music lessons.'

3

Luke looked back at the house and again heard the sound of weeping. Skin's voice came darkly back. 'You're either for us or against us, Luke. And you don't want to be against us. If you get my meaning.'

Luke stared into Skin's eyes and it was like looking at two black flames. Close by, he sensed Daz and Speed watching his face. He bit his lip and tried to shut the weeping from his mind.

'OK,' he said.

'Good boy,' said Skin.

They scrambled down to the track and ran along beside the wall as far as the gate. Skin stopped suddenly and glanced quickly round. All calmness was gone now; his face was as keen as a hunting dog's. From the forest end of the track came the sound of horses' hooves.

'Quick!' he said. 'Round the side of the house!'

They climbed over the gate, sped round the building to the back, and waited, pressed against the wall. The sound of the hooves grew louder as they approached the house. Luke peeped round the side of the wall.

'Who is it?' whispered Skin.

'Miranda Davis and her dad,' he said, watching the two riders disappear from view in the direction of Nut Bush Lane.

Speed chortled. 'Luke's girlfriend.'

'She's not my girlfriend,' said Luke.

'Oh, yeah? I've seen you two yakking at school.'

'Shut up!' said Skin. 'We've got things to do.'

He led them further round the back of The Grange and stopped on the lawn. The house now looked sleepy in the half-light; the curtains were drawn across, both upstairs and down, and there were no lights on that Luke could see. Skin pointed to the nearest window on the ground floor. 'That's the sitting room. That's where she was when I saw her with the box. Only I was looking in from the

4

other side. I managed to climb up the wall by the track and see over.'

'Maybe that's where the box is now,' said Daz. 'In the sitting room.'

'Doubt it. She'd keep it somewhere out of sight if it's really valuable. But we can check the room out. See if you can find a gap in the curtain to look through.'

Daz ran over, found one at once and put an eye to it.

'Bit of a weird place,' he said. 'Full of funny ornaments and stuff.' He went on peering through the gap. 'And it's really dusty in there. She doesn't do a lot of cleaning.' He gave a snigger. 'At least Luke'll feel at home. It's got a grand piano. He can play us some classical music while we're looking round.'

Luke ignored the sneer.

'Any sign of the box?' said Skin.

'No,' said Daz.

'Let me try.' Skin walked up to the window, squinted through the gap for a few moments, then spoke again. 'No, can't see it either. Doesn't matter. We'll have a better look round once we're inside.' He straightened up and turned. 'Right, it's time for Luke Stanton to deliver.'

Luke felt all eyes fix upon him. Skin walked up and put an arm round his shoulder. 'Come with me, Lucky Luke. I'll show you something me and Daz spotted from behind the wall while Speedy was gobbling his doughnut and you were staring into space.' He led them further round the back of the house and pointed upwards. 'There.'

Luke followed the boy's eyes, half-expecting to see a weeping girl, but instead he saw a drainpipe running up the wall, and two open windows, one a skylight in the roof, the other a window on the first floor below it.

'Now we've made it easy for you,' said Skin. 'Since it's your first job. And you've got to admit it's a doddle. She's even left you a nice metal drainpipe.'

Luke put a hand out and tested it. It seemed firm enough and Skin was right: it wasn't a difficult climb. Even the others could probably manage it, apart from Speed, obviously. But Luke knew well enough that this evening was not about testing the others; it was about testing him; and, of course, getting the box. Skin nodded towards the drainpipe. 'Off you go, then.'

Luke hesitated, looking from face to face. Skin took a step closer. The flames in his eyes now seemed darker, deeper, hotter; yet his voice was as cool as a knife. 'I said off you go, Luke. We're counting on you. We need you. You can climb better than any of us. Better than anybody I know. Do this one right and there'll be other jobs. Nice easy jobs, just like this one. No danger, no fuss. Stick with us and we'll all benefit. You wanted to join the gang and have a go at Mrs Little—here's your chance. So get going. And remember what I told you—don't hang about once you're in. Just let us through the front door and we'll do the rest.'

Luke ran his hand over the drainpipe, feeling more and more reluctant to get involved; yet he knew he had gone too far now to draw back from this; and refusal would bring terrible consequences. Everyone knew what Skin could do. He started to climb. It was a relief to leave the others below, yet somehow he felt more frightened than ever now. What would he find inside this spooky old house? He reached the level of the first-floor window and stopped for a moment, clinging to the drainpipe. From below came a scent of honeysuckle; from above, once again, the sound of weeping. And it seemed more desperate, more urgent than ever.

Who was this girl? And where was she? And why was she crying? He went on clinging to the drainpipe, trying to think and at the same time fight his old familiar doubts. What if this weeping were just his imagination? He knew his hearing was acute, much more so than most people's, and that he heard things long before others did, but he also knew that he heard sounds that no one else seemed able to hear at all; so much so that he was starting to suspect that they were just part of his imagination. And maybe this weeping girl was his imagination, too. Whatever the truth, he knew he had to go through with the break-in. The retribution Skin would exact for failure would be worse than anything a weeping girl—real or imaginary—could do to him. As if to prompt him, Skin called out from below. 'Go on, Luke! Get a move on! Even Speed could have got in by now!'

Luke glanced back at the window. It was a little further from the pipe than it had seemed from below but he should just be able to make it. He stretched out his left foot and positioned it on the window ledge, then caught hold of the frame and pulled himself across so that he was crouched on the ledge, square-on to the window. Through the opening he could see a small study with a writing desk and a swivel chair, and shelves covered with grotesque figurines that seemed to shriek at him as he peered in. Again he heard Skin's voice, now spitting with impatience.

'Get a move on! We're wasting time! Go down and let us in!'

He pulled himself into the room, glad to be out of sight of the others, but uneasy now that he was inside the house. The sound of weeping was louder than ever and it seemed to be coming from somewhere above him. He tiptoed to the door of the room and put his head round. A broad, unlit landing ran either side of him. To the left were three closed doors and one—half-open—at the end; to the right was a stairway down to the hall and, just beyond, at the other end, a small closed door raised slightly in the wall. Again he saw shelves bedecked with strange statuettes:

7

figures dancing, figures playing musical instruments, figures pulling faces. He frowned. Best just to run downstairs, open the front door and get the thing over with. Let Skin find his box. As for the weeping—it didn't exist; it couldn't exist. No one else had heard it so it was just his imagination playing tricks, like all the other noises he'd heard—or thought he'd heard—over the years, especially since Dad died.

He ran to the top of the stairs and started to hurry down. A loud sob, somewhere above him, froze him to the spot. He stood there, trembling, and listened. It's not real, he told himself. It's just imagination. Mrs Little lives alone. Everyone knows that. She hates people. There's no one here. He heard another sob above him, so loud this time it was almost a scream. He looked up to where the sound seemed to have come from and tried to picture the outside of the building and what was up there.

The open skylight. It had to be that. The Grange must have some kind of attic room. His eye fell on the little raised door at the far end of the landing and he stared at it, trying to find a reason not to go and inspect it; but he knew he had to. Breathing hard, he climbed back to the landing, walked over to the door and pulled it open. Before him was a narrow flight of steps twisting upwards. He stared at them, his mind a confusion of voices: voices shrieking at him to turn back, let the others in, get away from whatever this was; and other voices, urging him to go up and find out where this weeping was coming from. It might not be imagination. It might be real. There might be someone here, someone who needed his help. Clenching his fists, he started, as softly as he could, to climb.

The steps didn't run far and he soon found himself at the top, facing a small landing with two closed doors. There were no lights on and the air was dusky and grey. The crying was louder now and clearly came from one of these rooms. He stepped up to the first, braced himself, then turned the door-knob and pushed. It was a small bathroom and someone was obviously using it: he saw towels, a toothbrush, toothpaste, shampoo and other things; but no one was here. He turned to the other door and reached out his hand.

At that moment the weeping stopped.

An eerie silence fell. He stood there, motionless, his hand touching the door-knob. He must have been heard. He'd moved as quietly as he could but the girl must have picked up some sound, perhaps the slight click as he'd opened the bathroom door. Why else would she have fallen silent? And what was she doing now? He listened for some sound of movement. The girl, too, seemed to have frozen, yet he sensed her just behind the door, listening for him, no doubt, just as he was for her. Probably she was even more frightened than he was. He leaned his head closer to the door. 'I won't hurt you,' he whispered. 'I promise I won't hurt you.'

Still the eerie silence. It seemed to go on and on and on, and as it continued, it grew deeper and more frightening. He thought of Skin fuming outside with the others. They would be mad at him by now and wondering what the hell he was doing. And what was he doing? The doubts were coming back and the voice of logic chirping inside his head again: Mrs Little lives alone; everybody knows it; you've heard imaginary sounds before and these are imaginary, too. The room's empty.

But there was an easy way to test this. It just needed a tiny bit of courage. He squeezed his hand round the door-knob and turned. It was locked. He gave a sigh of relief. That settled it. There was no key in the door so he couldn't get in even if he wanted to. And there was no point anyway. Mrs Little might be ugly and unfriendly but she was hardly the kind of person to keep a girl imprisoned in an attic room. He listened for more sounds behind the door but all he heard now was his own restless breathing. On an impulse, he knelt down and put an eye to the keyhole.

There was no light on in the room but the skylight appeared to be letting in something of what was left of the day. He could see a bed and the edge of a radiator and some drab wallpaper, and a section of some shelves, though, unlike the ones downstairs, these appeared to have nothing on them. Suddenly a face appeared. He gasped. Only inches from the keyhole was a young girl, staring—it seemed—towards him. Nine or ten years old, she looked, with short black hair that seemed to shine. Her eyes were swallowed in tears; and there was a terror in her face beyond anything he had ever seen.

Suddenly he was stumbling towards the steps. He knew he should stay—try to speak to her, try to help, try to do something—but he couldn't. Her terror had mastered him, too. He reached the top of the steps and heard the crying break out again behind him, but it only spurred him on faster. He clattered down to the main landing, raced along it and plunged down the stairs to the hall, the weeping welling over him like a cloud of pain. It seemed to grow louder, the further away he ran. He reached the front door, wrenched it open and saw the others standing there, scowling. Skin cuffed him hard round the top of the head.

'What the hell's the matter with you? You've been ages! Hey! Wait a minute! Don't close the door!'

But Luke took no notice. Before any of the others could stop him, he slammed the front door shut, ran to the gate and vaulted over, then hared off down the track towards the forest. And the weeping ran with him, all the way.

2

He raced through the darkness into the trees, not looking back. The others would be after him—he knew that—but somehow the terror in the girl's face frightened him even more than the thought of what Skin was going to do to him. Never had he seen such fear, such pain, in a person's face. Who was she? Why was she locked up? What was she so frightened of?

Was it him?

Surely not. It had to be something else. He had heard her crying long before she could have heard him entering the house, unless her hearing was as acute—or as weird—as his, and that was hardly likely. He could hear her even now as he stumbled through the forest. Her weeping seemed to whisper through the leaves, through the earth, through the air. He heard shouts, too, far behind him: Skin's voice mostly, swearing and bellowing, but Speed's and Daz's, too, calling his name; then they fell silent.

But he knew they would be coming for him. They were just saving their breath. They would know they couldn't catch him when it came to running or climbing, but they would guess where he was heading: the place he always went to, the place Dad had loved. No doubt it would have been safer to run home, but home didn't feel particularly welcoming any more, whereas this place did. And Skin would get him in the end anyway, so what difference did it make where he ran for sanctuary? He sped on, anxious to put as much distance as he could between the others and himself; and soon he was at the clearing with the old oak.

The great tree seemed to sway in greeting, as though it had been waiting for him. He glanced up at the tree-house just below the canopy and started to climb. He would be safe up there, for the moment at least. None of the others could follow. Skin might like to pretend it was the gang's tree-house but Luke knew it belonged to him alone. He had built it long before he'd started hanging out with Skin and the others and he was the only one of them—indeed the only person he knew—who could get up the tree without assistance. The lowest branches were difficult to reach because of the texture of the bark and the lack of anything decent to hold or stand on, but after many years of coming here with Dad and then—after Dad's death—by himself, he had come to know every nub and crevice that could give him a hand-hold or foot-hold to help him scramble up to that first precious branch; and after that, the climb was easy. And without the rope ladder being let down, the others would be stuck on the ground. The only down-side was that he would be trapped up top, but hopefully they'd just swear at him for a bit, then get bored and go home. He wouldn't avoid the retribution but he might at least put it off for a while.

He clawed his way up the trunk, searching for the secret parts of the tree that offered purchase for his strong hands and feet. Even in the dark he found them easily. It was like clinging to a big, friendly brother who would pick you up and wrestle with you but never let you fall. The bark was warm and reassuring under his hands. He climbed on, breathing hard, and listening all the time for footsteps, but all was silent. He reached the first branch, swung his leg over and pulled himself up, then clambered into the darkening canopy.

He reached the tree-house just in time. He had barely

swung himself over onto the planks when he heard the footsteps below. He didn't look down. It would be Skin and Daz; Speed would struggle along later, out of breath, if he made it at all. Skin called up at once. 'Luke! You up there?' The voice didn't sound angry. It sounded friendly—but Luke knew this was just a trick. Skin was furious with him and nobody would be fooled. He said nothing.

'Luke! I can see you!'

Again he said nothing. He knew Skin was bluffing. No one could see him from the ground, especially now that darkness had fallen. They would guess he was here, of course, but that wasn't difficult to do. He was always here. Skin called out again. 'Let the rope ladder down!'

He glanced at it, curled on the planks close by, and again did not reply; but this time he put an eye to one of the gaps in the boards. Below him he could see the shadowy forms of Skin and Daz standing by the base of the tree. They weren't looking up and were talking in low voices. There was no sign of Speed. He had probably gone home. A moment later Skin looked up again and this time did nothing to hide the malice in his voice.

'Don't think you're escaping by hiding up there. You'll have to face us soon.'

And the two boys turned and disappeared into the forest, heading towards the village. Luke waited a few minutes to be sure they had gone, then rolled over onto his back and stared up through the murmuring branches of the tree. The leaves and sky were changing now: green to grey, blue to black, brightened by the moon and stars. The forest felt drowsy and all was silent; then, into the silence, came the weeping voice again.

He sat up, trembling. How could the girl's voice reach him like this? He pictured her face, with all its terror, and felt his guilt return. He should have stayed in the house,

13

spoken to her, tried to help her. He might have been able to do some good; and it was a long time since he had done something good, or so it felt. He didn't know why this was. Maybe he just wasn't a very nice person any more. Not like Miranda was anyway. She seemed to manage to be friendly to just about everybody; he found it hard even to talk to people nowadays.

He stared down at the darkening floor of the forest. Everything was going wrong in his life. He was in trouble at school for not doing homework, not working, for being rude to teachers; he seemed to fall out with Mum every time they spoke; he was getting a bad name in the village for hanging around with Skin and the others; and now he'd fallen out with them, too. Even playing the piano didn't seem to help any more.

He stroked the nearest branch, then held it tight. A pulse of energy seemed to run through it into his body. He breathed out hard and stroked it again. At least the tree was his friend; and he needed one badly right now, especially as he was losing Mum. He checked the ground again. The darkness had thickened round the base of the tree and it was hard to see clearly but he was pretty sure the others really had gone and weren't lurking anywhere nearby. It was time to get back or there'd be yet another row with Mum tonight. He frowned. There probably would be anyway.

He stared around him for a few final moments, unwilling to leave. The canopies of the neighbouring oaks were still but his own was swaying slightly, as though brushing the night sky. He started to climb back down the tree. The bark was moist now and he took more care, especially as it was dark, but he felt confident enough. He reached the lowest branch, climbed over, then, holding on to it with both hands, let his right leg slide down the bark, feeling with his foot for the familiar knobbly bit in the trunk. There it was. It was a little slippery now but he dug his toe in and let himself down further, his other leg straddling the trunk. The next knobbly bit was a few feet down to the left and just out of view but he found it easily from long practice. His cheek was hard against the bark now and he was still clinging to the branch above him with one hand while he gripped the body of the trunk with the other. He took a few slow breaths, then let go of the branch, gripped the other side of the trunk as tightly as he could, and started to edge down towards the ground.

He was still too high to jump but a few more feet would do it. He inched down the tree, feeling with his right foot for the little crack in the trunk. There it was, as sure and trusty as the tree itself. He pressed the toe of his shoe into it and let that leg take the weight of his body. He could feel a subtle pressure behind him now, as of a hand wanting to pluck him from the tree. He always felt that at this point, but he knew it was not the tree wanting to rid itself of him, just his fear of falling. He thrust it from his mind and eased himself further down until he felt the patch of rough bark against his instep. Darkness now enveloped him like a shroud. He twisted his head round and gazed into the blackness of the forest. The trees around the clearing looked like sentinels watching him but he didn't stare back for long. He was hungry for the ground now. He checked the forest floor below him, then pushed himself off from the tree, twisted in the air and landed on his feet, facing the path back to the village.

The air felt soft and sweet and still, and there was a deep silence all around him. Even the weeping voice had gone. He turned back to the tree, gave it a pat and whispered: 'Goodnight.' Then he set off across the clearing towards the trees on the other side. As he passed the old horse chestnut, a hand seized him and flung him to the ground. To his horror he heard Skin's voice snarling down at him.

'Little bastard!'

Before he could move, the boy fell on him, seized him by the hair and pounded his head back against one of the tree-roots.

'Chicken bastard!'

'Skin—'

'Chicken bastard!'

He felt a fist crash into his cheek, knocking his head to the side. As it moved, he caught a glimpse of Daz leaning against the next tree, watching. The fist drove in again, this time to his chin. He gasped as his head thumped back against the ground. 'Skin!' he mumbled through a mouthful of blood, but the fist simply pounded into him again. Then Skin seized him by the hair and jerked his face upwards.

'Little bastard! All you had to do was leave the front door open and that was you done. Now we can't get in till she goes out again and God knows when that'll be. So we've got to wait and watch all over again just because you got freaked by an empty house.'

'Skin, listen—' Luke was gulping for air now. 'That's what I'm trying to tell you. It wasn't . . . empty.'

'Don't be stupid.' Skin squeezed Luke's hair so tight that he yelped. 'It was empty, Luke. It was bloody empty. We could have gone in and done anything we wanted. She didn't even set the burglar alarm.'

'But Skin . . . it . . . it wasn't empty.'

'Who was in there, then?'

Luke's head was pounding, his heart thumping. All vision seemed to be fading and even Skin's face was growing fuzzy; only the black flames in the eyes were still visible. The boy spoke again, through clenched teeth. 'Who was in there?'

Luke tried desperately to think. He'd gabbled his words out quickly enough in an effort to stop the blows and it had worked. Now all he had to do was tell Skin about the girl . . .

But he found he could not.

The fist crashed into his face again. His head swirling, he felt himself dragged to his feet and thrust back against the trunk of the horse chestnut. The blurred outline of Skin's face appeared again. 'Next time you'll do the job properly, Luke Stanton. Because you're not finished. Not by a long way. I'm going to break into that place and you're going to help me whether you like it or not. Meet us first thing in the morning. Top of the track to The Grange. And don't try and avoid us because we'll find you.'

He stared into Luke's face a few moments longer, then, with a sneer, threw him to the ground again and spat. Luke felt the drip run down his cheek. Before he could wipe it away, a boot drove into his ribs. He doubled up and rolled onto his side, moaning. From behind him came the sound of Skin and Daz tramping away and, further off, an owl calling deep in the forest. But Luke barely heard these things. He was losing consciousness.

3

When he came to, he found himself curled up in a ball. His head throbbed as though Skin's fists were still pounding him, only from the inside. His body seemed to ache all over. He was lying on a bony cradle of roots and leaves and twigs and mossy grass. With an effort he stretched out and rolled onto his back to see the horse chestnut tree reaching over him, its leaves moving like tiny ghosts. Yet the forest didn't frighten him. It never had done. He had often come here at night, slipping out in secret on his own to climb the old oak and sit high up in the canopy, listening to the sounds. He had done so even in the days when Dad was alive; and much more since. He forced himself to stand up. Nausea swirled through him at once and he found himself swaying on his feet, the forest spinning wildly around him. He held onto the tree for a while, resisting the urge to sit down again, and gradually the nausea cleared. He stared through the darkness at the old oak on the other side of the clearing.

'Goodnight,' he murmured. 'For the second time.'

And he set off through the trees in the direction of the village. The pain was still thumping inside his head and his ribs ached where Skin's boot had driven in but at least nothing seemed to be broken. He reached into his pocket, pulled out his handkerchief and dabbed it over his face. It was hard to tell how much blood there was but there was certainly plenty caked round his mouth and nose. His left cheek was almost too painful to touch and no doubt there would be bruises to explain later. He plodded on, wearier than he'd been for a long time, and more anxious than ever about the future. Suddenly he stopped.

There it was again: the sound of the girl weeping, her voice as subtle as a zephyr yet as clear and as audible to him as his own breathing. Who was she and why was she so frightened? Mrs Little was obviously involved somehow. Even if the old woman wasn't keeping her prisoner, she must be doing something terrible to her. He wondered whether he should call the police but quickly dismissed the idea. Firstly, he'd have to tell them how he knew there was a girl in the house, secondly he didn't have any actual proof that Mrs Little was doing anything wrong, and thirdly he was starting to doubt again whether the girl existed outside his imagination. As if to justify that doubt, the voice faded and the silence of the forest returned.

He wandered on through the familiar glades and finally reached the main path, feeling slightly calmer now. His head still pounded, yet somehow the simple motion of walking seemed to have helped. He stopped at the outskirts of the forest and drank in the scent of the bluebells that carpeted the clearing close to the path. A faint breeze was wafting up from the south but the night air was warm. It was hard to believe it was almost Whitsun already and that Mr Harding's concert was drawing near. He wished he hadn't agreed to take part again this year but he couldn't think about that now. All he wanted to do was get home, climb into bed, pull the duvet over himself, and sleep. No questions, no explanations, no talk. Just sleep and forget, at least until tomorrow. He left the forest behind him, trudged up the track to Nut Bush Lane and set off towards the village. Exhaustion and pain were taking their toll now and he had to fight the yearning just to curl up at the foot of one of the hedgerows. He plodded on somehow, past the playing field and on to the lane that led down to Roger Gilmore's place.

There it was at the bottom by the hump-back bridge. He stared down at it with distaste: Stony Hill Cottage, an untidy bungalow with a tumbledown workshop in the garden—an appropriately eccentric dwelling for a man who made loopy sculptures out of twigs and branches he'd found in the forest and who kept turning up around the old oak when he wasn't wanted. But that was the very least of Mr Gilmore's crimes. Luke pushed on as far as the council houses by the children's playground and stopped again, swaying on his feet as before. Daz's house had curtains drawn and no lights on so Daz had probably gone back to Skin's place while their parents were all at The Toby Jug. From Speed's house further down came the sound of the television. Luke stared at the front-room window. The curtains were drawn back and he could see the portly frame of Mr Speedwell standing with his back to the pane. There was no sign of Speed or his mother and sister but Speed's bedroom light was on so he was probably up there playing computer games.

He watched for a moment to make sure Mr Speedwell didn't turn, then climbed over the low fence into the front garden and crept round the side of the house to the outside tap. Fortunately the television now had some blaring music on so he felt sure they wouldn't hear. He turned the tap a fraction and a hissing sound came out. He turned it a little more, the hiss stopped, and there was a satisfying gurgle of water. He cupped his hands under the flow and splashed his face. It felt good, though the parts with the blood stung badly. He washed himself as thoroughly as he could, listening all the while for sounds of someone coming or the television being switched off, but no one bothered him. He drank some of the water, then turned off the tap, wiped his face with the tail of his shirt, and crept back to the lane. The front-room curtains were now closed.

He hurried on to the village square and found cars parked everywhere. From The Toby Jug came the sound of slurred voices singing an off-key rendering of 'Old Man River'. Miranda's parents obviously had a full house tonight. He wandered across the square and down the lane past the primary school, now desperate for his bed. But first he had to get past Skin's house. He slowed down as he approached the gate but quickly relaxed when he saw the empty drive. The light in Skin's bedroom was on and the curtains were closed. He wondered whether Daz was there, too, and what they were talking about. He also wondered what state Mr Skinner would be in when he rolled back from the pub tonight. But that was Skin's problem, not his. He carried on down the lane and didn't stop until he saw Bill Foley's farm on the left and his own house on the right. He stared at it, thinking not for the first time what a stupid name The Haven was for a place that no longer felt like home. And there outside was one of the reasons why.

Roger Gilmore's car.

He walked up to it, rested his hand on the boot, and stared at the house again. The lights were on downstairs and the curtains drawn across but there were no sounds from inside. Then he heard voices: no words, just murmurs; then silence. He listened. They had come from somewhere near the front door but he couldn't see anybody because the side of the porch blocked his view. But he didn't need to see to know who was there, or what they were doing. The voices came back, this time with words.

'Thanks, Roger,' said Mum.

'For what?'

'For understanding.'

'It's OK. Look, I'd better go.'

'OK.' Mum paused. 'Take care.'

'And you, Kirsti.'

There was a long silence. Luke clenched his fists, knowing what that meant. Then Mum spoke again. 'Night, Roger.'

'Night.' Another long silence, then the sound of the front door closing and footsteps on the path. Luke turned to face away from the house. A moment later he heard the gate click, then the voice he hated. 'Luke? Is that you?'

'Who did you think it was?' He turned back, scowling. Mr Gilmore looked somewhat shamefaced, like a boy who'd just been caught scrumping, but he managed a lopsided smile that Luke just caught in the darkness.

'Sorry, Luke. Didn't recognize you for a moment. Are you all right?'

'Why shouldn't I be?'

'You're very late back from the youth club. Your mum was getting really worried about you.'

'She didn't seem all that worried a moment ago.'

Mr Gilmore looked down and seemed unsure what to do or say. Luke watched him a moment longer, then shrugged and made for the gate.

'Goodnight, Luke,' said Mr Gilmore.

But Luke simply walked up to the house, put his key in the door, and let himself in.

4

Mum came hurrying into the hall the moment he entered. 'Luke, you're really late. Where have you—?' She stopped suddenly, her eyes running over him. 'You've been in a fight!'

'I don't want to talk about it.'

'Luke—'

'I don't want to talk about it.'

She stepped forward; he stepped back. She stopped, her eyes still running over him. 'Luke, what's happened?'

'I don't want another row.'

'Neither do I.'

'Fine.'

'But what's happened?'

He looked towards the stairs. All he wanted was bed, sleep, oblivion. Not this, not now. Later maybe but not now.

'Who hit you?' said Mum. Still he didn't answer. She walked forward and took him by the hand. 'Well, at least let me sort out that face a bit.'

He let her lead him through to the kitchen and sit him down at the table. She fetched two ice packs, wrapped them in tea-towels, and handed them to him. 'Put those on either cheek. Just under the eyes. You're starting to puff up there already.' He pushed the packs against his skin and steered them into place. They felt good after the hot pain he had been feeling there. Mum looked him over, frowning, her fingers carefully feeling their way round the rest of his face. He shifted impatiently in the chair.

23

'There's nothing broken,' he said. 'You don't need to fuss over me.'

'I'm not fussing. I'm just making sure you're OK.' She went on checking him over. 'There's blood round your nose and mouth. We can wash that off. And you've got some nasty bruising round your left eye. Is your head pounding?'

'Yes.'

'Right, let's give you a painkiller.'

'I'm all right. I don't need one.'

'I'm only trying to help.'

'I know but I don't need one.'

'Do you want me to drive you to Casualty?'

'No.'

'I don't mind.'

'I don't want to go. I don't need all that. I told you. I'm all right.'

'Fair enough. If you insist.' She opened the medicine cabinet and pulled out some cotton wool, then filled a bowl with hot water, dabbed the cotton wool in it and started to clean the blood from round the nose. 'So who did this, Luke?'

'I told you—I don't want to talk about it.'

'Why not?'

'Because you'll get hysterical and we'll end up having another row.'

'Not if we tell ourselves we're not going to.' She tore off another piece of cotton wool, dipped it in the water and went on cleaning off the blood. 'We shouldn't be having rows anyway. Just because we've been through a couple of bad years. We should be sticking together. Isn't that what the British always do?'

'How would you know? You're Norwegian.'

'Luke!' She drew back and stared at him. 'I'm trying— I'm really trying—to make things work. Can't you meet me halfway?' He looked down, unable to answer. She continued with the cotton wool, tutting as she worked over his face. 'This is awful, Luke. You've been badly knocked about.'

'It looks worse than it is.'

'Have you seen yourself lately?'

He glanced round at the mirror and frowned at his reflection. Skin had certainly done a good job, especially on the left cheek. The bruises would probably be black in the morning. Mum went on working with the cotton wool. 'So who were you with at the youth club?'

He didn't answer. His mind was on the girl again—her face, her voice, her pain—and the unfinished business at The Grange. And Skin.

'Luke?' Mum's voice brought his mind back to the present. 'Who were you with at the youth club?' He could see the suspicion growing in her eyes as she searched his face. 'Luke, you were at the youth club this evening, weren't you?'

'Yeah,' he said, then, realizing how easy it would be for her to check, muttered: 'No.'

'You weren't there?'

'No.'

'So where did you go?'

'Nowhere special.'

'To the forest?'

'No.'

'Are you sure? You didn't go tree climbing again?'

'No.'

'Because you did promise me you wouldn't. Especially that oak tree. It's too dangerous.'

'I didn't go to the forest.'

'So where did you go?'

'I just said—nowhere special.'

'You must have gone somewhere.'

He folded his arms and said nothing. Mum frowned at him. 'I don't know why you won't tell me where you went. Or who hit you.' She drew back again for a moment and looked down at him. 'Just tell me you weren't with Jason Skinner again.' She searched his face again for a few moments, then gave a sigh. 'You were with Jason Skinner.'

'I might have been.'

'I'll take that as a yes. And I can guess who else was there. Darren Fisher?'

'Maybe.'

'Bobby Speedwell?'

'Maybe.'

'Three total wasters.' Mum scowled at him. 'As you well know. And which one of them hit you?'

'It's not a problem.'

'Which one was it?'

'For Christ's sake, Mum!' He glared up at her. 'It was Skin, all right?'

'Do you have to call him that?'

'What the hell does it matter what anyone calls him?' He was shouting now, unable to stop himself. 'Skin, Daz, Speed! They're just nicknames! Don't you have nicknames in Norway?' He regretted his outburst at once and tried to soften his voice. 'Mum, just lay off, can you? I had an argument with Skin—all right?—and I got knocked about a bit, but it's sorted now. And I don't want you taking it further with him or his family or anything. Especially his father, OK?'

She said nothing and turned away. He thought back to the days when they had been friends, when he had been so proud of her warm nature, her bright mind, her Nordic beauty, and the fact that so many men found her attractive. But that had been in the days when everything was safe, the days before Dad died and the light of his existence went out, before Roger Gilmore came to the village and into Mum's life, before rage and rebellion and hatred took him over like a poison. The days before old friends slipped away from the dark creature he had become and he sought refuge in a gang he was now too frightened to leave.

'What's happening to you, Luke?' said Mum.

He didn't answer.

'Luke?'

'What?'

'What's happening to you?'

'I don't know what you mean.'

'You go out every evening. You come back God knows when. You won't tell me what you've been doing or who you've been with. If I ask you, you bite my head off or just sit there saying nothing. I wouldn't mind so much if it was just me. I mean, I wouldn't like it but I could handle it better. But you're rude to people round the village, you're rude to people at school, you don't do your homework, you don't try in lessons—'

'I try in Music.'

'That doesn't count.'

'Why not?'

'You know why not.'

'No, I don't,' he lied.

'It doesn't count because you don't need to try at music. You're already brilliant at music. It's in your blood. You could do anything you want in music. Mr Harding says so. Mrs Parry says so. Your father said so. You could be a composer, a conductor, a concert pianist like Dad was. Mr Harding told me last week you're the most gifted young musician he's ever known, and that's quite a statement, when you think of how many people he must have worked with throughout his life. You've got something really special, Luke. It's something to treasure and make

27

use of.' She looked him over. 'Music's the greatest gift Dad ever gave you.'

'The greatest gift Dad ever gave me was himself.' Luke stared down at the floor, picturing his father's face in his mind. He felt Mum's hand on his arm.

'I know this is painful, Luke. I really do. But what I said is true—your music is a gift. Your father had it and you've got it, too. You mustn't waste it.'

'I'm not wasting it.'

'You are wasting it. You've stopped performing. You hardly ever practise the piano. You don't even want to think about how to advance your musical career. You've stopped all the things you used to do when Dad was—'

'I don't want to talk about this.' He looked up at her again. 'OK? And I haven't stopped performing. I still play the piano.'

'Occasionally.'

'I do all the stuff Mrs Parry gives me to do at school, even though it's so easy I'm falling over with boredom. I still go for my piano lessons with Mr Harding. I've even stupidly agreed to play in his retirement concert.'

'I know, Luke. I'm glad. I'm really glad.'

'So what's the problem?'

'We both know what the problem is.'

'Well, I don't.'

But he was lying again, and he could tell from Mum's face that she knew it as well as he did.

'Luke, some time or other you've got to bring yourself to talk to me about Dad.'

'I don't want to.'

'But, Luke—'

'I don't want to, OK?' He glowered at her. 'You said you wouldn't force me to talk about it until I was ready.'

'But that was two years ago.'

'So?' He was shouting again, uncontrollably. 'What's that got to do with anything?'

Again he regretted his outburst. He tried to think of something to say but she spoke first, in a small, almost frightened voice. 'You obviously think I'm the lowest of the low right now. Well, I . . . ' She took a slow breath. 'I'm just trying to do what's right for both of us. And— Luke, please let me say this—I do think that some time or other you've got to talk to me about Dad. If you go on bottling it up, we'll never come through this.'

'We?'

'Yes, we.' He heard a trace of anger in her voice this time. She narrowed her eyes. 'Do you really think you're the only person who's been hurt by your father's death?'

'No,' he said, reluctantly. 'I don't think that.'

'I've been finding things pretty difficult, too, you know.'

'You weren't finding things that difficult on the porch just now.'

She stared at him for a moment, then suddenly turned away, walked over to the window and pulled back the curtains. Through the glass he could see the night sky, brilliant with stars. She gazed out for a while, breathing slowly as though trying to calm herself. Then she spoke. 'I told myself I wasn't going to get into another row tonight. Not tonight of all nights.'

'What's that supposed to mean?'

'Never mind.' She went on gazing out of the window. 'It's so beautiful out there. I remember, when I was a little girl, I used to have this favourite place when we lived up in the north of Norway. It was a hill high up above the fjord and my English grandmother used to take me up there to see the stars. I can remember those nights even now. And my grandmother's face as she pointed them all out to me.' Mum stared at the stars in silence for a few moments, then went on. 'Do you know, I was actually happy earlier this evening. Before it got late and I started worrying about you again. I couldn't believe it—for the first time in ages, I was actually a tiny bit happy. For a few minutes anyway.'

'He's asked you to marry him, hasn't he?'

'Is that a question or an accusation?'

'What difference does it make?' He stared at her, wishing—without quite knowing why—that she would turn and look at him; but she simply went on staring out of the window.

'So has he?' he said.

'Yes.'

'And what did you say?'

'I said I needed to think about it.'

Still he watched her; still she gazed out of the window. Beyond her, through the pane, he could see shapes against the blackness: the outline of the shed, the whirligig, the silver birch at the bottom of the garden. He thought of the great oak—his tree, his friend—and wished he were up there now, cradled in the branches, listening to the night-songs of the forest. And yet his bed called him even more. He yawned.

'You don't need to think about it. You already know you want to marry him.'

'Would you hate it if I did?'

'What's it got to do with me?'

'It's got everything to do with you.'

'No, it hasn't. It's none of my business.'

She turned suddenly and looked at him. 'It is your business, Luke. I'd never take a big step like this without your approval. I couldn't. You're all I've got.'

'No, I'm not. You've got Mr Gilmore.'

'Roger. He's got a name. You don't need to be so formal with him.'

He stiffened suddenly. The sound of the girl's weeping had broken through the silence again. He listened, unsure yet again whether it was a real voice or just his imagination.

'What is it?' said Mum. 'You've tensed up.'

'Nothing.'

'But, Luke—'

'It's nothing, OK?' He drove the weeping voice from his mind. 'Don't worry about it. Go and marry Roger Gilmore. If that's what you want.'

Mum walked back to him and put a hand on his shoulder. 'Why don't you like him? Is it because you think he's going to take me away from you? Or is it just because he isn't Dad?'

'Who says I don't like him?'

'You do.'

'I've never said so.'

'Not in so many words. But you make it perfectly clear, believe me.'

He shrugged his shoulder away from her hand and stood up. He had to get out of the room. He was exhausted and angry and aching with pain, and he knew he was about to snap again; and this time he'd make her cry and end up hating himself as he always did. So many of their talks seemed to end that way now.

'I'm going to bed,' he said.

'I love you, Luke.'

'Yeah, yeah.'

He strode from the room and closed the door behind him, then leaned against the wall. It was no good. Already he could hear the sound of Mum sniffling behind the door. He turned and thrust open the kitchen door again. She was sitting at the table, her eyes streaming tears. 'Look, Mum . . .' He shifted on his feet. 'I just can't handle this marriage thing right now, OK? I've got too much on my mind.'

'OK, Luke.' She pulled out a handkerchief and started to wipe her eyes. 'Is it because you think I'm being disloyal to Dad?'

'We just agreed we wouldn't talk about that.'

'OK.' Her voice was barely audible now. 'OK. We don't talk about Roger and we don't talk about Dad. Is that what you want?'

'Yeah.'

'All right.' She wiped her eyes again and forced a smile. 'Thank you for being honest.'

'Yeah, well . . . ' He shrugged. 'Goodnight.'

'Goodnight, Luke.'

He closed the door behind him and this time walked on to the stairs and up to his room; and the sound of weeping followed his every step. Weeping from Mum and—again—weeping from the girl. He was living in a world of tears. Why couldn't he cry with them? But his eyes had long been dry and now his heart felt dry, too, as dry and barren as the whole of his life. He reached his room and opened the door, then stopped and closed his eyes, and leaned against the wall, listening. A new sound had broken through the silence, but it was not crying.

It was the sound of the piano down in the music room. He listened, his eyes still closed. It was so long since Mum had played but he knew this piece at once. He'd played it himself enough times, though not for a couple of years: 'Peace of the Forest' by Grieg, Mum's favourite composer. It was good to hear it again. The first two chords reminded him of distant bells, then came the soft singing melody, the left hand running up and down with a slow rhythmic bass while the right hand picked out the tune; and suddenly it was all bells, bells ringing in a forest. He saw pictures flooding through his mind as she played, pictures of Buckland Forest, of lush green canopies, of leaves dripping with dew, of light pouring

32

through treetops, and then—to his surprise—the girl's face, her black hair brightened by the sun; and she wasn't frightened: she was laughing, singing even, and he was with her, in the forest, in the music.

The tune paused for a moment, while Mum turned the page, then continued with those same two distant chords that had started the piece. The main melody returned and the pictures came back, of the trees in the forest and the sun on the girl's face; and he found himself dreaming of the high oak and the tree-house swaying in the breeze. The music moved on, playfully for a while, then more softly as it drew to its close. The girl's face slipped from his mind but the pictures of the forest remained in the tranquil final bars. The chords grew softer, each one more hushed than the last; and then there was silence.

He slipped into his room and closed the door behind him, then undressed, climbed into bed and turned off the light, and lay there, staring up at the ceiling. An owl called from somewhere over Bill Foley's farm, then fell silent. There was no more music from below. Instead he heard footsteps on the stairs. They reached the landing, approached his room and stopped outside. He closed his eyes and waited for the door to open or for Mum to call out; but the footsteps continued across the landing and a moment later he heard the sound of Mum's door; and then silence once more. A picture of the old oak floated into his mind as he fell asleep.

In the night he dreamt he was flying again. It was an experience he had had several times since Dad died and though he always thought of it as a dream, he still wasn't completely sure that it was. It felt so vivid and he was so conscious of himself that sometimes he was certain he was awake; yet the whole thing felt so strange. It started as it always did with him lying on his back on the forest floor at the base of the old oak, and he was gazing up through the canopy into a clear blue sky; and then suddenly it was as though he started to feel lighter, so light in fact that he simply stretched out his arms and with a soft shiver of his body floated up into the air.

At least, it felt like a shiver of his body, though he quickly realized that that heavier part of him was no longer there. It was behind him on the ground like a discarded skin, and now this lighter part of him, a part both airy and yet somehow more real than he ever could have imagined, was moving on towards the base of the tree, reaching out for the bark; and suddenly, by some slow rustling of the light, the roots and base of the trunk seemed to open and he floated into the warm, black tunnel of the tree and started to fly upwards through the darkness, straining to reach the crown; and then he was through that, pushing aside the leaves and flying up further, clear of the forest, clear of the ground, clear of all that had ever been, searching for the star he knew would be waiting for him. It was always there in this strange waking dream, even though this was the daytime sky, and here it was again, so bright it seemed to quench the sun itself. And he was not alone now. Dad was flying with him, and other presences he could not see but sensed all around him, familiar presences, though he could not remember who they were, and they flew on together, higher, higher, higher, towards the star, until it grew so brilliant they seemed to dissolve in light.

He heard a deep rumbling sound and opened his eyes. He was in bed and darkness was all around him. He was breathing hard and trembling, and there was a deep thrusting pain in his ribs and in the parts of his face where Skin had done his work. He lay still and stared up at the ceiling and after a while his breathing settled and the pain eased a little. The rumbling sound went on all around him. This was nothing new to him but simply one of many sounds that had rolled over him day and night since as far back as he could remember, but especially since Dad died. He listened to it and tried to work out where it was coming from but as usual its source eluded him. It seemed to come from everywhere and nowhere, and it changed constantly. Sometimes it was a roar, sometimes a hum, sometimes a soft murmur like the swell of an ocean far away. He listened to it for several minutes, then it, too, faded into the night and silence returned.

He thought of the day ahead. He desperately wanted some time to himself. He needed to think. He needed to collect himself somehow. He couldn't face seeing Skin again so soon after being beaten up; and he wasn't too keen on the prospect of more grief from Mum over the breakfast table either. He'd get up early, he decided, before Mum was awake, stuff some rolls in his pocket and head off on his own for a couple of hours, somewhere well away from The Grange. He had a piano lesson with Mr Harding at ten but if he slipped out early enough, he should at least have some time to himself. He'd wander past Frank Meldrum's pottery and find a secluded spot by the brook. Skin would never find him up there.

5

But Skin did. Luke had barely finished his rolls and settled back to enjoy the colours of the morning and the play of light over the brook when he saw the boy climbing over the stile from the lane and sauntering across the meadow towards him. Daz and Speed were close behind as usual, the sun bright upon their faces. He stood up at once, trying not to show the trepidation he felt inside. Skin didn't bother with preliminaries and simply grabbed him by the neck. 'So what are you doing here, Luke Stanton? I said to meet by The Grange.'

'I was just about to set off that way.'

'Liar.'

'I was. I was about to go.'

'But you're supposed to be there already. We've had to come and find you.'

'You didn't say what time we had to meet.'

'I said first thing.'

'I didn't know what time that was meant to be.'

'You liar.' Skin cuffed him round the face. 'You shit.' The boy looked him over. 'You came here to avoid us.'

'I didn't.'

'And you came here because you're scared. You were scared of the house when it was empty and you're even more scared now that the old girl's there.'

'It wasn't that.'

'So what did you come here for, then?'

36

'I was just sitting.' Once again he saw the flames in Skin's eyes. It was like watching a black fire reaching out to choke him. He swallowed hard and tried to match the boy's stare. 'Skin, let go, can you?'

But Skin tripped him up and dragged him closer to the brook. He heard the water rippling by, only inches from his head. Skin glared down at him. 'You're trying to avoid us, Luky.'

'I'm not.'

'Oh, right. You came here 'cause it's pretty. Nice little meadow, nice little brook.'

'I told you. I was—'

'Just sitting,' mimicked Daz. 'Looking at the flowers and the water. And eating. Hey, Speedy!' Daz pointed to the ground. 'Breadcrumbs! If we'd come a few minutes earlier, you could have shared his breakfast! You look like you need it!'

'Shut up!' said Speed.

'Leave it out, Daz,' said Skin, his eyes fixed on Luke. Luke lay still. The bank was hard, the grass damp, and he wanted to wriggle and try to break free. But he knew that was pointless. He couldn't escape. Skin was far too strong. Best to keep still and try not to provoke the boy to serious violence. Skin's hand flew out suddenly and cuffed him again. 'I hate people who lie to me,' he muttered. 'You came here 'cause you were scared. You came here to avoid meeting us. It's so bloody obvious. And there's another thing.' He hauled Luke to his feet. 'You think you're too good for us.'

'I don't.'

'Yes, you do. You don't want to get involved with us. Your mum's probably told you to keep away from us, right?'

Luke said nothing.

'Right?' said Skin.

'No.' He thought of all the arguments he'd had with Mum about Skin and the gang. But all he could say was: 'It's none of her business who I hang around with.'

'Good,' said Skin. 'So we'll see you tonight.'

'What?'

'We'll see you tonight. Just up from The Grange. Where you were supposed to have been meeting us this morning. We're going to have another go at the place. Only this time you're going to do it right.'

'But Mrs Little'll be there,' said Luke. 'She'll be in the house. I thought that was the point. Do it on a Friday evening when she's out at the shop.'

'We can't wait till next Friday. And since you're the one who messed up last time, you're going to be the one to put things right.'

'But we can't break in if Mrs Little's there. She'll hear us.'

'We aren't going to break in.'

'What do you mean?'

'You are.'

'What?'

'You are. You're going in.'

'What about you and Daz and Speed?'

'We'll be outside.'

· 'The back-up team,' said Daz with a snigger.

Luke looked from face to face. Daz was smirking, Speed staring at the ground as though he was slightly embarrassed. Skin, as usual, was in control: of himself, of the gang, of Luke, of everything. The boy continued, his eyes still on Luke. 'We can't all go in if Mrs Little's in the house. She'd hear one of us, probably Speedy bumbling about, knocking things over.'

'That's not fair,' protested Speed.

'But you can sneak in easy,' Skin continued, his eyes never leaving Luke's. 'As long as she's left a window open somewhere, which she's bound to do with the nights being so warm.'

'But why me?'

'You know why. Because you're the best at climbing. Because you're light on your feet.' Skin prodded him in the chest. 'And because you owe me, Luke Stanton.'

'I don't want to do this.'

'I don't give a shit whether you want to or not. I told you. You owe me. If you'd done things right yesterday, you could have left everything to us. All you had to do was open the front door and let us in. You could have gone home then if you'd wanted to. But you chickened out. You got scared of an empty house.'

'It—' Luke began, then stopped. Somehow, like yesterday, he knew he couldn't tell the others about the girl. They'd never believe him for one thing—they'd think he was just making it up to get out of going into the house again—but that wasn't the main reason for his silence. It was the thought of the girl, her terror, her pain, her vulnerability. What he'd seen and heard felt somehow personal to him now. He just couldn't tell the gang about her. Yet somehow he had to get out of this business tonight.

'It's really risky,' he said. 'I could easily get caught.'

'You won't,' said Skin. 'She's old. She's probably a bit deaf. Probably can't see very well, especially in the dark. It'll be a doddle. All you've got to do is climb in through one of the windows.'

'They might be all closed,' he said hopefully.

'Then we'll come back tomorrow night and the next night and the next night until there is a window open.'

'I still don't like it,' said Luke. 'If she catches me, I could get prosecuted.'

'She won't even know you're there. It'll be dark and she'll be asleep by the time you're in the house. And even if she does hear something, she'll probably be too scared to do anything. She'll more likely pull the sheet over her face and lie there quaking.'

'She wouldn't do that. She'd come looking for me. She wouldn't be scared of anyone.'

'Well, if you hear her coming, you can always run away. You're good at that. And she's so old you'll be out the front door and off before she even finds the light switch. There's no risk.' Skin glanced round at the others. 'Right, boys?'

'Right,' said Daz, smirking again. Speed said nothing, but nodded. Luke frowned. He knew there was no way out of this. Skin clearly had every intention of making him break in, whatever the risk. He even had the feeling that the boy wanted him to go in just so he could get caught. Perhaps Skin wanted that even more than the box now.

He thought of the old house and the mystery that hung over it. At least, if he went in again, he might have another chance to see the girl, and maybe even speak to her and find out what was wrong. And if he could somehow bring out the box as well, maybe Skin would leave him alone in the future. If he refused now, there was no telling what the boy would do to him.

'We'll meet at midnight,' said Skin.

'Midnight?' Luke stared at him. 'Has it got to be then?'

'Yeah.'

'What if I can't get away?'

'You'll get away. It'll be no problem at all. That's the whole point of doing it at midnight. We're all supposed to be tucked up in bed like good little boys. All you've got to do is turn in and make out you're asleep, then slip out. The village'll be quiet. Nobody'll see us. Mrs Little'll be snoring into her pillow. It'll be easy.' Skin leaned closer again. 'I want that box, Luke. And you're going to get it.

Don't bother with anything else you see in the house. Just creep round until you find the box. We can't come in and help you this time. If you'd done things right yesterday and let us in when the house was empty, it would have been a piece of cake. But you messed up so now you've got to do it on your own.'

'She'll hear me moving about. She's bound to.'

'Not if you're quiet. And anyway, I told you, she'll be fast asleep. So just creep around until you find the box, then bring it down to the front door and hand it over. If she doesn't wake up when you open the door, I might go in myself and have a look round. But you've got to do your bit first.' Skin's voice lowered. 'Because you don't want to fall out with me again, now do you?' The flames in the eyes seemed to grow larger, blacker, more dangerous. Luke looked away, unable to watch them any longer. 'Midnight, then,' said Skin. 'Don't be late.' And with a last cuff, the boy set off with the others, this time down to the gate at the bottom of the meadow. Luke waited until they had climbed over and disappeared from view, then slumped to the ground again and listened to the babbling water.

And with it came sounds he did not want to hear: the girl's weeping voice, and Skin's voice, too, like a whispering curse inside his head. 'Chicken bastard,' it said. 'Chicken bastard.' He put his hands over his ears, but the voice hissed on. 'Chicken bastard, chicken bastard.' And then: 'You don't want to fall out with me again, now do you?'

And that was the point. Much as he despised himself for being weak, he knew he couldn't afford to fall out with Skin again. The punishment for failure a second time would be worse than before. Skin had already been in trouble with the police for grievous bodily harm. Luke took his hands from his ears and tried to calm down; and gradually, to his relief, Skin's voice faded away. But the girl's remained, as though it were part of the air around him. He sat there for some time, listening uneasily to it. Then he heard a new voice—and a far less welcome one—behind him.

'Hi, there!'

He turned and saw Roger Gilmore standing in the lane just beyond the stile. He was in his tattered dungarees and had his sleeves rolled up as though he'd just emerged from his workshop. 'Are you all right, Luke?' he said.

Luke stood up and walked reluctantly over to him.

'Why shouldn't I be all right?'

'Lots of reasons. And I guess I'm probably one of them. Though I'd prefer not to be.'

'What's that supposed to mean?'

'It means I'd rather be a friend than Public Enemy Number One.'

Luke said nothing. Mr Gilmore watched him for a moment, then continued. 'Especially as you seem to have enough enemies as it is right now. I'm sorry about those bruises on your face. Your mum told me you got into a scrap last night.'

'I don't need any sympathy, thanks. Or any help.'

'No, of course you don't. But it's OK. You can relax on that score—I'm only doing this for your mum. She was worried about where you were. I gather you've got a piano lesson with Mr Harding at ten o'clock. I said I'd have a look round for you.'

Luke glanced at his watch. Half past nine. So the man had already been in contact with Mum this morning. Maybe she'd been to see him at Stony Hill Cottage or he'd been round to The Haven. They could have been together ever since he left the house. But Mr Gilmore seemed to guess his thoughts.

'No, Luke, I haven't seen your mum this morning. I've been working. She phoned me half an hour ago from The

Haven to say you'd slipped out of the house without saying anything and she was worried. She'd been out looking for you. I said I'd check this way. What made you come up here?'

Luke gave no answer but Mr Gilmore didn't seem to be expecting one because he was already dialling a number on his mobile phone. He waited for a moment, then spoke. 'Kirsti? It's me. I've found him . . . Yes . . . By the brook . . . No, he's fine . . . Clothes look a bit damp . . . Sure, if you like but, well, he probably won't want to . . . OK . . . OK . . . See you later.' He switched off the phone and put it back in his pocket.

'He probably won't want to what?' said Luke, climbing back over the stile into the lane.

'I beg your pardon?'

'He probably won't want to what?'

'She asked me to get you to come back with me to The Haven. I said you probably wouldn't want to.'

'Why wouldn't I want to go to my own home?'

'I meant you probably wouldn't want to come back with me.'

Luke glared at him but Mr Gilmore merely looked back without flinching. Luke shrugged. 'I'm going home. You can do what you like.'

'I'll come with you.'

'Suit yourself.'

And they set off together down the lane. Luke said nothing and was relieved to find Mr Gilmore seemed to have no desire to talk either. Skin's whispering voice had faded completely but the weeping presence of the girl was still there and with it, once more, he could hear the mysterious rumbling sound that had come to him last night. It was with him so often now. And gradually, as he walked, he found other sounds growing louder, sharper, more insistent: the clump of their footsteps, the

43

cawing of crows, the rumble of a tractor in one of the fields to the left, then, as they approached Frank Meldrum's pottery, the clip-clop of hooves round the bend in the lane. A moment later Miranda appeared on her bay mare, riding towards them. She saw them and waved.

'Hi!' she called.

Luke stopped and waited for her, hoping Mr Gilmore would walk on by himself, but there was no such luck. The man had obviously decided to go with him all the way to The Haven. Miranda drew level and reined in the mare. 'Hi, Luke,' she said with a smile; but the smile quickly vanished and her mouth dropped open. 'You've been in a fight!'

'Yeah, well—'

'Are you OK?' She leaned closer and looked him over. 'Who did that to your face?'

'It looks worse than it is.'

'Was it Jason or Darren?'

'Maybe.' He tried to look indifferent. 'But it's sorted now, OK? It's not a problem. How are you?'

'Fine but . . . Luke . . . I mean . . . '

'Honestly, it's not a problem, OK?'

'If you say so.' But she didn't sound convinced. She twisted round in the saddle and beamed at Mr Gilmore. 'Hi, Roger!'

'Hi, Miranda.'

'Mum's nuts about that sculpture you did for her. She's just gone totally stupid over it. She keeps grabbing people and pulling them over to look at it. It's getting really embarrassing. I think she's going to write you a note to say thank you.'

'She doesn't need to.'

'Well, I think you're getting one anyway.'

'I'm glad she likes it.'

'Where did you find the wood for it? In Buckland Forest?'

'Yeah.'

'Whereabouts?'

'By the big patch of bluebells.'

'The ones just up from The Grange? Where the young alders are?'

'No. Other side of the forest. There's a huge patch by the gate onto the Bramblebury road.'

'I know it. Dad and I went riding there yesterday. It's beautiful.'

'Certainly is. Anyway, that's where I found the wood. I knew it was right for your mum the moment I saw it.'

Luke listened, feeling awkward and even slightly nettled. He knew he couldn't stop other people using the forest but he still felt proprietorial about the place, and he especially disliked the fact that Mr Gilmore went in there to collect wood for his sculptures. He looked up at Miranda, reluctant to talk about Mr Gilmore's work but eager to regain her attention. 'What's this sculpture?' he said.

'It's beautiful, Luke. It's just so fantastic. You should see it. It's a carving Mum asked Roger to do for The Toby Jug. She wanted something that would make her think of the forest and also remind her of the days when she used to sing and dance when she was small, and Roger's taken a bit of wood from the forest and carved out this little girl. She's like a kind of sprite figure and she's got her arms out wide and she's dancing and singing, only she looks sort of sad and wistful, too, like she's all alone and in despair.'

A little girl. Sad, wistful, in despair. Luke frowned at the strange associations these words sent through his mind. Miranda turned back to Mr Gilmore. 'It's so beautiful, Roger. I just can't believe you made it.'

'I didn't make it,' he said. 'Nature made it. I just collected it.'

'But it wasn't like that when you found it.'

'Maybe not. But I was lucky with the piece I got.'

'You didn't cut it off a tree?' said Luke accusingly.

'Why would I need to do that?' said Mr Gilmore. His voice was calm, his face unruffled. 'The forest floor gives me everything I require. I don't have to steal from the trees.' He smiled at Miranda. 'I'm glad your mum likes the sculpture and thanks for telling me. People don't always give feedback. They usually just commission things, take the finished product, and send a cheque. And you often have to chase them for that.'

'Oh, yes,' said Miranda, 'that was another thing. Mum said you haven't asked her for any money yet. I heard her telling Dad this morning.'

'I was going to drop the invoice in later today. Haven't had time to do it yet. I had to come out early this morning.' His eyes flickered across to Luke, then back to Miranda. 'Will your mum and dad be in The Toby Jug this lunchtime?'

'When aren't they? I'll tell them you're coming.' She patted the great horse, who was becoming restless, then, to Luke's surprise, she turned to him again. 'Luke, I was going to ring you. Can you . . . ' She hesitated. 'Can you help me with something?'

'Sure—what?'

'I've told Mr Harding I'll do a flute piece at the concert but I need some help.'

'I can't play the flute.'

'No, I need someone to play the piano part.'

'I'm already doing a piece at the concert.'

'I know but . . . I mean . . . you're so good at music and everything and I just thought—'

'Can't Samantha play the piano part? Or Melanie?'

Miranda ran a hand down the horse's long brown neck. 'I suppose I could ask one of them,' she said slowly. 'If you really don't want to do it.'

Luke looked away towards the village. It seemed cruel to say no to Miranda when she so obviously wanted him to play the piano part, yet he wanted to have as little to do with the concert as possible. He wished he hadn't agreed to play his own solo piece. He wasn't interested in playing in public right now. There was so much other stuff going on in his life, difficult stuff, stuff he had to deal with. He hadn't got time to do party pieces. He heard the horse stamping and looked back at Miranda.

'What piece are you going to play?'

'"The Dance of the Blessed Spirits" by Gluck.'

'Good choice,' said Mr Gilmore. 'I've got a lovely recording of that at home.'

'You won't want to hear me play it, then,' said Miranda. 'I'm rubbish on the flute. That's why I was hoping Luke might help me. He's so good on the piano I thought it might cover up all the bad stuff I'm doing. Still, I don't want—'

'I'll do it,' said Luke.

She looked back at him. 'Luke, I don't want you to feel—'

'I'll do it. OK? It's no problem. I'll do it.'

'Are you sure?'

'Yeah.'

She stared at him for a moment, as though she was waiting for him to change his mind, then, when he said nothing, her face lit up with pleasure. 'Thanks, Luke. I never thought you'd say yes. I can't tell you what that means to me. I've been getting in such a state over this concert. I've never played in front of other people before. Can I give you a ring so we can arrange a practice session?'

47

'Sure.'

'Thanks.' She smiled at him. 'Thanks a lot. That's really great of you. I'll ring Mr Harding and tell him you're going to accompany me. He'll need to put it in the programme.'

'It's all right. I'll tell him. I've got a piano lesson at ten.'

'OK.' She smiled again. 'Thanks again, Luke.'

'No problem.'

'I'll see you later.'

'Yeah.'

'Bye, Roger.'

'Bye.'

And Miranda rode off, the smile still on her face. Mr Gilmore watched her for a moment, then smiled, too. 'That's a really, really nice girl,' he said.

Luke turned without a word and set off towards The Haven, more desperate than ever now to be left alone. But Mr Gilmore caught him up and kept pace with him. Luke turned his head away slightly, not just to discourage conversation but to focus on the sounds that were flooding over him again, among them the strange girl's voice. How he could hear it when he was this distance from The Grange was a mystery to him, yet the voice was there, demanding his attention. There were no words as before, just a constant weeping in the hinterland of his mind. And he could hear music now: a wistful, childlike tune that he'd heard before somewhere, yet he couldn't remember where or when or who it was by or what it was called. All he knew was that it was starting to haunt him. To his annoyance, Mr Gilmore chose this moment to speak again.

'It's good of you to help Miranda with her music.'

'It's an easy piece to play.'

'Is that an answer?'

'It's the only answer you're getting.'

Mr Gilmore tightened his lips but said nothing. They walked on, Luke praying that there would be no further conversation. But as they reached the lane up to The Haven, the wretched man spoke again. 'So if it had been a difficult piece to play, are you saying you wouldn't have agreed to help her?'

'How the hell do I know?' Luke flashed an angry glance at him. 'What do you keep asking me these stupid questions for?'

'I don't know. Maybe I'm nervous.'

'Nervous of what?'

'You.'

They stared at each other for a moment, then walked on in silence as far as The Haven. Luke pushed open the gate, then turned and scowled.

'I can't help the way you feel,' he said.

'That's true.'

'So you can't blame me.'

'You're absolutely right, Luke. I can't blame you.'

Luke felt the scowl deepen. Somehow this quiescent response from Mr Gilmore was even more irritating than the questions earlier. But there was nothing to be done about that and no point in hanging around out here. He shrugged and nodded towards the gate. 'You going in, then?'

'No.' Mr Gilmore looked calmly back at him and then—to Luke's further annoyance—had the nerve to smile. 'I'll be getting back, Luke. I've got an invoice to do. I'll catch you later.' And Roger Gilmore set off up the lane towards the square.

Luke stood there, chafing with resentment and at the same time feeling slightly guilty, though he didn't know why. He forced the thoughts of Mr Gilmore to the side and turned towards the house again. But as he did so, the weeping of the girl came back, and with it the strains of that simple tune he'd heard earlier, and the deep, distant roar that seemed to engulf all space. And that was not all. More sounds were coming—urgent, unsettling, unearthly sounds. Sounds that filled him with longing and disquiet.

6

M r Harding heard him through the Schubert, then sat in silence for some time, his ancient face craggier than ever now that he was frowning. Luke watched him for a moment, then, when the old man didn't speak, he turned and stared out of the window into the garden. Two cats were stalking a robin on the lawn but it saw them coming and flew off over the wall and they slunk out of sight. Luke looked back at Mr Harding. The old man was still sunk in silence on the chair next to the piano. Then suddenly, as though waking from a doze, he stirred.

'Luke,' he said, struggling to his feet, 'come and sit down for a moment.'

'I am sitting down.'

'I mean away from the piano.'

Luke gave him a quizzical look but the old man merely patted him on the arm and smiled. 'Luke, just do it for me, there's a good boy. I know you love questioning everything and everybody these days and you're no doubt thinking you just want to play your pieces and clear off without having to talk to a boring old windbag like me, but just for once, make my day and do as I ask.' The old man leaned forward suddenly and studied the bruises on Luke's face. 'Besides, you shouldn't be doing much anyway today after getting knocked about like that. Yes, yes, I know. You don't want to talk about it. Now come and sit down.'

And without waiting for an answer, the old man

hobbled over to one of the armchairs by the big bay window and, with something of an effort, lowered himself into it. Still feeling somewhat mystified, Luke stood up from the piano, walked over to the window and sat down in the armchair opposite, wondering what Mr Harding wanted. But Mr Harding didn't appear to want anything right now, except to gaze out of the window at the garden. Luke stared out, too, wondering what this strange behaviour meant. Mr Harding had always been a quirky old man but he'd never broken off a lesson before; and they weren't even a quarter of the way through this one.

Maybe he was ill. He was certainly getting on in years and he didn't move so well these days with his arthritis. He probably shouldn't still be teaching and he certainly shouldn't be organizing yet another village concert. But Mr Harding was a man in love with music and it was hard to imagine him giving up any of his activities. Luke fidgeted in the chair. Fond though he was of Mr Harding, it didn't really seem fair of him to take Mum's money without giving a lesson in return. The old man seemed to catch his thought. 'We'll make this lesson a freebie, I think, Luke. Since we're just sitting around.' His eyes still wandered over the garden. 'Look at that wisteria,' he said dreamily. 'It's starting to flower. Isn't it beautiful? And I gather the bluebells are out in the forest.'

'Yes.'

'Must be a lovely sight. I'm afraid I'll just have to picture them from this armchair. I'm too old to go rambling in the forest these days. I do rather miss it though. And I miss climbing trees. I really do. I used to do a lot of that when I was your age.' Mr Harding fell silent again, his eyes now half-closed; then, after what seemed a long time, he said: 'What is it you're hearing, Luke?'

'Eh?'

'You *heard* me,' said the old man, chuckling at his own joke.

Luke frowned, unsure what to say. Right now he felt as though every sound in the universe was somehow finding its way to him. He knew this could not be true— not even remotely—yet in spite of that his mind was awash with sounds: the song of a thrush, the laughter of children in next door's garden, the bounce of a football in the lane, and other sounds, softer sounds, so soft he knew that no one in the world should be able to hear them, yet they felt as loud to him as the beating of a drum. He heard the pounding of the old man's heart, the gurgle of saliva in his throat, the groan of his muscles, the murmur of his thoughts; and still more sounds came, sounds too subtle to believe in, too vivid to deny. He heard the breathing of the cats as they prowled through some unseen part of the garden; he heard the feather-touch of their paws in the soil, the swish of flower petals against their fur, the mad scuttling of insects over roots and twigs. He heard the whisper of clouds, the soughing of the air, the hiss and hum of the world as it spun through space. He heard the oceanic roar that dominated everything and the childlike tune that would not let him go, locked within it like a thread of light.

'The isle is full of noises,' said the old man in the same dreamy voice. He glanced at Luke and gave a languid smile. 'It was a quotation.'

'From what?'

'It doesn't matter. I'm sure you're not really that interested.' Mr Harding leaned his head back against the chair and closed his eyes completely. 'Your world has always been full of sounds,' he said. 'You are made of music, Luke.'

'What?'

'You are made of music. We all are but you're different.'

'In what way?'

'Because you experience it. You're one of the few who do. Music consumes you. But it comes at a price, doesn't it?'

Luke looked away. This whole thing was getting disconcerting. Mr Harding had always been whimsical but he'd never talked like this before. Mostly when they met he just listened while Luke played, made a few comments and suggestions, and that was it. In the early days when Luke was just starting, the old man had done a bit more, but not much because Dad had always been there to give help—when he wasn't away doing recitals—and Dad's help was real help, the best, most expert help anyone could ever have wanted. Mr Harding, for all his knowledge and enthusiasm, could not match that, but he had never really needed to.

Luke sensed the old man's eyes on his face and looked back. Mr Harding smiled at him. 'There's nothing I can teach you, Luke. Nothing at all. Not about music, anyway. There never really was. All I've ever been able to do is cheer you from the sidelines.'

'But I still make mistakes when I play the piano.'

'We're not talking about technique. We're talking about music. I thought you understood that.' There was a long silence, Mr Harding's eyes still fixed upon him; then the old man spoke again. 'But you do understand deep down. I can see that you do.'

Luke looked away again, feeling more and more uncomfortable at the way this conversation was going. His eye lit on a small wooden carving which he hadn't seen before on the mantelpiece. It was of a man sitting at a piano, bent so close to the instrument that he seemed to merge with it. There was no mistaking who had made it.

'Beautiful, isn't it?' said Mr Harding and Luke looked round to see him staring up at the sculpture as well. 'I asked Roger to do me something,' the old man went on, 'and he came up with this wonderful piece. And now I can't get him to take any money for it. He says it's a present.' Mr Harding shook his head. 'No wonder that man's always skint. But he's got a gift for beauty. There's no doubt about that. And he's really captured something here, don't you think? Man and instrument, made of the same substance.'

'Ash?'

'Yes,' said Mr Harding. 'But that's not the substance I meant.'

'What substance did you mean?'

'I meant music, Luke. Music itself.'

There was another long silence, both of them still staring at the sculpture; and the more Luke looked at it, the more uncomfortable he felt, though he wasn't sure why. Mr Harding spoke again. 'You have a gift for beauty, too, Luke. But it's not much use if you're not right in yourself.'

'What's that supposed to mean?' said Luke suspiciously.

Mr Harding went on studying the sculpture for a few moments, then he answered. 'Your gift could really help other people, Luke. But have you ever considered that it might help you, too?'

'I don't need any help.'

'You don't?'

'No.'

'OK.'

And Mr Harding turned back to the window and gazed out at the garden again. Luke scowled at the old man's averted head, angry with him for dropping these unwelcome suggestions into his mind. 'I don't need any help,' he repeated.

'You just said.'

'So why are you suggesting I do?'

'Because you're at war, Luke.'

'Who with?'

'Everybody. Especially yourself.'

Luke bustled furiously to his feet. 'I don't need to stay and listen to this.'

'You're absolutely right,' said the old man. 'But you did ask.'

Luke stood there, still glowering at the old man, yet unsure what to do. Part of him wanted to storm out, part of him wanted to stay and give Mr Harding a piece of his mind. The old man glanced up at him and gave a smile, as though nothing was wrong between them, then went on, in the same quiet tone he'd used all along.

'I'm leaving the village after this year's concert.'

Luke slumped back into the chair. 'What for?'

'Well, I'm retiring, as you know. I'm tired and—to be honest with you, Luke—I'm not really that well. That's why there aren't going to be any more concerts after this year's. I'm just going to do this last one and then I'm moving away.'

'Where to?'

'To Norwich. To stay with my sister. She's nearly eighty-five and she needs looking after.'

'You need looking after.'

Mr Harding gave him a wry look. 'I'll take that as an expression of concern for my welfare rather than a comment on my state of mind. But thank you for both.' The old man fell silent for a few moments, his chin resting on his chest as though he was about to take a nap, then he said: 'Play something for me, Luke.'

'What do you want me to play?'

'Oh, anything. Something you want to play. Something that's singing in your head. I can tell there's a tune of some kind doing that inside you right now.'

Luke thought of the piece that was haunting him,

the one that was so childlike and wistful and for some reason made him think of the young girl at The Grange. He tried to think of pieces he knew that had been written with children in mind. There was Schumann's *Scenes Of Childhood* but it wasn't one of those. 'Mr Harding?' he said.

'Yes, Luke.'

'Have you got the music for *The Children's Corner Suite*?'

'I thought you didn't like Debussy.'

'It's just some Debussy I don't like. Have you got the music?'

'Bound to have it somewhere. It's just finding it that's the problem.' Mr Harding hauled himself to his feet and shuffled over to the shelves, as packed with volumes of music as the shelves in the music room at The Haven. A few minutes later, after much searching, he pulled out one of the volumes and dusted it down. 'Must get all this stuff categorized one of these days,' he mumbled. 'A little job for my retirement perhaps. Anyway, here it is.'

Luke jumped up and walked over to him. The old man rested a hand on Luke's shoulder to steady himself and gave him the music. Luke opened it and they looked at the contents page together, Mr Harding running a finger down the titles. 'Some of these pieces are lovely, Luke. ''The Doll's Serenade'' is my favourite, I think, or ''The Little Shepherd''. They're both exquisite. You really should give old Debussy a second chance, you know. What made you ask for *The Children's Corner Suite*?'

'Just wanted to see it.' Luke leafed through the pages and scanned the opening bars of each piece, searching for the tune that ran through his head, but he couldn't find it. Not that he'd really expected to. Debussy's music was even less like the melody he was hearing than Schumann's was.

'Try this one,' said Mr Harding, hunting through until he found the page. ' "The Snow is Dancing". I've always liked it. Unless there's a particular one you want to play. Only don't do "The Golliwog's Cake-Walk". I know everyone else seems to love it but I can't stand the piece.'

'You really should give old Debussy a second chance, you know.'

'Touché.' Mr Harding raised an eyebrow. 'Things must be looking up if you're pulling my leg. Go on.' He tottered back to the armchair and sat down again. 'Play me something. Anything you want. Even "The Golliwog's Cake-Walk" if you really must.'

Luke started to play 'The Snow is Dancing'. He hadn't expected to know the piece but the moment he started, he recognized it. Dad had played it several times. It wasn't the wistful tune that even now was singing in his head like a cross-current of melody, but it was beautiful in itself and he played on, gradually settling into the music; and before long the snow was dancing in pictures before him, while the other tune, by some strange skill of its own, kept company with it.

Mr Harding did not move but Luke could feel him sitting there behind him, motionless. He played on, the pictures of snowflakes bright before him, and still the other tune clung there, tinkling in the back of his mind. The Debussy came to an end but the other piece went on, like a whisper; then it, too, died away. All sounds seemed to be gone now. He sat there in the silence, staring at the piano. Mr Harding gave a sigh.

'You have your father's touch, Luke. Thank you. And good luck.'

'Good luck?' Luke twisted round on the piano seat and stared at him. 'Are you dismissing me?'

'I told you. You don't need me. You need a new

teacher. Someone far more advanced than me. Someone you can really respect.'

'I respect you.'

'Thank you, Luke. But you still need a new teacher.'

'But what about the concert? I need to practise the Liszt you wanted me to play.'

'Oh, don't play that,' said Mr Harding with a wave of the hand. 'Virtuoso stuff, I know, but it's not really your cup of tea. I don't know why I was so keen on you doing it. Perhaps I just wanted your brilliance to somehow reflect on me. What a silly notion at my age.'

'You mean I'm not good enough to play it?'

'Of course you're good enough. With practice, Luke, you could probably play just about anything in time. That's how good you could be. But I told you, this isn't about technique. It's about music. It's about what sings in your heart. You play the Liszt quite well but it doesn't sing in your heart. I should have got you off that piece ages ago. It's just the vanity of an old man, like I say. Play whatever you want at the concert. And by the way, help Miranda with her piece, too, can you? She's so nervous about it. I've been trying for weeks to get her to pluck up courage and ask you for help but I bet she still hasn't done it.'

'She has. And I've agreed.'

'Oh, good.'

'But I don't know what to play for my solo piece now. And what about the programme? You've got to get it printed and—'

'Luke, will you relax?' Mr Harding smiled at him. 'It's been my concert for the last forty years and if I can't mess around with it, who can?'

'But you can't print the programme until you know what I'm going to play.'

'Don't worry. We'll just print your bit as: *Luke Stanton: Personal Choice.* How does that sound?'

'Pretty weird.'

'Good. So go away and choose whatever piece you want—something weird if you prefer it—and then come along on the night and play it. We'll keep your piece last as before, to round off the evening.'

'So when do I need to let you know what I'm playing?'

Mr Harding rolled his eyes. 'Luke, you do love to complicate things. You don't need to tell me anything, OK? Just turn up on the night and play and make us all happy.'

Luke stared out of the window again and saw the cats padding across the lawn once more. A moment later they slipped from view behind the shed. The roaring sound returned, growing louder and louder until it seemed to race through him and around him from every particle of space; and amidst the roar, as though curled up inside it, he heard the weeping voice of the girl, and the strange plaintive melody. The old man rested his head against the top of the chair again and slowly closed his eyes.

'The isle is full of noises,' he said.

7

Luke waited till Mum had driven off to town for the shopping, then hurried upstairs to her study, switched on the computer and keyed in his password. It was good to be alone. He needed to be alone. He'd had too much of people lately. Yet even now his solitude did not feel complete. He could hear the girl's voice again, breathing through his thoughts. He tried to ignore it and concentrate on checking his e-mails. There were two waiting for him, one from Miranda, the other from an address he didn't recognize; but he knew at once who the message was from. It was just one word and Skin hadn't even bothered to sign it.

Midnight.

He frowned, deleted the message and checked Miranda's.

Hi, Luke!
THANKS for saying you'll help me with my piece at the concert. I just feel so much better knowing the piano bit will be OK even if the flute's going to sound rubbish. I promise I'll try really hard not to embarrass you. I did try the piece with Melanie at the piano but she's not very confident (like me!!!!) and keeps having to stop and she also fidgets and sniffs a lot when she's playing and that puts me off. I won't worry nearly so much if you're doing the piano part. Can we meet up and practise some time soon? I know you don't need to because you're so brilliant on the piano but I do. It would really mean

61

a lot to me if we could practise together. Are you free tomorrow morning around 11? You could maybe come to The Toby Jug and use our piano or I could come to your house. I don't mind. I've got to help Mum and Dad quite a lot tomorrow so I'm a bit busy but I've got some free time around 11 and it would be really great if we could practise then. Can you let me know if that's OK and where you want to meet up? Thanks again, Luke. This means such a lot to me. I've never played in front of other people before and I really want to do it well. See you soon. Love, Miranda :-) xxx

He e-mailed straight back.

Tomorrow is fine. I'll come to The Toby Jug at 11. See you then.
    Luke

He sat back in the chair and stared out of the window. Across the lane the fields of Bill Foley's farm were a brilliant gold in the late-afternoon sun. He saw house martins flitting round the barn and watched them for a moment, then turned back and ran his eye over the Norwegian dictionaries and other reference books that Mum used in her translation work. Close by on the wall was the framed photograph of Dad outside the Albert Hall in the days just before the chemo took away his hair. At the bottom was the handwritten inscription that Mum had scrawled before giving Dad the picture.

To Matt, my beautiful husband. With love, Kirsti.

He closed his eyes, unable to look at it any longer, and to his surprise saw a blue light spreading under the darkness of his brow. It was like a ripple moving across a pond and he watched it for a while, finding it strangely

62

comforting. The familiar rumbling sound started. It was more of a hum than a roar this time, yet it was as powerful and as clear as ever. He squeezed the edge of the desk and listened. What was this sound? Where did it come from? It seemed to be there all the time now. Even when he didn't hear it, he could feel it reverberating through him like an engine that never stopped. He heard other sounds, too—the chatter of birds, the drone of an aeroplane, the fruity chuckle of Bill Foley as he talked to someone by the barn—but the hum, subtle though it was, seemed greater than all these sounds. The blue light deepened and he saw splashes of gold around the edges of his inner sight.

He snapped open his eyes, uneasy at what was happening. These sights and sounds didn't feel scary, yet they were unsettling. He remembered what he'd come here to do and stared back at the screen—but he was dreading this. The thought of nosing through Mum's private e-mails filled him with distaste, not so much because he felt guilty about it—which he did—but because he was frightened of what he might find. The only time he'd done this before was when he'd thought Mrs Searle from school was e-mailing Mum about his behaviour in class, and he'd felt bad enough then, even though he'd found nothing. But he had to check again. He had to know about Mum and Roger Gilmore. If they were corresponding by e-mail, they would probably have discussed the marriage thing. And he had to know what they'd said.

He hoped she hadn't changed the password she'd used last time he broke into her system. That one had been easy to crack. She'd simply chosen the full name of her favourite composer. Holding his breath, he keyed in the word again.

edvardgrieg

And a moment later he was browsing through Mum's e-mail inbox. It was full of messages, mostly from her translation clients in Norway. He ran down the list of senders, checking them one by one, and right at the end found the name he was looking for:

Roger Gilmore

He frowned and checked the date and time of the message. It had been sent while he was out at Mr Harding's. He hesitated, then clicked on the box and brought the message to the screen. Like Skin's, it was short and unsigned.

I'll wait forever if that's what it takes.

And below was the message from Mum to which he was replying.

Roger, please be patient and wait. I promise I'll give you an answer soon. Kirsti.

He returned to his own e-mail system, glad to be out of Mum's but feeling worse than ever now. *I'll wait forever if that's what it takes.* He frowned. Why did Mr Gilmore have to be in love with Mum? Why couldn't he be in love with someone else? There were plenty of other beautiful women around. Mum wasn't the only one. And why did he have to be the kind of man he was? Luke clenched his fists, determined to hold on to his anger, but it was no use. No matter how hard he tried, he was finding it increasingly difficult to accept his own assessment of Roger Gilmore. If the man had been arrogant or boring or stupid, then in some strange way that would have made things easier, though he'd still have hated him. But even in his most cynical moments, Luke knew that Roger Gilmore was none of those things, and that his only real flaw was that he'd fallen in love with the woman who had once been Dad's wife.

Dad's wife.

The words tore at him and he felt tears starting. He squeezed his fists even more tightly. He wouldn't give in to this. He'd fight it, he'd . . . he'd do something. He glared at the screen, then, on an impulse, clicked New Message. The box appeared before him, the cursor flashing in the space for the recipient's address. He started to type:

dad@heaven.com

Then stopped. What the hell was he doing? This was only going to upset him even more. But he couldn't hold back now. He glowered at the words in the imaginary e-mail address, then clicked on the subject box and typed:

Why?

He was crying now, uncontrollably, but he clicked the message box and went on typing:

Why won't you answer?

He sent the message, switched off the computer and thrust his face in his hands. He was acting like an idiot. He knew that. The message would come straight back from the server with the address unrecognized and he'd end up feeling more miserable than when he'd started, if that was possible. But he couldn't think about that now. He went on crying, his face still pushed into his hands, his mind centred on Dad. It was some minutes before he calmed down. He took his hands away, wiped his eyes and leaned back in the chair, staring out of the window. The sky was now cloudy and the fields a steely grey. The voice of the girl and the deep humming sound were gone and all that reached him was birdsong. Then, to his surprise, he heard music.

It was so quiet he barely caught the notes but it sounded like the piano down in the music room. Yet that was ridiculous: there was no one in the house but him. It must be coming from somewhere else. He listened again. No, it was definitely coming from downstairs. But what was it? It wasn't like anything he'd ever heard before and it had an eerie beauty. Yet the strangest thing of all was that it was unfinished. It ran for a while, then stopped in the middle of a bar and started again from the beginning. He listened to it a few times, then it faded away. He walked to the door of Mum's study and stood there. All was silent now and he was beginning to think he'd imagined the music, then he caught it again, soft but clear and unquestionably coming from the music room. He started to walk downstairs, frightened now at the thought of what this might mean.

The music grew fainter as he descended the stairs but it was still audible, stopping as always at the same point, then returning to the beginning and starting again. It was like listening to someone practising a few bars of something again and again in order to perfect them. He reached the hall, walked up to the door of the music room, and, after a moment's hesitation, pushed it open. As he did so, the sound died away. The house fell silent, yet the music still hung upon it like a scent. He could hear it in his mind like some half-uttered snatch of improvisation. He walked over to the piano and sat down; and heard the music start again. He stared down at the keys. They were unmoving, yet they seemed bright with energy. He ran his

66

fingers soundlessly over them, following the pathway of the tune as it coursed over him; then he pressed down. The sound of the instrument startled him for a moment— it felt strange to be tracking another melody like this— but he played on, anxious at first in case he broke the thread of notes that he was hearing, then with more confidence as he realized how strong they were; and suddenly he realized he was enjoying himself, listening and playing, listening and playing, and the piano was starting to speak—then the tune ran out.

And silence fell once more.

He sat there, rudderless, his hands resting on the keys. The tune had stopped mid-bar, mid-thought, in exactly the same place. Where was it meant to go next? He had no idea. He stared towards the window and saw a shaft of sunlight break through the clouds and brighten the old harp that Dad had bought all those years ago in a sentimental moment; then the clouds closed again, the sunlight vanished, and the sky darkened over Bill Foley's farm. He thought of the business of the night that lay before him and frowned, wishing now that he'd never had anything to do with Skin and the others. But he knew he was too deeply involved and that he'd pay an even heavier price than before if he failed to deliver again. Even the prospect of seeing the mysterious girl was not enough to make him feel better about what was to come. He stared down at the piano and tried once again to hear the unfinished tune, which for some reason made him think of Dad. But, like his father, it was gone.

8

The Grange at midnight was an even scarier place than it had been before. He stared over the wall at its shadowy outline, then turned to the others. They were watching him in silence but he knew what was in their minds. They were waiting to see if he would fail them again. Skin spoke, his voice hard and low. 'All yours, Luke. Time to show us you're not the chicken we think you are.' There was a murmur of agreement from Daz. Skin glanced round at the house, then turned back to Luke. 'And you've got lots of open windows to choose from this time. Now isn't that nice?'

It was true. There were three open on the first floor, one to the study he had climbed into yesterday and two to the left of it, plus the skylight at the top of the house. He stared up at it and thought of the girl again but Skin prodded his arm to make him look back; then held out a balaclava. 'Put that on. Just in case you bump into the old crow.'

'I don't want it.' Luke pushed it away. 'I need to be able to hear properly.'

'Suit yourself.' Skin thrust the balaclava back in his pocket and leaned closer, his eyes smouldering with the same black fire Luke had seen in them before. 'Now remember—it's different this time. She's in the house so you've got to be really quiet. When you get inside, you just look for the box. You don't fiddle about with anything else, no matter how tempting it looks. If you see something worth nicking, make a note in your head and we'll come back for it another time. All you want right now is the box. It's about this size.' Skin held out his hands as a measure. 'And it's got—'

'I know what it looks like. You've told me.'

'All right.' Skin's eyes ran over him again. 'So go and get it.'

'What if it's in her bedroom?'

'Then you'll have to be extra quiet, won't you?'

'Like a little mouse,' put in Daz. 'Squeak squeak.'

'Only no squeak squeak,' chortled Speed. 'She might hear that.'

Luke looked round and saw both boys smirking; but Skin's face didn't even flicker. 'She won't hear you if you're careful,' he said. 'Just don't rush it. Creep about until you find the box, then bring it down to the front door and let yourself out. That's the only risky bit. She might hear you when the door clicks so don't move away from the house until we give you the signal from behind the wall. We'll be checking the windows above to see if she's looking out. When you get the all-clear, bring the box to the gate and hand it over and you're done.'

'What if she's looking out of one of the windows?'

'Then we'll give you the signal to stay put.'

'I can't just hang around in the doorway. Not if she knows someone's there.'

'Yeah, you can. She won't be able to see you from any of the windows, not if you keep close to the door. The moment she leaves the window to come downstairs or call the police or whatever, we'll give you the signal and you can run for it. We'll be out of sight before she gets anywhere near the front door. Nothing to it.'

Luke glanced from face to face but it was clear there was no way out of this. 'I'll see you later,' he said. He left them in their hiding place behind the wall, slipped down to the track and cut along to the gate of the house. The building rose above him, tall and silent in the darkness. Over to the right he could see the trees of Buckland Forest moving against the night sky. He climbed over the gate, crept across the gravel to where the lawn started, then ran round the back of the building. He had already decided to use the same window as last time. It was the easiest route into the house and since the room was a study and not a bedroom, he was less likely to bump into Mrs Little, as long as she didn't hear a noise and come to investigate. He reached the drainpipe and started to clamber up it, the scent of honeysuckle heavy upon him, and was soon level with the first floor and stretching across towards the window. Yet again he found himself feeling grateful for his strong hands. He remembered Dad taking them in his own that time after they'd been climbing together in the Lake District: 'Good hands, Luke,' he'd said. 'Special hands. Strong and sensitive. Good for climbing and good for piano playing. You can do anything you want with hands like these. So don't ever put them to bad use.'

And here he was, doing exactly that. He bit his lip and swung himself into the study, moonlight pouring through with him. He moved to the dark side of the room and held himself still, listening. There were no sounds of movement or voices in the house, not even weeping from the girl. He listened for several minutes, then crept to the door of the room and stared round it. The landing was dark, though moonlight from the window was pushing through the open doorway and catching the figurines on the shelves opposite. They seemed to stare at him like miniature gargoyles. Further down to the left another snatch of moonlight was breaking through from the door at the end. He frowned. If that was the old woman's bedroom and she had the door open, he would have to be even quieter to avoid being heard. And what if she kept the box by her bed?

But he turned the other way. The box would have to wait. He had to find out about the girl first. He knew this was probably even more risky than trying to steal the box—she could panic and scream before he could say a word to her—but he had to try and find out who she was and what was wrong. He knew she was somewhere in the house. He could sense her, even though, for once, he couldn't hear her. He crept towards the little raised door at the end of the landing. She had been in the attic room before, locked up like a prisoner, and it was the obvious place to try first, though the thought of going up there and seeing that terrified face again now filled him with dread.

He reached the raised door, opened it as softly as he could, and paused, listening. Still no voices or sounds of movement in the house. He stared at the steps that led up to the attic room, his heart thumping inside him, then started to climb. The silence around him was now so deep he felt as though his steps were resounding all round the house. He reached the upper landing and stopped. The bathroom door was open but he didn't even glance in. He knew she would not be in there. His eyes were fixed on the bedroom door. It was closed, as before. Would it be locked again, too? He tiptoed up to it, leaned closer, and listened for sounds inside the room. There were none—at least, none that he could hear. He gripped the door-knob, took a slow breath and turned. It was not locked. There was a light click; he froze, waiting for a scream from inside the room, but none came. He took another slow breath and pushed open the door just enough to peer into the room.

The light was off but he could see by the moon-glow falling in through the skylight that there was no one here. Yet clearly the young girl had been—and presumably still was—living in this room. Her day-clothes were strewn about the floor, though the bed did not appear to have been slept in. He looked uneasily around him. Where was she? He glanced at the bed again. If she were hiding underneath, she would be even more terrified if his face suddenly appeared; but he knew he had to check. He knelt down, paused for a moment, then whispered: 'Don't scream. Please don't scream. I promise I won't hurt you. I'm your friend.' And he looked underneath.

All he saw was a pair of tiny slippers. He stood up again and turned to face the door, his own fear deepening by the second. The house now ached with silence. He crept back down the steps to the raised door and stared along the main landing. It stretched away before him, eerie and still, brightened only by the splashes of moonlight through the open doors of the study and the room at the end. He started to make his way down towards them, slowly, warily, feeling the silence, feeling the presence of the girl somewhere nearby and wondering, too, about Mrs Little.

He stopped at the study door and glanced towards the window. Through it he could see the branches of the silver birch at the southern end of the garden and the night sky speckled with stars. He felt a sudden urge to climb back down the drainpipe and race off into the darkness, away from this place. But he knew what Skin would do to him if he returned empty-handed after such a short time in the house. It would be no use saying he hadn't found the box. Skin would just beat him up worse than before and make him go back another time.

He stared down the landing towards the room at the far end. It was the obvious place to start. The other doors on the landing were closed so there might be a click or the sound of squeaky hinges when he opened them but the moonlit opening to this farthest room should be no problem. All he needed to do was put his head round the half-open door. He stole down towards it, watching, listening, trying to sense where Mrs Little and the girl were. The moonlight ahead of him grew brighter and sharper and as he drew near, he saw that it was catching a corner of the shelving on the opposite wall and illuminating one of the statuettes: a small dancing figure with a flute that reminded him for some reason of Roger Gilmore's sculpture in Mr Harding's music room. The door was only a few feet away. He held his breath and listened.

Still silence. He moved closer to the door. He could feel his hands sweating now, and his cheeks, and his brow. Who was in this room? Mrs Little or the girl? Or both of them? Or were they somewhere else in this ghostly house? He took another step, then stopped again, now level with the half-open door. Through it he could see a window with curtains roughly drawn and moonlight pouring through several gaps onto the floor, over the landing, over him. Beneath the window was a dressing table with bangles, curlers, a hairbrush, a pin-cushion, nail-scissors, tweezers—and something that made him stiffen with excitement.

A large box.

He stared at it. It had to be the one. It was exactly as Skin had described: black velvet sides, thick silver beading on the lid and a funny tassel thing at the front. He clenched his fists. He was so close to success now. He hadn't found the girl but at least this box would get Skin off his back. All he had to do was creep in and take it. He edged forward, still hidden by the door. The bed— assuming this was a bedroom—should be somewhere behind it, over to the right, possibly with Mrs Little or the girl in it. He listened for the sound of breathing but all he heard was his own. He steeled himself, then peeped round the door.

He relaxed at once. The room was empty. There was indeed a bed on the other side of the door but it had nobody in it, though someone had clearly been sleeping here: the sheets and duvet were bundled together in a huge, untidy pile. He frowned. It was unsettling not to know where Mrs Little and the girl were but from the point of view of clearing himself with Skin, things were looking good. He started to creep towards the box, then, to his horror, heard a sound behind him: a small, deliberate cough.

He whirled round in panic and saw Mrs Little standing in the doorway.

9

She was holding a cordless phone in one hand and a stick in the other. He turned away to shield his face from view. It was just possible she hadn't recognized him in the darkness and if he brushed straight past her now before she could switch on the light, he might just get away before she worked out who he was. She gave a little snort of contempt, as though she'd read the thought the moment it entered his mind.

'Don't even think of running,' she said. 'You'll only make it worse for yourself. I know exactly who you are. You're Luke Stanton. You hang around with those louts from the village, Jason Skinner and Darren Fisher and that fat boy—what's his name?' She didn't seem to be asking him so much as herself. 'Speedwell,' she went on. 'Bobby Speedwell. Losers every one of them.' She looked him over. 'I've phoned the police so all we need to do is wait.'

He stood there, trying not to betray his fear. He knew she was right. There was no point in running. He could get past her easily enough but what good would that do? She knew his name. She no doubt knew where he lived. If not, she could easily find out. She'd probably even watched him breaking in. Once again she seemed to read his thought. 'Yes, I saw you climbing over the gate. I don't know if the others are with you.' He could tell this was a question but he said nothing. Her eyes narrowed. 'I suppose you're the one who broke in last night.'

Again he knew this was a question; again he said

nothing. He stared back at her as defiantly as he could but it was hard. He felt only fear: fear of the consequences of all this but, most of all, fear of Mrs Little herself. She was old and frail but she was chilling. She watched him for a moment in silence, then gave another snort of contempt.

'I don't expect you to tell me. But I know it was you. It was obvious someone had climbed in through the study window. There were little bits of earth on the carpet and I certainly didn't put them there. But that's not the only way I know someone was here. I was told.' And, to his surprise, she looked towards the bed and spoke in a strange voice, so different from the cutting tones she had used on him. This other voice was soft, slow, almost coaxing. 'It's all right,' she murmured. 'You can come out now. He's not going to hurt you.'

At first nothing happened, then suddenly the swirl of bedclothes started to move and finally a face appeared. Luke stared. It was the girl he had seen in the attic room. There was no mistaking those tiny features, that glistening black hair. Her eyes moved in a strange, questing way, her head turning this way and that, then she spoke, in a small, anxious voice: 'Nana, Nana . . . '

'Here, darling,' said Mrs Little, struggling towards the bed. The girl's arms were outstretched yet her eyes went on searching as though she found it hard to see the old woman in the darkness. Mrs Little put down the cordless phone and the stick and sat on the bed. The girl's arms were round her at once. 'Nana,' she murmured.

'Nana,' said the old woman, holding her, too, and now stroking the girl's hair and face. Luke watched, unsure what to do. He could get away easily now but somehow there seemed no point; and in spite of the trouble he was in, he was somehow mesmerized by this scene: the ugly old woman he'd always regarded as a dragon and the girl clinging to her as though her life depended upon it. Mrs Little went on stroking the girl without even a glance in his direction and her only words were whispers of reassurance, which seemed to be working as the girl was clearly starting to calm down. After a while the old woman kissed her on the head and spoke in a slightly louder voice. 'He's over by the far wall. Don't you want to say hello to him?'

The girl didn't speak and simply buried her face in Mrs Little's neck. Luke caught a sharp glance from the old woman.

'Hello,' he said awkwardly.

Again the girl said nothing. There was a long silence, Luke still standing there, the girl still clinging to Mrs Little but calmer now; and Mrs Little went on stroking her, kissing her, holding her. Luke watched with uneasy fascination. Suddenly the old woman looked up at him and spoke again. 'She's terrified of you. She's been terrified all day after last night's experience when I was out of the house. That's why I've had her sleeping with me tonight.'

'I'm not going to hurt her.'

'I know you're not.' It sounded to Luke more like a threat than an expression of confidence in him, but when she spoke again, he found he was wrong. 'I know you wouldn't hurt her. You're not like the boys you're stupid enough to hang around with.'

He looked away towards the window. Somewhere outside they would be wondering what was going on. Or perhaps not. Perhaps they didn't care. Perhaps the whole plan for tonight had just been to set him up as a kind of punishment for yesterday. His eye fell on the box. No, it couldn't be a set-up. This was for real. Skin really wanted that box. But now it didn't look as though he was going to get it. The game was up. The police were involved and there was going to be nothing but trouble. He thought of Mum and what this would do to her. Then Mrs Little spoke again.

'I haven't called the police.'

'What?'

'You say "Pardon", not "What".'

'Pardon?' he said sullenly.

'I haven't called the police. That's not to say I won't. But we can talk about that.'

He looked at her, trying to work out what this all meant. He was still afraid of her, yet she had softened in his eyes a little, perhaps because of her manner with this frightened girl, perhaps simply through what she had just said. He tried to think of the best way to answer but she spoke again first.

'We'll talk downstairs.'

She eased back from the girl, who still clung to her and clearly didn't want her to go. 'It's OK,' murmured the old woman, smoothing the girl's cheek with her hand. 'It's OK. Nana back very, very soon.' Gradually the girl let go. Mrs Little leaned over her and started to rearrange the bedclothes, talking softly to the girl all the while. 'There you are. Let's tuck that bit in there, shall we? Good girl. And that little bit there? OK. That better? Good. Now lie back and close your eyes. What's that?' The girl had whispered something. Mrs Little leaned closer and the girl spoke into her ear. Luke did not catch the words but the old woman did and answered at once. 'No, he won't hurt you. I promise. He won't hurt you.' She stroked the girl's face once more. 'Now, then. Off to sleep. I'm going downstairs for a few minutes but I'll be back soon and then we'll cuddle up together. Night night.'

The girl didn't answer but she seemed calm now. Her eyes were closed and she was snuggled under the duvet, only the top of her face showing. Luke watched, uncomfortable at the thought of her being so frightened of him. Could he be responsible for the terror he had seen on her face that time he looked through the keyhole? Yet he had heard her weeping before she had even known of his existence. He couldn't be the sole cause of her distress. There had to be something else. Mrs Little stood up and turned towards him.

'Come with me,' she said curtly. The sweetness was gone; the hard voice was back and, with it, the hard face. She hobbled out to the landing and down the stairs and he followed, in a daze, trying to make sense of all this and thinking again of the gang outside. She hadn't switched on any of the lights yet but the moment she did, they would realize something had gone wrong, especially if she took him to one of the rooms on their side of the house. But she didn't. She took him to the kitchen at the opposite end, a room they could not see unless they had moved from their hiding place. She switched on the light, sat down at the table and nodded to a chair on the other side. He hesitated, then sat down and waited for her to speak. She did so at once, in the sharp, snapping voice he was used to. 'The girl's blind. You realize that?'

'Blind?'

'You didn't notice?' Her eyes ran over him scornfully. 'Don't tell me *you're* blind. Blind as well as stupid.'

'I don't have to listen to this.'

'Yes, you do. Oh, you can run out of here. Even you ought to be able to escape from an old woman. But where are you going to run? I'll have spoken to the police before you even reach Nut Bush Lane.'

'You can't prove anything.'

'I've seen you in my house.'

'You can't prove that to anyone else. It's your word against mine.'

'And yours is going to count for a lot round here, isn't

79

it?' The old woman gave a mirthless chuckle. 'You forget just how much I know about you. Have you got the faintest idea what's being said about you and your friends in this village?' Luke said nothing. The old woman watched him for a moment. 'One of these days,' she went on, 'instead of trying to burgle my house, why not do an undercover job and sneak into the village shop? Not to steal anything, of course—though I don't doubt you've taken a good few things from there—but just to hide in a cupboard and listen to what Miss Grubb and her customers talk about. You might find it interesting.'

Luke shrugged and looked away but Mrs Little continued.

'They talk about your little gang. They talk about Jason Skinner and what prison he's going to end up in. And Darren Fisher stealing money from his auntie and from the younger kids when he was at the primary school. And how that Speedwell boy used to be such a nice kid before he got mixed up with Skinner and Fisher. But most of all, they talk about you.'

He looked back at her. 'Me?'

'Yes, you.'

There was a silence between them. He took a slow breath. 'Why me?'

She stood up, walked somewhat painfully over to the window and stared out. 'They're out there now, are they? Your friends?'

'Why do people talk about me?'

'Where are they hiding? Behind the wall by the track round the forest?'

'Why do people talk about me?'

'Or are they on this side of the house?'

He didn't answer. She went on gazing out of the window for a few moments, then spoke again. 'They talk about you because you're not like the other boys. You're

80

different. You're special. So people say.' She paused. 'I think they're wrong. I don't think you're special at all. I think you're stupid. Are your friends hiding out there?'

'Why do they say I'm special?'

'Are they out there?'

'Why do they say I'm special?'

'Are they?'

'Yes.'

She paused again, as though winning this admission from him had cost her some effort. When she spoke again, it was in a less censorious voice. 'And are you going to get into trouble with them for not bringing something back? Some spoils? Some booty?'

'Maybe.'

The old woman turned suddenly. 'They say you're special because of your gift.' He said nothing. She studied his face for a moment. 'You're the son of Matthew Stanton, aren't you?'

'What if I am?'

'And you play the piano. Like your father.'

'Like my father *did*,' he spat, glaring at her. Her face seemed to soften a little, though the anger and scorn were not far away.

'I read about the cancer,' she said.

'Bully for you.'

She watched him in silence for what seemed a long time, then looked away. 'Your father was a wonderful pianist,' she said. 'I heard him play at the Festival Hall ten years ago. He was—'

'I don't want to talk about this.'

'He was magnificent. He played like a god.'

'I just told you—' He stood up. 'I don't want to talk about this, OK? Do you understand English? I don't want to talk about it.' He glowered at her. 'I'm going home. Do what you like about the police.'

81

'And the little girl upstairs?'

'What about her?' He tried to harden his expression but he could feel his will weakening at the thought of that frightened face he had seen upstairs. 'What about her?' he said again. For answer, she pulled open a drawer, crumpled something inside her fist, and walked up to him.

'You can help her,' said the old woman.

'But she's frightened of me.'

'She's not frightened of you. She's terrified of you.'

'So I can't help her.'

Mrs Little looked into his eyes so deeply he felt as though she was staring right through him. 'You can't walk away from this,' she said. 'You think you can be hard like those other boys but you can't. Because you're not hard. You just want to be hard. You want to rage against the world because the world took away your father. But now you've got a chance to do some good.' And before he could speak, she took his hand, prised open the fingers and thrust the contents of her fist into his palm. He looked down and saw a small bundle of notes. 'Something to show your friends,' she said. 'It's not a lot but it might keep you on the right side of them. You'd have found the money anyway if you'd looked long enough.' She held his eyes steadily. 'Come back when you can and don't tell anyone what you're doing. Not a word. I'll tell you how you can help another time. But come. I'll be waiting for you. And so will my granddaughter.'

He frowned at the mention of that last word. Somehow, even though the girl had called the old woman 'Nana', it hadn't occurred to him that the two might be related. Mrs Little was such a solitary person it was hard to imagine her having a family. He looked down at the money in his hand, then pushed it back into hers, and turned towards the door. 'I can't get involved in this,' he said, and set off out of the kitchen. She called after him at once.

'You'll come back, won't you?'

'No.'

'But you can help.'

'I can't. And it's not my business.'

He strode off down the hall. The old woman didn't follow. He reached the front door and made to open it, then stopped and turned. She had walked as far as the entrance to the kitchen and was standing there, remote and proud, yet somehow less fearsome than she had been. Above him he heard the weeping sound that was now so familiar. He looked up. The girl had appeared at the top of the stairs and was feeling her way round the wall as though searching for the banister rail. Her face was drowned in tears. Mrs Little hurried up and put her arms round her before she drew too close to the edge.

'Nana,' murmured the girl.

The old woman pulled out a handkerchief and dabbed it over the girl's face, then looked down at Luke, who was still standing by the front door. 'You'll come back,' she said. 'Won't you?'

He stared up at the two figures, locked together as though they shared the same pain, then he turned without a word and left the house.

10

He didn't check for Skin's signal, but climbed straight over the gate, set off up the track and stopped by the turning to Nut Bush Lane. He didn't have long to wait; within seconds three shadows had emerged from the darkness. They moved towards him like ghosts and stopped a few feet from him.

'You didn't wait for the signal,' said Skin.

'I forgot.'

'I told you to wait by the front door in case she heard you leave and looked out of the window.'

'Yeah, sorry.'

'And you haven't got the box.'

'Couldn't find it.'

The three moved closer until he could see their faces. He braced himself to fight or run. Without the box he knew that in their eyes he had failed them yet again. If he said or did the wrong thing now, Skin would fall on him for sure, and Daz, too, probably. He glanced down the track at the moonlit roof of The Grange, then quickly back at Skin. 'Can we get away from here?' he said, as casually as he could. 'The old woman might hear us.' He turned to set off down Nut Bush Lane but Skin caught him by the arm.

'She can't.'

'Can't what?'

'Hear us.'

'She might.'

He tried to move off again but the grip tightened and stopped him. Skin leaned closer. 'I just told you,' he said through gritted teeth, 'she can't hear us.' He kept his hand locked round Luke's arm. 'So you can tell us what happened—or what didn't happen—inside the house.'

'You're hurting my arm.'

'Tough. What happened?'

Luke stared back at him in the darkness. 'I didn't find the box.'

'We've established that.'

'But I had a good look round. There was nothing worth nicking.'

Daz snorted and moved closer. 'Nothing worth nicking? What about those ornaments?'

'All rubbish,' said Luke, keeping his eyes on Skin. 'Just statues and stuff. Cheap and tacky.'

'Never mind the ornaments,' said Skin, still watching him. 'What about the box?'

'I told you. I didn't see it.'

'Where did you look?'

'All over the house.'

'Every room?'

'Yeah.'

Daz spoke again in his thin voice. 'I reckon you didn't bother looking.'

'I did.'

'I reckon you just got inside and curled up in some dark corner, all scared in case the old girl caught you.'

'So how come I left through the front door?'

'That's no big deal,' said Daz. 'You still could have spent the rest of the time doing nothing.'

Speed yawned. 'If he hasn't got the box, can we go home? I'm tired.'

'Nobody's leaving,' said Skin. 'Not till I've found out exactly what happened.' He fixed his eyes on Luke again. 'Tell me everything you did from the moment you got in.'

Luke tried to look steadily back. He knew his safety depended not just on the answers he gave but the way he gave them. He had to act confident, even if he didn't feel it. He took a deep breath. 'I climbed in through the same window as last time. It opens into a kind of study. There's not much in there, just statues and things, and—'

'Never mind all that. Did you look for the box?'

'Yeah.'

'Where?'

'Well, in the room. I mean, under the desk, on the shelves, behind the—'

'Yeah, yeah. Then what?'

'I went through to the landing.'

'And?'

Luke remembered the dark, silent space; the moonlight pushing through the doors. 'I had a look round there,' he said, 'then I went upstairs.'

'Upstairs?'

'Yeah, there's a sort of attic room. So I checked it out.'

'And?'

'Nothing.'

'Then what?' Skin's questions were coming faster, his voice growing louder. His grip on Luke's arm was tighter than ever. Luke tried to stay calm.

'I went back down to the landing and searched the bedrooms.'

'What about the old woman?'

'Didn't see her.'

'But you just said you checked over the whole house.'

'Yeah.'

'So you must have seen her.'

'Yeah, well . . . what I meant was . . . I saw her but she didn't see me. She was asleep.'

'Which one's her room?'

'Far left of the house as you look up from the garden. First floor.'

'The room with the two windows open?'

'Yeah.'

Skin frowned. 'I thought that had to be her room. So you saw her asleep?'

'Yeah.'

'You actually looked in on her while she was in bed?'

'Yeah.'

Speed gave a giggle. 'Was she wearing curlers? What did she look like?'

He thought of the old woman's angry face as she had stood there in the doorway; then that different face she had shown when talking to the girl; and her strange request that he go back and help. Though how he could do so, he could not imagine. He looked back at Speed. 'She wasn't wearing curlers.'

'But I bet she looked ugly. I bet she looked really gross.'

'Maybe.' Luke shrugged. 'Anyway, I didn't see the box.' He glanced back at Skin. 'Can you let go my arm now? And can we go home?'

But Skin shook his head. 'You haven't finished talking yet.'

'There's nothing more to tell.'

'Sure about that?'

'Yeah.'

Skin watched him in silence for a moment, his grip still tight round Luke's arm, then suddenly he let go, only— in the same movement—to seize both Luke's hands and pull them, palms-upwards, in front of him.

'Let go!' said Luke.

But Skin gripped them like a vice. 'I just want to look at them,' he said. 'If that's all right with you.' There was something disturbingly polite about his voice now. Luke knew there was nothing he could do. Out of the corner of his eye he saw Daz and Speed watching, too, but Skin was the one who worried him. The boy's eyes wandered over the hands for a few moments, then he spoke, in a chillingly casual voice. 'Good hands these, Luke. Very good hands. Very, very, very good hands. No wonder you're brilliant at climbing.' He looked up and met Luke's eyes. 'And playing the piano.'

Luke felt a shudder pass through him. It was not so much the uncanny repetition of Dad's words as the realization of where Skin's mind was moving. The boy's grip tightened round his fingers. Luke tried to look unconcerned.

'Glad you like them,' he said. 'Can I have them back now?'

'Do you like to click the joints?' said Skin.

'Can I have them back?'

'Speedy does that. Go on, Speedy. Make 'em pop.'

Speed duly clicked the joints of his chubby fingers. Skin listened and chuckled. 'I don't know anyone who makes them pop as loud as that.' He pulled Luke's hands higher. 'Do yours make as much noise as that?'

'I don't know. I don't like clicking them.'

'It doesn't hurt. Here, I'll do 'em for you.'

'Don't.'

But already Skin was fiddling with the hands. He went through the fingers one by one, yanking each joint roughly about until it clicked. Luke squirmed but bit off further protest. He knew it was useless. Skin finished at last but kept both hands tightly clasped in his own. 'You can do the thumbs as well,' he said.

'Don't!' said Luke.

'But you've got to be careful.' Skin paused. 'You can break them quite easily.' He gripped the fingers more tightly and started to run his thumbs over the palms in a mocking caress. Then he went on, in the same conversational voice, his thumbs still wandering over the hands. 'I wouldn't want you to lie to me, Luke,' he said.

'I'm not lying to you.'

'Because we don't want anything nasty to happen to you.' The thumbs went on stroking, stroking, stroking. 'And we don't want anything to ruin your . . . ' Skin thought for a moment. 'Your musical career.'

'I'm not lying to you.'

'You've told me everything?'

'Yeah.'

'The old woman was asleep?'

'Yeah.'

'And she stayed asleep?'

'Yeah.'

'Then what?'

'I checked the downstairs rooms.'

'And?'

'I found nothing.'

'And the old woman didn't wake up?'

'I just told you.'

'So how come the kitchen light went on?'

Luke tried desperately to think but the speed of Skin's questions had filled him with confusion. Fortunately, Daz cut in. 'I didn't see the kitchen light go on.'

'Neither did I,' said Speed.

'You wouldn't have done from where we were hiding,' said Skin. 'It was when I left you two and wandered up the track to the other side of the house. I saw the light go on in the kitchen.'

Luke was still thinking frantically. It was possible to see the kitchen window from the track if you hauled yourself up the wall but he was sure the curtains on that side had been drawn across. So it was possible Skin had spotted the light on but hadn't seen him talking to Mrs Little inside; unless there had been a gap in the curtains. Once again he tried to act more confident than he felt. 'I put the light on,' he said, trying to ignore the thumbs still moving over his palms. 'The old woman was asleep upstairs and I felt sure she wouldn't wake up so I put the kitchen light on when I was down there. I thought it might help me see things better.'

'So why didn't you put the lights on in any of the other rooms?'

'Didn't think it was a good idea. The kitchen's the room furthest from her bedroom. I reckoned it would be safe.' He paused. 'Can you let go my hands?'

'Why were you in the kitchen so long?'

'Can you let go my hands?'

'When I'm ready. Why were you in the kitchen so long?'

'I wanted to have a good look through all the drawers and things.'

'She'd hardly keep the box in there.'

'Yeah, I know.' Luke shifted on his feet, at a loss for a convincing answer. Skin stared at him a while longer, then slowly released his hands. Luke let them fall by his side and moved the fingers a little to ease some of the tension from them. Skin stared at him a moment longer, then turned to the others.

'Go back to your beds. And make sure you don't wake anybody up. Meet tomorrow afternoon. Usual time, usual place. Anybody got a problem?'

Daz and Speed shook their heads.

'Luke?' Skin looked him over. 'Got a problem?'

Luke thought of the old woman, the girl, Mum, Roger Gilmore, Dad, school, the concert, the strange sounds he was hearing—and this. No, he didn't have a problem; he had a cartload of problems. But he shook his head. 'No problem.'

'Good.'

Speed pulled an apple from his pocket and took a bite. 'So are we giving up on The Grange, then?'

'Giving up?' Skin looked round at him. 'We haven't even started on The Grange, Speedy.'

'But Luke didn't find anything,' said Speed, chewing noisily.

Skin's eyes flickered round at Luke. 'Luke's job's not over yet.'

'OK.' Speed took another bite. 'So what's the plan?'

'I'll tell you tomorrow,' said Skin.

They wandered back down Nut Bush Lane, none of them speaking. The air was still and the loudest sounds were their footsteps and Speed crunching his apple. The sky was darker now, the moon muffled in cloud, and a feathery rain was starting to fall. They walked on in silence and finally drew close to the centre of the village. Speed and Daz headed off to their houses and Skin and Luke walked on across the square and down the lane towards their own, Skin striding ahead, silent and grim; then suddenly, in front of his gate, he stopped and turned. Luke made to walk past, but Skin moved across and blocked the way. They faced each other in the darkness.

'You were lying to me back there,' said Skin quietly. 'I don't know what you haven't told me but you were lying. I could see it in your face.'

'I wasn't. I—'

But before he could finish, Skin stepped forward, clasped him by the throat and drove him back against the gate. Then he thrust his face close to Luke's ear and muttered into it, the words falling like chipped glass. 'Just remember, Luke bloody Stanton—you're still in one piece because that's the way I need you right now. And if you want to stay that way, you'll do exactly what I say.' And with a snarl, Skin threw him to the side, vaulted over the gate of his house, and disappeared into the darkness.

Luke half-stumbled down the lane towards The Haven, still shaken by Skin's words. The rain, light though it was, felt strangely reassuring and before long he saw the welcome sight of Bill Foley's farm on the left and The Haven on the right. There were no lights on at the house and all was silent, so Mum did not appear to have woken up; but he would know for certain the moment he entered. He slipped round to the back door, put his key in the lock and turned. There was a faint click but no more. He gave a sigh. He'd been right to use this door; it was so much quieter than the front door. He closed it softly behind him and listened.

All was still in the house. The utility room was as he had left it and so was the kitchen. He crept through to the hall and stopped at the foot of the stairs. Again no sound of Mum stirring or her voice calling for him. If she had detected his absence she would have been up waiting. He tiptoed up the stairs to the landing, stopped and listened again, then continued as far as his room. Still no voice called out to him. He pushed open the door, slipped in and eased it closed behind him, then sat on the edge of the bed.

He was shaking. Skin's final words still rang in his head and he knew he was in desperate trouble. This business with the box was far from over and, to make matters worse, his connection with The Grange had now become more complicated than ever. He thought of the blind girl and her fear, and Mrs Little's grandmotherly concern for her, and the box, sitting there on the dressing table, waiting; and he thought of himself: his body, his hands, his music—how far would Skin's anger go if his cat burglar failed him a third time? It would not just be bruises on the face and sore ribs. It would be much worse.

It could be torture, mutilation, maybe even death. He didn't doubt Skin was capable of all these things.

He lay back on the bed and tried to calm himself by thinking of Dad; and, to his surprise, the strange unfinished melody that had come to him earlier slipped back into his mind. It was so beautiful and this time he heard new harmonies with it, though the tune was the same and still ended in the middle of a bar. He pulled off his clothes and dumped them in a pile on the floor, then put on his pyjamas and lay back again; and still the music played on inside his head. The tune had started again from the beginning, the melody unchanged but the harmonies different again, as though it was a piece of improvisation. He closed his eyes and saw the deep blue appear under his brow again, then the splashes of gold, much clearer this time, like two half-moons, left and right, which gradually moved closer until they formed a circle: a gold ring around a blue lake. The music faded and a new sound came: a tinkling of tiny bells, as soft as wind chimes, as numerous as stars; then they, too, faded, and the familiar rumbling sound took over, low at first, rising to a hum and then a roar, like surf pounding on a beach—a pulsing wave of sound, without beginning or end. He fell asleep with it rolling over him.

11

It was still there when he woke, together with the noise of geese honking in Bill Foley's yard and snatches of Dad's tune, as he now called the strange unfinished melody. Then another sound came, a voice: 'Luke? Are you awake?'

It was Mum. He opened his eyes and saw her standing by the bed with a mug of tea. 'It's nine o'clock,' she said. 'I thought you'd want to be woken by now.'

He rubbed his eyes and stared up at her, confused at the mixture of sounds all around him and inside his head. It was hard to tell sometimes where they all came from. He felt tired and groggy and worried, not just about the business with Mrs Little and the girl, and the danger of Skin and the others, but about Mum. She looked so unsure of him as she stood there. He sat up in bed and took the mug of tea.

'Thanks,' he said.

'You've done it again,' she said, nodding down at the clothes he had dropped on the floor last night. 'Dumped your stuff all over the shop.' He felt a moment of alarm. If she picked the clothes up for him and they were still damp from last night's rain, she would realize he'd been out. But she looked up again and smiled. 'It's OK. I didn't say that to nag you. I'm through with nagging. But you won't mind if I let you pick them up for yourself.'

He took a sip of tea.

'Is it all right?' she said.

'Is what all right?'

94

'The tea.'

'Yeah, it's fine.' He saw her watching him and added: 'Thank you.'

She gave another smile. 'I wasn't waiting for that.'

'Waiting for what?'

'For you to say thank you. Like Dad and I used to when you were young and you forgot. Do you remember? If we offered you something, like a piece of cake, and you took it and forgot to say thank you, we used to sit there and watch you until you noticed us and realized it was a prompt. And then you'd say thank you. But we didn't have to do it much. You were always very good.'

He stared at her in disbelief. What was she doing, dredging up all this old stuff? He remembered it well enough but he didn't want to because it made him think of Dad and that always made him miserable. 'I didn't think you were waiting for me to say anything,' he said. 'I just said thank you because I wanted to, not because you were sitting there watching me.'

'OK.' She forced another smile. 'Well, anyway, I'll let you get up. See you downstairs.' And she leaned across, gave him a kiss, and left the room.

He stared after her, more confused than ever. She was so awkward with him these days. Maybe it was just this marriage business. Maybe she was trying to pluck up the courage to tell him she'd said yes to Roger Gilmore. Perhaps he'd hear about it over breakfast. Not that he wanted to; it was hardly news he was looking forward to. He climbed out of bed and sloped off to have a shower. The water on his body felt good but it didn't wash away the burden of his thoughts. What did Mrs Little want him to do? Why did she think he could help her granddaughter? What was Skin planning next? And why was Mum so nervous of him? He dried himself, wrapped the towel around him and padded through to Mum's study to check his e-mails. The words appeared on the screen:

Receiving Message 1 of 2.

He frowned. He wasn't expecting anything but perhaps this was Miranda reminding him about their practice session this morning, or Skin putting more pressure on him. But the name that appeared in the sender's box was Mum's. He frowned, wondering what she could possibly want to send him an e-mail about.

Receiving Message 2 of 2.

Here was the second message coming through. He watched the screen again, waiting to see who it was from. He didn't care who had sent it as long as it wasn't Skin. If it was a message from Skin, he was going to delete it unread, he decided. The name of the sender appeared at last.

Heaven.

His mouth dropped open. He'd completely forgotten the message he'd sent in a moment of craziness to *dad@heaven.com* yesterday. It should have come back unrecognized from the server yet this clearly wasn't a reject but some kind of answer. He clicked open the message and the foolish hopes that had momentarily rushed through his mind vanished in an instant. There at the top was his original message: *Why won't you answer?* And underneath was the reply.

Hello there!
Thank you very much indeed for your enquiry. I'm so sorry that we seem to have failed to answer you. We do receive a

huge number of enquiries and we pride ourselves on our ability to respond promptly to all but clearly in your case the system has broken down! In fact, I have not even been able to trace your original enquiry so all I can do is apologize once again and ask if you would be kind enough to write to us a third time and let us know how we may be of service. I do sincerely apologize for the inconvenience caused. However, at the risk of sounding smug, I feel fairly confident that you will forgive us once you've heard a little more about some of the exciting new products we are offering this summer.

Heaven Scent Natural Perfume Supplies Dot Com is the no-hassle way of meeting your natural perfume requirements from the comfort of your own home. By ordering our products on-line, you can save . . .

Luke didn't bother to read any more. This seemed the cruellest of mockeries. He scowled at the e-mail address: *heaven.com*. It seemed to laugh at him. 'Damn you!' he muttered. 'Damn you!' And he spat at the words. A little drip of saliva ran down the screen. He wiped it dry with the end of his towel and went on scowling. Heaven was not a place of joy but of jeers. Yet he had sent his message to Dad. He had written Dad's name in the address. So who had sent this back? He scrolled to the bottom of the text; and there was the sender's name.

Daniel Adams-Day.

He clenched his fists. D.A.D. The final joke. Mr Adams-Day would never know how deeply he was hated for having a name with those letters in it. He deleted the message and glowered up at the wall. Before him Mum's dictionaries and reference books sat neatly on the shelves. She had rearranged them and they were now grouped according to language and subject areas. She had even tidied away the loose papers on her desk and put next week's translations in order in the tray. He stared about him. So everything was neat now, everything was fine, everything was dandy. She had a nice, ordered office and plenty of work and a new man in her life. What more could she want? He glanced at the photograph of Dad. At least she hadn't tidied that away—but maybe that would be the next thing to go. Maybe he'd be looking at a picture of Roger here a few days from now. He clicked angrily on Mum's message and opened it. There were only four words but they sprang at him from the screen:

I love you, Luke.

He felt a rush of shame—then suspicion. Was this message for real or was it just another part of the mockery? She'd loved Dad, too, loved him to bits, just as Dad had loved her to bits. And where was that love now? Where, for that matter, was his own? He heard Mum call up the stairs. 'Luke! Breakfast in two minutes!'

He deleted the message, switched off the computer, and hurried back to his room. The clothes on the floor were not wet at all. He dressed, then pulled back the curtains and stared out. The sky was clear and bright; it was going to be a hot day. He made his way down to the kitchen and found Mum cutting bread.

'Thanks for your e-mail,' he said. He sat down at the table and poured some cereal into the bowl, then looked up to see her watching him.

'I meant it,' she said.

'Thanks.' He swallowed hard and looked down again. What was the matter with him? Was his heart turning to stone? He'd never have shut her out like this in the old days. But all he could do was say 'Thanks' again and then pour the milk and start eating.

Mum spoke. 'How many eggs?'

'Two, please.' He didn't look up. He couldn't look up. He didn't know why. In desperation he listened for music, any music: the wistful tune that made him think of the girl; Dad's unfinished piece; anything. But all was silent in his head. He glanced up at last and saw that Mum had turned away. She had her back to him and was standing by the cooker, preparing the poached eggs. How often had he seen her do this for his father? More times than he could remember. It always had to be poached eggs for Dad when he was home. Nothing else would do. 'Nobody makes poached eggs like you,' he'd say. And he'd stand there next to her with his arm round her waist while she made them. Mum turned suddenly, as though she'd sensed she was being watched.

'What?' she said.

'Nothing.' He looked back at his cereal and went on eating. He heard her pull out the grill pan and turn the toast, then, as though she had read his thoughts, she spoke again.

'I've never stopped loving him, Luke. I couldn't stop loving him any more than I could ever stop loving you.'

'Don't,' he said, still unable to look at her.

'Luke—'

'Don't. Just don't say any more, OK? It screws me up when you talk like this.'

He heard her footsteps approaching, felt her arm round his shoulder. He reached a hand out to pull her to him, then let it drop back. She pulled him to her and he let her do it, trying to make himself hug her back. He could feel tears wanting to come but they seemed locked inside him as though pride or stubbornness or some other part of him wouldn't let them out. But he managed to speak. 'How can you . . . how can you . . . love Dad . . . and Roger?'

She stroked his cheek. 'That's the first time I've heard

you call Roger by his Christian name.' She kissed his head and whispered: 'Hang on.' She hurried back to the cooker and checked the toast and eggs. 'Just give me a moment, Luke, OK? I don't want to mess this up for you.' She gave the toast a few more seconds, then buttered the pieces, put the eggs on top, and walked back to the table. 'Here,' she said. She put the plate in front of him, sat down, and put an arm round his shoulder again. 'Go on eating,' she said.

He finished his cereal, pushed the bowl to the side and started on the poached eggs, Mum watching him quietly, her arm still round his shoulder. It felt strange sitting here like this: strange yet not unpleasant. 'Are the eggs OK?' said Mum.

'They're great. They always are. No one makes poached eggs like you do.'

'That's what your father used to say.'

'I know.'

'They're very easy to do. I don't suppose I'm really that special at making them.' She watched him eating for a while longer, then looked down. 'Love's a strange thing, Luke. You think you've lost it and then it creeps up on you again. When your father died, I thought I'd never love again. Romantically, I mean. I'm not talking about you. I'll always love you. But . . . another man. I just never thought that was possible. I'm still not sure what I feel about Roger.'

'You like him.'

'Are you asking me or telling me?'

'I'm telling you.'

'Yes, of course I like him. I wouldn't see him if I didn't like him.'

'No, I mean you really like him a lot. You sort of brighten up when you see him.'

'Do I? I wasn't aware of that.'

100

'And when you talk to him on the phone, you've got this kind of different voice.'

'What do you mean?'

'Sort of like . . . I don't know . . . '

'Tell me.'

'I can't describe it. Sort of like . . . you're a girl Miranda's age and he's a boy in the village and he's asking you out and you want to go but you don't want to sound too keen in case he thinks you're cheap.'

'Are you serious?' She stared at him. 'Do I really sound like that?'

'Yeah. Well, maybe. I don't know. Not all the time. Just sometimes. I hear it in your voice.'

'You hear lots of things. The way your father did.'

He wished she wouldn't keep mentioning Dad. But perhaps it was his own fault. He was the one who'd asked about love. He went on eating the poached eggs, hoping now that Mum would drop the subject. But she spoke again.

'I don't want to be like some love-struck schoolgirl. I don't . . . feel that's how I'm behaving. I don't feel that way towards Roger. I just feel . . . confused. And guilty. About hurting you. And about your father, though I know he'd want me to accept love from another man if it was offered and it made me happy.'

'Does it make you happy?'

'Yes. A bit. But not truly happy, not completely happy. I can't be completely happy if you're not happy as well.' She ran her hand over his neck. 'I just . . . I just suppose I've come to realize that the heart's got room in it for a lot of loving. You know? And it's not a betrayal of someone you've loved and who's gone if you then give love to another person. As long as that person is worthy of it.'

'And is he? Roger?'

'Yes. He's worthy of it. Everyone's worthy of it really. But we can't spread our love too wide.'

'I thought you said the heart's got room in it for a lot of loving.'

'Yes, but there's a limit to how many people you can love deeply.' She frowned. 'I'll never stop loving your father, Luke. Never ever ever. But I'm trying . . . I don't know . . . I'm trying to go on living the way he would have wanted me to. He wouldn't have wanted me to spend the rest of my life moping and grieving and wearing black. And if some man found me attractive—'

'Some man?' Luke stopped eating for a moment. 'Are you kidding? Some man?'

'What do you mean?'

'Half the men in this village fancy you.'

'Don't be silly.'

'I'm not. It's obvious. Skin's dad does, for starters—'

'He's revolting.'

'And so does Bill Foley. And Mr Nettles. And Mr Robinson. And that guy from the delivery firm who came to the door the other day. And those men on the building site whistled at you last week, remember? And what about that plumber who came round to fix the—'

'All right, all right.' She started to chuckle. 'Don't make me big-headed.'

'Men talk to you in a certain way. I've seen it. They either flirt with you or they go all gooey, like they're shy.'

Mum was looking awkward again, as though this subject embarrassed her. Then she said: 'What about Roger? How does he act? Is he a flirty one or a gooey one?'

Luke looked away.

'How does he act?' said Mum again.

He looked back at her and saw how much she needed him to say what they both already knew.

'He's different,' he said. 'He's not like the others.'

'How's he different?'

'You know the answer.'

'Tell me anyway.'

Luke pushed his plate to the side and leaned forward on his elbows. 'He doesn't just fancy you,' he said. 'He really loves you.'

'And is that such a terrible thing?'

'Maybe not.'

'Maybe not?'

He looked round at her. 'Maybe not.'

She watched him for a moment, her eyes searching his face. 'Luke?'

'Yeah?'

'It'll be all right.'

'What'll be all right?'

'Everything.' She smiled at him. 'Everything'll be all right.' She paused, still watching his face. 'And since you've been giving me your observations on matters of the heart, I'll give you one of my own. You say I've got admirers. Well, you've got one, too.'

'Who?'

'You're going over to see her this morning.'

'Miranda?'

Mum nodded. Then she reached out and touched him on the arm. 'Don't hurt her feelings, Luke.'

'I won't. I wouldn't.'

'She's a nice girl.'

'I know.'

'And very attractive.'

'I know.'

'But she's sensitive. So don't give her a hard time.'

'I won't. I told you. But she doesn't feel that way about me anyway.'

'Oh, sure.'

'She doesn't.'

Mum took his empty plate, then leaned across and kissed him. 'Believe that if you want. Only don't hurt her feelings.'

12

But he knew he was going to hurt Miranda's feelings the moment he left the house. He couldn't go to The Toby Jug yet. The sounds were starting to overwhelm him again. He stood in the lane outside The Haven, listening, trembling. They seemed to roll over him, through him, around him, sometimes loud, sometimes soft, sometimes just a presence he seemed to feel rather than hear. He heard Dad's unfinished tune, he heard the plaintive childlike piece that kept haunting him, he heard other music, some known to him, some unknown, the melodies speaking to him as clearly as if he were playing them himself; he heard the sounds of fields and hills and hedgerows, the murmur of voices in distant places, and one in particular: a voice that was growing louder by the minute.

'Nana, Nana, Nana.' The words were so distinct it was as though the little girl were right here beside him. Yet he was still standing in the lane, alone, and nowhere near The Grange. 'Nana, Nana, Nana.' It was a voice on the cusp of tears. He tried to imagine what could have caused this girl's pain, and why Mrs Little should think he could help. But it was all a mystery. He wandered through to the churchyard, slumped to the ground by Dad's grave, and went on listening. It was well over an hour before the sounds left him and he felt able to make his way to The Toby Jug.

Laughter and chatter burst through the open windows of the pub. He stood outside, the memory of the girl's voice still whispering through his mind, and steeled himself to go in. He knew it was an insult to Miranda to turn up as late as this but he had to see her. He had to see a friendly face; someone who wouldn't lecture him; someone who . . .

He frowned.

Just someone.

But maybe Miranda wouldn't be free now. She'd said she had to help her parents today and it was clear from the noise that Mr and Mrs Davis were having another busy lunchtime. But this was normal nowadays for The Toby Jug. The old pub, for all its ramshackle eccentricity, or maybe because of it, had become something of a magnet for tourists in the summertime. He entered the saloon and found it crowded with bikers, backpackers, cyclists, and other visitors, plus the usual Sunday lunchers and other regulars from the village. Mr Davis had a throng of people round the bar, clamouring for drinks, and Mrs Davis, Sophie, and Verity were hurrying round the tables with trays of food. Luke pushed forward and somehow jostled his way to the bar where he found the burly figure of Bill Foley. Next to him, slumped on a bar stool, was a haggard-looking Mr Skinner. Bill Foley saw Luke coming and bellowed at him at once in his booming voice.

'Luke Stanton! You can't come in 'ere! Got to be eighteen to come in 'ere!'

'I'm not after a drink.'

'It was a joke, you turnip! Where's your sense of humour?'

'Dropped it in the square. Sorry.' Luke glanced at Mr Skinner. The man's eyes were glazed already and he was staring down at his glass. He didn't look dangerous yet but it probably wouldn't take many more drinks before Bill Foley and his mates had to get him out. Mr Davis was pulling a pint nearby but he spotted Luke and shouted across at him.

'Where the hell have you been? It's nearly half twelve!'

'Sorry.'

'She's given up on you and I don't blame her. I told her she was daft expecting you to show up when you said.'

'I got held up.'

'Couldn't you have rung?'

'Yeah. I mean . . . no. Look, I'm sorry. Is she still here?'

'She's up in The Eyrie. Go and see her if you want. But don't blame me if she bites your head off.'

'Stood her up, have you?' said Bill Foley. The farmer prodded Luke in the chest. 'That's not the way to treat a nice girl like Miranda.'

'Yeah, yeah, OK,' said Luke. He pulled away from Bill Foley and forced his way back through the crowd, only to bump into Mrs Davis on her way to the kitchen. She looked him up and down.

'Don't know why you bothered turning up,' she said.

'Sorry.'

'Got a reason?'

'I was held up.'

'By what?'

'I . . . ' He looked away, fumbling in his mind for an answer. 'I . . . '

'Don't bother. I'm busy.' Mrs Davis sniffed. 'She's upstairs.' And she brushed past him without another word. Feeling more guilty than ever, he let himself through the side door and closed it behind him. As if by magic, the babble of the saloon fell to a manageable drone. He took some slow breaths to calm himself, then walked through to the lounge at the back of the pub. He liked this room with its squashy sofa and ancient fireplace, and the rickety old piano in the corner: a hideous instrument with blotchy wood and discoloured keys, which played surprisingly well considering how often it had the life thumped out of it by Mr and Mrs Davis playing duets.

He walked over to the window, taking more slow breaths. His mind was still full of the girl's voice and all the other strange things he'd heard, and he knew he couldn't go up to Miranda in this state. He gazed out at the Davis's private garden at the back of the pub. Beyond the low wall at the end the churchyard stretched away, peaceful and still. He stared at it for a moment, trying to catch a glimpse of Dad's grave, but it was hidden from view by the side of the church. He swallowed hard. What was the point of looking? He'd just been to the grave, for God's sake, and no doubt he'd be back there again soon. He turned to the piano and saw Miranda's flute resting on top with some music beside it. He glanced at the title. *'The Dance of the Blessed Spirits' by Gluck. Arrangement for Piano and Flute*. He braced himself and set off down the corridor towards the stairs.

There was no doubt about it: The Toby Jug was a strange place. He had always had mixed feelings about it. It wasn't just that parts of it dated back to the fourteenth century and looked even older; it was such an untidy, unconventional place. There were no carpets, only hard stone. The corridors were narrow and low, and the steps up to the guest rooms spiralled like the stairway of a castle. The windows were so small and the lighting so poor that the place seemed permanently dull; and since the rooms had no toilets, washbasins, baths, or showers and the only facilities were on the ground floor, Luke didn't imagine guests would be too happy making their way down those cheerless stone steps in the middle of the night. Yet Miranda, whose room was right at the very top of the building, would live nowhere else.

He started to climb, counting the steps to himself as he always did: 'One, two, three . . . ' And so he went on, passing landing after landing, glancing out of the tiny windows whenever they appeared, not so much to see the garden or the churchyard below as to reassure himself that daylight still existed. 'Fifty-nine, sixty, sixty-one . . . ' He was growing breathless now but the end was in sight. He had left behind him the last of the guest rooms and there was only one more landing. Here it was, with Mr and Mrs Davis's room to the left, Sophie's in the middle and Verity's to the right, and a few steps further up, all by itself at the highest point of the pub, Miranda's room; on the door the familiar plate with the words: *The Eyrie*.

No sound came from inside. He hesitated, then knocked. There was a murmur from within, but he caught no words. He twisted the door-knob and pushed. Miranda was standing by the window with her back to him, staring out across the square towards Buckland Forest in the distance. She glanced round, saw him there, and frowned.

'I'm sorry,' he said.

She didn't answer.

'Miranda? I'm sorry. It's just—'

'You don't need to do this, Luke,' she said, still staring out of the window.

'Do what?'

'Apologize. I expect you had something important come up. It's no big deal. I know you're busy.'

'Listen—'

'And you don't need to bother about the concert. That's no big deal either. Anyway, it's a bit stupid, don't you think? You accompanying me. I mean, I'm so useless on the flute and you're so brilliant and everything and—'

'Miranda—'

109

'Only the thing is, Luke . . . ' She turned and faced him for the first time. 'I don't think it's fair if you say you're going to do something and then you just leave me hanging around when, you know, like I told you, I've got to help Mum and Dad with a lot of things today and I've only got a bit of time for practising. I'm not even supposed to be up here now, you know? I'm supposed to be downstairs helping out, only Dad told me to have a bit of a break as I was getting worked up about the concert and worrying and stuff.'

'Miranda—'

'It's OK. All right? It's really OK. I mean, I can understand you not wanting to do it. I know it must be really boring for you to have to accompany me on the flute. And if you don't want to do it, it's no problem. I'm OK about it. Just . . . don't tell me you're going to help me when you don't want to.'

'I do want to.'

'You don't. And it's OK. I told you. It's OK.'

'Miranda, listen, I do want to help. It's just that . . . ' He sat on the edge of the bed. 'I don't . . . really know what's happening to me.' He frowned. 'I'm getting more and more mixed up. I'm sorry I hurt you. It was wrong. You're the last person I want to hurt. Please don't be angry with me. I'm just not doing very much right at the moment. I've been falling out with Mum and she's got Roger Gilmore coming round all the time and I'm screwed up about that, and there's . . . ' He thought of the girl and Mrs Little, and Skin and the gang; and the strange sounds he was hearing. 'There's . . . other stuff. Stuff I can't talk about.' He frowned again. 'I'm sorry.'

He stared down at the floor but out of the corner of his eye saw her move towards him and sit down on the bed beside him. Then he felt her hand on his arm. 'It's OK,' she said.

He looked round at her and smiled; and she smiled back, a shy smile that quickly vanished. He took the hand that was resting on his arm and gave it a squeeze. 'Come on,' he said. 'Let's try the music. If you've got time.'

'I have—just about—but are you sure you still want to? I mean, since your life's falling to pieces—'

'I didn't say it was falling—'

'Since your life's falling to pieces,' she continued, giggling now, 'don't you think you maybe ought to sort it out before you try playing the piano? I mean, I don't want you making loads of mistakes and spoiling my act at the concert.'

'Shut up,' he said, laughing, too. He stood up and pulled her to her feet. 'Do you think a minor problem like my life falling to pieces is going to mess up my piano playing?' He realized with a start that he was still holding her hand, and let go of it, feeling slightly embarrassed. 'Come on,' he said. 'Let's have a go at the music.'

They made their way down to the lounge and he took his place at the piano. 'Hope your parents have had this thing tuned since I last played it,' he said. He tried a couple of runs up and down the keys, then nodded. 'Much better. I still can't believe it plays so well, considering the punishment it gets from your mum and dad.' He knew he was forcing himself to be jocular, though whether it was to make himself feel better or Miranda he didn't know. He played a couple more runs to loosen up, then, remembering the piece they were going to practise, started to make it up from memory while he waited for Miranda to arrange her music stand nearby. But after a few bars he realized she hadn't moved. He stopped playing and looked round to see her staring at him.

'How do you do that?' she said. 'You haven't even got the music in front of you.'

'I can remember it. Sort of.'

'So you've already learnt it? Did you do it with Mr Harding?'

'No, I've just heard it a few times. Dad played a piano version of it once, years ago. It's a nice piece. I'm probably playing it all wrong.'

She picked up the music for the piano part and propped it open in front of him. He glanced over it. 'Told you,' he said. 'I was in the wrong key for a start.' He began to sight-read the piece, again waiting for Miranda to get herself ready, but she went on just watching him. He stopped playing again and looked round at her.

'What?' he said.

'You've got such a gift, Luke.' She shook her head. 'There can't be that much wrong with your life if you can play like that.'

'There's plenty wrong with it, I promise you, but we've done that subject. Come on. Let's have a go at this.'

She opened her own music and placed it on the stand, then picked up her flute. 'Luke, listen, can you be really patient with me?'

'Sure.'

'I mean, I know I was joking earlier about you making mistakes and spoiling my act and everything but I'm really bad at this. I'll probably stop a lot.'

'Don't worry about it. Just have a go.'

'OK.'

They started, slowly, and Miranda lost her way almost at once.

'Sorry, Luke.'

'Don't worry. Just go on from where you are.'

'Can we start again from the beginning? I sort of need a run-up at it.'

'OK.'

They started again and this time she made it a little

112

further, only to stop again a few bars later. She coloured. 'I'm pathetic at this. I don't know why I bother.'

'Just do your best.'

'I can play it on my own. Honestly. Not very well but I can get through the whole thing, as long as I don't go too fast.'

'It's not meant to be played fast anyway.'

'I know but . . . I mean . . . I can play it. It's just that with you I feel kind of nervous.'

'You don't need to.' He thought for a moment. 'Look, just pretend you're playing it on your own, OK? Pretend I'm not in the room, not even in the building. Stop and start as much as you want. I'll fit in my bit round you. Go as fast or as slow as you like.'

'It'll be slow.'

'OK.'

'Really slow. You'll get bored.'

'I won't. Go on. Slow as you like. Super-mega-slow, if you want.'

They started again, from the beginning. She didn't play slowly. If anything she played fast, as though she wanted to get the thing over and done with as quickly as possible. But the music was starting to flow. He watched her as he played, secretly, trying not to make her feel she was under scrutiny. Her face was creased in a frown, her eyes fixed on the music, her body slightly tense, but he could feel her growing more confident. He relaxed a little himself and started to enjoy the music. It was good to hear it again. He had forgotten what a pleasant piece this was. He remembered the time Dad had played it back in the days when they lived in Strawberry Hill, and how Mum had hummed the melody line as she sat on the sofa, listening. He pictured Dad's face and played on, happily—then suddenly stopped. The sound of Miranda's flute came to an abrupt end.

'What's wrong?' she asked.

He said nothing. He could only listen to what had caught his attention: the sound of another flute cutting through the silence. It was so subtle and so intimate it seemed to creep out of him as though it were his own voice. He listened, transfixed, and then realized that more sounds were coming, strange sounds that seemed to well up from deep inside him: a buzzing sound, a harp sound, a bell sound, and, all round his head, a sound of rushing water, the flute-song weaving its path through them like a river of air.

'Luke?' said Miranda. 'What's wrong?'

The sounds faded and silence returned. He felt a stabbing pain at their loss. He looked round at her. 'Did you hear?' he said.

'Hear what? ''The Dance of the Blessed Spirits''?'

He saw confusion in her face, even a touch of fear, and smiled at once, anxious to put her at ease again. But her face remained dark. 'What did you hear?' she said.

He looked away, unwilling to answer.

'Luke, please say something.'

He looked round at her again. 'I heard . . . ' He saw the fear still in her face and forced himself to smile again. 'Nothing. Honestly. I heard nothing. It's just my imagination playing tricks.' He turned back to the piano. 'Come on. Let's get back to the music.'

13

Skin and the others were waiting by the young alder just down from The Grange. Daz was up the tree, half-hidden by the foliage, his gaze directed towards the old house. Luke joined them and looked warily around him. There was no sign of Mrs Little and he was glad of it. He had no desire to see or be seen by her right now. But he could hear the sound of the girl weeping again. It was like a one-way conversation inside his head and for the moment had taken over all other sounds; and it was more intense, more urgent than ever.

Skin looked him over. 'Half an hour late. Thought you weren't going to turn up.' Luke hadn't wanted to turn up but he knew what the price of that would be. He said nothing. Skin eyed him a moment longer, then glanced up at Daz. 'Any sign of the old bird?'

'Nah,' said Daz. 'Haven't seen her once.'

'She's probably seen you,' said Speed, squinting up. 'You keep bobbing your head around and moving the branches and stuff.'

'Least I can get up the tree,' retorted Daz. 'That's more than you can do, fat boy.'

'I can get up the tree.'

'Only with help.'

'You need help yourself to get up the oak.'

'So do you. So does Skin. So does everybody. Except the piano player.'

'Easy, girls!' said Skin. 'Cut out the bickering. It's like a cat fight, listening to you two. There's no need to worry

115

about getting up the oak.' He swivelled his eyes at Luke. 'We've got our specialist climber with us now.' He watched Luke a moment longer, then called up to Daz again. 'Come down. We're off to HQ.'

Daz shinned down the alder and, to Luke's relief, they set off through the forest. Much as he hated the gang using the tree-house in the old oak, he was desperate to get away from The Grange. The mere sight of the place tugged at his conscience in more ways than he liked to admit. Skin threw another taunt at him as they walked.

'Thought you'd bottled out again.'

'What's there to bottle out of?' said Luke, trying to sound as brash as he could.

'Seeing us,' said Skin. 'Since you've bottled out two nights in a row now.'

'I didn't bottle out last night. I went in. I looked round the house. I just didn't find the box.'

'Never mind.' Skin watched him for a moment. 'You'll have another chance to prove yourself tonight.' He winked at Luke. 'Aren't you a lucky boy?' Before Luke could answer, Skin stopped and whistled to the others. 'Hey! Smokey time!'

The four boys drew together under a horse chestnut tree and Daz pulled out a packet of cigarettes.

'Is that all you got?' said Skin.

'Yeah.'

'Brilliant. Bloody brilliant. I'm going to get dead high on that.'

'Sorry, I haven't had time to get anything else.'

'Never mind.' Skin took a cigarette and put it in his mouth. 'Have to do.'

Daz handed round the packet. Luke took one like the others and Daz struck a match. They all leaned forward to share it.

'Bonding,' said Skin. He stuck the lighted cigarette in

his mouth, then reached out both arms and pulled the others close. 'Serious bonding.' His eyes moved from face to face as they huddled together, cigarette tips glowing in their mouths, a cloud of smoke rising from the centre. 'One for all and all for one. That's the deal. Come on—squeeze.' And they all reached out their arms and squeezed. 'Squeeze,' said Skin. 'That's it. All one. Right? All one. We stick together. We're there for each other.' Luke caught the glance that Skin intended for him and looked away. Speed started to cough.

Skin burst out laughing and they broke apart, Speed still spluttering from the smoke. Skin slapped him on the back. 'OK, Blobby. We're done now. You can move on.'

'I am moving on,' said Speed, already lumbering off through the trees.

'Moving?' called Daz. 'Call that moving? Waddling, more like.'

Skin laughed again. 'Don't think I've ever seen that kid do anything fast.'

'You obviously haven't watched him eat a burger,' said Daz.

The two chuckled and walked on together after Speed. Luke followed uneasily. Why was he here? He didn't want to have anything more to do with these boys but how was he to break free? If it were just Daz and Speed, there'd be no problem, but Skin was different. He was afraid of Skin—and Skin knew it. He trudged on through the forest, taking the occasional drag of the cigarette but not enjoying it very much. At last he reached the old oak tree. The others were already there. All eyes fixed on him.

'Right,' said Skin, throwing his cigarette down at the bottom of the tree. 'Over to the specialist.'

'The cat burglar,' said Daz.

Luke looked round at them. He hated the way Skin had thrown his cigarette down by the tree. He had stubbed his own out earlier and buried it under some loose earth. Daz and Speed dropped theirs, too, both boys watching him as they did so. He frowned and started to climb. He'd clear the butts away later, even if he had to come back specially for it. But at least he was climbing again and it felt good to touch the warm bark of the tree. He'd missed his old friend, though he knew he was going to enjoy today's experience less than he normally would, given the company he had to keep. More and more he was finding he resented anyone else climbing the old oak and the thought of Skin and the others pawing their way over it was particularly disturbing.

He reached the first branch and rested a moment, looking down. As usual he saw the grudging admiration in the eyes of the others. He didn't know why no one else seemed able to climb up to this point. It didn't feel that difficult—but it wasn't the time to think about that now. Skin was already nodding him towards the top. He climbed on through the familiar tangle of branches and finally reached the tree-house. It was good to be back. He hauled himself over onto the planks and lay there, relishing the moment; but his pleasure was cut short as Skin bellowed up from below.

'Come on, Luke! What are you doing up there? Playing with yourself?'

He heard goonish laughter from the others. With great reluctance, he pulled the rope ladder towards the edge and let it down, paying it out hand-over-hand until it touched the ground. Skin took hold of it below.

'Is it made fast?' he shouted.

'Yes!'

Skin started to climb. Despite his muscular frame he was heavy and awkward on the rope and it always gave Luke a certain amount of satisfaction to see that there was at least one area where Skin was less than confident. It took the boy a considerable time to reach the lower branches, but once there his confidence returned. He left the rope for the others and started to haul himself up towards the tree-house. Daz was next on the rope and with his lighter frame he swung and writhed his way up much more quickly. He reached the first branch and let go of the rope ladder but, unlike Skin, did not climb on further. Instead he grinned down at Speed, now standing somewhat forlornly on his own.

'Don't bounce around too much, Speedy,' he said. 'You might pull down the tree.'

'Shut up!' said Speed.

Daz looked up at Skin. 'Do you reckon we should have used a thicker rope? This one nearly broke last time he used it.'

'Don't know if they make rope strong enough,' said Skin.

'Maybe I should have brought some chain,' said Daz.

'Shut up!' said Speed.

Daz and Skin dissolved in laughter.

'Shut up or I'm not coming!' shouted Speed.

'Go on, Speedy!' called Skin. 'We love you really!'

Speed reached for the ladder and started—ponderously—to climb. Skin and Daz whooped as the rope took the strain.

'Speedy!' shouted Daz.

'Speedy-weedy!' shouted Skin. 'The flying blob!'

Speed struggled on up the ladder, grunting with the effort, his face creased in concentration. There were more hoots from Skin and Daz but Speed ignored them and forced himself on. Luke watched in silence for a moment, then turned away, lay back on the planks and stared up through the canopy; and, to his surprise, the waking dream came back—of him flying up through the tree and out into the sky and away with Dad towards the lambent

119

star. He closed his eyes and pictured himself flying towards it, chasing his father's presence just ahead. Then he heard a voice.

'Bloody hell! That's some climb.'

Luke broke from the dream and opened his eyes to see Skin's face peering over the edge of the tree-house at him. 'What did you have to build the thing up this tree for?' the boy muttered. He hauled himself over the top and sat there, breathing hard but watching Luke all the while. 'Still,' he went on after a moment, 'I suppose it's good once you're up here.' He pulled off the little rucksack he'd been carrying and dropped it on the planking. 'Bit of light refreshment,' he said, then turned, peered back down the tree and chuckled. 'Speedy's going to be yonks. We'll be leaving by the time he gets here.'

But even Speed finally made it to the tree-house. The boys sat round on the planks, all out of breath, it seemed, apart from Luke. Skin opened the rucksack and pulled out a large bottle.

'What we got today?' said Daz.

'Whisky,' said Skin. 'Straight from my dad's cupboard.'

'Won't he miss it?' said Daz.

'Have you seen how much he's got in there? Anyway, I don't care if he does miss it. He'll have to put up with it.' He took a swig from the bottle. 'If he doesn't like it, tough. I can take any shit he gives me now.' He handed the bottle to Speed. 'Looks like you need this more than I do.'

'Speedy!' said Daz.

Speed took the bottle.

'Don't drink the lot,' said Daz. 'Save a bit for us.'

'It's a full bottle,' said Speed.

'Exactly.'

Speed glared at him and took a couple of swigs, then passed the bottle to Luke. Luke took only one small swig, though he tried to make it look as though it were more. He had no taste for whisky. They'd given it to him the last time they met up in the tree-house and he'd felt so queasy and light-headed he'd nearly slipped when he was climbing down. He wondered again what he was doing here. He wasn't part of this gang. He wasn't born here like the others. They'd grown up in the village and been in and out of each other's pockets since primary school. He'd only been drawn in since Dad died two years ago. He'd thought he'd find strength here and so he had.

Only it was the wrong kind.

Daz took the bottle and handed round more cigarettes and they sat there, smoking and drinking, as the sun slowly moved towards the west.

'So,' said Skin, looking round. 'Midnight again, then. And this time there'll be no mistakes.' Luke saw the boy's eyes on him again and looked down.

'I'm going to be knackered,' said Speed. 'I couldn't hardly sleep last night when I got back. I don't know if I can keep awake two nights in a row. Specially after drinking this stuff. And it's Monday tomorrow. I've got to be up for school.'

'Your mum'll wake you if you oversleep,' said Skin. 'You'll be fine. Everyone'll be fine.' There was a pause in the voice and Luke looked up to see the others all watching him.

'What?' he said.

'We're wondering,' said Skin.

'Wondering what?'

'If you're going to turn up tonight.'

'Why wouldn't I turn up?'

'I don't know. You tell me.'

Luke looked away through the trees. From deep in the forest came the sound of wood pigeons calling. He thought of Mrs Little and the girl and knew he had to protect them somehow, especially the little girl. But refusing Skin would mean danger for him and he couldn't face that right now. Especially up here. He'd have to think of something later. He looked back at them.

'I'll be there,' he said.

'I hope so,' said Skin. 'For your sake. Because you still haven't delivered.'

'I did my bit last night. I broke into The Grange. And the night before.'

'And we still haven't got the box.'

'I didn't see it last night. I told you.'

'Are you saying it doesn't exist? Do you think I imagined it?' Skin watched him for a moment, then went on, his voice low and hard. 'You'll do the same as before. You'll climb in through the window. Only tonight'll be a bit different. This time we're going in, too.'

'What?' said Luke.

'We're going in, too. Me and Daz, anyway. Not Speedy.'

'Why not me?' said Speed, the disappointment in his voice somewhat at odds with the relief on his face.

'Because if the old girl wakes up, we may need to run,' said Skin. 'And running's not exactly your strong point. And you'd probably give us away. You're a bit distinctive.'

'Is that another word for fat?' said Daz.

But Skin didn't answer. His face had become chillingly serious. 'We meet at midnight,' he went on. 'It's a balaclava job. We'll send the cat burglar in first to open the front door and then me and Daz'll go in to look for the box. If we're quiet, the old bird won't even wake.'

'What if there's no window open that he can climb in?' said Daz.

'Then we'll come back night after night until there is. But there'll probably be lots. It's going to be warm again tonight. There'll be no problem.'

Speed sniffed and wiped his nose with the collar of his

122

T-shirt. 'What about the burglar alarm? She might have it on in some of the other rooms while she's asleep.'

'It didn't go off last night,' said Skin. 'And Luke says he went round all the rooms.' He glanced at Luke again. 'That's assuming our boy told us the truth. Which I'm not sure about.'

'I did,' said Luke.

'Even if you didn't,' said Skin coldly, 'you're going in again tonight. You're going to climb in and sneak down to the front door and let me and Daz in. Then we'll find out if you really were telling the truth about the box.'

Luke thought of Skin and Daz roaming the house; he thought of Mrs Little; he thought of the blind girl cowering in terror. 'It's not there,' he said. 'You're wasting your time. I looked in every room. You won't find it.'

Skin studied him in silence for a moment, then gave a steely smile. 'Midnight,' he said. 'Make sure you're there—for your sake.'

14

'You've been drinking,' said Mum. 'And smoking. I can smell it on your breath.'

She straightened up after putting the supper on the table in front of him. He turned his head away.

'Luke?' she said.

'What?'

'I'm not telling you off.'

'Sounds like you are.'

'I'm not. I told you—I'm through with nagging.'

'What, completely? Even if I do something really, really stupid?'

'Well, I might make an exception.'

He saw her smiling at him, trying to be friendly, but he couldn't even think about being friendly back. He was drained with worry about tonight. He didn't want to have to sit here and talk. He wanted to be alone to think. He thrust his hands in his pockets and felt the cigarette stubs he'd managed to pick up from the base of the tree without the others seeing him do it. He'd forgotten they were in there.

'Aren't you going to eat?' said Mum.

He took his hands from his pockets, picked up his knife and fork, and started to cut open the baked potato.

'Butter?' said Mum.

'Yeah.' He paused. 'Please.'

She passed him the butter. He scooped out the potato onto the plate, put some butter on the skin and started on that first.

'Salad?' said Mum, holding out the bowl.

He took it with a grunt, the closest thing he could manage right now to another thank-you. But the food tasted good. He hadn't realized just how hungry he was; and how tired. After being awake so much of last night, all he wanted to do now was sleep. But even in this state, thoughts of what lay ahead still preyed upon him. He had no idea what he should do. If he went to The Grange and let Skin and Daz into the house, the consequences could be terrible for Mrs Little and her granddaughter. If he didn't, they could be terrible for him. Having Skin as a friend was dangerous enough but having him as an enemy could be fatal. Mum spoke again.

'What were you drinking?'

'Eh?'

'I think you heard, but I'll ask again—what were you drinking?'

'I don't want a row.'

'Neither do I, so that makes two of us. What were you drinking? It smells like whisky.'

'It was.'

'And where did you get it from? Don't tell me—Mr Skinner.'

'He doesn't know about it.'

'I wouldn't expect him to. He's too drunk to know much about anything. How much did you have?'

'Hardly any. Honestly. Just one sip. I don't like the stuff.'

Mum leaned across and he waited for the inevitable lecture, but all she said was: 'Luke, did you try and phone me this afternoon?'

'No.'

'Did any of your friends?'

'How should I know?'

'I mean . . . were any of you mucking around or anything?'

'What's happened?'

'Oh, it's . . . ' She shrugged. 'Nothing really. I've just had some silent calls.'

'Silent calls?'

'Yes. You know, someone rings and you answer it and there's just silence at the other end. You ask who's there but there's still no answer.'

'Then what?'

'Then they hang up.'

'Did that happen this afternoon?'

'Yes. A couple of times while you were out . . . wherever you were.'

'What time?'

'The first one was about half past four, the second about fifteen minutes later.'

'How long did the person stay on the line before hanging up?'

'Oh, only a few seconds. It wasn't like some of those nuisance calls where the person just stays there and tries to intimidate you. I suppose it was someone wanting to speak to you and when they got my voice, they just hung up. But it seems a bit strange. A friend of yours would surely have asked for you. Unless it was one of the boys from the gang. I mean, they must know I don't like them very much.'

Luke ate in silence for a few moments and tried to think. Skin and Daz both had mobiles but he'd been with them at the time the calls were made, so it couldn't have been them. He tried to look unconcerned. 'Don't know who it was,' he said. A thought occurred to him. 'Unless it was Mr Gilmore.'

She gave him a pained look. 'So it's Mr Gilmore again now, is it? It was Roger last time. I was beginning to think we were getting somewhere.'

He said nothing. She watched him for a moment, then went on.

'It would hardly be Roger. Why would he phone and then just stay silent at the other end?'

'Maybe he's secretly a pervert trying to scare you.'

'Don't be silly,' said Mum.

The phone rang suddenly and their eyes met.

'That's probably him now,' he said.

She stood up, walked over to the phone and picked it up. 'Hello?' she said, somewhat edgily, but almost at once she turned her back to him and in a soft voice that he'd heard all too often lately said: 'Hi, how are you?'

He frowned. Talk of the devil. He watched as Mum took the phone through to the sitting room and closed the door behind her. Roger bloody Gilmore. Luke attacked his food again but his appetite was leaving him. From the sitting room came the faint sound of Mum's voice but he couldn't catch the words; and just as well, he thought. It was probably gooey talk, baby talk, pet-name talk. And no doubt they'd had plenty of pillow talk as well while he was out of the house.

He pushed his plate to the side, the food half-eaten, and stared over at the photograph on the mantelpiece of Dad, standing next to a piano, taking the applause at that concert in South Korea. He looked so young there—and he was young: just forty-two. It was hard to imagine he had only eleven months left to live. The evening sun broke through into the room and brightened the silver frame round the photograph. He stood up, walked over to the mantelpiece and stared hard at the face, then turned towards the window—and stiffened.

Mrs Little was standing in the lane, staring towards him. Their eyes met and he felt himself shiver. What was she doing out there? She hardly ever left The Grange and he had never even seen her in this part of the village before, yet here she was, staring through the window at him. He saw her head move, just a fraction, but enough for him to recognize that she was beckoning him out to the lane. He shivered again. What did she want? Was she going to threaten to speak to Mum about him breaking in? He glanced towards the sitting room door. It was still closed and Mum had not yet finished speaking. He could hear the murmur of her voice. He hurried to the back door, slipped out as quietly as he could, and made his way round the side of the house and across the front garden to the wall. She hobbled up to the other side and started speaking at once.

'You've got to come to The Grange. My granddaughter needs you.'

'I can't help her. And I never promised I would anyway.' He looked round at the house, uneasy at the thought of Mum catching a glimpse of them through the sitting room window. Mrs Little spoke again.

'She hasn't seen us.'

'What?' he said, looking back at her.

'Your mother. She hasn't seen us. She's in the sitting room, talking on a cordless phone. I can see her from here through the window. She's on a stool, facing towards your back garden. If she turns round, I'll walk on and she'll never know we've been speaking.' The old woman leaned closer and went on, a sudden urgency in her voice. 'I rang you twice this afternoon. I found your number in the book. I was hoping you might answer but your mother picked up the phone so I hung up.' She narrowed her eyes and looked at him so hard he felt she was squeezing two knives into him. 'You must come. You must. My little girl needs you. You can help. You really can. Only you mustn't tell anyone. It's got to be a secret. That's why I didn't speak to your mother.' She leaned closer still. 'Do it for my granddaughter's sake if you won't do it for mine.'

'But—'

'Please. Don't let her down.' Mrs Little glanced up the

lane in the direction of the square. 'I've got to get back now,' she said. 'I'm taking a terrible risk leaving her alone as it is.'

'But—'

'I can't stay any longer. You don't understand how terrified she gets when I go out. I have to lock her up in her room so she can't wander off and fall down the stairs or have some terrible accident. But she gets really distressed when I do that. It takes me hours to calm her down afterwards. Please come to The Grange. As soon as you can.'

'Look, I . . . ' He clenched his fists. 'I can't handle this. I don't know what's going on but there's got to be someone else who can help her. I mean, if she's ill or something, there's got to be . . . I don't know . . . authorities or something. People who specialize in kids like her. I can't do anything. I mean . . . look . . . I'm fourteen years old and I'm in trouble with just about everybody right now, including you.' He thought of Skin and the others, and their plans for tonight. 'It's no good. I just can't help.'

He saw the hope fade from her eyes. She stared at him a moment longer, then turned without a word and shuffled away towards the square.

'I'm sorry,' he called after her. She didn't answer, didn't look back. The late sun fell upon her straggly hair and crooked shoulders. She was ugly even from behind; yet she didn't look scary any more. She just looked sad and old and ill. He called out again. 'I'm sorry. I'm really sorry.'

She shambled round the bend in the lane and disappeared from view. He stared after her, filled with guilt yet also angry at her for making him feel this way. Who did she think she was? She hadn't even told him how she wanted him to help the girl, yet here she was, pressurizing him to go back to The Grange. At least it was Monday tomorrow so he had the excuse of having to go to school. But before that he still had to decide what to do about tonight. He turned back to the house, slipped round the side again and into the kitchen. The sitting room door was still closed and the murmur of Mum's voice continued as though nothing had happened.

Half an hour before midnight the alarm sounded under his pillow. He fumbled for it and switched it off, then lay back, listening. There were no noises from Mum's room. He slipped out of bed, opened his bedroom door as softly as he could and stole down the landing. Mum's door was ajar but he could see through the gap that she was fast asleep. He felt sure she wouldn't hear him if he decided to leave the house tonight.

But even as he tiptoed back to his room, he knew in his heart that he wasn't going. It was no use. He simply could not let Skin and Daz into The Grange. He would never forgive himself if something terrible happened to the girl, or to Mrs Little. What he would do tomorrow, how he would face the boys, he did not know. All he knew was that after tonight he would be in danger.

He closed the door of his room behind him and sat on the bed, not wanting to turn on the light. The electric clock on the bedside table read twenty-five to midnight. The others would be setting off about now. They would be making their way out into the night and by ten to midnight they would be waiting for him. By midnight they would be doubting him. By ten past they would be cursing him. By half past he would be their enemy.

He lay back on the bed and stared up at the ceiling. Darkness had not smothered it completely; moonlight was breaking through a gap in the curtains and throwing a limpid glow over the surface. He closed his eyes and saw under his brow the deep blue that had appeared there before, and the splashes of gold against it, forming slowly into a circle; and now, in the middle, something new: a tiny white speck. The sounds he had heard earlier started to pour through him again. He heard the bell sound and the flute sound and the harp sound and the buzzing sound and the sound of rushing water, all playing together in a weird, ethereal symphony, then somehow, as he listened, it was as though the different sounds all merged into one: the deep oceanic roar that seemed to pervade everything. He stared through the golden circle at the white speck in the middle and saw at last what it was.

A five-pointed star.

He felt his body shake, then some inner part of him seemed to stir, as in the waking dream that visited him so much, and the next moment it was as though that inner part of him were being pulled through his forehead in the direction of the star, which was now growing bigger and bigger, and seemed to be opening before him. The roaring sound grew louder until he felt certain it was about to consume him. He opened his eyes in panic and found himself lying on the bed as before, staring up at the ceiling. The room was still and the sounds and images were gone. But he was still shaking. He put his mind on Dad and tried to calm down, and the strange unfinished melody came back, and he hummed it, hearing in his head the harmonies that seemed to want to go with it; and somehow, still humming, he fell into a doze.

When he woke, he found he had twisted right round on the bed and was now curled up, hugging the end of the duvet into his chest. He sat up and rubbed his eyes, feeling disorientated and frightened. The clock read half past one. Moonlight was still filtering into the room through the gap in the curtains. He stood up to close it out, then realized with a start that another light was pushing through with it; but this was no natural beam. It was a torch and he knew whose it would be. He edged closer to the window, keeping well behind the curtain, and made to squint out through the gap; then stopped. Whether it was from bravado or just plain foolishness, he didn't know, but instead of peeping through unseen as he had intended, he took a deep breath, then thrust apart the curtains on either side, and revealed himself. From down in the lane, on the spot where Mrs Little had stood earlier, the beam of the torch fell hungrily over him, then went out; and he saw Skin standing there in the moonlight. And the two boys watched each other in silence and contempt.

15

The alarm woke him at half past six and he reached out to switch it off, wishing he could switch off the day that came with it. He felt groggy and sluggish and frightened of what lay ahead, and he resented this early start, even though he knew it was necessary for what he had decided to do. He was also itching for a shower and a hair wash. He climbed out of bed and pulled aside the curtain to check the lane. There was no sign of anyone and no indication from up here that Skin had done any damage last night. A snowy mist hung over the fields of Bill Foley's farm but sunlight was already breaking through and it looked as if another hot day was in store.

First things first, he told himself. You've made your decision so get on with it.

He hurried to the door and listened. Mum wouldn't be up for half an hour so he should have plenty of time for what he needed to do. He slipped out to the landing and hurried down to Mum's study. To his dismay she was already there, sitting in her dressing gown at the computer. She looked round at him and smiled. 'Hello, Luke.'

'Hello.'

He stared at her, unsure what to do. She looked back at the computer and tapped a few keys. 'Just got to sort this out,' she said.

'What is it?'

'E-mail from Berit. About a translation.'

'Oh.'

'It's only a query but she needs a quick answer. Won't be a minute.'

'Has it just come in?'

'Yes. Well . . . ' Mum checked the original e-mail on the screen. 'She sent it at half past three this morning, Norwegian time. I sometimes wonder if that woman ever sleeps.' Mum went on typing and Luke said nothing this time, anxious for her to finish the e-mail and send it as quickly as possible. 'Right,' she said after a moment. 'I'm done. Hang on while I just send it.'

They watched the e-mail go, then Mum leaned back in the chair and looked him over. 'You're up early.'

'So are you.'

'Lots to think about. Mind racing all over the place. I'm as bad as Berit. Do you want some tea?'

'Yes, please.'

She gave him a kiss and wandered off down the stairs. He waited until he heard her moving about the kitchen, then sat down at the computer and went into his e-mail program. Now, more than ever, he was glad that his e-mail address only gave away his surname and some numbers, but no initials. He must have known something like this was going to happen when he'd fixed it last year. It was tempting to send a message from Mum's e-mail for extra authenticity but he knew there was too great a danger of her receiving a reply, so it was best to use his own. He clicked on New Message and then hunted through Mum's bottom drawer for the letter Mrs Searle had sent her three months ago. There it was, in the folder with the others. He glanced over the first lines again.

Dear Mrs Stanton,

I am sorry to have to report that Luke has once again been involved in an incident at school in which he was extremely

*rude to a member of staff. The teacher concerned on this
occasion was Mrs Dawson and . . .*

And blah blah blah, he thought, skimming down to
the bottom. *Yours sincerely, Mrs Searle. Head of Year.* And
there was the thing he wanted: her e-mail address. He
started to type it into the recipient's box on the screen,
then stopped. He was doing this all wrong. He should send
the e-mail to the school secretary, not the head of year.
Mrs Searle was such a canny woman, she'd be much more
likely to smell a rat than Mrs Jay, who never quite knew
what day of the week it was and was usually too harassed
to chase things up anyway. He ran his eye over the
letterhead, found the e-mail address of the school office
and typed that in instead, then put the letter back in the
folder and closed the drawer. The subject box on the screen
awaited his attention. He thought for a moment, then
typed: *Luke Stanton—absence.*

And on to the message. This was the tricky part. It
didn't need to be long but it had to be right, with no
spelling mistakes. He stared at the screen, thinking hard,
and listening all the while to Mum downstairs in the
kitchen. She would be here any moment. He started to
type.

> Dear Mrs Jay,
> *I am afraid that Luke has a bad cold so I have decided to
> keep him at home today.*

He stopped for a moment. Yours sincerely or yours
faithfully? He could never remember. What had Mrs Searle
said in her letter to Mum? He bent down to open the
drawer again, then stopped; footsteps had sounded down
in the hall. He looked frantically back at the screen. Yours,
he thought. Yours . . .Yours . . .

The footsteps started on the stairs. He typed feverishly on.

Best wishes,
Mrs Kirsti Stanton

And clicked on *Send*. The message disappeared to the outbox just as Mum entered the room.

'Checking e-mails?' she said.

'Yes.'

'Here's your tea.'

'Thanks.' He took the mug from her and put it down on the desk.

'I'm off to have a shower and a hair wash,' she said.

'Can you leave me some water? I wanted one, too.'

'Don't worry. There'll be plenty.'

And she left him again. He waited until he heard the shower start, then went on-line, dispatched the e-mail and waited to see if there were any incoming messages. There was one, sent at two o'clock this morning. It didn't need to be signed.

You're DEAD.

He felt a shiver pass through him. He had expected something like this, yet seeing it here in front of him still made him shudder. There was no doubting the danger he was in. He would avoid Skin and the others as long as he could but he knew that sooner or later they would catch up with him, either at school or around the village; and if he was on his own, there was no telling what they would do to him. He thought of Mum, and Mrs Searle, and wondered whether to tell them.

But he knew he could not. This was his fight, and besides, what could anyone else do? He'd been hanging around with Skin and the gang and nobody was going to have any sympathy for him now that he'd fallen out with them. And they hadn't actually done anything to him. A threatening e-mail was hardly something for the school to take action over. No doubt that was how Mrs Searle would see it. As for Mum . . .

He listened for the sound of the shower and to his surprise heard her humming. He frowned, unsure whether to be happy or angry. He hadn't heard her hum since Dad died but what was disturbing was that she was humming the tune of 'I Love Thee' by Grieg, the piece Dad used to play for her. She wasn't humming boisterously, just very quietly to herself, almost as though she didn't want him to hear her. Perhaps she didn't realize that he could. But who was she humming 'I Love Thee' to, now that Roger Gilmore was part of her life?

He scowled and drank the tea, then went back to his room, put on his school uniform and wandered downstairs. Mum was out of the shower now and he could hear her moving about upstairs. He entered the music room and hunted along the shelves for the dusty green jacket he remembered so well. There it was. He pulled it out and glanced over the title.

'I Love Thee'
By Edvard Grieg (1843–1907)

He sat down at the piano, propped it open in the holder and started to play. Almost at once he heard footsteps on the stairs and a moment later Mum appeared in the doorway. She was wearing a dressing gown and had a towel draped round her hair, and she looked beautiful and happy, not at all like someone whose racing mind had kept her awake, as she had said. He stopped playing.

'Don't,' she said. 'Please, Luke. Play a bit more.'

He carried on playing.

'I was humming it in the wrong key,' Mum said. 'Well, a different key anyway.'

He started to transpose the tune to the key she'd been humming it in. Out of the corner of his eye he saw her shaking her head.

'That's such a gift, Luke,' she said. 'Have you any idea how few people can do that? Just look at a piece of sheet music and then play it in a different key?'

'Dad could do it.'

'I know.'

He stopped playing, thoughts of Dad heavy upon him again. Mum spoke.

'You're so beautiful, Luke.'

'I don't feel very beautiful.'

'Well, you are. Take it from me.' She kissed his head. 'I didn't expect to see you dressed. I thought you wanted a shower and a hair wash.'

'I'll have one this evening.'

'You've got time if you want one. And there's plenty of water.'

'No, it's all right.' He looked down. 'I'm not fussed.'

'OK.' Mum paused. 'Luke?'

He looked up at her again. 'Yeah?'

'Things'll be better by this evening.'

'What do you mean?'

'They just will. OK? I promise.' She smiled and kissed him again. 'I'll get the breakfast going.'

There was no sign of Skin and the others in the lane but that meant nothing. They would probably be waiting for him on the school bus. The treatment would start then. Words to begin with, since others were around. Or maybe no words. Maybe just silence and stares. The heavy stuff

138

would start in the playground or outside the school gates. Except that today he wasn't going to give them the chance.

He waited, sitting on the ground inside the entrance to the churchyard and hidden behind the old stone wall. There was something reassuring about this place, especially with Dad's gravestone in view over in the corner. From the square came the sound of the school bus revving up. He checked his watch. Ten past eight. It should have left by now. The driver must have realized he wasn't coming. He thought of Skin and the others watching for him and the glances that must be passing between them as they realized he was avoiding them today. He wondered whether Miranda was watching for him, too.

At last he heard the tone of the engine change. The bus was finally moving off. He listened as it rumbled across the square, past the shop, and away down the lane to town. He looked about him. Now was the really difficult part: getting where he wanted to go without being seen. He decided to avoid the village square with all the mums and toddlers heading for the primary school and Miss Grubb with her suspicious little eyes peering out through the door of the shop. He cut across the churchyard, stopped for a brief moment at Dad's grave, then slipped out of the gate at the far end and took the footpath that ran past the village hall and across the fields to Roger Gilmore's lane. To his relief, he saw no one on the way and he was soon at the stile just down from Stony Hill Cottage. He ran his eye over it. The curtains of the bungalow were drawn across but the door of the workshop was open. From inside came what sounded like the tap of a chisel on wood.

He climbed over the stile and crept closer, watching the open doorway all the while, but no face appeared and the tapping continued. A few moments later he was past and racing up to the junction with Nut Bush Lane. He stopped at the top to catch his breath, his eyes on the lustrous green of Buckland Forest just beyond the playing field; but the trees were not his destination this time, much as he wanted them to be. He turned down Nut Bush Lane and ran on, and didn't stop until he had reached The Grange.

16

M rs Little didn't look pleased or grateful to see him. She simply stared at him through narrowed eyes as though his presence on her doorstep was an affront and she showed no signs of wanting to let him in. 'I thought you'd decided you weren't coming,' she said eventually. Her voice was frosty and hard. She didn't wait for an answer but went straight on in exactly the same tone. 'Aren't you meant to be on the school bus?'

'Yes.'

They stared at each other in silence. From the direction of the forest came the scratchy sound of pheasants croaking in the still air. The old woman frowned. 'So who knows you're here?'

'Nobody.'

'What about your friends from the gang?' Her eyes flickered round for a moment as though she was searching for them. 'Are they truanting as well?'

'They don't know anything about this.'

'And your mother?'

'She thinks I'm on the way to school.'

'So what will happen when you don't turn up?'

'I've sorted that. You don't need to worry about it. No one knows I'm here. And no one'll find out.'

'I hope not. Because I don't want people turning up at the door asking questions. If they do, I'll deny ever having seen you.'

He shrugged and tried to look unconcerned but the coldness of this welcome was starting to make him regret

141

his decision to come here. Then, to his surprise, the hardness in her face seemed to melt—just for an instant—and he saw what he imagined was the best she could manage of a smile. It was barely a twist of the mouth and it lasted no more than a second before the severity returned but it was the only smile he'd ever received from her and he felt it had to mean something.

'I'm glad you're here,' she said. 'Come in.' The voice was a little softer, too, but this—like the smile—was not to last. When she spoke again, as she led him towards the sitting room, the formality was back and the distance between them re-established. 'There are a few things we need to understand,' she said.

She reached the sitting room, held open the door, and ushered him through, then nodded towards the nearest armchair and closed the door behind her. He sat down, wondering where the girl was. There was no sign or sound of her yet. On the wall before him was a picture of a large, multicoloured star. Below it were several shelves stacked with the weird, foreign-looking figurines Mrs Little appeared to like so much. The star image shone as the sun caught it and it was strikingly beautiful, in contrast to the slightly grotesque objects beneath it. Mrs Little caught the direction of his gaze.

'I brought the statuettes back from India,' she said. 'They're mostly Hindu deities and sacred figures. I like to have lots of them around because it makes me feel safe. Now, if you've satisfied your curiosity, I'd like to get on. Do I have your full attention?'

'What?'

'Don't say "what"!' she snapped.

He turned quickly back and saw her watching him disdainfully.

'You'll speak politely when you address me,' she said. He scowled at her. It was one thing Mum ticking him off for bad manners but who the hell did this woman think she was? She watched him impassively for a few moments, then continued in the same haughty voice. 'If we're going to spend time together, you'll speak to me respectfully.'

'Who said we're going to spend time together?'

'You're here now, aren't you?'

'That doesn't mean I'm ever coming back. I mean, we haven't exactly got much in common, have we?'

'You're not coming to see me. Do you think I want that any more than you do?' Mrs Little watched him for a moment with obvious scorn. 'I don't want to see you. I don't want to see anyone. And I don't suppose anyone wants to see me.'

He searched the ugly face before him for some trace of self-pity but found none. The features were hard and proud. Yet this woman had a granddaughter who had clung to her and who needed her; and if there was a granddaughter, there must be—or must once have been— a mother and a father; and a Mr Little. Someone at some time must surely have loved this woman, perhaps still did love her, in spite of the person she had become.

'No,' Mrs Little went on, her voice as imperious and uncompromising as ever, 'I have no desire to see you, any more than I imagine you want to see me. I don't like you very much and I certainly don't trust you.'

'The feeling's mutual.'

'And yet . . . ' She studied him for a moment. 'Underneath that rudeness, I sense you're quite a different person. Not nearly as bolshie as you're trying to appear. So I'm going to take a chance on you. And you do owe me something. You broke into my house, remember. And I promise you this: I won't hesitate to contact the police and let your mother and all the village know what I've seen—if you fail to help my granddaughter.'

143

Luke looked away. There was no doubt this woman had some power over him. She could not prove that he had broken into The Grange—it was her word against his—but as she had reminded him when they spoke in the kitchen, his word no longer counted for much in this village. Two years ago it would have been different. Two years ago people would have believed him without question. But in the days when his word had meant something, there would have been no need to pledge it because there would have been no acquaintance with Skin, no break-in at The Grange, no contact with this horrible old woman. Luke frowned. It seemed to him suddenly that in his fourteen years he had had two different lives: there had been life with Dad and now there was life without Dad. And life without Dad was like a kind of death.

'So let's not beat about the bush,' said the old woman. 'You're not here to get to know me or for me to get to know you. You're here to help Natalie.'

Natalie. So that was the girl's name. He'd been wondering what it was. He pictured her face in his mind for a moment and listened again for sounds of her in the old house. But as before, he heard none.

'You still haven't explained how you want me to help her,' he said.

'All in good time,' said the old woman. 'There are a few things I have to tell you about her first. And we need to establish some ground rules.' She walked over to the piano, rested her hand on the top, and looked sternly down at him. 'Any visits you make to this house will remain a secret. I will tell no one. You will tell no one. Is that absolutely clear?'

'OK.'

'The answer is either yes or no.'

'Yes.'

144

'I shall deny ever having seen you if anyone asks me about you.'

'You've already said that. It's not a problem. Look, if this is such a big deal, we'll just forget it, OK? I don't have to come here. I don't have to risk getting into trouble for you.'

'For me?'

'Well, for the girl. Natalie.'

'All right. Just as long as we understand each other.' The old woman sat down in the armchair opposite. 'Natalie's ten years old but she has a mental age of four. She's been mentally handicapped all her life but to make matters worse she was in a car crash just over two years ago. Her mother and father were both killed. Natalie survived but the impact caused her to lose her sight. And of course that's only been part of the trauma. She had enough problems as it was before the crash but now— especially not being able to see—she's become very confused and very frightened. She's unsure of everything. Who she is, who her parents were, who I am.'

'But she calls you Nana.'

'That's only because I've taught her to do that over the last couple of years. She knows me now as Nana but I'm not sure she remembers me as the Nana I was to her before. She's never been able to express herself very much and it's hard to tell what she knows or remembers. It's as though she's had to learn to love me all over again. Fortunately she's good at loving and that side of things hasn't been so difficult for her.'

'And she's been living in this house ever since you moved here?'

'Pretty much.'

'But I've never seen her round the village.'

'No one's seen her round the village because she's never been round the village. She's never left this house. Nobody else knows she's here. Apart from you.' Mrs Little paused for a moment, then went on. 'You're wondering why I don't take her out. Two reasons. Firstly, she's too frightened to go out. In fact, she's mostly too frightened even to come downstairs.'

He turned away and stared out of the window, his unease mounting. He could feel this situation moving more and more out of his control. He gazed at the forest beyond the garden wall. Deep in there was the oak tree, his oak tree, his friend, waiting for him, calling to him. That's where he should be right now, not cooped up here with this strange woman. Yet her story compelled him to speak again. 'What's the second reason why you don't take Natalie out?'

'Because I'm not supposed to have her.' The old woman's eyes darkened. 'Natalie's mother was my daughter and when she and my son-in-law died in the accident, I was getting ready to return from India. I'd lived out there for most of my adult life but had bought The Grange because I wanted to spend my last years in this country with my daughter and son-in-law, and get to know Natalie a little better as she grew older. I was her only relative, apart from her parents, and I'd only ever seen her a few times, being abroad. I'd got my furniture and effects installed in The Grange but was still tying up loose ends out in India when I heard about the accident. I rushed through things out there and got away as quickly as I could but by the time I reached England, the funeral was over and Natalie was in a home—blind and in a terrible state. She was frightened and confused and in shock and the people in charge had no idea what to do with her. As far as I could tell, she'd received no medical care appropriate to her condition. And I know what I'm talking about here. I was a nurse for over forty years out in India. I've worked with accident victims and I know what severe trauma can do to people. So I waited till no one was watching, then took her away.'

'You . . . ?' He stared at her, thinking for a moment he'd misheard her.

'Yes,' she said, 'I took her away. Sneaked out with her. It was easy enough. The people at that place were a bunch of amateurs. No one saw me and I don't think anyone even suspected me. I'd only made one appearance at the home and I acted the doddery old biddy who'd gone a bit gaga. I brought Natalie secretly back to The Grange and looked after her. There was an investigation, of course, but nothing was found and no one suspected me. I got a routine call from the police after they discovered I was Natalie's grandmother and her only surviving relative but they didn't find anything.'

'How come?'

The old woman snorted. 'It was easy. Natalie had quickly become attached to me and I told her she had to keep very quiet if anyone ever came to the house or they'd take her away from me. She hid under the bed and didn't make a sound when the police turned up. But they didn't even bother to search the house. They took one look at me and the doddery old biddy routine did the rest. They were gone in no time at all and no one's bothered us since.' She levelled her eyes at Luke. 'Until you turned up.'

He forced himself to look steadily back. 'So you've kept Natalie a secret because you think she'd be taken back to the home.'

'I don't think—I know. She'd definitely be taken back to the home. And there's no way I'm going to let that happen.'

'But you're her grandmother. Her only living relative, you said. Surely she'd automatically be put in your care.'

'It doesn't work like that. They would argue that with her blindness and trauma, and her low mental age, she needs special care. Something an old woman like me, who's lived in India away from the family for so many years, cannot provide. But they're wrong. I've cared for her as well as anyone could have done. We've kept ourselves to ourselves and Natalie's had a chance to get better. Only things haven't gone so well for her lately. In fact, they've been really tough for her. She's still in a very vulnerable state and there are lots of things coming to the surface that she finds it hard to deal with.'

It seemed incredible, all this, and Luke still wasn't sure what to make of it. To keep a traumatized blind girl hidden for so long without anyone—apart from himself—finding out was no mean achievement. It also explained a lot about Mrs Little's behaviour.

'So that's why you hardly ever go out,' he said. 'Because you have to look after Natalie and you can't take her with you in case she gets discovered.'

'I only go out to buy a few essentials,' said the old woman. 'I have as much as I can delivered to the house. I don't encourage visitors for obvious reasons.'

'I thought that was just because you didn't like people very much.'

'I don't like people very much,' she answered bluntly. 'But Natalie's the main reason why I don't go out and why I keep people at a distance. And now that you know the secret, you mustn't give us away. For Natalie's sake, not mine. Keep quiet about this and I'll keep quiet about your breaking into my house.'

'But I still don't see how I can help Natalie,' he said. 'I mean, I'm not a specialist or anything. What can I do?'

She leaned back in the chair. 'You can play the piano.'

'What?' He saw her raise her eyebrows and quickly corrected himself. 'I mean, pardon?'

'You can play the piano,' she went on. 'I can't. If I

could, I wouldn't ask you to help. But you owe me something and you have a gift. So I want you to use it for Natalie. And it shouldn't be too onerous a task. You might even enjoy it.' She glanced round at the piano. 'Don't you want to play on a beautiful grand like this? It's been tuned.'

'I thought you said you didn't like people coming to the house.'

'The piano tuner I used was blind.' She gave him a wry look. 'Which was slightly ironic but very handy. He never saw Natalie and she never saw him. She didn't come downstairs anyway. The sound of someone in the house pounding the keys the way piano tuners do frightened her but then, after he'd finished, he started to play. Just a few pieces to try out the piano. And suddenly she changed. Something happened to her. I was sitting with her up in her room and I saw that she was spellbound. She even seemed to be humming. Then, when the music stopped, she was so wretched I almost wished he'd never started. So when you turned up, I thought . . . ' She paused. 'I thought perhaps you might be able to play for her. And make her happy again.'

'Can't you put the radio on for her? Or play a CD or something? There's plenty of music she could listen to.'

'It doesn't have the same effect. I don't know why. She listens to it and seems to like it but it doesn't grip her in quite the same way. It must have been the living sound of the piano that time the tuner came. I don't know— maybe it won't work with you. It's only happened that once, with the tuner. But I'd like you to try. And as I say, you should enjoy it. It's a magnificent instrument.'

He glanced round at it again. 'What did you buy it for if you can't play it yourself?'

'That's none of your business,' she said sharply.

'And why keep it tuned if no one else uses it?'

'That's none of your business either.' The old woman's tone grew more censorious still. 'You're not here to ask questions. You're here to play the piano.'

'Is that an order?'

'No, it—'

'Because it sounded like an order.' He could feel his anger rising again. 'And I don't take orders from you, OK?'

'It wasn't an order. It was a . . . ' The old woman softened her voice almost grudgingly. 'It was a request. I'd . . . I'd like it . . . if you'd play for my granddaughter.'

He frowned at her, wondering yet again whether he should be getting involved in all this. 'All right,' he said eventually. 'I'll do it this once. How long do you want me to play for? And what sort of stuff do you want? Classical, jazz, rock?'

'You're that good, are you? Able to pick and choose?' Her voice was a curious mixture of mockery and respect. He didn't answer and she went on. 'Play whatever you like. And play as long as you like. That's all I ask.'

So he played. Mrs Little left him and went upstairs and he sat down at the great grand piano and simply started. The old woman was right. Dusty though it was, this was a magnificent instrument with a rich, sonorous tone. He played whatever pieces took his fancy. He played Chopin and Schubert and the Beatles and the Bee Gees, and Simon and Garfunkel, and Fats Waller and Billy Mayerl and Scott Joplin, and then Bach and Scarlatti and Haydn, and simple Grade One pieces he'd learned years ago. He played and played. He didn't care that he was improvising half the time and often hitting wrong notes. He just played on, alone in the great room, wondering about Mrs Little upstairs, and the frightened girl with her, and for some reason thinking about Dad; and for a strange, unsettling moment, he felt a presence near his shoulder. It was nearly noon when he stopped. His wrists were aching and he was tired. No one had come down to the sitting room. The sun was high and the sound of birdsong had closed upon the stillness that the music had left behind. The presence by his shoulder was gone; but he suddenly realized he was not alone.

A tiny figure was standing in the doorway.

17

S he was staring towards him, as though she could see him sitting there at the piano, though he knew she could not. Her eyes were wide open, as was her mouth, and she was motionless, transfixed. She did not speak; she did not move her head; she seemed not even to blink. She simply stood there, alone, in the doorway. He spoke, as softly as he could. 'Hello, Natalie.'

The effect of his words was immediate. She turned in panic and disappeared from view. He gave a start of dismay, then heard another voice just outside the room. It was Mrs Little, speaking in those softer tones she reserved for Natalie alone. 'It's all right, my love. It's just a friend. A really good friend. We've just been listening to him, haven't we? Let's go and ask him if he'll play some more.'

There was a sound of snuffling outside and light footsteps moving about, not walking away, just pacing this way and that. Still the girl did not speak but she did not need to. It was easy to feel her fear of this terrifying new presence in the house. Yet all he had done was say two friendly words. He tried to think of something he could do to make amends; and the answer was obvious. He started to play again, Ravel's 'Pavane' this time, a piece he hadn't played since he was Natalie's age, but he remembered it well enough. It was perhaps a little mournful and he wasn't sure he should be playing something that had once been written in memory of a dead child, but in a strange way the music seemed to mirror the mood he felt; and as he played, he wondered about the part of Natalie that had died in the accident, and whether it would ever come to life again. He played on, through the opening bars into the hushed magic of the second section, still alone in the great room; then suddenly, out of the corner of his eye, he caught a movement in the doorway again.

He glanced towards it, still playing, and saw the girl standing there as before, and this time Mrs Little close behind her. The old woman caught his eye and put a finger to her lips. He nodded, though her warning was unnecessary. The one thing he was not going to do was speak. Not yet, anyway. He played on, enjoying the piece more and more as it came back to him. Once again he felt the presence by his shoulder, but this time it didn't unsettle him so much. He almost found it comforting. It was as though Dad were standing there, watching him play, as he had done so many times in the old days when life was good. The final bars seemed to come too soon. He took the chords slowly, then lifted his hands from the keys and let the stillness settle. Neither of the figures by the door spoke. He sat there and waited; then the girl moved. He said nothing and simply watched, as she walked towards him, slowly, hesitantly, feeling her way from object to object. Mrs Little was still close behind, one hand on the girl's shoulder. The old woman caught his eye again and nodded towards the piano.

And he played on, Grieg's 'Nocturne' this time, and very quietly. The girl was barely a few feet from him. She had made her way towards him with lots of stops and starts but now she was almost within touching range. He glanced at her as he played, feeling slightly nervous at her closeness, and anxious in case he frightened her again. He took the lively section of the piece much more slowly than it was meant to go, and with no crescendos at all.

Too much sound and movement and he felt certain he would lose her again. She had stopped now, her eyes still wide open and staring towards him, as though she could see him as clearly as he could see her. Mrs Little stood behind her as before, the hand still on the girl's shoulder. He played on, through the repetition of the main theme and up to the high peak of the music, still keeping the sound low for fear of startling the girl, then he eased the melody towards its conclusion. As the notes faded away, she stepped towards him.

Mrs Little took her hand away and did not follow. Natalie took another step until she was only inches from him. He did not move or speak. He simply watched and waited to see what she would do. Close by he saw Mrs Little watching, too. At first Natalie did nothing but stand and stare towards him with her unseeing eyes, then she reached out towards the piano. Her hand found the keyboard and she traced a path along it with her fingers, feeling her way round the black notes. Then she stopped, her hand still poised over the notes, and looked towards his face. She had not touched him but he felt sure she must realize how close he was. Suddenly she pressed a key. It was Middle C. She pressed it again, then took her hand from the piano and reached towards him.

He watched, unmoving. The hand touched his arm and he felt the fingers close round it. They were slender and delicate, yet surprisingly firm. Her eyes flickered this way and that as though she was searching for some glimpse of what this strange person looked like, then her hand moved again, up his arm to the shoulder and along towards his face, where it started to stroke the cheek. He knew this was curiosity rather than affection on her part, yet her fingers felt light and pleasant on his skin. They moved to his mouth and ran slowly around it, then on to his nose, and up between the eyes to his forehead, and then on to his left ear—at which point she suddenly giggled. He stared at her in confusion, sensing the reason for her laugh but unprepared for it, and unsure of his own response. Her hand moved round to his other ear and she giggled again. He glanced at Mrs Little but her face gave no clue as to what he should do. He decided to take a risk and speak again.

'Funny ears?' he said softly.

Natalie didn't answer, but she didn't run away either. Instead she touched the ear and giggled again.

'What's wrong with my ears?' he said, his voice as gentle and self-mocking as he could make it. 'I think they're rather good, don't you?'

Still she played with the ears, first one, then the other. He hesitated, then reached out and—very lightly—touched one of hers. She drew back at once and turned away, her face clouded with fear. He forced a chuckle and quickly spoke again, in the friendliest voice he could manage. 'I think your ears are funny, too, Natalie.'

She froze, half-turned away but not moving any further from him. He lowered his voice. 'OK, Natalie, what piece shall we play next?'

She didn't speak. She simply stood there, her mouth tight.

'I know what,' he said. 'Here's one you'll like.'

He chose 'To A Wild Rose' by MacDowell. It was nice and simple and it seemed a good piece to play for Natalie right now. He glanced down at her. She had turned back towards him and her eyes were darting about the room as though the notes were flashes of light and she was trying to catch them. He played on and soon saw her moving closer again. A moment later he felt a hand on his forearm. He glanced at her again. She seemed to have no desire this time to run her fingers up to his face but simply wanted to rest her hand there as he played. It was a little distracting but he continued somehow, her hand bobbing about as his arm moved over the keys. When the piece was over and he sat back in the silence, he found her hand still there. On an impulse, he put an arm round her shoulder. To his surprise she moved towards him straightaway. He had expected her to pull back or run away; but she moved closer still and even snuggled against his body.

Mrs Little spoke. 'She's very trusting.'

He heard the threat inside the words and answered at once.

'I won't hurt her. You don't need to worry.'

He wondered what the old woman was thinking; whether this was what she had wanted for Natalie or not. It was hard to tell from her expression. Mrs Little watched him for a moment, then reached out and stroked Natalie's hair.

'Did you like that, Natalie?' she said. 'Did you like that?'

There was no answer from the little girl. She simply moved closer to Luke. Luke looked down at her and spoke. 'You don't even know my name, Natalie. Do you want me to tell you what it is?'

And Natalie looked up at him and spoke for the first time.

'Funny ears,' she said.

18

He lay back on the floor of the tree-house and gazed up through the canopy at the sky. It was a deep blue with clouds that seemed hardly to move; but his thoughts were running fast. Funny ears—she'd said he had funny ears. Or maybe she'd meant it as a name for him. If so, it wasn't a bad one for a boy who kept hearing funny things. Strange things, anyway. Yet right now it was not sounds that were pressing upon him but the strange presence he had felt earlier, close to his shoulder. It was still there, never quite in one place but always somewhere near. He tried to tell himself it was Dad. He didn't care if this was fanciful. It was nice just to imagine Dad was here, even though he was quite sure his father was far away and probably incapable even of thinking of him right now. He moved his head to the right, then to the left, and as usual saw nothing.

'Why can't I see you?' he muttered. 'Eh? Why can't I see you?' He pictured Dad's face as if his father were lying right next to him in the tree-house. 'You're not scared of me, are you?'

The only answer was a murmuring of leaves.

'But maybe you're not Dad anyway,' he said to the empty space. 'Maybe you're someone else. Or maybe you're nobody at all. Maybe I'm just imagining you.' He frowned. 'I'm probably just talking to the air.'

But even as he said this, he sensed he was wrong.

At least this presence—whatever it was, whoever it was—didn't feel like a threat. He looked at his watch:

157

three o'clock. He'd been lying up here for two hours since leaving The Grange but it was time he was moving. He was due at Miranda's to practise their piece straight after school and he ought to be at The Toby Jug waiting for her when she came in from the school bus, otherwise she might ring his home to find out why he wasn't in school today, and Mum would find out he'd truanted. He climbed down the tree and set off back through the forest, the strange presence still close by. There was no sign of Natalie or Mrs Little as he passed The Grange.

He reached the top of the track and turned down Nut Bush Lane in the direction of the village. Half past three. It was a question of timing, he decided. If he reached the square too early, it would be obvious to any nosy parkers like Miss Grubb that he hadn't been in school today; if he arrived at the same time as the school bus, he'd have to deal with Skin and the others; and if he arrived too late, Miranda would ring his home. He needed to get there just a few minutes early, hang around the churchyard out of sight until the bus had arrived and Skin and the others had gone, then slip into The Toby Jug as quickly as he could. He decided to cut down past Stony Hill Cottage and head back to the village the way he had come this morning. He was less likely to meet anyone on the footpath and the only really difficult bit would be getting past Roger Gilmore's place unnoticed. But when he reached Stony Hill Cottage, he found a bigger problem waiting for him.

Mum's car was outside it. He frowned. So she couldn't even manage a ten-minute walk to get here. She was in such a hurry to see the guy she had to take the car. He wondered how long she had been here. Maybe hours, maybe the whole day. He stared down at the bungalow with loathing and caught a movement in the kitchen. Someone was standing there, just back from the window— no, two people, close together, very close. A shiver ran through him and a voice inside his head told him to turn back to Nut Bush Lane, go to the village that way, keep away from this place. But already he was moving closer to the bungalow. He felt the presence by his shoulder draw near, heard the voice inside his head again. Turn back, it said. Turn back, turn back. But still he was moving towards the bungalow, yearning to call out, charge, throw stones, rocks, anything at the window. He stopped at the fence, breathing hard, and waited for their faces to turn towards him.

But they did not.

Miranda found him in the churchyard, slumped against the wall by Dad's grave.

'Luke?' She sat down beside him. 'Are you OK?'

He said nothing. He hardly noticed her. All he saw was a picture in his mind that he yearned to forget.

'Luke?' She put an arm round his shoulder. 'Are you ill? You weren't in school today.'

'I'm not ill.'

'And you didn't turn up at The Toby Jug either. I thought maybe—'

'That I'd stood you up again.'

'You didn't stand me up last time,' she said. 'You turned up. In the end.' She watched him in silence for a moment. 'No, I thought maybe something was wrong so I came out to look for you. I was going to give you a ring but I was a bit worried I might get you into trouble if . . . you know . . . your mum maybe didn't know you weren't in school or something. I mean, I'm not suggesting . . . '

He started to cry and that made him feel worse. Crying in front of Miranda. She would think him weak now. Everyone would think him weak. And he was weak. He was so pathetically weak. She'd been tactful and kind, not wanting to get him into trouble with Mum, and all he could do was blubber. She'd push him away now and he didn't blame her. But to his surprise she pulled him close and just held him. When he'd finished crying, she took her arm away.

'Is it Jason Skinner and the others?' she said. 'Have they done something to you?'

'Not yet.'

'What does that mean?'

'Doesn't matter. It's not them anyway. Not right now.'

'What, then?'

He looked round at her through blurred eyes. 'I'm losing her.'

'Who?'

'Mum. I'm losing her—to that man. I've already lost Dad. Now I'm losing Mum as well.'

'What's happened?'

'I saw them. I shouldn't have. I know I shouldn't have. I didn't go to school today. I can't tell you why but you mustn't let on to anyone.' He waited for her to show some sign of disapproval but she simply watched and listened. 'I saw them,' he went on. 'I was outside Stony Hill Cottage and I looked through the kitchen window. They were kissing. And it wasn't just a little peck, you know? It was . . .'

The picture filled his mind again and he looked away. She put her arm round him once more. 'Did they see you?'

'No, they were too wrapped up in themselves.'

'How long were you there for? Watching, I mean.'

'Long enough.' He shook his head. 'They just kissed and kissed and kissed. And then they left the kitchen.' He scowled. 'I know where they went after that. I saw them drawing the curtains.'

'So what did you do then?'

'I ran off.' He felt tears in his eyes again. 'I know it sounds stupid but I've never seen them kissing before. Not like that. I mean . . . I knew they did it but they've never . . . you know . . . if I was around. Or if I ever came upon them, they'd stop or I'd look away or whatever. Only this time, they didn't know I was there and . . . '

He fell silent. Miranda gave his arm a squeeze.

'Was it so terrible?' she said.

'No.' He pushed his face into his hands. 'That's the problem. Don't you see? It wasn't terrible at all. He was . . . he was tender with her. He was so . . . bloody . . . tender.' He swallowed hard. 'I couldn't bear to see it.'

Miranda pulled him closer. 'Luke?'

'Yeah?'

'Roger's a nice man.'

'My dad was a nice man.'

'I know he was.'

He took his hands away from his face and stared over at Dad's gravestone. Miranda spoke again. 'If your dad was standing here right now, if you could look up and ask him if he thought it was OK for your mum to be with Roger, what do you think he'd say?'

And Luke looked up—but as in the tree-house saw only an empty space; and this time the presence was gone, too.

'He's not here,' he said bluntly, 'so there's no point in asking, is there?'

'Yes, but just imagine he—'

'He's not here!' he snapped. 'OK? He's not here. He's not anywhere. He's gone. That's what happens when you die. You disappear. Goodnight, Vienna.' He saw the distress in her face and quickly softened his voice. 'I'm sorry.'

'It's OK.'

'I didn't mean to bite your head off.'

161

'It's OK. Really.'

'It's not OK. I was horrible.' He looked away over the churchyard again, then back at her. 'I'm sorry.'

'Don't keep saying sorry. I'm fine.'

He took a deep breath and tried to calm down. 'Do you want to go back to The Toby Jug and practise?'

'Are you sure you want to? You wouldn't rather go home?'

'Go home?' He stood up, dusted the grass off his legs and reached out a hand to pull her up. 'What on earth would I want to go there for?'

19

He found Mum in the sitting room when he returned from The Toby Jug. She was in Dad's old armchair and had the television on with the sound turned off. She was staring at the far wall but she looked round as he approached. 'It's half past six, Luke,' she said.

'I've been at Miranda's. We've been practising.' He sat on the edge of the sofa. 'I did tell you I was going to The Toby Jug straight from the school bus.'

'Yes, I know.' She looked away again as though unwilling to discuss the matter further. He watched her in silence and felt a few seconds of disorientation. It was hard to connect the person he had seen in those guilty moments back at Stony Hill Cottage with this other person sitting here; and it wasn't just his own confusion that was causing this feeling: there was something strange about Mum, too. Her eyes were glazed; she looked deeply distracted. 'There's been a phone call,' she said.

He thought at once of school and Mrs Searle, but he was wrong. 'Three phone calls actually,' Mum said. 'All between five and six o'clock this afternoon. Same thing as before. It rings, I pick up the phone and say hello, there's a pause, then the phone goes down the other end.'

He tried not to betray his relief; or his disquiet.

'Did you try and trace the number of the caller?' he said.

'Yes. Nothing. Number not given.'

'Probably some nutcase with nothing better to do.'

163

'Probably Jason Skinner or one of those other misfits,' she said.

He tried to look indifferent but his thoughts were racing back to The Grange. What was happening there? It had to be Mrs Little who was ringing and that could only mean a problem with Natalie. Mum spoke again, her voice as listless as her eyes.

'What's going on, Luke?'

'Nothing's going on.'

'Don't lie to me. Please don't lie to me. I'm not stupid.'

'I'm not lying. Nothing's going on.'

'All these strange phone calls.'

'Nothing to do with me.'

'Sure about that?'

'Yeah.'

She frowned. 'You're out all the time. You never tell me where you're going.'

'I told you about Miranda.'

'Yes,' she sighed. 'All right, you told me about Miranda. But most of the time you tell me nothing. Usually I haven't got the faintest idea where you are or when you're coming back. I sometimes even wonder if you're coming back.'

Luke sloped over to the window and stared out of it for a few moments, then turned back to her. There was something strange about this conversation. It wasn't like their usual rows. Something was wrong and for once it wasn't just him. He glanced at the flickering television screen. 'What have you got the sound off for?'

'I put it on to watch the news and lost interest.'

'So why don't you turn it off?'

She gave him a baleful look, then reached for the remote and pressed the button. 'Satisfied?' There was something in her voice, something other than disapproval;

164

a kind of sadness that didn't make sense after what he'd seen earlier. She spoke again. 'I've finished with Roger.'

He gave a start. 'What?'

'I've finished with Roger.'

'When?'

'Today. This afternoon. While you were at school.' She gave him a weary smile. 'So it's over. OK? All finished.'

He stared at her, too stunned to speak. This couldn't be true. It made no sense at all, unless something terrible had happened after he'd run away from the bungalow. She watched him for a moment, then yawned. 'Fancy a walk?'

'Not particularly.'

'Well, I do.' She stood up. 'I'll make supper when I get back. I won't be long. If you're hungry while I'm out, you can always hit the bread bin.'

'Mum—' He looked at her, unsure what he wanted to say; and she looked back, her face dark and sad. He remembered how she had hummed Grieg only that morning in the shower; how happy she had seemed. 'Mum, he hasn't . . . I mean . . . he hasn't done something horrible to you, has he? Hit you or anything?'

She gave a tired laugh. 'No, he hasn't hit me, he hasn't done anything horrible, he hasn't said anything nasty, he hasn't been unkind. In fact . . . ' She bit her lip. 'I can honestly say he hasn't done anything wrong at all.'

'What, then? What's happened?'

'Nothing's happened, Luke.' She reached out and touched him on the cheek. 'Nothing for you to worry about. And certainly nothing for you to be angry with Roger about. He's been fantastic, OK? You can stop hating him now.' She leaned forward and gave him a kiss. 'I won't be long.'

'I'm coming with you.'

'I thought you didn't want to.'

'I've changed my mind.'

They set off down the lane, heading away from the village. He was glad Mum hadn't turned in the direction of the square because that would have meant going past Skin's house, but she usually took this route when she wanted a stroll. It was the way they'd often gone as a family when Dad was alive. The evening felt soft and mild and there was a warm glow over Bill Foley's fields. A buzzard glided overhead, splintering the sunlight as it passed. Mum walked slowly and seemed in no hurry to talk. He thought of Natalie and Mrs Little; and Skin; and Dad; and now this business with Roger Gilmore. It was as though whichever way he looked there were problems. To add to his confusion, he could hear the roaring sound again. It had started the moment they left the house, a low hum at first, then the familiar rumbling sound, growing gradually louder until now it rolled over him like a great billow of sound. He saw Mum glance at him quizzically.

'What's wrong?' he said.

'Funny.'

'What's funny?'

'Your father used to do that.'

'Do what?'

'Narrow his eyes slightly when he was hearing something unusual.'

Luke said nothing, his mind still absorbed by this strange roaring sound. As usual it seemed to be everywhere, as much inside him as outside. Mum hooked her hand round his arm. 'You're so like him,' she said. 'You even hear the same sounds.'

'How do you know?'

'I just do. I can't hear them because I'm not sensitive that way but I know you hear them because you're like Dad. Anyway, he said you did.'

'I never told him.'

'You didn't need to. He could tell.' They reached the T-junction at the end of the lane. 'Left or right?' she said.

'Neither.' He nodded straight ahead towards the gate into the field opposite. Mum smiled.

'OK,' she said.

They walked forward, leant over the gate and gazed down the field. At the far end the cattle turned from their leisurely munching to stare up towards them, then resumed their feeding.

'I know why you like this spot,' said Mum.

'Dad.'

'Yes.' She chuckled. 'He loved leaning over this gate, didn't he?' She reached out and put an arm round him. 'You're so like him, Luke. He was always hearing strange things. I'd wake up in the middle of the night and find him lying there with his eyes closed, but dead still, rigid almost, and I'd know he was listening to something. And I'd put my arm round him and ask him what he was hearing.'

'And what did he say?'

'It varied. He heard so many different things. Sometimes he said he heard bells or gongs. Other times it was wind instruments or plucked strings like a harp, or buzzing sounds, or rushing water. Sometimes it was actual music. He'd hear melodies and harmonies and things, music he knew or music he'd never heard before. There were lots of things he heard. But the main sound he heard was a kind of deep humming or roaring. He said it was a combination of all the other sounds and it was the most powerful of all. He used to call it the engine.'

'The engine?' said Luke, listening to the sound even as he listened to Mum.

'I think it was partly the noise it made,' she said. 'It reminded him of an engine for some reason. But he said

167

something else about it, too. Something a bit weird.' She looked at him. 'He said it's the engine that started creation and keeps it running. He said it's there all the time, even if we can't hear it, and it'll never ever die. I know that sounds a bit strange but that's what he said. I've no idea if it's true or not. I don't hear any of these things myself. But your dad did. And I know you do.'

The roaring sound went on and it did indeed sound like an engine. He had thought that before. It was comforting to know that Dad had used the same word to describe it.

'But he didn't like talking too much about the sounds he heard,' Mum went on. 'He only ever spoke about them to me or Mr Harding.'

'Mr Harding?'

'Oh, yes. They talked quite a bit. They were closer friends than you probably realize. But your dad didn't say much about the sounds even to us. He felt they were sacred and he was frightened that if he spoke too much about them, they'd leave him. So he told me never to press him too much on the subject and never to press you either, once he'd realized you were hearing them, too.'

Luke pictured Dad's face, as if his father were standing next to him right now, leaning on the gate with them. 'I . . . I don't like speaking about the sounds either,' he said. 'But not for the same reason as Dad. I just don't want people to think I'm off my head.'

She laughed. 'Well, there was probably an element of that with Dad, too. He always said he couldn't tell people about the sounds because they'd think he was talking rubbish. But deep down I know the real reason was that the sounds were just very special to him, very sacred, like I said. So he kept quiet about them. But . . . ' She paused for a moment. 'I'll tell you one thing your father said. I remember it because it involved you, in a small way.' She paused again, as though she was uncertain whether or not to continue.

'Go on,' he said.

She frowned. 'It was when we were living in Strawberry Hill. You were about eighteen months old. I woke up one night in the small hours and found your dad wasn't in bed, so I got up and went to look for him. He was downstairs, sitting at the kitchen table in his dressing gown with some blank paper and some coloured crayons in front of him. He was holding you in the crook of his left arm while he drew a picture on the paper with his right hand.'

'I don't remember this.'

'You wouldn't. You were much too young. And you were fast asleep anyway. He said he only picked you up because he wanted to hold you. But that wasn't what I remember most.' She ran her eye over the field again. 'What I remember most was that he was crying.'

'Crying?'

'Yes. He had tears streaming down his face. I put my arm round him and asked him what was wrong. He said nothing was wrong at all. He said he was as happy as he'd ever been in his life. And then he looked up at me and you know what he said? I remember his exact words. He said: ''The firmament is singing.'' '

'The firmament?' Luke stared at her. 'What's that?'

She pointed upwards. 'It's what you see above you. The expanse of the sky and everything in it. The sun, the moon, the stars. All the celestial bodies. But that's only one meaning of the word. It means something else, too.'

'What else does it mean?'

'Heaven,' she said.

He stared up into the sky, where the buzzard was circling again. 'If heaven's up there in the—what's it called?—firmament, there won't be any singing going on.

169

It'll be a miserable place because it's full of people like Dad who've been taken away from their loved ones.'

'Maybe.' She pulled him closer. 'But I don't think that's how your dad saw the firmament. I think he saw it as a place of beauty. And he used to say it's not just above us but inside us as well. He said we carry our own firmament with us. It's physical and metaphysical. He said some of the sounds he heard—some of the sounds you hear—can't be measured or recorded because they're too subtle and the only instrument sensitive enough to pick them up is the human soul.' She ruffled his hair. 'This is getting a bit serious, isn't it? Come on, let's walk.'

They set off down the lane in the direction of Frank Meldrum's pottery, Luke's mind now full of strange new thoughts. His anger was gone—that was one thing. So was Mum's listless manner. So, too, was the roaring sound. It had simply faded away. Yet he knew it was still there, just below the surface. He could feel it, even though he couldn't hear it any longer. Perhaps Dad was right. Perhaps it really was there all the time. But was it the engine that drove creation? He remembered something else Mum had said and turned to her. 'What was the picture Dad was drawing? That time he said the firmament was singing.'

'He said it was a picture of what he was hearing,' she answered. 'He used to say that you can draw sounds if you hear them clearly enough because sounds have got colours and shapes. But I expect you know that as well as he did.' Luke said nothing. 'Anyway,' Mum went on, 'he didn't talk much about what he saw any more than he talked about what he heard. It was all sacred to him. And he was no scientist anyway. He wasn't interested in analysing things. He was too busy experiencing them.'

'But what was he drawing?'

'A pentagram.'

'A what?'

'A pentagram. A five-pointed star. He coloured it, too, while I was there in the kitchen with him. I remember I had to hold the paper for him to stop it slipping about on the table as he drew, since he had his other arm tied up holding you. It was a beautiful drawing. It had a blue background with gold all around it but the star itself was—'

'White,' he said.

'Yes.' She stared at him. 'How did you know?'

He shrugged and looked away, thinking of the image he had seen under his brow and hoping Mum wouldn't besiege him with further questions. He felt as reluctant to talk about this as Dad had been. Mum touched him on the arm. 'Don't worry,' she said. 'I know you don't want to say any more about it. You're not your father's son for nothing.'

'What happened to the picture?' he said.

'Don't know. Got lost, I think.'

They walked on down the lane, past the pottery and on towards the brook. The sun was still bright on the fields but the air was starting to cool a little. They reached the stile into the meadow where Luke had tried in vain to hide from Skin and stopped again. 'Your dad used to like this spot, too,' said Mum, gazing over at the running water beyond.

'I know.'

'This and your favourite oak tree.' She threw a mock-serious glance at him. 'The one you're not supposed to be climbing.' He didn't respond to this but she didn't seem to expect him to. She pointed further up the lane. 'Saw a stag here once. Did I ever tell you that?'

'No.'

'It was the year we moved to Upper Dinton. Our first autumn here. You'd just caught the school bus in the

171

morning and your dad and I went out for a walk. It was really misty, I remember. Anyway, we got to this stile and we were just about to climb over it and walk by the brook when we saw this huge stag up there on the lane. It was standing sideways-on so we could see its profile. Its head was slightly raised and it looked really proud and fierce. I'll never forget it.'

'What happened?'

'It just glanced in our direction, then trotted through that gate into the field and vanished in the mist. Your dad said he could hear the animal's song as it loped away.'

'The animal's song?'

'Yes.'

'What did he mean?'

'I think you know deep down. But you've probably never thought about it before.' Mum was silent for a moment, then she went on. 'It's something your dad believed in very strongly. He used to say that every single thing in creation—every human being, every creature, every flower, every tree, every blade of grass, every speck of sand—has its own special song, different from all other songs. He said you can hear those songs if you listen hard enough.' She frowned. 'I don't know if that's true. I don't hear any special songs when I see people and stags and trees and things. But he did. And I know you do. Your father told me it would happen.'

'Can we drop this?' said Luke. He looked down. 'I just feel a bit—'

'It's OK. I understand.'

'Thanks.' He hesitated. 'Mum, this thing with Roger—'

'Is over,' she said.

Their eyes met and he saw she was as reluctant to pursue this subject as he was to pursue the other. He thought again of what he had seen at the bungalow.

'Completely over?' he said.

'Yes.' She gave him a kiss. 'Completely over. It's just you and me now, Luke. You and me and nobody else.'

Except Dad, he thought.

20

And Dad felt close that night when the waking dream returned. It had the usual mysterious beginning. One moment he was lying in bed, staring up at the ceiling, the next he was in the forest, floating, flying, straining towards the old oak; and the roots seemed to open as if to embrace him, and he flew into the gap and upwards through the tunnel of the tree, and out into the sky, Dad's presence drawing quickly near. He did not see his father or hear his voice or feel his touch—he never did. It was just a presence, close and familiar; and then the other presences started to appear, also close, also familiar, though he couldn't remember who they were; and they flew on together, towards the luminous star. But the dream was cut short by a loud *crack!*

To his surprise and dismay, he found himself lying in bed again. The house was still and he was wide awake—and scared.

Crack!

He gave a start. It was the window. Something had struck the pane, a stone by the sound of it. He slid out of bed and peeped round the edge of the curtain. Beyond the wall of the front garden a shadow was moving in the lane. There was no mistaking who it was. He searched to see if Daz was there, too, and spotted him over to the right, crouching behind the wall. There was no sign of Speed. He saw Skin's arm whip through the air.

Crack!

Another stone hit the window. He thought of Mum, sleeping on the other side of the house, and hoped she wouldn't hear. This was his battle, not hers. He glanced at the clock—half past midnight. Hopefully, if he failed to appear at the window, they'd get bored with this soon and go home. They couldn't keep it up all night.

Crack!

Another stone from Skin, then the two boys started to climb over the low wall into the garden. Luke clenched his fists. This was different. This was more serious. This wasn't just throwing stones now. They landed on the other side of the wall and stood there for a moment, staring up at his window as though they knew he was there watching. He kept to the side, trying not to show himself, then he remembered what he'd done last night; and on an impulse pulled back the curtain. The boys stiffened at the sight of him and fixed their eyes on his. He stared back as defiantly as he could but his resolve was weakening already. Even from this safe place he found Skin's menace terrifying. He wanted to run, call Mum, ring the police, anything but stand here and face this. He wondered how he could ever have thought these were his friends. They drew closer, their eyes never leaving his, and finally stopped below the window, glaring up. Skin's face was aflame with hatred. Neither of the boys moved at first; they simply watched and snarled. Then Skin bent down, wrenched a clod of earth from the flowerbed and flung it up against the pane. It struck with a thud, then fell back in a lump on the path. Skin didn't even glance at it. He simply glowered up at the window, thrust two fingers in the air, then turned and set off back across the lawn, Daz trotting at his heels like a faithful dog. A few moments later the boys were gone.

Luke closed the curtain and sat on the bed, breathing hard. He felt full of fear, full of uncertainty about what

175

lay ahead. He tried to coax Dad's presence back to him but nothing came, only more fear, more uncertainty. He thought of Natalie, locked in her own world of pain, and for some reason found himself humming the wistful melody that haunted him so often when he thought of her. It felt good to hum and in a strange way the tune seemed to push away some of his fear. He pondered the melody. It was so childlike, so innocent, so like Natalie herself. Maybe that was why it made him think of her. But what was it called? And why did it sound so familiar? He'd heard it before somewhere. He knew he had. But where? Perhaps he would never find out.

But even as he sat on the bed, humming the tune to drive away his fear, the answer came, as though the music itself had transported it. He saw a picture in his mind of their old house in Strawberry Hill, and it was a hot summer's day with all the windows open, and he was four years old, standing in the hallway, listening to the sound of his father as he played the piano in the music room, not practising or performing but just playing for himself, thinking no doubt that he was alone in the house with Mum and Luke down the road at the shops. Except that they were not at the shops. They had returned and Mum was outside the house, talking to a neighbour, while Luke had run on ahead to see his father—only to stop in the hallway, mesmerized by the tune that was coming from the piano.

And he had walked down the hallway and up to the threshold of the music room, and then stopped, and listened through the half-open door, not wanting to go in. He remembered that feeling even now, so clearly: he hadn't wanted to go in. Somehow he'd known, even at that young age, that if he went in, Dad would see him and smile and hold out his arms and pick him up—which would be wonderful—but the music would stop; and he couldn't bear it to stop. It had to go on. So he'd stood there and listened, just as now, sitting here on the bed, he was listening to that same tune again as he hummed it to himself. He dived back into his memory, searching the picture again, and saw himself once more, waiting there for the music to reach its natural end before he ran into the room. And Dad had seen him and picked him up and spoken to him.

'Did you like that, Luke?'

He had nodded; and Dad had smiled.

'Then it's for you.'

And now, just for this moment, the tune was his again, and he was a small boy standing on the threshold of a room, listening to the dream-music of his father.

The alarm woke him at six, much earlier than he wanted to get up, but after yesterday he was taking no chances. He slipped out of bed, pulled on his dressing gown and hurried through to Mum's study. But he needn't have worried. She was not there this time. He switched on the computer and listened while it booted itself up for sounds from Mum's room. But all was silent. Perhaps she had slept well this time. Perhaps, now that Roger Gilmore was out of her life, things would be different. Yet the picture of what he had seen at the bungalow yesterday still bothered him and he knew Mum was keeping something from him. However much she denied it, she couldn't have broken up the relationship straight after something like that unless the man had done something horrible to her. And although he despised himself whenever he poked his nose into Mum's e-mails, he knew he had to do it again. The computer was ready. He keyed in her password and ran his eye through her inbox. Sure enough, there was an e-mail from Roger Gilmore.

He opened it and scanned the contents. There were only two lines, one a message from Mum, the other an answer from him, both sent yesterday evening. She had written:

Thank you for understanding about Luke.

And he had replied:

Thank you for your parting gift.

Luke stared at the screen, struggling with a mixture of emotions. Any satisfaction he had felt at the thought of Mum being free again now vanished as guilt started to take over. Because for the first time he was starting to understand just what had really happened yesterday. He read the lines again. *Thank you for understanding about Luke.* He frowned. Understanding what about Luke? But he already knew the answer—it was pointless pretending he didn't. *Thank you for your parting gift.* He knew what the gift was, too—and that the parting was for him.

He squeezed his hands tight round the edge of the keyboard. Was he really the cause of all this? He had wanted Mum to be free but not at the cost of her own happiness. And he had seen her happy, truly happy, only yesterday. Now that was gone, and he was responsible. He thought over the things he had said and done since Dad died and realized suddenly that in a perverse way all he had been trying to do over the last two years was love his father; yet all he had managed to do was hate himself.

He took a deep breath and looked at the screen again. At least there was one thing he could do that might help someone, even if it wasn't Mum. He entered his own e-mail program and prepared a new message.

Dear Mrs Jay,

I am very sorry but Luke is still not feeling well so I have decided to keep him home another day.

Best wishes,

Mrs Kirsti Stanton.

21

Mrs Little scowled at him as he stood before her on the gravel. 'So you've truanted again, have you?'

He returned her scowl with one of his own. 'You don't have to look so disapproving. You're the one who rang up three times yesterday afternoon to get me to come over and see you.'

'To see Natalie, not me.' She looked him over haughtily. 'I told you before. I have no personal desire to see you at all. And it was yesterday she needed you.'

'I was here yesterday.'

'I meant yesterday afternoon. Or even the evening would have done. She was fine for a couple of hours after you went. She even seemed happy for a bit. Then she started crying again, and banging the keys of the piano, as though she was trying to make it sound like it had done when you were here, and she just got worse and worse, and wanted to go up to her room again, and she's been there ever since. I can't make her come down. It's just like it was before, only worse somehow.'

'So you needed me yesterday but you don't need me today,' he said coldly. But he knew the answer even before she gave it.

'I need you today. Natalie needs you today.' The old woman stood aside in the doorway. 'Just come in and play the piano for her again. I'm sure that will bring her downstairs.'

He walked past her into the house and headed for the

sitting room. The great grand piano looked warm and bright in the morning sun, in spite of the dusty wood. He listened for sounds upstairs but heard none, not even the familiar weeping.

'She's so quiet,' he said. 'It's like there's no one in the house apart from us.'

'She's here,' said Mrs Little. 'She just goes into a kind of deep, silent pain sometimes. She's very frightened and confused but let's see if we can make things a little better for her this morning.'

It was strange how the old woman's fierce manner grew milder the more she talked about Natalie. He thought over what piece to start with. 'The Dance of the Blessed Spirits' seemed a good choice, especially as he'd been practising it with Miranda. He began to play, adding Miranda's flute melody with his right hand. Mrs Little left him and he played on, wondering whether Natalie would be too upset to come down today.

He needn't have worried. He had barely played the opening bars when he heard footsteps upstairs and a voice calling 'Nana! Nana!' He went on playing and the music started to flow, and he found himself wishing Miranda were here, too, playing the piece with him. He felt sure Natalie would enjoy the sound of the flute. There were footsteps on the stairs now, and murmuring voices, and a kind of soft, bustling excitement; then Natalie was in the doorway, staring towards the piano with her sightless eyes, Mrs Little holding her hand.

'Hi, Natalie,' he said, playing on.

Natalie didn't answer but instead tried to pull Mrs Little by the hand towards the piano. The old woman allowed herself to be led forward and Natalie moved closer, feeling her way past the furniture with her free hand. A moment later she was at the piano. She let go of Mrs Little and started to trace her hands over the wood, round to the keys, then over to Luke's body and up the side of his face.

'I know,' he said. 'Funny ears.'

She flicked at the lobes a few times, then ran her fingers down his left arm to his hand.

'How can I play if you keep fiddling with me?' he said gently, hoping she wouldn't think he was being serious. But she seemed completely unafraid of him now. She was smiling up at his face, a big smile so trusting it unsettled him slightly and even made him stumble on the notes for a moment. He played on somehow, her fingers still running over his hand. 'Funny how it moves,' he said. 'Eh, Natalie? Funny how the hand keeps moving all over the place.' He stopped playing suddenly and took her hand in his. 'Here,' he said. 'Let's get you to play something.'

She stared up at him.

'It's OK,' he said. 'I promise it'll be fun. Look, here we go. We'll do "Twinkle, Twinkle, Little Star".' And he straightened out her index finger and lightly pressed the keys with it. She didn't pull her hand back and simply giggled as he picked out the tune with her finger. '"Twinkle, twinkle, little star",' he sang. '"How I wonder what you are." Do you know it, Natalie? Can you sing it with me?'

But she merely stared back at him with the same unseeing gaze. He thought for a moment. 'Natalie? Do you know what a star is?' Her face remained blank. He glanced up at Mrs Little's multicoloured star picture on the wall. 'Natalie? Can you draw me a picture of a star with your finger? You can draw it on the piano if you want.'

She didn't move or speak and he wasn't sure she'd understood him at all. He glanced at Mrs Little but the old woman's face was impassive. Suddenly, without warning,

182

Natalie reached out and with the finger that had picked out the tune she started to draw something on the piano top. It was a very lopsided picture but there was no mistaking what it was meant to be: a five-pointed star, etched in the dust.

'Well done, Natalie,' he said, staring at it. 'That's a very good star.' He glanced at Mrs Little again and lowered his voice. 'So she can remember things she's seen, even if she can't see them now.'

'Some things,' said the old woman. 'But I'm not sure how much. It's hard to know.'

'What about me? Does she know my name?'

'I've told her but I don't think she's really taken it in. Not yet anyway.'

'Natalie?' Luke stroked her on the arm. 'Natalie, what's my name?'

She started to run her fingers up his arm again.

'What's my name?' he said. 'Do you know?'

The fingers reached his ears and started to play with them again. He laughed. 'Funny ears, I know. What's my name, Natalie?'

'Funny ears,' she said.

'Funny ears? Is that my name? Or are you just saying I've got funny ears?'

'Funny ears.'

And Natalie turned back to the piano. She was frowning and seemed slightly agitated, and he could tell she wanted more music. He thought for a moment of what to play, then remembered 'Peace of the Forest'. He hadn't played it for ages but his fingers found the notes at once, the two opening chords that made him think of distant bells, and suddenly the music was flowing out of him like running water, the song of the forest speaking through the notes. Natalie moved closer, her body pressed against his, almost to the point where he found it hard to play, but he went on somehow. After a while she spoke, in her small, dreamy voice.

'Trees.'

He looked at her but kept on playing. 'Trees?' he said.

'Trees.'

'Can you see them in the music?'

It didn't seem possible. He hadn't told her the name of the piece and she surely didn't know it.

'Big, green trees,' she said.

'And leaves?' he said, still playing. 'Can you see the leaves?'

'Lots of leaves.'

'Lots of leaves?'

'Lots and lots.'

'What else?' he said, thinking of sunlight.

'Sunlight,' she said.

As she spoke, the sun burst through the window and splashed his hands with dancing light. He played on to where the bell-like chords come back, his mind running ahead as he tried to remember how the music went; but his fingers knew the path. Natalie wriggled a little closer, knocking his left arm again, but he held the notes somehow and played on, aware of her close to him, aware of Mrs Little standing rigidly nearby, watching them both; and aware of the forest and the music, whispering now as it moved towards the end. The bell sounds returned, more softly, the slow final chords opening like petals. He felt the rustling of leaves, the movement of treetops, the stillness of hidden glades; then silence. The forest slept. And Natalie wriggled again.

He looked down at her. She had closed her eyes and tipped her head into the crook of his shoulder. He eased his left arm back from the piano, put it round her waist and held her close to him. Mrs Little watched, her small eyes dark and remote. It was hard to tell whether she was jealous or angry or sad or pleased, or something else. She turned suddenly towards the door. 'I'll make some tea,' she muttered.

He watched her go, unsure what to make of her. He supposed it was a measure of her trust that she felt able to leave him alone with Natalie like this, yet the old woman's feelings were hard to gauge. She was such a strange, solitary figure, so full of contradictions. She could be snappy and rude and disdainful, and she made no secret of her dislike of other people, including himself; yet she had also taken care of Natalie, and Natalie clearly loved her. It was strange to think that he had once found this old woman frightening. He looked down at the little girl, who was now clinging to him as though he might vanish at any moment.

'Natalie?' he said softly.

She didn't answer.

'Natalie?' He lowered his head so that his face was close to hers. 'Can you still see the trees?'

Silence. He thought for a moment.

'Natalie? Can you remember where you used to live?'

Silence.

'What's your surname? Your second name?'

Silence.

'Do you know the name of this village?'

Silence.

'Have you got any brothers and sisters?'

Still no answer, not even a movement of the head. He thought of playing the piano again and started to take his arm away from her. She gave a squeal of anxiety and clung to him more tightly than ever.

'It's OK,' he said, pulling her close again. 'I'm not going to let you go.' He looked down at her and frowned. 'You can remember trees,' he murmured. 'You can remember leaves. You can remember stars.' Keeping his left arm around her waist, he stretched out his right hand and began to play the singing melody at the start of 'Peace of the Forest'. To his surprise, Natalie started to hum. He stopped playing and looked down at her again but she went on humming. It was a strange sound, very disjointed and way off-key, and it clearly wasn't meant to be 'Peace of the Forest'. It was some other tune; and as the notes slurred out, he realized with a shock what it was.

C, D, E, E, A, A, went the notes. She paused a moment, frowning, as though she was struggling to remember more. He listened tensely. They were the opening notes of the wistful tune that Dad had played all those years ago; the tune he had come to associate with Natalie. But how could she know the piece? He waited for the next phrase, hearing it already in his head, but she went back and repeated the phrase she had just hummed: C, D, E, E, A, A. And then she hummed it again, several times, as though she needed to reassure herself that it was right. Each time he heard it, the notes were clearer. It had to be coincidence—the notes were not that special and she had simply hummed them as though they were all crotchets, which they weren't in the tune Dad had played. Then she hummed some more notes: D, E, F, F, B, B. He felt a shiver run through him. She had hummed the next phrase of the same piece. There was no mistaking it. Yet how could this be? He forced himself to speak as gently as he could.

'That's a nice tune, Natalie. What's it called?'

No answer. He wondered whether to play the next few bars of the piece on the piano. He could remember it well enough and it might make her hum a little more. It might even encourage her to talk about how she had come to know it. But she had started crying. He reached out and stroked her head. 'It's a nice tune,' he said quietly. 'And can you see pictures in it, too? Like you did with the other piece?'

'Barley,' she said.

'Barley?'

She dug her face into his chest. He stroked her head again. 'Yes,' he lied, 'that's just what I see. A nice field of barley, swaying in the breeze, and maybe wheat, too, and corn and maize and long grass. Can you see the long grass?'

'Barley,' she murmured, and went on crying. And as she cried, the melody ran through him again as though she were humming it still.

22

Mr Harding opened his front door and raised an eyebrow in his quizzical way. 'Hello, Luke. You look as though you've been climbing trees all day. But I know you'd never dream of bunking off school to do a thing like that. What time is it?'

'Quarter past four.'

'We don't have a lesson, do we?'

'No.'

'I thought not. I might be getting old but I'm not so gaga I can't remember who I'm supposed to be seeing, though it's only a matter of time before I get that way.'

'Have you got someone with you?'

'No, I was having a sleep. I've got Miranda coming at five thirty but that's about it.' The old man scratched his head. 'Actually, come to think of it, you can't be here for a lesson anyway. I seem to remember telling you that you didn't need to come any more because there's nothing I can teach you.'

'I think you were wrong.'

They looked at each other in silence for a moment, then Mr Harding stood to the side. 'Come in, Luke,' he said. The old man led the way through to the music room, lowered himself into one of the armchairs by the window and motioned him to the other. Luke sat down, feeling more awkward than ever. 'What's up?' said Mr Harding.

Luke took a deep breath and wondered how to start. Even now, as he sat here, trying to phrase his thoughts, the sounds were starting to engulf him again. They had begun the moment he left Mrs Little's house and stayed with him while he was up in the tree-house, waiting for the school bus to return so that he could come here: the buzzing sounds, flute sounds, harp sounds, bell sounds; the deep ocean roar rolling inside him and around him; the sound of Natalie's voice in his head, humming that strange melody; and against all this, the cacophony of noises from the outside world, noises he knew he should not be able to hear.

'Sounds,' he said. 'Everywhere. Around me, inside me.'

'I know.'

'Do you hear them, too?'

'No,' said the old man. 'To me we're sitting in silence. The village is silent, the house is silent, my head is silent. Which is rather nice. There's usually a lot of nonsense going on in there.'

'So how do you know about the sounds?'

'Because I know you, Luke, and because I knew your father, and because I've known or read of others who have heard these things, too. I know the sounds exist, though I don't experience them personally.'

'They're not unpleasant. They're just—'

'Disturbing.'

'Yes.' Luke frowned. 'They don't come all the time. Sometimes everything's silent for me, too, just like it is for you now. But then it's like I'm suddenly surrounded by sound and filled with sound. Sometimes it's an actual piece of music but other times it's like a jumble of instruments playing together. I hear these buzzing sounds and flute sounds and harp sounds and bell sounds, and sometimes I hear rushing water and stuff. But most of all I hear this . . . kind of . . . '

'Deep roar,' said Mr Harding.

'Yes.' Luke looked at him, both startled and relieved.

189

'A deep, booming roar,' said the old man. 'Sometimes a low hum, sometimes a rumbling sound, sometimes the sound of an ocean swell. Yes, I know. There's nothing wrong with you, Luke. These are things others have experienced since time immemorial. You're just a highly sensitive, highly strung, highly gifted boy. Very like your father. So like him, in fact, I almost feel as though I'm sitting talking to him rather than you right now.'

Luke thought back to his conversation with Mum while they were out walking. 'Mum told me Dad heard all these things, too,' he said. 'She said he talked to you about them.'

'He did. He used to say that the roaring noise is the primal sound that started and now perpetuates creation.'

'Perpetuates?'

'Keeps it going. That's why he called it the engine. He saw it as the motive force that drives the cosmos and everything that exists.'

'But how does it do that?'

'Through vibration. All matter—if I understand this right—is in a state of constant vibration. I read an article only the other day about this. It said that each individual atom and each individual molecule has its own unique vibratory fingerprint. Your father would certainly agree with that. He used to say that every single thing—whether it's a stick, a stone, a cloud, an animal, a human being, whatever—has its own unique song. He used to say creation is buzzing with all these different vibratory energies. He could hear the sounds these things made, he said. But he went further than that. He used to say that thoughts have vibrations, feelings have vibrations, desires have vibrations. He said he could hear love, hear anger, hear fear. And he went further still. He said there are subtle realms beneath the physical universe, and subtle bodies beneath our physical bodies, all of which have

190

vibrations and therefore sounds, too. If he were sitting here now, he'd say that the primal sound you're hearing is the origin of all this. It's the parent of all sounds, all vibrations, all things.'

'I can't get my head round this,' said Luke.

'Well, I'm no expert on it either,' said Mr Harding.

'And I don't even think I believe in what you just said. So how come I keep hearing these sounds?'

'You don't have to believe in anything to hear the sounds,' said Mr Harding. 'You just have to be very sensitive, as you've proved yourself. Very few of us appear to be able to tune in with these vibrations. You can. Your father could. I can't. So I can only approach these things from a theoretical viewpoint, and that's not enough to truly understand them. Theoretical study, without experience, can only take us so far. Scientists can measure external sounds but many of the things you're hearing are too subtle. Your father once said they're subtler than the ether, subtler even than thought. So if I can't hear them and I can't measure them, it's pretty hard for me to believe in them.'

'But you do believe in them.'

'Yes, I do. And it's largely as a result of knowing your father and hearing him speak about these things that my intellectual curiosity has been transformed into what one might modestly call belief.' The old man was silent for a moment, then he went on. 'He was a remarkable man, your father, one of the most extraordinary people I've ever known, and some of the things he claimed to have heard were astonishing. I mean, he didn't just hear subtle internal vibrations. He heard external things, too, that were simply mind-boggling.'

'Like what?'

'Like sounds that should have been way beyond his auditory range.' Mr Harding gazed out of the window at the garden. 'He once told me that when you were a toddler, he heard you crying when he was on a tube train rattling towards Hammersmith and you were miles away in Strawberry Hill. And when he got home, your mother told him you'd fallen over and hurt yourself and bawled your eyes out at exactly the time he heard you. He heard you, Luke. He said he physically heard you. How do you explain that?'

'I can't.'

'Neither can I. Neither could he. Neither can anyone probably.'

Luke thought of Natalie's weeping, and how he had heard that, too, from far away.

'And he heard other incredible things,' the old man went on. 'Not all the time, he said. Just occasionally. It was as if he had these moments when he experienced some kind of expansion of consciousness and he could hear things that no one should be able to hear. Insects crawling on the ground, the footsteps and voices of people miles away, things like that. He even once told me he'd heard the planets moving through space. He said there's a harmony to the cosmos and if you listen carefully enough, you can hear it.' Mr Harding looked round at him again. 'He was either lying or deluded or telling the truth. Make your choice.' The old man smiled suddenly. 'It's all right, Luke. You don't need to choose and neither do I. You have the integrity of your own experience. I have the integrity of your father's words.'

They fell silent, Luke still listening to the sounds, though they were fading now to a murmur. 'These sounds,' he said after a while, 'I still find them disturbing.'

'I know.' The old man leaned forward. 'But the thing is, Luke, they're not going to hurt you. I know that's what your father would tell you. He'd say they're nothing to be frightened of. You'll probably even find them comforting one day. I know he found them so.'

192

'Did he talk to you a lot about this?'

'Not much. We talked a great deal about all kinds of things, especially music, of course, but not a lot about this. He was wary of discussing it—and I respected that—but every so often he'd open up and I always felt very privileged when he did. Just as I do when I listen to you. He was just the same as you, Luke. Just as sensitive, just as easily hurt, just as musical—'

'More musical.'

'No, Luke, not more musical than you. And he'd be the first to agree with me on that point if he were sitting here right now—which I sort of feel he is in a funny kind of way.'

Luke stiffened, partly at the strangeness of this last remark but mostly because he, too, had been feeling Dad's presence close by. It was as though his father were only inches away. Yet the only other person he saw was Mr Harding, watching him through half-closed eyes.

'Yes, Luke, he was very, very like you. Not quite so mixed up, though. But then, he hadn't recently lost his own father like you.'

Luke looked away, his mind still focused on Dad. His father was here somewhere. He could sense him. Why couldn't he see him? He remembered the other things he had wanted to ask Mr Harding and forced himself to turn back to him. 'Mr Harding?'

'Yes, Luke.'

'It's . . . it's not just sounds that are bothering me.'

'I know. It's the things you see, too. The colours and shapes and what have you.'

Luke stared at him. 'What is it with you? How come you know all this? Are you living inside my head or something?'

'Fortunately not,' said Mr Harding. 'That would be a troubled place to be right now. Inspiring from a musical point of view, I admit, but rather more than I can handle. But then geniuses have always lived close to the edge.'

'I'm not a genius,' said Luke. 'Dad was but I'm not.'

'Ah, there you go again, running yourself down alongside your father. Well, we won't quibble over a word.' The old man smiled at him. 'I know you see colours and shapes when you hear music because you're so like your father, and he saw them, too. As others have done.'

Luke thought back again to the things Mum had told him about Dad yesterday. He thought of the kitchen at the house in Strawberry Hill; the pentagram on the table; the crook of his father's arm that held the sleeping boy who once was him. To his surprise, Mr Harding opened his mouth and without warning sang a note. It was a slightly shaky sound and the old man dissolved into laughter the moment it was over. 'Yes, Luke, I know,' he chortled. 'I make truer notes farting than singing these days but that's what happens to your voice when you get old. Anyway, what note did I just attempt to sing?'

'It was between D and E flat. Closer to D.'

'Hmm.' Mr Harding watched him for a moment, a half-smile on his lips. 'And what colour did it give you?'

'Green.'

'You said that without the slightest hesitation.'

'I just saw the note straightaway as green.'

'I see. Sing me a note of your own.'

'What one do you want?'

'Sing me a B.'

Luke sang. Mr Harding hauled himself to his feet, hobbled over to the piano and played a B. 'Spot on,' he said. 'Though no more than I expected.' He turned and looked back at Luke. 'And what colour does a B give you?'

'It varies. B major usually gives me a bright red colour.

B flat major makes me see more than one colour. I usually see bits of blue and bits of yellow.'

'Fascinating.' Mr Harding returned to the armchair and sat down again. 'Just like your father.'

'Did he see the same colours?'

'I don't know if they were the same colours as you see but he certainly saw colours. Do you see colours with all sounds?'

'Not always. Sometimes it's shapes. Or pictures.' He thought of 'Peace of the Forest', and the images of trees and leaves and sunlight that had come flooding to him. He thought of Natalie, pressed against him, seeing those same things in the notes. Mr Harding stroked his chin.

'Strange, isn't it?' said the old man. 'To think of music having colour and shape. But perhaps not so strange to you. Did you know you can scatter sand on metal discs and then play different musical notes and the sand will shift to form patterns? They've done experiments.'

'Who?'

'Oh, I don't know. The clever people who understand these things. Scientists, whatever. They've taken powders and liquids and filings and played music and found that as the pitch changes, so the shapes change to form geometric patterns, perfect circles and concentric triangles and squares and things. I've seen pictures. They're absolutely beautiful. They've even created a special gadget that transforms sounds into a picture on a computer screen. Isn't that amazing? I'm told that the final chord of Handel's *Messiah* produces a five-pointed star.'

He thought again of Dad's pentagram. He thought of Natalie's drawing on the piano; Mrs Little's picture in the sitting room. He thought of what he saw sometimes under his brow, and the luminous star he flew towards in his waking dreams. And now all this from Mr Harding. He looked down, more confused than ever. 'I . . . I don't understand what's happening to me. These sounds and shapes and colours.' He heard the sound of hammering from Mr Tyson's garage next door. 'Why can I hear that hammer's playing a G? Why can't everybody hear that?'

'We just can't, Luke.'

'We?'

'I can't hear that Jim Tyson's hammer's playing a G. I haven't got perfect pitch like you.'

'It's not really a G,' said Luke. 'It's just off a G. About a quarter tone.'

Mr Harding chuckled and said nothing.

'But why?' said Luke. 'I don't understand.'

'It's just the way it is, Luke. It's not a strength on your part or a weakness on the part of those who can't experience these things. It's just the way you're made. The way your father was made. He heard things others don't hear. As I said earlier, he could even hear the individual songs of people and animals and trees and other things. I expect you have that same experience, too.'

Luke thought of Natalie, and Mum, and Roger Gilmore, and Skin, and Mr Harding, and Miranda, and Dad. It was true: each one of them had a kind of unique song, a fingerprint, as Mr Harding had put it, too subtle to notice, unless you really listened for it. He'd been hearing them all this time without realizing it consciously. Perhaps, if he'd seen the stag that day, he'd have heard its song, too, like Dad.

'And what kind of a song do I have, Luke?' said the old man suddenly.

'A nice song.'

'Liar.' Mr Harding gave him a prod. 'Stop being polite and tell me.'

They sat in silence for a while, Luke listening intently, then he shook his head. 'Can't hear anything. I reckon that's something I can't match my father on.'

Mr Harding watched him for a moment, then smiled. 'If my song's the same as the feelings in my heart, then I know what it is even without hearing it. But you heard it. I know you did. You just didn't want to tell me it. It's all right, Luke. I understand. You think it will make me sad to hear you say how lonely I am.'

'I—'

'It's all right, Luke. We've talked about this enough.' The old man glanced at the clock. 'I really should be getting ready for Miranda.'

'Oh, right.' Luke made to get up, then suddenly remembered his original reason for coming here. 'Mr Harding?' he said quickly.

'Yes, Luke.'

'There's a piece of piano music. It just keeps haunting me. I heard someone play it years ago. Well, Dad. Anyway, I just wondered if you knew it.'

'Play the melody line for me.'

Luke hurried over to the piano and played the notes Natalie had tried to hum: C, D, E, E, A, A and then D, E, F, F, B, B, only this time with the proper rhythm. He was about to continue when Mr Harding motioned to him to stop. ' "Reverie", ' said the old man. 'By Tchaikovsky. I'm sure that's what it is. Play me a few more bars.' Luke played on and Mr Harding nodded. 'Yes, it's from *Album for the Young*. Stop a moment.'

The old man struggled to his feet again and wandered over to the shelves, then, a moment later, pulled out a slim green volume. He stared at it for a while with obvious affection, then brought it over to the piano. 'They're lovely pieces, these. I'm surprised you don't know them. You're playing "Reverie" or rather "*Douce Rêverie*", as Tchaikovsky called it. Here, let me find it.' He leafed through the book until he found the piece, then propped it up in the holder and smoothed the pages flat. 'Now play it.'

And Luke played; and as the notes moved, so the presence of his father—still close by—seemed to move, too, through his fingers, through the music, through all his emotions. He played on, fighting hard to keep his composure, but the poignancy of the piece, and the thought of his father playing it all those years ago, mastered him. He stopped, halfway through. Before him on the page, the printed notes awaited his attention; yet he could not play them. He felt Mr Harding's hand on his shoulder.

'Stand up, Luke. Let an old man have a try.'

He stood up and let Mr Harding take his place on the piano seat. The old man's hands stretched out and he started to play, at the point where Luke had left off. Luke closed his eyes as the melody ran through him; then a moment later he heard Mr Harding's voice, musing as he played. 'Yes, it's rather nice, isn't it? More like a lullaby than a reverie really. You could imagine someone playing this as a cradle song.'

Luke kept his eyes closed and felt his father's presence again, and with it the presence of the little girl who could not see; the girl who had tried, with a voice as feeble as the gnarled, arthritic fingers of this old man, to hum the piece that Dad had played all those years ago. The music ended and he fell into the silence. Mr Harding did not break it and simply waited. When Luke opened his eyes, he saw the old man watching him. 'And what colours did you see this time, Luke?' he said quietly.

'Blue. Deep blue, like the sea.'

'And?'

'Gold. All around it.'

'Anything else?'

'A tiny speck of white in the middle. I don't know what it was.'

But he knew what it was well enough. What he didn't

know was why he felt he needed to conceal it from Mr Harding. But Mr Harding was more than a match for such concealment.

'It was a star, Luke,' he said.

'How did you know?'

'Oh, so you did recognize it.'

'Yeah, but . . . how did you know?'

'Just a hunch.'

'More than a hunch. You knew.'

'Maybe.'

Luke stared at him. There was something uncanny about the way the old man seemed to see inside his head. He thought of the image that kept forcing itself into his mind. 'I keep seeing it,' he said. 'This . . . this star.'

'So did your father.'

'I've even started . . . looking for it.'

'Looking for it?'

'Yes.'

'Well, maybe you don't need to.'

'What do you mean?'

'Maybe you don't need to look for the star. It sounds to me as though the star's looking for you. And it doesn't seem to be having much trouble finding you.'

'That sounds weird.'

'I suppose it does.'

'But what is it—this star?'

The old man smiled. 'I asked your father the same question once.'

'And what did he say?'

'He said it's a symbol of the primal sound.' The old man paused. 'And the gateway to another world.'

There was a long silence between them, then Luke looked away. 'I still don't understand all these things.'

'Well, I'm not sure I do either,' said Mr Harding. 'But we don't necessarily have to understand everything that happens to us in order to live a happy life. It's like the sand patterns on the metal discs. The sounds create the shapes whether you believe in the principle or not. Maybe it doesn't really matter how much you understand. The main thing is just to know that these sounds and colours and pictures won't hurt you.'

'So what do I do with them?'

'Make friends with them, Luke, like your father did. Trust them. They mean you no harm. As I said earlier, you may even find them comforting one day.'

Luke frowned. 'Why me? Why do I hear these things and see these things?'

Mr Harding didn't answer at first. Instead, he stood up from the piano, took the volume of music and handed it to Luke. 'Here. Take this and keep it as a present. I'd like you to have it.'

'I couldn't,' said Luke. 'I mean, I can get a copy myself. We've probably got it at home anyway. Only I can't say I've seen it.'

'Take it,' said Mr Harding. 'Do it for me. Only—wait a second.' The old man took a pen and wrote inside the front cover.

> To my good friend Luke,
> Wishing you a safe and happy journey.
> Best wishes,
> Graham Harding.

'Journey?' said Luke, who'd been watching the old man write the words. 'What journey?'

'Oh, I think you'll understand that one day. And if you don't, it won't matter. Don't ask me what I'm going on about. I don't really know myself half the time.' Mr Harding handed Luke back the music and put an arm round his shoulder. 'I'm going to have to kick you out now, Luke, I'm afraid. I've got a few things to do before Miranda gets here, and she's usually early. She's worked out how much I enjoy having a chat, so being the little poppet that she is, she usually turns up early to indulge me. I'm such a lucky man, really, to have so many nice people around me.'

The old man frowned suddenly.

'You ask me why you hear these things and see these things. I don't know, Luke. I don't know why people like yourself and your father and certain others have such experiences while the rest of us don't. But I'll tell you one thing I do know: I know that if you strike a tuning fork, it'll make any other tuning fork within hearing range vibrate at the same frequency.'

Luke waited for him to continue but the old man remained silent, as though he felt he had said enough with this cryptic statement.

'I don't understand what you're saying,' Luke said eventually.

Mr Harding walked with him to the front door and stopped. 'Well, Luke, maybe we're all tuning forks of a kind but some of us are more sensitive than others. Maybe the sensitive ones—people like yourself and your father— can pick up the vibrations of other people, other creatures, humming in the ether. Maybe even the vibrations of creation itself.'

'The firmament singing,' said Luke, remembering Mum's words.

'Yes,' said Mr Harding quietly. 'As your father would have put it. The firmament singing, above and below.'

'Above and below?' said Luke, but he was already thinking back to the other things Mum had said.

'Yes,' said Mr Harding. 'Don't be fooled into thinking the firmament's only up in the sky. But let's leave it there. One can overcomplicate things by too much philosophizing.' The old man opened the front door. 'And maybe things are really much simpler anyway.' He nodded to the volume of music under Luke's arm. 'Maybe at the end of the day our lives are no more than tunes, brief little reveries like Tchaikovsky's. And then we wake up and find we were dreaming them all along.'

Luke stepped out onto the path, then turned and looked back. 'If our lives are just dreams, why do they hurt so much?'

And the old man smiled. 'I don't know, Luke,' he said.

23

Mum was sitting, tight-lipped, at the kitchen table and one look at her eyes told him he was in trouble. 'I've had a phone call from Mrs Searle,' she said. She didn't shout. She didn't scream. Her voice was under control—just. She breathed out hard. 'I feel so betrayed, Luke. I mean, I've tried not to hassle you. I've tried not to nag at you. I've tried to give you time to get over Dad. I've tried to be there for you. I've tried to . . . trust you. And it's like you're just laughing at me.'

'I'm not laughing at you.'

'You hang around with those revolting boys, you get into trouble, you tell lies, you're rude to people when you never used to be, and now you play truant two days in a row. Did you really think Mrs Searle was going to believe an e-mail claiming to be from this house? Especially when it wasn't from my own e-mail address. She said she was going to follow it up yesterday only she decided to check first whether the other boys in your gang were in school, and they were, so she left it for a day. But this morning her suspicions got the better of her and she rang me.'

'I'm sorry.'

'I feel cheap, Luke.' She stared up at him. 'I feel cheap. And you know why? Because you make me feel cheap. You make me feel cheap for committing the unforgivable sin of enjoying the company of a thoroughly decent man who doesn't happen to be your father—as though you somehow think it means I haven't grieved and don't still grieve as much as you do. And you make me feel cheap because other thoroughly decent people like Mrs Searle and half this village probably now think I'm as wayward and untrustworthy as you are because I can't keep you on the straight and narrow.'

'Mum—'

'And you make me feel cheap, Luke, because I've even found myself lying for you. Trying to make other people think that deep down you're still a lovely boy with a heart of gold underneath all that aggression and surliness, and if they just keep looking, they'll find it.'

'Mum—'

'Go away, can you?'

'Mum.'

'Just go away!' She put a hand over her eyes. 'No . . . don't go away. Just . . . I don't know . . . '

He looked down at her. 'I'm sorry.'

'Why, Luke?'

'Why am I sorry?'

'Why did you truant?'

He thought of Natalie and her dark world of confusion; he thought of the gruff old woman who looked after her and who'd warned him to keep his mouth shut; he thought of the boys who wanted his blood; and he knew he couldn't speak of these things.

'I just did,' he said.

'You just did.'

'I needed to be by myself.'

There was a long, tense silence.

'I'll go to school tomorrow,' he said.

'I know you will.' She took her hand from her eyes and looked up at him. 'I'll be driving you in myself. We've got a meeting with Mrs Searle at nine o'clock.'

But the meeting with Mrs Searle next morning was the

least of his worries. It went exactly as he knew it would. Questions from her, lies from him. Where did you go? To the forest. Both days? Yes. You spent the whole time in the forest? Yes. Doing what? Climbing trees. Why did you truant? I needed to be by myself. Which was sort of true, just as the forest bit was sort of true. But his mind was barely on this conversation. Even as the answers flowed from him, he was thinking of his greatest fear.

The gang.

They would be stalking him today for sure.

The meeting ended in the usual way. Reprimands from her, contrition from him, more reprimands, more contrition, conciliatory words from her about giving him another chance, pretend gratitude from him. Then he looked at Mum; and for the first time felt truly guilty. But by then the meeting was over. Within minutes she was gone—and the real business of the day started.

At least he didn't have any lessons with Skin and the others today. They weren't in the same set for anything except English and he'd missed that legitimately for the meeting with Mrs Searle. But there was still break and lunchtime to get through—and the bus home. He decided to go to the music room at break. With any luck Mrs Parry would be in there and none of the boys would mess with him if she was around. He found her there listening to a couple of Year 7 girls playing keyboards. She saw him approach and raised an eyebrow. 'Saints preserve us,' she said in her lilting voice. 'The maestro himself.'

The girls stopped playing and looked up. Luke stood there before them, unsure what to say.

'Miranda Davis was looking for you,' said Mrs Parry. 'I told her you don't bother coming in here any more because you're too good for the likes of us.'

Luke said nothing. He was used to Mrs Parry's jokes.

She turned to the girls. 'The most naturally gifted musician I've ever come across but can I get him to play in the school concert? No chance. Now is that crazy or what? It's like Achilles refusing to fight.'

'Who?' said one of the girls.

'Tell you later.' Mrs Parry turned back to Luke. 'So what can I do for you? I'm sure it's not a piano lesson.'

'I just . . . ' Luke shrugged. 'I just wanted to come in. I heard the music.'

'Good, wasn't it?' Mrs Parry grinned at the girls. 'They're great, these two. They've composed this piece all by themselves and we're just tinkering with it a bit and seeing if we can make it even better. Come on, girls. Let's give the expert another blast.' Both girls looked at her in alarm but she simply beamed back. 'It's OK. I know it's not tidied up yet but it doesn't matter. Luke won't mind. He's a nice lad really, underneath all that macho nonsense.' And the girls started to play. He sat down and listened, and waited for break to end, his mind fixed on the gang.

They caught up with him at lunchtime. He'd thought he'd be safe in the canteen, surrounded by the clamour of kids and dinner staff, and he'd found a table with just one free place among a crowd of younger lads. But within minutes they'd finished and gone; and some very different boys sat down: Speed and Daz opposite, Skin next to him—close. They didn't speak at first but simply glared; then Skin leaned towards him and hissed: 'You're finished.'

'What's that supposed to mean?' said Luke, trying to sound confident; but his words came out like a croak. Skin's answer was chillingly direct.

'It means you're going to die.'

He felt a coldness run through him and his muscles tightened. Suddenly someone tapped him on the shoulder.

He jumped and looked round to see Miranda standing there.

'Hi,' she said.

'Hi.' He stared awkwardly up at her, aware of Skin and the others watching; but Miranda didn't seem to notice them.

'Have you got a minute?' she said. 'Mrs Parry wants to see you in the music room. If you've finished eating.'

He'd hardly started but he picked up his plate and stood up at once. 'Sure, let's go. I'm done here.'

'Miranda?' said Skin. She looked at him for the first time. He gave a sickly smile. 'Hi.'

'Hi,' she said.

'How are you?'

'Fine.'

Skin reached out and took a chip from Luke's plate. 'Seeing as Luky's not eating his din-dins,' he said. He put the chip into his mouth and glanced back at Miranda. 'Still riding?' he said, chewing slowly.

'What?'

'Still riding your horse?'

'Yeah.'

'Only I haven't seen you go past my house for a while. Used to like looking out of my bedroom window and watching you.'

Miranda said nothing.

'Speedy's interested in riding,' said Daz, also reaching for one of Luke's chips. 'But they can't find a horse strong enough to carry him.'

Speed looked angrily away, but Skin and Daz took no notice. Their eyes were now running over Miranda with leery interest. Luke shifted on his feet, desperate to get her away from all this, but she spoke first. 'Look, I'm sorry, only—' She turned back to Luke. 'Mrs Parry said now, if you're free.'

'Sure,' he said.

They made their way out of the canteen and down the corridor. To his relief, the others didn't follow. Miranda caught him by the arm and stopped him the moment they were out of sight of the canteen. He looked round at her in surprise.

'What's up?' he said. 'I thought we were going to Mrs Parry's.'

'What's up?' She stared at him. 'What's up with you, more like? Mrs Parry doesn't want to see you. I just made that up to get you out of there. What's going on, Luke? Jason Skinner and the other two looking at you like that. I mean, I couldn't believe their faces, Jason's especially. What's happened?'

'It's a long story.'

'Tell me.'

'I can't.'

'Well, tell someone. Tell your mum. Tell Mrs Searle. Whoever.'

'I can't. It's not something anyone else can sort out.'

'But Jason looks like he wants to kill you.'

'I think he does.'

'Luke! You must tell someone what's going on. Whatever it is.'

He frowned and looked away. 'I can't. I just . . . can't.'

They stood there in the corridor, other pupils rushing and brushing past them on their way to and from the canteen. 'Come outside,' she said. 'It's too crowded here.'

They wandered out through the main entrance and headed round the playing field towards the sixth form centre.

'You weren't in morning registration,' she said.

'I had to see someone.'

'Someone at school?'

'Yeah.'

'Mrs Searle?'

'Yeah.' He glanced at her. 'I bunked off yesterday. And the day before.'

They walked in silence for a while, then Miranda spoke again.

'So you're in trouble with Mrs Searle and you're in trouble with Jason Skinner.'

'Yeah.'

'Nice one.'

He looked down, unwilling to say more. Somehow he knew that if he told Miranda part of this business, he'd end up telling her all of it, and that meant the break-ins and Natalie; and he couldn't do that. Whatever his feelings for Miranda—and they were growing stronger by the day—he knew he couldn't involve her, any more than he could involve Mum. Miranda lowered her voice and spoke again.

'Luke, listen—you don't have to tell me anything, OK? But if you ever want to, that's OK, too. All right?'

'Thanks,' he said.

They fell silent again and walked on, and finally reached the wall round the sixth form centre. Miranda turned and leaned her back against it, and Luke did the same, and they gazed over the playing field together. Then a thought occurred to him.

'Miranda?'

'Yeah?'

'Can you sit with me on the school bus going home? I don't want Skin to grab the place next to me.'

'Oh, thanks,' she said. 'That's really flattering.'

'I'm sorry.' He looked quickly round at her. 'I didn't mean it that way.'

'You want me to sit next to you just so someone else doesn't. That makes me feel great.'

But he could hear her chuckling.

'I didn't mean it that way,' he said.

'I'm offended now,' she said primly.

'No, you're not.'

And he heard her chuckle again.

'I do want to sit with you as well,' he said.

'Well, you can't anyway,' she said. 'I'm not going back on the school bus today. Mum's picking me up. She's shopping in town this afternoon so we agreed she'd come and get me on the way home.' Miranda reached out suddenly and touched him on the arm. 'Why don't you come back with us? We could give you a lift. That way you can avoid Jason and the others and still get to sit next to me.'

'Won't your mum mind?'

'Are you kidding? You know she's got a soft spot for you. Don't ask me why.'

'She didn't have a soft spot for me last time I saw her.'

'That's only because she knew you'd upset me by turning up so late for the practice session. She's still got a soft spot for you underneath. Come back with us. It won't be a problem.'

'OK. Thanks a lot.'

He smiled at her and she smiled back, then looked quickly away. He watched her for a moment, grateful that she was there with him, then turned and gazed over the playing field again; and as he did so, he felt his mind move back to The Grange, and to the tiny blind girl who needed him.

24

S he was in distress. He knew it. He could hear the weeping again, just as Dad had once heard him crying from far away. He heard her as he sat through afternoon lessons, he heard her as he talked with Miranda and Mrs Davis in the car going home, he heard her as he walked from the square back to his house. As he entered The Haven, Mum said: 'There's been another silent call.'

'When?' he said, trying to look unconcerned.

'Just a few minutes ago.'

'Did you try and speak to whoever it was?'

'Didn't get the chance. The moment I said hello the person hung up. I couldn't trace the number.' Mum looked at him hard. 'Are you sure you don't know anything about this? Don't you think it might be one of your gang?'

'Doubt it. Why would they hang up?'

'Because they know I don't like them. They want to speak to you but they can't face the thought of having to deal with me first.'

'I don't think they're that scared of you, Mum.' He was trying to sound jokey but it was hard. His mind was racing. He had to get to Natalie as quickly as possible. Yet if he rushed out now, so soon after hearing about the silent call, it would look suspicious. He fumbled in his mind for a believable excuse and clutched at the first idea that came into his head. 'I'm sure it's nothing to worry about. Some nutter with time on his hands. He's probably bothering loads of other people, too. Anyway . . . ' He glanced at his watch. 'I'd better get going or I'll be late. I'll just get the music.'

'What music?'

'Tchaikovsky.'

'What Tchaikovsky?'

He fetched *Album for the Young* from the music room. 'Mr Harding gave it to me. Look—he's written inside it.' He opened the volume at the inscription and Mum read it.

'That's so nice of him,' she said. 'And so typical.' She smiled. 'I remember your father playing these pieces at a concert once. Long time ago. Must be ten years at least. We used to have the music somewhere but I don't think I've seen it since that time he played it. It wasn't the same volume as this one. It had a light blue cover, I remember.'

'I was thinking of playing one of the pieces at the concert,' he said. 'Anyway, I'd better be going.'

'Where are you off to?'

'Mr Harding's. I promised him I'd go through the pieces with him and see if there were any that might be suitable for the concert. I thought I told you.'

'You didn't but it doesn't matter.' Mum took the volume from him and leafed through it. 'They're a bit easy for you, Luke. Aren't you going to play something a little more challenging at the concert, like the Liszt you were practising?'

'You just said Dad played them at a concert.'

'Yes, but he played the whole cycle. And that was just part of an evening's programme. He played other things as well. Some Chopin, I seem to remember, and some Debussy and other things.'

'Well, I was only thinking about it. I haven't decided or anything.'

'It's just that—' Mum caught the expression on his face

and quickly handed back the music. 'OK, sorry. It's none of my business what you play. And to be honest, Luke, I'm just pleased you're taking part in the concert at all, after all the trouble I had getting you to play last year. Give Mr Harding my regards.'

'OK.'

'And tell him none of us in the village want him to retire and we all hope he's joking with this talk about moving away to Norwich.'

'I don't think he is.'

'What? Joking or moving away?'

'Joking.'

'Hm, you're probably right.' She looked at him for a moment, then reached out her arms and pulled him to her; and they held each other. 'Did it go all right today?' she said.

'Yeah.'

'You weren't upset after seeing Mrs Searle?'

'No.'

'Things'll be better now, Luke. OK? They'll be much better.'

'Yeah. I know.'

She let him go and drew back. 'Supper at half past six.'

'OK.'

'You'll be here?'

'Promise.'

She gave him a kiss. 'I'll see you later.'

'OK.'

He turned to the front door, taking care not to appear too hurried; but the moment he was out in the lane, he started to run.

From inside The Grange came the sound of Natalie screaming. He stood on the doorstep and listened. This was even worse than he had expected. It wasn't just weeping now; it was hysterics. He gripped the music tight and rang the bell. Mrs Little appeared. She looked white and haggard. Her eyes were bleary. Her hands were trembling. She didn't speak. She simply stood aside to let him in. He stepped past her into the hall.

'What's happened?' he said.

The old woman was breathing hard and looked as though she was about to collapse. But she managed to speak. 'Natalie's in a terrible state. It's never been this bad before. I can't seem to calm her down at all. She was all right for an hour or so after you left yesterday, but then she started crying and moaning, and she just went on like that all day and all night. I can't get her to eat. I can't get her to go upstairs to her room. She won't leave the piano. She keeps banging the keys as if she's trying to make the music come back and then she gets more upset when it doesn't. She didn't sleep at all—not a wink—and neither did I, and she's just been crying and moaning all through today. And now, over the last hour or so, she's started screaming. She's never ever done that before. I don't know what to do next. I rang you the moment I thought you were back from school but your mother answered so I hung up.'

'I guessed it was you.' He frowned. 'Come on. Let's see if the piano will help her again.'

They hurried through to the sitting room. Natalie was on the sofa, dressed in a nightie, her face running with tears, her body twisted out of shape like an abused doll. She didn't seem to hear them come in, didn't turn their way, didn't speak—she simply went on screaming. The only pauses were when she gathered breath. Mrs Little waited for one of these and then spoke. 'Natalie, guess who's here.'

Natalie screamed again.

'It's me,' called Luke over the scream. 'Natalie, it's me. The boy with the funny ears.'

Natalie went on screaming. Mrs Little waved him desperately towards the piano but he was already stumbling towards it. He propped Mr Harding's volume open in front of him and started to hunt through the pages for 'Reverie'. Natalie paused for breath, then screamed again.

'What's that music?' said Mrs Little.

'Something I think Natalie will like.'

He found 'Reverie' and started to play. The effect was immediate. Natalie's scream broke off as though he had flicked a switch. He played on, enjoying the feel of the keys under his hands and the relentless beauty of this little piece that had haunted him for so long. Why it should haunt Natalie, too, was still a mystery to him, but he didn't care about that now. All that mattered was that it was working its magic. He glanced over his shoulder as he played. Natalie was sitting bolt upright with that same transfixed expression he had seen before. He played on, as gently as he could, putting all the feeling he could muster into the music; and the piano sang on, through to the end.

Silence fell. He sat still, not wanting to move in case he broke the spell. Out of the corner of his eye he could see Mrs Little slumped in an armchair. She was exhausted and he knew Natalie must be, too. They both needed sleep badly. At least the music seemed to have calmed the little girl down. But it didn't last. A few moments later there was a sniffle from the sofa, then a moan, then the screaming began again.

'Natalie, no,' murmured Mrs Little.

Luke started to play once more, 'Peace of the Forest' this time, but the screaming went on. He stopped halfway through and started 'The Dance of the Blessed Spirits'. Still the screaming went on. He tried 'Jingle Bells', and 'Twinkle

Twinkle Little Star', and 'Bridge Over Troubled Water', again with no result. Finally he tried 'Reverie' a second time; and the screaming stopped at once.

What was it about this piece? It seemed to affect her like no other music. He played on, trying to think what he should do when he reached the end. She couldn't go on screaming forever. Surely, at some point, exhaustion would master her? She was quiet again now but he couldn't keep playing this piece indefinitely. He reached the end again and stopped, and waited, tensely. This time the silence lasted longer. He turned and looked towards the sofa. Natalie's eyes were half-closed and her head was tipped back against a cushion, but she looked anything but comfortable. She was still sprawled there in an untidy tangle of limbs, and though she was quiet for the moment, she was not asleep; indeed, he could already see her mouth shaping for another scream.

He started to play again, 'Reverie' as before, and this time, when he reached the end, he waited only a second or two before beginning it all over again; and so it went on, like an endless dream, as he played and played the same tune. He ignored the printed notes now—he had hardly needed them in the first place—and put his whole mind into the music; and, to his surprise, he found that rather than lose interest in the piece, now that he was playing it so much, he merely grew into it more and more. Or perhaps the music was growing into him—he wasn't sure. It certainly seemed to feel that way. But the strangest thing of all was that the more he played, and the more the silence from the sofa continued, the more he himself calmed down. The piece came to another end and he made ready to start from the beginning again; then realized he didn't need to.

Natalie was asleep.

He stared at her. She had curled up into a ball and

was sucking her thumb, her eyes tightly closed now, her breathing soft and regular. He looked at Mrs Little. She was still slumped in the armchair and was clearly struggling to stay awake. He wondered how she would cope with another night of screaming from Natalie, if that was what was in store. But for now the girl was asleep. He caught Mrs Little's eye and whispered to her.

'What do you think we should do now? Leave her to sleep where she is?'

Mrs Little shook her head. 'She needs her bed. She'll sleep better there. But I hardly dare leave her for a moment right now. We'd better put her in my bed. She's happier there anyway. Well, up until last night she was. There's no guessing what she'll be like tonight.' The old woman yawned. 'All I know is I don't think I can get through another night like the one we just had.'

'Maybe she'll sleep right through.'

'Maybe. I hope so. Still, we'd better get her upstairs.' The old woman started to heave herself out of the chair but Luke held out a hand and stopped her.

'It's OK. I'll do it. You're exhausted.'

Mrs Little slumped back without the slightest resistance.

'You won't need to do anything,' she said tiredly. 'She's already in her nightie from my attempts to get her to go to bed last night. Just pop her in my bed and tuck her up and make sure she's sleeping all right. I'll . . . ' The old woman leaned her head back. 'I'll . . . '

'Just stay here,' he said. 'You don't have to do anything.'

'You'll have to carry her up.'

'I know.'

'But she's only light. You'll manage that easily enough.'

'It's OK. Don't worry. I can do it.'

'All right.' Mrs Little's eyes met his and for the first

217

time he saw in them a flicker of warmth towards him. 'Thank you,' she murmured. There was no smile, but smiles, he already knew, were not a part of this woman's life. Perhaps they had been once. Perhaps long ago there had been smiles but, if so, they had stopped now. He found himself wondering when that had happened; and why.

He glanced down at Natalie. She was still fast asleep and showed no signs of waking. She made only the faintest moan as he picked her up, but otherwise remained as she had been, curled up, sucking her thumb, eyes tightly closed. Her body was indeed light, so light it felt as though he were holding a baby. He pulled her close into his chest and turned towards the door. Mrs Little rubbed her eyes. 'Are you sure you don't want me to help you?' she mumbled, now barely awake herself.

'I'll be fine,' he said. 'You just rest here for a bit while I put Natalie to bed.'

'I'll probably fall asleep.'

'You probably will.'

'Can you stay with her for a bit? Just watch over her. Make sure she's all right. While I'm getting some rest down here.'

'I can stay till about a quarter past six. Then I've got to go.'

'That's all right. If I'm asleep, wake me when you leave. And wake me if there's a problem with Natalie.'

'OK.'

And without another word the old woman closed her eyes. Luke glanced down at Natalie, adjusted his grip to make her more secure, then set off with her out of the sitting room, down the hall and up the stairs. It felt so strange to be walking through the house like this. So much had happened since he first broke in. He reached the top of the stairs, turned down the landing and made his way to Mrs Little's bedroom. The bed was already made and he simply turned back the duvet and laid Natalie carefully down. She rolled into a ball straightaway, still sucking her thumb, still fast asleep. He pulled the duvet over her and tucked it in at the sides, then, on an impulse, leant forward and kissed her on the temple. She murmured slightly but did not move or wake. He straightened up and turned to fetch the chair by the dressing table so that he could sit on something while he watched her. But his eye caught something else instead.

Mrs Little's box.

He stared at it, still in its original position on the dressing table, and remembered Skin's dream. How crazy that all seemed now. He wondered how he could ever have become involved. Robbing Mrs Little held no attractions for him now, even with the box unguarded before him; yet curiosity still drew him towards it. It was so striking with its bright silver beading and black velvet sides. The only bit he didn't like was the tassel at the front, which seemed showy and ridiculous. He sat down at the dressing table and pulled the box towards him, then listened for sounds: slow, regular breathing from Natalie; nothing at all from downstairs. He looked back at the box and the temptation grew. To look, just to look—and to find out whether Skin had guessed right about its contents.

But Skin had guessed wrong. There were no jewels inside, only—at first glance—some old black-and-white photographs. He pulled one out. It was a picture of a young man standing by a Spitfire. He was in flying gear and seemed about twenty or twenty-one, and he had an open, boyish face. He was smiling slightly self-consciously at the camera. Luke stared at the face and for a moment it didn't seem that much older than his own. He turned the photograph over and saw some words, written in a girlish hand: *Bill at Biggin Hill, August 1940*.

He picked up another photo, again a picture of Bill, but this time with other young men, all in flying gear. They were sitting in an airfield, playing cards, with several planes in the background. Most of the men were smoking cigarettes, including the one called Bill. He turned the photograph over and found more words written in the girlish hand: *Bill and the boys, Biggin Hill, August 1940*. He looked quickly through the other photographs. They all seemed to feature the man called Bill, sometimes on his own, sometimes with the other men, and always in flying gear. All the pictures were taken at Biggin Hill and all were dated August 1940. Usually the men were sitting around smoking and playing cards, but there was one of them kicking a football, and one of Bill by himself, whittling a stick. Then he found a completely different photograph.

It was Bill again, this time in uniform, but with a young woman. She was wearing some kind of party frock and they were standing outside what looked like the entrance to a pub. They had their arms round each other and were both smiling at the camera. She looked about the same age as Bill and he knew exactly who she was even before he turned the picture over and read the words: *Bill and me outside The Black Horse, August 1940*. He looked back at the smiling woman in the picture, and thought of the old woman downstairs. So there had once been smiles. Back in 1940. And was that the time when they had stopped, too? He looked back into the box and saw there were no more photographs, only a folded piece of paper and a tangle of brown hair, tied together with string. He knew from the photographs who the hair belonged to, and he left it well alone—it seemed disrespectful to touch it—but the piece of paper . . .

He stared at it, sitting there on its own, the last mystery to discover in this box. Maybe it was his conscience—he didn't know—but as he looked down, the paper seemed to look back up at him and reproach him for even thinking of running his eyes over what was not his business—and he knew he should not. This was her history, not his. Yet he also knew that however wrong this was, he had to find out what had happened to Mrs Little; though he was starting to sense the answer already. He took a deep breath, picked up the piece of paper and slowly unfolded it. It was a letter sent from Biggin Hill, dated 18th September 1940, and written in a strong, forceful hand, very different from the girlish writing on the backs of the photographs. He took a second deep breath, and started to read.

> *Dear Mrs Little,*
>
> *It is with great regret that I write to inform you that Bill was shot down earlier today by enemy aircraft during an engagement off Beachy Head. His plane crashed into the sea at around 0930 this morning. Unfortunately he did not have time to bale out and I am sorry to say there is no possibility that he could have survived.*
>
> *It grieves me immensely to have to be the bearer of such dreadful news and I can only imagine what you must be feeling to lose a husband so soon after your wedding. Bill was a wonderful man, greatly respected by all of us here, and he will be sorely missed.*
>
> *I enclose some photographs of Bill and one of the two of you together, which we found among his things, and also your letters to him at Biggin Hill. The rest of his effects will, of course, be sent on to you.*
>
> *Once again, I am so sorry to have to give you such shattering news. If you have any queries or require any assistance whatsoever, please do not hesitate to contact either myself or Group Captain Hugh Philips at Biggin Hill.*
>
> *Yours sincerely,*
> *James P. Hutchinson*
> *Squadron Leader*

Luke felt a sick stab of guilt and pain. She had lost her husband in 1940 and had never married again. He reread the words that she had written in that girlish hand. If these were the photos the squadron leader was referring to, she must have written those words after learning of her husband's death. He found himself trying to picture that young woman in a room somewhere, writing the name of a man she knew she would never see again. It was a picture he could not bear to contemplate. He clenched his fists. He had no right to be poring over these things. He'd put them back right away. He folded the paper, arranged the photographs in the order in which he'd taken them out, and was about to replace everything when something in the box caught his attention: something small and bright, almost hidden beneath the tangle of hair. He had been wrong. The letter was not the last mystery in this box. There was another. He bit his lip and reached in.

It was a silver identity bracelet.

He read the name.

Barley May Roberts.

To his surprise there was a telephone number underneath the name. He didn't recognize the code and it certainly wasn't a local number, but it seemed very strange. Identity bracelets didn't normally have telephone numbers, like tags for pets. And the name—Barley May Roberts—that was strange, too. He supposed it must be Mrs Little. He had no idea what her Christian name was and Roberts might well be her maiden name, yet there was something about this name that sounded familiar to him. He'd heard it somewhere. He was sure of it. He caught a sound downstairs and stiffened. Mrs Little was moving through the hall towards the foot of the stairs. He hurriedly put the things back in the box and returned it to its former place on the dressing table.

Only to find he was still holding the identity bracelet.

He didn't know why he hadn't put it back; or why, a moment later, he slipped it into his pocket; or why, when Mrs Little finally entered the room, he had moved away from the dressing table and was sitting on the floor by Natalie's side of the bed, as though he had never been anywhere else; or why, late that night, after Mum had turned in, he climbed out of bed, went onto the Internet, found his favourite search engine, and typed in the words: *Barley May Roberts.*

25

He had several hits right away. He stared at the screen, trembling with excitement. 'Barley May Roberts,' he murmured. 'You do exist.' Suddenly he stiffened. He could feel someone close by his shoulder, watching him. He whirled round, expecting to see Mum standing there; but the room was empty. He relaxed, though his eyes still searched the space before him. Then he frowned. 'It's you, Dad,' he said softly. 'I know it's you. I can feel you. I felt you before. But why can't I see you?'

The room remained empty, silent; yet he sensed Dad was still near. He spoke to the space again. 'You're watching all this. I know you are.' And then he smiled. 'You want to find out who Barley May Roberts is, too. OK.' He turned back to the screen. 'We'll find out together.'

He ran his eye down the entries. The first one said:

Barley May Roberts. Official Website.

That seemed the obvious place to start. He clicked on the link and waited, holding his breath. It seemed to take an age to download the site, but suddenly it was there; and, to his amazement, he found himself staring at a photograph of Natalie. There was no doubt about it: the tiny face, the black hair, the trusting smile. It was her. All that was wrong was the name. Because this was not Natalie after all. This was someone called Barley May

Roberts. It said so underneath. A twin maybe? Something told him no. This was the girl he had met at The Grange. He knew it. He scrolled down the page and read on.

Barley is ten years old but she has a mental age of four. She has been missing for over two years. She was last seen . . .

He read on, still trembling, still feeling Dad's presence close by. The site was only a small one but little was needed to tell the story of this girl. Her name was not Natalie but Barley. Her surname was Roberts. She came from Hastings. She was friendly and trusting. She liked animals. She liked music. She smiled a lot. She went to a special school for mentally-handicapped children. And on a fateful day just over two years ago she had somehow managed to become separated from her mother and father and wander away unnoticed; and she had never been seen since.

Barley May Roberts. He remembered now where he had heard the name. It was on the news, when the police hunt was at its height. But he'd taken so little notice of it, with Dad being ill and then dying at around the same time. His attention had been all on that. There was no mention on the site of Barley being blind, nor was there any suggestion that her parents were dead. On the contrary, at the end of the site there was a photograph of them with an anguished appeal for information, followed by an e-mail address and a police contact number.

He pulled out the identity bracelet and studied the telephone number there. It was not the same as the one on the site. This must be the home number of Mr and Mrs Roberts. He checked the screen again. Barley came from Hastings, it said. He pulled out the telephone directory and found the code for Hastings. It was the same as the one on the bracelet. Barley's parents must have put their home number there so that if she ever got lost, anyone finding her would be able to contact them. But it clearly hadn't worked. He leaned back in the chair and tried to piece together what must have happened. But he found he could not. One thing, however, was clear: Mrs Little had been lying to him.

'Barley,' he murmured, staring at her photograph again. 'Barley, Barley, Barley.' And then he remembered something, something she'd said to him that time she had tried to hum 'Reverie' to him, and he had asked her what she saw in the music. She had said: 'Barley'. And he had thought she meant barley swaying in a field, when all the time she was saying her own name. He thought of Mrs Little again. How much had she been concealing? And what was her part in all this?

He went out of the website and checked all the other links he had found but there was nothing new in them. They were simply reports on the hunt for the missing girl and covered only the same ground as the official website. He went back to it and stared at Barley's photograph again; and he knew what he had to do. He had to phone her parents. He had to pluck up the courage and do it. It needn't be difficult. He didn't have to give his name. He could just give them Mrs Little's address, tell them that was where Barley was, and put the phone down. He checked the clock. Half past midnight. Not a great time to call anyone but he didn't imagine Mr and Mrs Roberts would mind in special circumstances like these. All he had to do was pick up the phone.

But an hour later he was still sitting there, hesitating. What if this whole thing backfired? What if Barley's parents turned out to be difficult or aggressive? They looked pleasant enough in the photograph but there was no telling what they'd be like towards someone who knew where their daughter was. And once he was involved, that was it. No matter how little he told them about himself, they'd contact the police, the police would go to The Grange, find Barley, arrest Mrs Little—and she would give them his name. Why should she cover up for him? She'd know he was the one who had given her away and she'd shop him immediately. She'd mention the break-in and blacken his name in any way she could. By tomorrow he could be sitting in a police station answering questions. And everyone would know about it. Mum would know, Miranda would know, Mr Harding would know, the whole village would know, and the school. He couldn't get involved in this.

Yet the picture of the little girl forced him from these thoughts. He stared back at the face on the screen, and the smile seemed to speak to him like a reproach. He felt Dad's presence draw close again and spoke into the living space. 'I know, Dad. I know.' He checked the number on the identity bracelet and picked up the phone. His heart was pounding now. The handset felt slippery against his palm. He tried to calm down, tried to keep his mind clear and work out what he was going to say. The phone at the other end seemed to ring for ages but he held on, half-hoping no one would answer. Then he heard a woman's voice.

'Hello?'

It was a soft voice, a tired voice; but not an unpleasant one. He tried to force himself to speak but found he could not.

'Hello?' repeated the voice.

He tried again. He had to speak. He had to make himself.

'I'm sorry,' said the voice wearily. 'I haven't got time for silent calls. We get enough of those as it is, thank you. Goodnight.'

'Wait!' he said.

There was a silence; a deep, tense silence. Then the woman spoke again.

'Who is this, please?'

He took a slow breath, again struggling to speak. The woman sighed.

'If you've got something to say, then say it. If you haven't, then I'm putting the phone down. It's half past one in the morning and I'm not in the mood for games.'

Still he couldn't speak. He tried again to make himself but it was no use. He felt Dad's presence draw closer.

'Goodnight,' said the woman.

'Wait!' he said. 'Please don't hang up.'

There was another silence at the other end, but no click of the phone. He took a deep breath and spoke again.

'Are you Mrs Roberts?'

'What's it got to do with you who I am?'

'Please, are you?'

'It's none of your business who I am. Get to the point.'

'It's about Barley,' he said.

There was another silence. Then the woman spoke again, her voice no longer impatient, but wary. 'What about Barley?'

'I know where she is.'

There was yet another silence and he sensed she was trying to work out how to play this. He also realized suddenly just why she was so suspicious of him. She must have had to put up with countless disappointments from hoax callers since Barley disappeared. Despite his determination to say as little as possible, he felt a desperate urge to reassure her.

'Listen,' he said. 'I'm not a hoax caller, OK? I do know where she is, so can you just listen to me? Only don't bother trying to trace this call. I've made sure you can't, but that's only for my own protection. I can help you but I don't want the police involved.'

'Where is she?' said the woman, her voice tense and frightened.

'She's safe. I promise you she's safe.'

'But where is she?'

'She's . . . she's being looked after by someone who loves her very much.'

'Who?'

Luke tried to control his racing thoughts. He had to keep calm. He had to watch every word he said. He was starting to see a way he might be able to get Barley back to her parents without compromising himself too much but he had to handle this right. And he had to have an answer to a question that now nagged inside him.

'Mrs Roberts—I'm going to assume you're Mrs Roberts—has Barley got any other relatives?'

'What?'

'Any other relatives. Has she got any?'

'What's that got to do with anything?'

'Just tell me. Please.'

'She's got an uncle in Broadstairs. She's got an aunt here in Hastings. Why's this important?'

'Nobody else? No other relatives?'

'No.'

'No grandparents or anything?'

'No, they all died before she was born. Please . . . whoever you are . . . she's our daughter. She's—'

'It's OK. I'm going to help you. I promise. I'm a friend. It's just that . . . ' He heard a listening silence at the other end of the phone. 'It's a bit complicated.'

'Why?' said the woman. 'How? Barley belongs to us. She doesn't belong to anyone else. She's our daughter.'

'I know. I understand. And . . . ' He could feel the situation slipping out of control. He tried again to keep calm, to think of what he needed to say. 'I'm going to help,' he said. 'You've got to listen to me. Please, just hear me out.'

He could hear another voice now at the other end of the phone, a man's voice speaking in the background, not to him but to the woman. 'It's about Barley,' the woman whispered back and Luke heard an intake of breath.

'Mrs Roberts?' he said. 'I want to help you. I want to help . . . ' He thought of the girl he had only ever known as Natalie. 'I want to help Barley. But you must do exactly what I say. And there's something else you need to know.'

He waited for one of them to speak but nothing came from the other end. He took a deep breath and spoke again.

'She's blind.'

'What!' shouted the woman.

Before Luke could answer, the man seized the phone and bellowed down it.

'What have you done to her?'

'I haven't done anything to her.'

'And who the hell are you?'

'It doesn't matter who I am. Look—'

'What's happened? Where is she? What have you . . . ?' The man's words were punctuated by pleadings from the woman, begging him to calm down, to give her back the phone; but the man went on thundering down the line. 'I don't know who the hell you are or what you've done, or what you know, but I'm telling you, there's such a thing as retribution and if you've got any shred of decency or conscience—'

'Stop it!' Luke snapped at him with as much force as he could manage. He wanted to shriek back but did not dare raise his voice for fear of waking Mum. But he'd stopped the man's rush of words. 'Please,' he went on quickly, 'you've got to trust me. I'm trying to help.'

He heard the woman still urging the man to give her back the phone and a moment later her anxious voice was on the line again. 'Are you still there?' she said.

'Yes.' But he felt shaken now and he was starting to wonder how much further he could go with this. The man's anger was terrifying. Was it really right to hand Barley over to someone like this? Then the woman spoke again.

'Please . . . you must understand . . . we're in a terrible state over this. I've no idea if you're genuine. Maybe you are. Maybe you're not. Maybe you're just another one of those jokers who get a kick out of doing things like this to people in distress. I hope you're not.'

'I'm not.'

'And now you tell us she's blind. Oh, my God . . . '

Her voice trailed away and he heard her crying at the other end. He thought of Barley again, her distress, her screams, her tears, her loneliness, her confused memories; and the sightless world she now inhabited. He listened to the woman weeping at the other end of the line, and after a moment heard the man weeping, too. The doubts he had felt a moment ago started to fade, though he was still wary. He waited till they had calmed down, then spoke again.

'Mrs Roberts?'

'Yes.'

'This is real. I promise. It's going to be all right. If you can just trust me.'

'How can I trust you?' she said. 'How can I know you've even met her? You could be making this up. Her photograph's on the website. You could describe her to us and we'd have no way of knowing whether or not you're lying.'

231

He closed his eyes and listened to the hum of the night, then, on an impulse, started to hum, too. A tune he knew Barley loved. Whether or not it would mean anything to this woman, he didn't know. But she started to cry again the moment she heard it.

'Oh, God, this is torture,' she said.

He stopped humming. 'You know that tune?'

'You obviously know I do.'

'I didn't know. But I know Barley loves it. I heard her trying to hum it.' He hesitated, confused by memories of his own. 'Can you tell me . . . why it's special for her?'

'I used to play it to her when she was in the womb.' The woman was still crying, but she had calmed down a little. 'My husband and I went to a piano recital just after I got pregnant. The pianist . . . I can't remember his name . . . ' She paused, then the man spoke in the background.

'Stanton.'

Luke felt a sharp pain run through him. Dad's presence closed round him like an embrace.

'Yes,' said the woman. 'That's it. Matthew Stanton. He played lots of things . . . but the one I'll always remember is . . . the Tchaikovsky. He played all the pieces in *Album for the Young* and "Reverie" was the one we liked best. But we didn't know what it was called so we . . . ' She sniffed and blew her nose. 'We went up to him after the concert and asked him what the piece was called. We had to sing it to him, I remember. But he knew which one we meant.' She blew her nose again and went on, still sniffling as she spoke. 'He was so nice. He said he'd send us a photocopy of the music so we could play it for ourselves, so we gave him our address and in the end he sent the whole volume with a lovely signed message inside. It was such a kind thing to do. I was so sorry when I heard he died a couple of years ago.' The woman gave a sigh. 'And so I played that piece to Barley when I was pregnant, lots and lots of times, and again after she was born. I played other things, too, because she always loved to hear the sound of the piano, but "Reverie" was her favourite. It was special to her. I don't know why. It just had something that felt right for her. It used to calm her when she couldn't sleep.'

There was a long silence. Then Luke spoke. 'Keep playing that piece to her. When she's with you again.'

At this the woman broke down. He listened to her sobbing at the other end of the line, then after a moment the man spoke into the phone. He did not bellow as he had done earlier. His voice was calm and grave.

'Tell us what we have to do,' he said.

26

L uke watched the school bus from his hiding place behind the wall of the churchyard. The other kids were clambering aboard but Skin and Daz still hung about by the door, looking around them. He had no doubt they were searching for him. He kept his head as low as he could but went on watching. Speed appeared at the far end of the square, eating what looked like the remains of his breakfast as he bumbled towards the bus. He reached the others and they spoke for a few moments, then all three started to look around the square.

Luke ducked his head below the wall. They mustn't see him today of all days. He decided to wait until he heard the bus leave. He slumped on the ground, his back against the wall, and waited, staring over the gravestones. The early morning sun was already warm and there were no clouds in the sky. It was clearly going to be a very hot day. After a while he heard the engine rev up but he stayed where he was, hidden behind the wall. The bus pulled away, crossed the square, and headed down past the shop. He listened to the drone of the engine as it faded away, then strained his ears for the sound of voices in the square. But there were none. He waited a few minutes, still listening hard, then eased himself to his feet and checked over the wall. The square was empty. Skin and the others had gone to school and he wouldn't have to face them today. That was one problem solved. The problem of what to say to Mum and Mrs Searle when they confronted him over today's truanting was another matter, but he'd have to think about that later.

He didn't risk crossing the square, not with Miss Grubb's door wide open, but took the route he had used last time, along the footpath and past Stony Hill Cottage. Roger Gilmore was busy tapping away at something in his workshop but the door was closed and it was easy enough to slip by without being seen. He was soon at the end of Nut Bush Lane, staring down the track towards The Grange. He moved to the side of the lane, keeping out of sight of the windows and well out of hearing, then pulled Mum's mobile from his pocket and the scrap of paper with the number the woman had given him last night. Her husband answered on the first ring. 'Yes?'

'Mr Roberts?'

'Yes.'

'It's me.'

'I gathered that.'

'Where are you?'

'Where you told us to be. At the motorway services. What do we do now?'

'How many of you are there in the car?'

'Just myself and my wife.'

'No police with you or anything? I mean, you didn't—'

'Listen,' the man cut in. 'We've just driven through the night from Hastings to get here. We're exhausted. We're overwrought. We don't need any hassle and we haven't come to play games. We just want our daughter. We've done everything you've said. We haven't contacted the police, we haven't spoken to anybody, we haven't tried to trace your number. We don't know your name and we don't want to. We don't want to see you any more than you want to see us. We just want Barley, OK? We'll do everything you say but don't play around with us. What do we have to do next?'

'Have you got a map of the area?'

'I just told you!' snapped the man. 'We've done everything you wanted us to do!'

Luke bristled at the angry tone in the man's voice. Then he heard the woman in the background, whispering urgently to her husband. 'Keep calm,' she was saying. 'Keep calm. Don't snap at him.'

There was a silence, then the man spoke again, slightly less irritably.

'We've got a map.'

'OK,' said Luke, fighting the unease he was starting to feel once again about the prospect of handing Barley over to this man. He glanced towards The Grange. 'Now listen, the next bit may take me some time. I'm going to direct you to a place where I can leave her for you. It's nowhere near the place where she's been kept so don't even bother trying to trace—'

'We've been through this,' interrupted the man. 'For Christ's sake, we've been through this.'

'OK, OK.' Luke took a slow breath. 'I want you to find a place called Bramblebury. It's only a tiny hamlet so it might not be marked on your map but it's just a couple of miles up from the village of Sedgecombe, which you should find on the map.'

'Where's that?'

'About twelve miles from where you are now.'

'Yes, but where?' said the man curtly. 'North, south, east, west? Where do I look on the map?'

Luke gave him the directions and the man heard him through in tense silence.

'Then what?' said the man when he'd finished.

'Just wait for me to call again. OK? Get to Bramblebury and wait. You can turn your mobile off now and save the battery. Switch it on again when you get to Bramblebury. I'll phone you when I'm ready for the next stage.'

'When will that be?'

'I don't know.'

'Now look here—' began the man.

'No, you look here!' shouted Luke. 'You bloody well look here!' He took a deep breath, struggling to control himself, but it was no good. He was beside himself with rage. 'I'm trying to help you, OK? I'm not an enemy so don't treat me like one. Just . . . just . . . '

He heard the woman's voice, speaking softly to him. 'Thank you, whoever you are.'

'I'm not an enemy!' he shouted down the phone.

'I know.'

'I'm not! I'm not!'

'I know you're not,' she said. 'It's all right. I know.' Her voice was calm, almost motherly. It even sounded for a moment as though she was anxious for him. She went on, in the same quiet voice. 'Don't be angry with us. Please don't. We've worked out that you're a friend to Barley. But we're upset and we're tired and we're very frightened, so we maybe don't always say things right.'

He took another slow breath; and the woman spoke again.

'We'll drive to where you want us to go and speak to you when you're ready to ring us. We'll do everything you say.' She paused, then added: 'Be careful.'

Her last two words took him by surprise. He had expected the tension and wariness from these people. Maybe even the anger. He hadn't expected concern for his safety. He wasn't sure how to respond and in the end could only say: 'I'm ringing off now.'

'OK,' she said. 'We'll speak to you later.'

The woman's voice wavered only once.

Mrs Little's relief at the sight of him was obvious the

moment she opened the front door. 'Thank God you're here,' she said. 'I didn't expect to see you till tonight and she's in a terrible state again. Have you truanted?'

But she didn't wait for an answer. She simply turned and led the way towards the sitting room. He followed, his hands twitching at his sides. The little girl was curled up on the sofa, still in her nightie, but she wasn't screaming this time. She was snuffling and moaning, her face a pool of tears. Luke stopped on the threshold and looked down at her, reminding himself that he had to call her Natalie; then he glanced at the old woman. She, too, looked in a dreadful state. If the girl was suffering, so was she. He wondered again what part Mrs Little had played in all this; and what losing Barley would do to her. But that was not his concern right now. The little girl was his concern; and he had to concentrate. He had to do this right. If the old woman started to suspect anything, there was no telling what might happen.

'Hi, Natalie!' he said brightly.

The little girl stopped moaning at once and turned her head towards the door.

'Hi, kid!' he said. He walked over, bent down by the sofa and took one of her hands in his. Over by the door he sensed Mrs Little watching intently, but he kept his eyes on the girl. 'Natalie?' he said softly. 'Remember me?'

She sniffed and reached out her free hand to his face, then traced a path with her fingers round the side of his head to his left ear; and then she giggled. He laughed, too.

'Funny ears,' he said. 'Just like yours.' He reached out and gently flicked the lobe of her left ear. She giggled again. He started to hum 'Reverie', and her manner changed at once. From being upset to being playful, she now became still. Utterly still. But her eyes were shedding tears again. He squeezed her hand, just a little, and felt a

238

tiny pressure back from hers. She lay there, curled up before him, and he watched her, thinking as he did so of the broken vision and broken memories that had engulfed her; and of Mrs Little standing near, the key to whatever it was that had happened here; and of the two anxious people driving from the motorway, praying that their nightmare would soon end.

He slid his arms under Barley's body and pulled her gently to him. She did not resist. She even turned slightly towards him, as though she wanted to be held. Still humming the tune, he pulled her close until he was holding her against his chest, then he carefully stood up. Once again he was struck by how easy it was to carry her. She was as light as air. It was like carrying a spirit. She was humming, too, now, well out of tune as before, but clearly thinking of the music her mother had played to her when she was in the womb. He carried her over to the window, both of them still humming, and stopped there for a moment, staring out over the garden towards the forest; then he turned back into the room. Mrs Little was still standing there, watching, her face a mixture of relief and envy.

'You've obviously got the magic touch,' she said somewhat grudgingly. Then she gave a sigh. 'I just don't understand it. Natalie was fine for most of the night. She slept right through after you left. But then she woke up around half past five this morning and started all this moaning and weeping. I just couldn't make her stop. I don't know why she's become like this.'

Because she's not yours, he wanted to shout back at her. Because she's missing her parents and her friends. Because she can't see. Because she doesn't live here. Because she's unhappy and confused. Because she keeps remembering the music her mother played to her. And because she can't express herself and tell you all this.

But all he said was: 'Mrs Little, could you make us something to drink? I expect Natalie could do with something and I certainly could.'

'I'll get you some orange juice.'

'Something hot would be nicer.'

She looked at him warily. He tried to keep his own gaze steady as he spoke again.

'Anything'll do. Cup of tea, hot chocolate, whatever.'

It was a harmless enough request, he knew. Harmless and normal. So why was the old woman watching him in that suspicious way? Had his voice or his manner betrayed something? Then she shrugged. 'I'll make some hot chocolate. Natalie likes that.'

'Great. Sugar for me, please.'

She gave him another wary look and he started to worry that his efforts to sound normal were having the opposite effect. To avoid her eyes, he turned back to Barley, dipped his head close and rubbed noses with her. She gave a little giggle and he did it again, then started to hum the tune once more.

Mrs Little didn't go.

He felt the tension inside him grow. Why wouldn't she leave the room? Why was she staring at him like that? Then she spoke. 'How many spoonfuls?'

'What?'

'I told you,' she said sharply. 'I don't like it when you say "what".'

'Sorry—pardon?'

'How many spoonfuls of sugar do you want?'

'Oh, two. Please. Thanks very much.'

And he went on humming as he carried Barley round the room. Mrs Little stared at him a while longer, then, to his relief, she turned and set off down the hall. He watched her walk away. He watched her enter the kitchen. He waited to see if she would close the door. She did not.

240

From where she was standing, she could see right down the hall into the sitting room. But she had taken the kettle and in a moment would be facing the other way to fill it at the sink. He looked down at Barley, clinging to him as though she never wanted to let him go; he thought of her parents, only a few miles away; he thought of his father; he thought of the music running through all their lives. Barley was silent now and he was glad, for this was the moment. The old woman had turned towards the sink. She was bending over the tap. It had to be now. There might not be another chance. He tiptoed out of the sitting room, holding Barley close to his chest, then turned and, without looking towards the kitchen, made his way as softly as he could towards the front door. No voice called after him; no footsteps sounded in the hall. He pulled the front door towards him, glad that he had thought to leave it ajar when he came in so that it wouldn't click now; then, not closing it behind him, he stole out through the gate and down the track towards the forest. As he entered the trees, Barley opened her eyes wide and stared up so brightly he almost felt she could see again. A shaft of sunlight broke through the canopy and lit her face. He pulled the identity bracelet from his pocket and fastened it round her wrist, then leaned down and kissed her on the brow.

'I'm taking you home, Barley,' he said.

27

He carried her deep into the forest, praying they wouldn't meet anyone out walking, but he saw no one. It was as though the forest belonged to them alone. Barley was silent, her head turned in to his chest but her eyes still open as though to drink in the sunlight that came dancing through the overhanging trees. He couldn't believe how light she was. She seemed almost to be floating in his arms. She turned her face upwards suddenly and wrinkled her eyes.

'You OK?' he said.

She didn't answer. He wondered what sense, if any, she made of all the things that had happened to her and all that was happening now. He remembered the words on the website: *Barley is ten years old but she has a mental age of four. She has been missing for over two years.* What was she feeling right now? What did she remember? Did she have any memory of the day she was taken away? She spoke suddenly, in a voice so tiny it was barely a whisper.

'Trees,' she said.

'What did you say, Barley?'

'Trees.' Her head moved slowly from side to side, as though she were staring at the forest around her. He hesitated, then moved his left hand round and held it in front of her eyes. She seemed unaware of it and he felt sure she couldn't see anything. Then she spoke again.

'Trees.'

'Can you see them?' he said.

'Hear the trees.'

'Hear them?'

'Hear the trees.'

He stopped for a moment and listened. The forest was still. Not even a wood pigeon called. How could she know they weren't walking across a field or through a churchyard or down a deserted street? Perhaps it was the scent of the forest she was picking up.

'Hear the trees,' she said again. 'Hear the trees.'

He leaned closer to her and started to hum 'Peace of the Forest'.

'Remember that, Barley?' he said, walking on again. 'I played it to you.'

She said nothing and simply pressed her head against his chest again. He walked on, still humming, and didn't stop until he reached the old oak. It was good to be back with his old friend again and he had wanted to bring Barley here. It was such a special place for him that he wanted to share it with her. He sat down, still cradling her in his arms, and rested his back against the trunk. High overhead, the canopy swayed in the breeze. He stopped humming and looked down at Barley's face again. Her eyes were closed now and she looked as though she was falling asleep; but then she spoke again.

'Barley,' she murmured. 'Barley.'

'That's your name,' he said, stroking her hair. 'That's who you are. Barley. Beautiful Barley. Beautiful Barley May Roberts.'

'Where Nana?'

He wondered what the old woman was doing, what she was thinking, what she was feeling. It was hard to know. She must realize by now that he'd worked out who the girl was. No doubt she thought he was taking Barley to the police and that they would be turning up at The Grange very soon. He hoped she wouldn't do anything rash. But Mrs Little was the least of his thoughts right now. There were far more important things to sort out first. He lifted Barley carefully from him and placed her on the ground with her back against the trunk of the oak. Then he took her hand. 'Nana not very far away,' he said. 'Nana loves you very much. Like I do. OK, Barley?'

She moved her head again from side to side, her eyes still closed.

'Can you still hear the trees?' he said.

'Hear the trees.'

'Let's just sit here for a bit, then, and listen to them.' She seemed content to do this and even rested her head back against the oak. He watched her for a moment, then, as quietly as he could, stood up. She did not stir, did not turn her head in his direction, and seemed unaware that he had moved. He watched her a moment longer, then, keeping her in view, tiptoed over to the far side of the clearing, pulled out the mobile phone and dialled the number. As before, the answer was immediate, but this time it was Mrs Roberts.

'Yes?' she said.

'It's me. Have you reached Bramblebury?'

'Yes.'

She sounded calm but he sensed the tension just below the surface of her voice.

'Where are you?' he said. 'In the hamlet, I mean.'

'Outside a thatched cottage with a big white gate and a paddock with—'

'I know it. Which way are you facing?'

'I beg your pardon?'

'Which direction?'

'Oh, I see.' Again he heard the tension beneath the desperate normality of her voice. 'Just a moment,' she said. 'I'll check the map.' There was a pause, then: 'We're pointing towards the village of Wedburn.'

'Right, you need to turn round and head the other way.'

244

'Towards Upper Dinton?'

He stiffened at the sound of his own village. He had hoped to keep it out of the conversation altogether but it couldn't be helped now.

'Yes,' he said. 'Head off in that direction for about a mile. You'll be driving round the edge of a forest.'

'Buckland Forest?'

'Yes,' he said, again uncomfortable at the sound of the name. 'Keep on that road until you come to a lay-by on your left. It's next to a field with loads of meadow buttercups in it. You can't miss them. They're so bright. There's a fence along the field with nettles and bracken and stuff, and a sweet chestnut tree just before you get to the lay-by. On the other side of the road, about a hundred yards further down, there's a track that leads into the forest. OK?'

'What do we do?'

'I want you to pull into the lay-by and wait.'

'Until you phone us?'

'Yes.'

'And you will phone us, won't you?' she said suddenly, all calmness gone. 'Please tell us you're going to phone us. You're not going to just raise our hopes and then—'

'It's OK,' he said quickly. 'It's OK. I will phone.' He heard her breathing hard at the other end of the line. He glanced across the clearing at Barley, sitting with her back against the oak tree and still apparently unaware that he was not with her. He spoke again. 'This is for real, Mrs Roberts. I promise. You'll have Barley back very soon.'

He heard her voice at the other end, and it was so tiny, he could almost have mistaken it for Barley's. 'Thank you,' she said. 'Whoever you are. Thank you.' And then she rang off.

He walked back to Barley and knelt down. She was still leaning against the tree, her eyes closed. He reached cautiously out, not wanting to startle her, and took her hand. She stiffened for a moment, then relaxed again.

'Only me, Barley,' he said quietly. 'Only me.'

She turned her face towards him. 'Singing,' she said.

'Singing?' He picked her up again. 'Who's singing? The birds?'

'Tree.'

'The tree?'

'Tree singing.'

He pulled her close and saw that her eyes were open again, and that her hands were reaching past him towards the oak. He moved closer to it so that she could touch the trunk. Her fingers played over the bark. 'Tree singing,' she said.

He listened, and after a moment heard it, too: a low murmuring melody, subtler than breath. He leaned down and kissed her on the head. 'Tree singing,' he said. And he set off with her again, heading east towards the Bramblebury end of the forest. And as he walked, he heard the murmuring songs of the other trees all around them. 'Lots of trees singing now, Barley. Can you hear them?'

'All singing,' she said.

'Yes, they're all singing. And there's lots and lots of them. There's oak and spruce and birch and larch.' He walked on, holding her close. 'And a hazel tree,' he said, walking over to it. 'Feel?' He stretched her hand out until it touched the bark, then moved her fingers slowly round the trunk. 'Feel that? Ivy round the tree.'

'Singing,' she said again, tracing it with her hand.

'I know. It's singing, too. Everything's singing.'

He walked on, humming 'Reverie' now, and Barley hummed with him, her own tune mingled with his, and theirs mingled with those of the trees, until at last the forest came to an end. He stopped, well back from the road and just to the side of the track that led down to it. Before them a carpet of bluebells threw up a heady scent. He looked down at Barley, still comfortable in his arms, still light, still humming, and wondered how he was going to manage to say goodbye. He carried her over to a young fir tree and placed her on the ground, just as he had done by the oak, her back against the trunk; then he sat down beside her and took her hand again. She turned towards him and reached up with her free hand and felt round his face. He chuckled.

'I know what you're doing,' he said.

She giggled and flicked his ear-lobe.

'Funny ears,' she said.

'Funny ears.' He stared at her. What was it about her manner that made him feel she knew he was about to leave her? He pulled her close. 'I'll always think of you,' he whispered. 'I'll always love you.' He thought for a moment. 'And Nana will always love you.' Barley stared up at him, wide-eyed and trusting, and he wished she could see the smile on his face. He gave her one final kiss, then said: 'And your mummy and daddy will always love you, too.'

'Mummy and Daddy,' she said, still staring up at him.

'They'll be with you very soon.' He stroked her on the cheek. 'They're going to look after you from now on.'

He slid his arm gently away from her, placed her hands on her lap, then moved a few inches to the side. She did not stir. Her face was as still as stone. He started to hum 'Reverie' again, and she hummed it, too, in her funny, out-of-tune way.

'Keep humming, Barley,' he whispered. 'Keep humming. It's nice to hear your voice.'

She went on humming, softly.

'I'm going to just sit here and dream for a while,' he said. 'I'm feeling a bit sleepy. I might even have a doze. Can you just keep on humming?'

She went on humming, and as he slipped quietly away from her, he thought she looked as happy as he had ever seen her. He hid in the shadow of the trees over to the right. She seemed unaware that he was no longer beside her and she was still humming. He could hear her voice clearly against the murmuring of the trees. He pulled out the phone and spoke, then moved back further into the shadows and watched from behind an old sycamore tree.

They did exactly as he asked. They did not rush. They did not drive up the track. They did not call out. They walked slowly forward, two figures, instantly recognizable from the website: a tall man with a light grey beard, a small woman with short black hair. He saw Barley's face in both of theirs and any doubts he might have had left about giving her back to them vanished forever. But he did not dwell on them, nor did they search for him. The eyes of all of them were on the girl sitting against the tree, bluebells spread before her like a sea. She was still humming—he could hear that even from this distance— but she had closed her eyes again and was sucking her thumb, just as she had done that time on the sofa when she was falling asleep; and perhaps she was now falling asleep. He bit his lip, and watched; and the two frightened people reached her at last, and bent slowly down, not touching her yet, and he heard the woman murmur something in a soft, loving voice.

He did not catch the words and did not want to. This moment was no longer his but theirs. Barley stirred, but not with fright. Her eyes opened and she leaned forward, feeling the air; then her mother picked her up and held her; and her husband moved closer and put his arms round them both, and they stayed like that for some minutes, all three together, in a closed circle of love. And as Luke watched, he felt his own father's presence encircle him. He closed his eyes and whispered into the silence:

'Thank you.' And then dropped his head and cried, silently, for what felt like a long time. When he looked up again, Barley and her parents were gone.

He walked back through the forest, his head down, still hearing the murmur of the trees and now, strangely, Barley's voice, humming, even though she was gone. He wondered what she was feeling right now, in the car heading back towards the motorway. Confusion, no doubt, at this strange mixture of loving people, coming and going in her life. But her parents would make things right again now. The sight of them standing there, holding her, had given him all the reassurance he needed. Any sense of loss Barley might feel for the Nana who wasn't her Nana or the boy with the funny ears would no doubt soon be gone, and perhaps even the memory of them, too; and in a way, he hoped it would be so. She needed to move on from all this. She needed to start again. But she would remain in his memory forever.

The sun was now high overhead and it seemed to be growing hotter by the minute. He checked his watch. Five past twelve. Had the whole morning really gone? He felt as though he had been frozen in time and still was. He was close to the old oak now and he couldn't wait to get up there and rest in the tree-house and think. But something made him stop. He scanned the path in front of him, trying to work out what it was that had unsettled him. Then he understood. Dad's presence had drawn closer, much closer. There was no mistaking it. He leaned against a small ash tree and went on staring at the path.

'Where are you?' he murmured. 'Please, Dad. Where are you?'

No figure appeared before him.

'Please, Dad. Please show yourself. Just once.'

Again he saw no one. But Dad's presence remained, close by, closer than it had ever been; and Luke sensed an urgency, as though his father were trying to communicate with him. Suddenly he felt a second presence. He stiffened. Someone else had drawn near, someone he knew. He ran his eyes over the path again. But at that moment a hand seized him from behind.

28

He tried to turn but, before he could do so, he was flung to the ground. The jolt stunned him and jarred his vision but through a blur he saw the figure of Skin looming over him. 'Bastard!' muttered the boy. 'Shitty, shitty bastard!' Daz appeared at Skin's shoulder, then Speed, and the three looked down at him for a moment, their faces grim; then Skin stepped forward and kicked him in the ribs.

'A-ah!' Luke gave a gasp of pain and curled up in an effort to protect himself. Another kick drove in, this time from Daz in the small of his back. The next moment kicks were raining in from all sides as Skin and Daz vented their rage upon him. Luke writhed over the ground, crying, moaning; then Skin seized him by the hair and twisted his face round. 'Don't think we're finished,' he hissed. 'We've hardly started.'

He dragged Luke to his feet and threw him against the ash tree. 'Pin his arms back!' he shouted. Before Luke could move, Daz and Speed seized his wrists and jerked them back round the trunk. He struggled to free them but the boys only held on more tightly. Skin looked him over with scorn. 'Thought we were in school, did you?'

Luke said nothing.

'Eh?' said Skin. 'Thought we were in school?' And he drove his fist into Luke's stomach. Luke doubled up with a groan, only to be yanked upright again by Daz and Speed. 'Well, you obviously got that wrong, didn't you?' said Skin, watching his face. Luke looked dully back, still trying to catch his breath. He remembered the school bus. He'd watched them in the square but he hadn't seen them get on. They must have waited for him, then, when they realized he wasn't coming, decided to truant themselves. They could have been wandering through the forest all morning, looking for him. He shivered at the thought of what might have happened if they'd found Barley. But there was no time to dwell on this as Skin's fist crashed into his stomach again. He doubled up once more, again gasping for air, then an uppercut smashed into his chin. He felt his head thump back against the tree; his vision flickered again but somehow he remained conscious. He heard Speed talking in a low, nervous voice.

'Skin, leave it there, OK? It's enough.'

'It's not enough.'

'Skin—'

'Shut up!'

And Speed shut up. Luke rolled his eyes to the left and saw fear in the fat boy's face; fear of what was happening but an even greater fear of disobeying Skin. There would be no help from Speed and certainly none from Daz, who had points of his own to prove. He saw Skin moving closer again, and it was clear from the boy's expression that this was where the retribution was really meant to start.

'The stupid thing is,' said Skin, 'that none of this had to happen. All you had to do was keep your word. Do the business. The rest of us do the business. Even Speedy, when we push him a bit. But not you. You wanted to be part of the gang and we gave you the chance, but you let us down. And then you stopped showing respect. And that was bad, Luke. You stopped showing respect. We don't forgive that. We don't ever forgive that.'

Skin pulled out a cigarette lighter and snapped it. A bright yellow flame flickered before them. Skin held it up to Luke's eyes and moved it this way and that. Luke shrank back as far as he could go before the tree stopped him; but the flame followed, moving ever closer. 'We don't forgive,' murmured Skin. 'We don't ever forgive.'

'Skin,' said Speed. 'Skin—'

'Shut up and hold him!'

'Skin—'

'Do as I say!' Skin snapped.

Luke looked desperately from side to side. Daz's face was fixed, dark, eager, but Speed's was a battle-zone of conflicting emotions. Luke spoke to him, urgently. 'Speedy, don't let him do this.'

Speed looked away, as though unable to face him.

'Speedy!' said Luke. 'Help me!'

Luke felt Skin's hand slap him on the cheek and looked back to see the flame only inches from his eyes, and, behind it, Skin's face, peering at him. 'Speedy's not going to help you,' the boy said, 'because he knows he'll get the same treatment if he does.' Skin watched the flame for a moment as it danced before them. 'I told you what would happen if you messed with me.' He started to move the lighter down Luke's right arm, just close enough for the heat to tickle the skin. Luke felt his arm twitch and tried to pull it back but Daz's grip tightened around it. Skin watched for a moment, then suddenly pulled Luke's hand from Daz's grasp and held it out in front of him; and looked up, the flame in one hand, Luke's wrist in the other.

'I did warn you, Luke. You can't say I didn't.'

Luke tugged frantically at both hands in an effort to escape.

'Hold him!' roared Skin. 'Hold him tight!'

He felt Daz seize him round the neck and pin him back against the tree. Speed still clung to his other hand, though Luke could feel the boy's fear growing by the minute. Skin spoke again, in the casual voice that always signalled the greatest danger. 'The thing about being a pianist, I suppose, is that you need a good pair of hands. If your hands aren't right, you're finished. I guess that's why some pianists get their hands insured.' He paused for a moment, his eyes on Luke, then said: 'Are yours insured?'

Again Luke tugged wildly at his hands; again the others restrained him. Skin waited for him to stop struggling, then gave a mock sigh. 'It's obvious from the way you're reacting that you're not insured. Which is a bit of a shame really, since you're not going to be able to play the piano again after today. Or do anything else for that matter.'

Luke felt a sick chill run through him. Speed spoke again, feverishly.

'Skin, listen, we—'

'Shut up, Speedy,' said Skin.

'Skin, we—'

'Shut up, I said!' Skin glared at Speed. 'We agreed on this before we came. Daz was in, I was in, you were in. We were all in.' His eyes slanted back towards Luke. 'All except this piece of chicken shit who's never going to be in.' Skin thrust his jaw close to Luke's. 'Because by the end of today he's going to be dead.'

And he jerked Luke's hand forward and ran the flame over the palm. Luke squirmed and squealed and thrashed his arms as the heat licked over the palm; then the lighter moved closer still, and the flame became a burning knife. He opened his mouth and howled as the unspeakable pain seared through him. Skin started to laugh. 'You really should have insured your hands,' he chuckled. 'I'm sure your stupid old pop must have done.'

It was all Luke needed to galvanize his will. With a scream of fury that startled even him, he wrenched his left arm from Speed's loosening grip, knocked the lighter to the ground and somehow—in the mad confusion that followed—wrestled himself free.

'Grab him!' bawled Skin.

Luke stumbled down the path, fear driving him beyond the pain it cost to run. Skin and Daz thundered after him, their hands grasping at his body but unable to catch hold. Somehow he pulled a few feet clear but they were still close behind, shouting abuse as they ran. He drove himself on, desperate to put more distance between them. Normally he would have outrun them easily but he knew he would not be able to this time. He was too badly hurt and he didn't have much energy left. He'd never make it all the way to the village before they caught him. But there was one place he could go that was safe. If he could just get there. He glanced over his shoulder. They'd fallen back a little but he was tiring now, and hurting badly. He put on speed somehow, desperate to reach the old oak, and suddenly there it was, just ahead. He threw himself against the trunk and started to scramble up. Never in his life had he climbed so recklessly, so painfully, so frantically. He knew he had only seconds to get clear. Any moment now and the hands would be clutching for his feet.

He was just in time. He was only inches clear when the other two arrived. They jumped and tried to catch him, then, realizing it was useless, stopped and glowered up at him. 'Don't think this is going to help you,' snarled Skin. 'Because it won't. I told you. This is the day you're going to die.' Luke hauled himself over the first branch and sat there, breathing hard. Speed stumbled into the clearing, his face bathed in sweat. Skin turned to him at once. 'Right, you and Daz know what to do. So get going!' Daz set off at once across the clearing but Speed remained, as though unwilling to move. 'Get going, Speedy!' Skin shouted. 'Don't waste my time!'

'Come on, Speedy!' Daz called over his shoulder. 'Come on, Speedy boy!'

Speed glanced up at the tree and Luke saw a look of anguish in the boy's face; but then he was gone. Skin turned back to Luke with a sneer. 'We thought you might try something like this so we made a few preparations.' He threw himself on the ground and cushioned his head on his arms. 'I'll just relax here till the others get back. If I were you, I'd do the same. Make the most of your last few moments on earth.'

Luke started to climb. Whatever Skin had planned for him, he had no wish to stay here on the lower branches and be jeered at. His body was aching, his head pounding, his right hand throbbing where the flame had scorched it, and the last thing he wanted to do was climb, but the tree-house beckoned and should at least offer him some kind of security and privacy. He clambered painfully up, Skin still shouting the occasional taunt from below, but at last he reached the tree-house. He hauled himself over onto the planks and lay back, out of sight of the ground. Skin had fallen silent now and all he heard was the sound of rustling leaves. He pulled out the mobile, dialled and waited.

'Come on, Mum,' he murmured. 'Pick up the phone, pick up the phone.' But there was no answer. She was probably out looking for him, he thought. She must know by now that he hadn't turned up at school. Mrs Searle would have rung for sure. The answerphone cut in. He waited for the tone, then gabbled a message down the line: 'Mum, it's me. I'm in trouble. I'm in the forest, up in the tree-house of the old oak, and Skin's down below, and the gang are after me. They want to kill me. They can't get up the tree but they've got something planned. I don't know what they're going to do. Get a ladder or something probably. Please help. I can't escape.' He thought for a moment. 'Only, Mum—don't come on your own. It might be dangerous. Get Roger to come with you, or Bill Foley or someone. Don't come on your own, OK?' He paused. 'I love you, Mum.'

He rang off and tried to remember the other number he wanted. He'd only ever rung it once to pass on a message from Mum and he wasn't sure about all the digits. To his relief, he was right first time; but it was another answerphone: 'Hi, this is Roger Gilmore. I'm not here at the moment but leave a message and your number after the tone and I'll get back to you.'

He waited for the tone, then gabbled a second message: 'Roger, it's me . . . Luke. I'm in the forest, up in the tree-house of the old oak. Please help. I'm in danger.'

He rang off and lay still, listening for noises below. There were no voices or sounds of activity. He decided not to keep looking down to see what Skin was up to. He felt sure he'd hear if they brought a ladder or tried to climb the tree. In the meantime, he'd keep himself hidden. If he showed himself, that would only encourage further taunts. He wondered whether to call the police but quickly dismissed the idea. Once they were involved, there was no telling what other things would come to light. They'd question everybody, and that meant they'd probably find out about the break-ins, and maybe even about Barley, and Mrs Little's involvement; and somehow, though he knew Mrs Little had done wrong, he had no wish to be the cause of her prosecution—not, at least, until he'd had a chance to speak to her himself. With any luck Mum would turn up with Roger Gilmore or Bill Foley or someone else and he'd be able to escape without the police ever getting involved. It still didn't solve the problem of what to do about Skin and the gang but if the boys knew some of the adults in the village were on to them, they might just ease up a bit and maybe the whole business would fizzle out in time.

But he still had to get out of this present predicament.

Every part of him now seemed to ache. He tried to ignore the pain and put his mind on other things, and found himself thinking of Barley. Where was she now, he wondered? On the motorway, probably, heading for home. He pictured her face and wondered whether she ever tried to picture his. Probably not. Probably, if she thought of him at all, it was of his voice, or maybe the music he had awoken in her. She would never know how much she had awoken in him. He closed his eyes and looked into his brow for the pool of blue he so often saw there, with its glowing golden rim and the white star in the centre, but all he saw was a dark, empty space; and he lay there for some time, watching it, as in a kind of fitful dream. Skin's words came back, not from the forest floor, but from the darkness of his mind: 'This is the day you're going to die.'

Then he caught the smell of smoke.

Thick, acrid, clinging smoke. He opened his eyes in horror, scrambled to the edge of the tree-house and looked over. Down on the ground were Skin and Daz grinning up at him. At the base of the tree was a burning pile of twigs, branches, leaves; and, heaped on top, some old car tyres. Skin held up a can for him to see. 'Diesel oil!' he shouted with a demented laugh. 'Specially for you!' In a panic Luke started to claw his way down the tree. He knew there was not a second to lose. Diesel oil and car tyres—he'd have two minutes at the very most before the smoke killed him. But already his eyes were smarting and he was struggling to breathe. He started to cough, wheeze, dribble as the smoke swirled around him. He tried to hold his breath but it was no good. He was gasping, spluttering, retching as the fumes engulfed him. He felt spasms round his lungs as he gulped in the hideous black mist; and as he gulped it in, so it seemed to gulp him in, too, as though

it were a huge, gobbling mouth. He was barely halfway
down the tree and he knew he wouldn't make it to the
ground before the smoke overwhelmed him. He started to
haul himself out along the nearest branch, desperately
seeking the outer edge of the tree. If he could just get away
from the main body of the smoke, perhaps he could find
some clear air; but he was losing consciousness now.
Somehow he forced himself on, his head whirling, his
lungs burning, his eyes narrowed to slits, on, on, towards
the end of the branch. He heard the manic screams of
Skin and Daz below, the crackle of branches and twigs,
the eerie hiss of burning tyres; he heard his own hoarse,
hacking, drowning voice. He crawled on, choking,
choking, choking, as the smoke went on billowing over
him in an all-enveloping cloud. The end of the branch was
upon him and he crawled out through the foliage to the
tip, his mind swimming, his heart faltering, his mouth
aching for air. But there was no air, only more black,
murderous smoke. The bough started to tip under his
weight. He clung on somehow, dangling high over the
ground. Far below him, the forest floor was spinning, but
he saw the two boys running away and another shadowy
figure racing into the clearing.

And then he fell.

He remembered no jolt, only a feeling of lightness and
a realization that he was no longer falling but flying. He
was moving upwards, as though through the tree itself,
and the tree had become a tunnel, and the tunnel a place
of sound, and he could hear the deep omnipresent roar
that was now so familiar to him; and he went on flying
through the tunnel, upwards, upwards, past the lower
sections of the tree, past the middle and upper sections,
until finally he broke clear and burst out into the sky. It
was only then that he looked back. He saw Skin and Daz
running away through the forest; he saw the great tree,

259

maimed by smoke; and there, to the side of it, his own body sprawled on the forest floor. Someone was bending over it but he could not tell who it was. He felt presences around him now, Dad's presence and the presences of others he seemed to know from times long past, all crowding round him, urging him, it seemed, to turn away from the forest, away from the figures on the ground, away even from his own body; and so he turned and saw a light opening before him. It was like a star, a star so vast and radiant and blissful he never wanted to be apart from it. He heard a voice speak, as if from the star itself.

'Are you ready to die?'

He stared into the light and saw it grow brighter and brighter and brighter; and it seemed to him there could be no greater beauty than this. He made ready to fly towards the star; then the voice spoke again.

'Or are you ready to live?'

He looked back at the body on the ground, and the figure bending over it. He thought of Mum, and Miranda, and Mrs Little, and Barley, and Mr Harding; and Dad, with him here, now, as he had always been; and all these other loving presences he had somehow forgotten, though they had not forgotten him. He would never feel alone again. He listened for a moment to the music of the light, then turned to the star again.

'I'm ready to live,' he said.

29

He opened his eyes to find himself lying on his side on the forest floor. His vision was blurred but he could see Roger Gilmore's worried face looking down at him against a background of leaves, smoke, and sky. His chest felt as though someone had been pounding him with a hammer. He was still coughing and wheezing and the taste of smoke in his mouth made him want to retch. He tried to speak but could only croak.

'Easy,' said Roger. 'Too early to talk. Save your strength. You need everything you've got right now.' He patted Luke on the hand. 'I'm going to phone the emergency services.'

'Mum,' he spluttered. His voice sounded so rough and strange it seemed to belong to someone else. 'I want . . . Mum . . . '

'I know,' said Roger. 'I'm going to phone her, too. I just—' A grimace of pain crossed his face and he broke off for a moment. 'I just haven't had a chance to ring anyone yet. Things happened so quickly.' He gave another grimace and turned away, as though he wanted to disguise it. Luke tried to work out what had happened but it was hard to think straight. He wished the ache in his chest would go, and the foul taste of smoke in his mouth and lungs, and the blurred vision; and he wanted Mum here. He wanted her here so much. Over to the right he could see black smoke still billowing up from the base of the tree. The tyres were still hissing and tongues of flame still licked over the branches and twigs. The trunk of the old oak was turning black. He started to cry.

'I know,' said Roger, following his gaze. 'It's probably going to die, I'm afraid. There's not many trees'll survive that kind of treatment. There's nothing we can do about it, or the fire. It's a job for the professionals. That Skinner boy sprinkled diesel oil all over the tyres. I saw him running away with the empty can in his hand. Stupid kid! He must be out of his mind. Still, the police can deal with him, and his mate.' Roger pulled out his mobile. 'Right, Luke, I'm going to ring for the paramedics, and get a message passed on to the police and the fire people.'

'And . . . and . . .'

'And then I'll ring your mum. It's OK. I know. You just rest for a bit and try to get some strength back.'

Luke listened as Roger made his call, his voice faltering now and then as he explained what had happened, and gave directions on how to find them in the forest. It was obvious he was in great pain and that even talking was difficult, but eventually he was finished and it was time to phone Mum.

'I'll ring her at home first,' said Roger, dialling the number, 'and if she's not there, I'll try her mobile.'

'I've . . . I've . . . got her mobile.'

'OK.' Roger said nothing more. He was already listening for an answer at the other end. But to Luke's dismay, Mum was still out. There was a pause, then he heard Roger leaving a message: 'Kirsti, it's me. Luke's had a fall. He's OK, but he's going to have to go to hospital. I've called the emergency services and they're on their way. We're in the forest at the moment, by Luke's oak tree, and the paramedics are going to have to park the ambulance as near as they can get it and then come the rest of the way on foot. There's been some trouble with Jason Skinner and Darren Fisher as well and the police are going to be involved. If you get back in the next few minutes, by all means come to the forest, but otherwise I suggest you go straight to the hospital and meet us there. I'll leave my mobile on so you can ring me when you get a chance. And Kirsti—' He paused. 'Don't worry. It'll be all right. I'll speak to you later.'

Luke waited until Roger had rung off, then murmured: 'Thank you.' And Roger looked back at him and smiled. They fell silent, Luke still lying there, Roger kneeling beside him. The fire burned on, though the fumes did not reach them. It was only then that Luke realized with a start that Roger must have moved him. He could not possibly have landed here. He would have fallen much closer to the fire but he was now several yards back from the tree, almost in the middle of the clearing. No doubt Roger had moved him because of the danger from the smoke. Luke wondered what carrying him had cost the man in terms of pain. When they were both well again, he would make sure they talked about this. There was lots he wanted to say. But for now silence seemed most comfortable for both of them. Against it, and the ever-present hiss of burning tyres, he could hear wood pigeons calling, and, further off, the sound of a cuckoo. He thought back to what he'd seen in that magic place of light; what he'd felt, what he still felt, even in this present distress. He thought of those he loved and those who loved him, both here and in that other place; and it seemed to him suddenly that he had been on a long, long journey to somewhere deep inside himself, but that now he was coming back.

The paramedics arrived, a man carrying a large green rucksack and a long flat board, and a woman holding a red, cylindrical case. They knelt down quickly.

'Hello, Luke,' said the man. 'I'm Tom. This is Mary.

She's just going to have a quick word with Mr Gilmore while I take a little look at you, OK? Now, first of all I'm going to put my hands round your neck and keep them there for a bit. We want to make sure you haven't done anything nasty to your spine. Can you feel as though anything's broken anywhere?'

'No,' Luke murmured.

'Good. OK, lie still.'

Luke felt Tom's hands close gently but firmly round his neck. A few yards away the woman called Mary was talking to Roger in a low voice. He didn't catch the words but the conversation was soon over and he found himself surrounded by the three of them again. Mary glanced at her colleague. 'Mr Gilmore says he moved Luke from where he landed.'

'Wish you hadn't done that, sir,' said Tom.

'I had to,' said Roger. 'He'd have been overwhelmed by the smoke if I'd left him where he fell. I knew it was a risk but I had no choice.'

'I see,' said Tom, his hands still firmly round Luke's neck. 'Well, in the circumstances, I'm sure you did the right thing, and with any luck there won't be anything to worry about. But to be on the safe side, I think we'll strap Luke onto the board and make sure he can't come to any harm. But let's give him some oxygen first.'

Luke felt an oxygen mask pressed over his face. An immediate sense of relief came with it after the hideous taste of smoke in his mouth.

'That should help a bit,' said Mary. 'OK, Luke, what we're going to do now is put a collar round your neck and get you strapped up nice and secure on the board. You'll feel a bit funny but we need to do that as a precaution. All right?'

Luke said nothing. He was still savouring the relief that the oxygen was giving him. The paramedics attached the collar, then, holding him rigidly straight, rolled him carefully onto the board and strapped his body and head down.

'OK, Luke?' said Mary.

Luke murmured some kind of assent.

'Now what we're going to do next,' said Tom, 'is run a few checks on you before we take you back to the hospital. Mary's going to fiddle around with all the little toys we've brought with us, and I'm going to give you a quick physical examination. Nothing remotely nasty, I promise, so don't worry. Just make some kind of noise if I touch anything that really hurts, OK? Otherwise, lie still.'

And Luke was happy to do so. Even with the help of the oxygen, he felt as though all energy had drained from him. He thought again of that magic place, that other world. He had not felt tired there. He had felt full of life. But he was spent now.

The paramedics set to work. Mary fitted a clip to his finger, attached a drip, stuck patches on his chest with leads running to a portable monitor, then squeezed a blood pressure cuff round his arm. While she was doing this, Tom checked him over, calmly and methodically, talking to his colleague as he did so. 'No breaks, as far as I can tell. Lots of scratches on the arms and legs, probably from scrambling over the tree. Some nasty cuts and bruises on the face. More round the ribcage. Looks like he's been punched and kicked pretty badly. And there's a bit of a gruesome burn mark on his right palm that I don't like the look of.' He glanced at Luke. 'Falling from a tree isn't the only thing that's happened to you lately, is it?' He touched Luke quickly on the hand. 'It's all right, lad. No need to answer that. This isn't the time for talking.'

So Luke said nothing, and the paramedics continued their work. Roger sat close by, silently watching, one hand on Luke's shoulder; and the smoke went on rising from the base of the tree. Luke closed his eyes and felt his mind drift away—he did not know where it went. After a while, he heard Mary speak.

'OK, Luke, we're ready to take you to the hospital now. We're going to do some precautionary tests on you. Chest X-ray, blood samples, check your airways, that kind of thing. Now, just to let you know, there may be a bit of noise and commotion on the way back. Tom's just spoken to the other emergency services and they're not far away now so we could well bump into them as we carry you to the ambulance. But it's nothing for you to worry about.'

'How will the fire people get their gear through the forest?' said Roger.

'They've got special smaller vehicles and equipment for jobs like these,' said Mary. She turned quickly back to Luke. 'And the police will be coming out as well, Luke. But no one'll be asking you any questions until we've checked you over at the hospital and made sure you're absolutely OK.'

'He is going to be OK, isn't he?' said Roger quickly.

'He's going to be fine,' said Mary. 'Thanks to you. But we need to get him to hospital now and take it from there. And you need to be looked at, too, Mr Gilmore. I'm sorry I didn't have a chance to give you a proper check-up just now, but we needed to get Luke sorted first, obviously.'

'Don't worry about me. I'm fine.'

'You're not fine at all, sir, with respect, but thank you for being so patient. It's just that we do have to keep a really close eye on Luke for the moment. But if you can make it with us to the hospital, we'll get you looked at properly.'

'Sure.'

'All right,' she said. 'Let's get Luke away.'

And they carried him off through the forest, the oxygen

mask still over his face. On the way, as Mary had predicted, they saw the first of the vehicles from the fire service bumping along one of the narrow tracks over to the right. It was followed a few minutes later by a second. Luke barely glanced at them as they passed. All he could think of was that they were too late to save his tree. But at least his head was starting to clear a little and it was a relief to see as they moved further away from the fire that the blue of the sky was no longer tainted by black smoke. He thought of what Mary had said to Roger: 'He's going to be fine. Thanks to you.' He wasn't sure what that meant, but he was starting to guess. He looked up at the man he had once hated, now walking painfully beside him; and took his hand, and held it tight.

The hospital bed felt warm and soft after the forest floor. He relaxed into it, enjoying the late-afternoon sun that filtered in through the window and relieved that the checks had revealed nothing unpleasant. He was also glad that Roger was being taken care of at last. But what was most wonderful of all was that Mum was here now; and they'd been left alone.

'You're going to be fine,' she said, smoothing his brow. 'A few days' rest here, they said, and you should be able to come home.'

'Where were you when I rang and left the message?'

'Out looking for you. Driving round the lanes. I got a phone call from Mrs Searle this morning to say you weren't in school so I went off to try and find you. She told me the other boys in the gang hadn't turned up either so I guessed you must be with them. If it had just been you on your own, I'd have gone straight to the forest but I didn't think Jason Skinner and the others were as keen on trees as you are, so I decided to try some of the other

places they've been seen hanging around. I've been just
about everywhere—apart from where you actually were.'

'I'm sorry,' said Luke. 'I'm really sorry. I've messed
everything up.'

'No, you haven't.' Mum put a hand on his shoulder.
'It's nothing we can't sort out between us.'

'How's Roger? Have you seen him?'

'Not yet, but I've spoken to him on the phone.'

'Is he all right?'

'He's in a lot of pain but he's going to be OK. You're
the one everybody's been worried about, including Roger.'

'What happened to him? And how did he get hurt?'

'Don't you know?'

Luke shook his head. 'I don't remember anything about
the fall from the tree. Well, I remember falling and then
. . . ' He thought back to that magic place again; and his
brief, precious time there. He remembered that well
enough and always would. But this was not the moment to
speak of it, if indeed he ever did. 'I don't remember
much,' he said eventually.

'Well, I'll tell you what happened,' said Mum. 'I got
back to the house, heard your answerphone message, and
Roger's, and rang Roger straightaway on his mobile. You'd
reached the hospital by that time and he was about to go
in for an X-ray, but we had a brief talk. He said he was on
his way to his workshop when he heard the phone ring
in the bungalow, so he went back to check who it was. He
missed speaking to you by about two seconds but he
listened to your message and then rushed straight off to
the forest. And he said he was just in time.'

'He was,' said Luke, thinking back to those desperate
last moments up in the tree. 'I remember this figure
running forward as I fell. But I couldn't see who it was
because my head was spinning and there was all this
smoke and stuff.'

'It was Roger,' she said. 'He said he saw you about to slip from the end of the branch, so he ran forward to try and catch you or cushion the impact somehow. It was a reckless thing to do with you falling from such a height. He must have known he'd hurt himself. Anyway, he managed to get between you and the ground so that you fell on top of him. But he paid the price. He dislocated a shoulder, broke his right wrist, and cracked two ribs. He must have been in agony, especially during the things he did next.'

'What do you mean?' said Luke, though he sensed the answer.

'He had to move you,' Mum said. 'He didn't want to because of the danger of causing you spinal injury, but he knew he had to take the risk because the smoke would have killed both of you if you'd stayed at the place where you landed. So he carried you back across the clearing away from the fire. God knows how he managed it with his injuries and all the smoke and everything. Anyway, he put you down, he said, and then checked your pulse— and found you had no heartbeat or chest movement. Nothing.' She put a hand over her face. 'You'd gone, Luke. You'd gone. You'd slipped away.' She wiped the corner of her eyes with her hand. 'If Roger hadn't been there and known what to do, you wouldn't be alive. He gave you mouth to mouth, then chest thumps—which must have been excruciating for him with a broken wrist—and then more mouth to mouth, and more chest thumps. He had to repeat the process several times, he told me, and he was terrified you weren't going to make it. Then—thank God— you came back.'

She pulled out a handkerchief and wiped her eyes again. Luke reached out and took her hand. 'I'm sorry, Mum,' he said, close to tears himself. 'I'll put it right. I'll—'

'It's OK, Luke. It's OK. We're going to be fine.'

'I'll put it right.'

'We'll both put it right. It's nothing we can't fix.' She blew her nose. 'Nothing . . . we can't fix.'

They fell silent, as though they each needed a few moments to calm down; then Mum spoke again.

'One strange thing I must tell you: I was just driving out of the village on my way here—well, racing, more like—and I bumped into Bobby Speedwell in the lane. I nearly didn't see him but I happened to look in my wing mirror and I saw him running after me, frantically waving. So I stopped. I didn't want to—I was desperate to get to the hospital—but I pulled over anyway. He was in a terrible state, out of breath and coughing and crying his eyes out and God knows what. I could hardly get any sense out of him at first but in the end he blurted out the story of what they'd done to you. You can imagine what that made me feel like. Oh, Luke . . . ' She squeezed his hand tight. 'Thank God you're safe now. I can't bear the thought of—'

'It's OK, Mum.'

'What they did to you . . . I mean, it's just . . . it's just . . . '

'It's OK, Mum. I'm all right now. I promise. Tell me about Speed.'

'Oh, him.' She collected herself again. 'He just said he'd run off before the other two started the fire because he couldn't bring himself to go through with it. He said they'd been planning the thing for a couple of days. They'd had the tyres and the diesel and everything hidden away not far from the old oak and they were intending to light a fire the very next time you went up the tree.' She shook her head. 'I just can't believe they could even think about doing something like that.'

'But what did Speed do after he ran away?'

'Came haring over to our house, he said, and rang the bell, but of course I wasn't in.'

'So what then?'

'He told me he'd spent the rest of his time rushing round the village looking for me. He didn't appear to have the brains or the presence of mind to phone the police or tell his mother or someone—that was obviously asking too much of him—but I suppose I feel a little better disposed towards him than I might have done. Anyway, I left him in the lane and came on here.'

Luke looked away towards the window and took a long, slow breath. So Speed had had a crisis of conscience. Perhaps that was no great surprise. But he didn't imagine the other two would feel any remorse; probably just disappointment that they hadn't managed to kill him. He wondered what they'd say to the police; and what he himself would say to the police. The time for questions would soon be here and there were things to tell; and perhaps things to conceal. He didn't know what he would say if they asked him about Mrs Little. He felt Mum squeeze his hand again and looked back at her.

'It's going to be all right, Luke,' she said. 'You just need a bit of time. I'll give Miranda a ring and tell her what's happened, and obviously let Mr Harding know you're not going to be playing in the concert.'

'No!' he said, slightly startled at the force of his own reaction.

Mum looked at him. 'No to what? No to Miranda or no to the concert?'

'No to the concert. I mean, yes to the concert. I want to play.'

'Luke, it's only a few days away. You're not well enough.'

'I want to play,' he said firmly. 'I know I'll be OK.

271

And I promised Miranda I'd accompany her with her flute piece.'

'Somebody else can do that. Melanie or Samantha or someone.'

'But I want to do it.'

'What about your injuries? Your bruises? Your right hand, for God's sake!'

'It's OK. I can still move my fingers.'

'But what about the burn?'

'It's not too bad to stop me playing.'

'You haven't tried yet.'

'It'll be fine. And the rest of me's all right, too. I just ache a bit, that's all.'

Mum frowned. 'Well, I'm not sure you'll be up to it. You might think you will be but don't be surprised if you find yourself too tired or out of sorts to want to play when the time comes. Tell you what—I'll explain to Mr Harding what's happened and tell him to be prepared for you not to play. Then, if by some miracle you feel able to, it'll be a bonus.'

'I'll be OK for the concert.'

'We'll see.'

'I will be.'

She shook her head, but with a smile. 'You can't be that bad if you're arguing with me and being stubborn.' She leaned forward. 'But no arguments about me phoning Miranda, I presume?'

'Definitely not.'

Mum picked up her mobile phone. 'And now that I've finally got this thing back from you,' she said, with a mock-baleful look, 'I can ring her right away.'

'No, you can't.'

'What do you mean?'

'You're not allowed to use mobiles in hospital. They interfere with the equipment.'

'Oh, God, of course. I'd forgotten.' Mum frowned and put away the mobile. 'But they've got a special phone here for patients, haven't they?'

'Yeah. Only you've got to ask the nurse to bring it.'

'OK. I'll go and get her.' Mum stood up and turned towards the door. But Luke caught her by the hand again.

'Mum?'

She stopped and looked back at him.

'Yes, love?'

He studied her face for a moment, then spoke again.

'You are going to marry Roger, aren't you?'

30

Three days later he was home. He walked in through the front door, while Mum put the car away in the garage, and stopped in the hall. For some reason he felt as though he had been away for years. He looked around him, feeling vulnerable, yet also strangely at peace, though how these two things could exist together he didn't know. What he did know was that he felt different. Something had happened, beyond the shock of the fire and the fall from the tree. Something had happened that had changed him; and in that sense he realized that he was right: he had been away for years.

Two years, in fact. Or, to be precise, two years, one month, and six days. But why was he still counting? Couldn't he cherish his memories without notching up every day, every hour, every moment that he had run away from life, being focused only on death? It was time to move on; and Dad could still come with him. Indeed, Luke sensed him here again, close by even now, just as before. He closed his eyes and whispered into the silence. 'I can feel you. I can't see you but I can feel you.'

The front door clicked and he turned round to see Mum standing there. He walked over and hugged her. She chuckled. 'I can't get over this.'

'Over what?'

'I've had more hugs from you in the last few days than I normally get in a month.'

'You're not grumbling again, are you?'

'Do I sound like I am?'

They both laughed, then Mum spoke again. 'I forgot to tell you—I've invited two guests for dinner tonight. It was maybe a bit rash of me. You might not be up to it. So don't worry if you're too tired. I can always—'

'Mum.' He looked at her. 'I'm fine. I keep telling you. I'm fine for seeing people tonight and I'm fine for the concert tomorrow evening.'

'Hm,' she said. 'I'm still not sure about the concert.'

'I really want to do it. It's important to me.'

'Well, it's certainly important to Miranda,' said Mum. 'She's so keyed up about it, isn't she? I guess I can't stop you but you must promise to tell me if you suddenly feel you don't want to do it. You can always drop out at the last minute. Everybody'll understand.'

'I won't need to. I'll be fine.'

Though, in truth, he was exhausted. He knew he would need lots of rest before he started to feel fully well again. But he also knew that he had to play at the concert, not just for Miranda but for himself. It was as though there was something he had to say—he didn't know what—and music was the only way he could say it.

'So who's coming?' he said, as brightly as he could. 'No, wait—let me guess. Roger and Miranda?'

'Yes. Miranda's coming earlier with her flute, just in case you're up to practising. But remember, Luke, if you're too tired—'

'Mum.' He put a finger on her lips. 'Will you stop worrying?'

'Probably not.' She smiled and kissed him. 'But I promise to try.'

Miranda arrived just before seven. She had her flute in one hand and a bunch of red peonies in the other. She smiled at Luke and he smiled back, feeling for some reason slightly awkward. But it was good to see her. Mum came out of the kitchen. 'Miranda! I thought I heard the bell only I wasn't sure because I had my head in the oven.'

'You're not that desperate, are you, Mrs Stanton?'

Mum laughed. 'Not quite. What beautiful flowers.'

'They're for you. From the garden.'

'That's very kind of you. I'll just go and find a vase for them. Would you like a drink? I've just made some orange juice.'

'That would be lovely. Thank you.'

'I'll bring it through. You two go on ahead.'

Luke led the way to the music room and closed the door behind them. Miranda walked into the centre of the room, staring round at the busts of composers, the shelves of music, the piano, the old harp by the window. 'I love this room,' she said. 'It's got your father's personality stamped all over it. And yours.'

'Not sure about mine. Dad's, yes.'

'No, yours, too. Definitely.' She nodded towards the old harp. 'Did your father ever play that?'

'Not really. He just saw it in a shop collecting dust and bought it because he felt sorry for it. He used to strum it occasionally but it wasn't really his thing.'

'So doesn't anybody play it?'

'No. Bit of a waste really. I mean, I know it's pretty ancient but the tone's still good. We ought to sell it, I suppose, but we rather like having it there, even though it never makes any music.'

Mum appeared with the glasses of orange juice, left them on the piano, and vanished again. Miranda waited until the door was closed, then looked round at him. 'Are you all right?' she said.

'Fine.'

'You look really tired.'

'No, I'm OK. Honestly.'

'And are you still OK about playing at the concert? I mean, I really will understand if you—'

'Miranda, listen—I'm OK. All right?' He smiled at her. 'You're starting to sound like my mother.'

'Thanks a lot!' She pushed him over to the piano and sat him down. 'Come on, then. Let's practise.' She raised her flute, then suddenly lowered it again. 'Oh, my God!'

'What's wrong?' he said.

'I didn't bother bringing any music. You've got nothing to follow.'

'It's OK. I can remember it.'

'Oh, sorry.' She gave him a wry look. 'I was forgetting you're a genius.' She raised her flute again. 'Come on, then.'

'Hang on,' he said. 'If you didn't bother bringing any music, does that mean you've learnt your part?'

'Don't sound so surprised.'

'I'm not surprised.'

'Yes, you are.'

'No, I'm not. I'm not surprised at all.'

She looked away suddenly. 'Luke?'

'Yeah?'

'I've really worked hard at this.'

'I know you have.'

'I don't want to let you down at the concert.'

'You won't.'

'And I don't want to let myself down either.'

'You won't. You'll be great. Come on, let's give it a go.'

They started to play and he quickly found she was right. She really had worked hard at the piece. 'The Dance of the Blessed Spirits' flowed from beginning to end without a single hitch. There was a long silence afterwards that neither seemed willing to break. Then Miranda shrugged.

'Do you think I took the middle section too fast?'

'No.'

'What about—'

'Miranda.' He looked up at her from the piano. 'It was great.'

'You're just saying that to be nice to me.'

'I'm not just saying it. I mean it. It really sounded good and you're getting a great tone from the flute now.'

'Thanks.' She looked down. 'That means a lot, coming from you. And Mr Harding said the same thing, so maybe you're not just making it up.'

He laughed. 'Are you ever going to learn to take a compliment?'

'Maybe.' She smiled at him. 'Do you think we ought to play it again? I mean, just once more to make sure we—'

'No.' He shook his head. 'We don't need to. Just remember how you played it here and then try and do the same tomorrow. It won't be the same—it never is—but it'll be good. And it might even be better.'

'Did your hand hurt while you were playing?'

'What—you mean the burn?'

'Yeah.'

'It hurt a bit to begin with, when I had to stretch, but it sort of eased up as I got going and by the end I'd forgotten about it. It's not a problem.'

Miranda rested her flute on top of the piano and took a sip of orange juice. 'Wasn't it weird about that girl?' she said.

He'd been wondering when she would mention Barley. The story had been all over the news. His own story had been covered, too, briefly and with no names mentioned, but Barley's had dominated every headline. The mentally-handicapped girl, missing for over two years and now dramatically rediscovered in the forest. *Lost and Found*,

278

one headline said. *Babe in the Woods,* said another. Some boffin on the radio had called Barley *Perdita,* whatever that meant. All speculated on the identity of the anonymous young woman who had phoned Mr and Mrs Roberts and guided them to the place where Barley was to be found. He smiled inwardly. So in the eyes of the media he had become an anonymous young woman. Well, he didn't mind that, if it kept his name secret. He hadn't expected Mr and Mrs Roberts to shield him like this—he had even thought they might try to trace him—but they had left him alone, it seemed, and he was grateful for that. Perhaps they really had understood that he was Barley's friend. He remembered Miranda's question and said: 'Yeah, it was weird.'

'And to think you were going through your ordeal in the forest at around the same time the girl was there. Is that spooky or what? You didn't see anything, did you?'

'No.'

'I suppose you couldn't have if she was found over by the Bramblebury end and you were the other side of the forest. Weird, though.'

'Yeah.'

He heard a ring at the front door and a moment later Mum's voice calling: 'Luke? Can you get that? I've got my hands full!'

'OK!' he shouted back. He walked with Miranda through to the hall and opened the front door. Roger was standing there, his right arm in plaster and held up by a sling. In his free hand he was holding a bunch of red peonies. Miranda saw them and gave a chuckle.

'Lovely flowers, Roger.' She walked up to him and gave him a kiss on the cheek. 'Do you want me to take them?'

'Thanks.'

'And can we sign your plaster?'

'Only if you're gentle with me.'

'I promise I will be.'

'It was Luke I was worried about.'

Mum came out, holding some oven gloves, and caught sight of Roger. 'That was good timing,' she said. 'It'll be ready in about five minutes.'

'Roger's brought some flowers, Mrs Stanton,' said Miranda. 'See?' And she held up the peonies.

'Oh—' said Mum. She and Miranda exchanged the faintest of smiles.

'I hope you like them,' said Roger. 'I picked them from the garden.'

'I do,' said Mum quickly. 'They're lovely. Thank you.' She gave Roger a kiss, then took the flowers from Miranda and turned back towards the kitchen. 'Excuse me if I dash. I've got something about to boil over. Luke, get Roger a beer, can you?'

'OK.' Luke fetched a beer, poured it into a glass and hurried back to the hall where Roger and Miranda were still standing, deep in conversation.

'Thanks,' said Roger, taking the glass. 'How do you feel?'

'OK.' Luke yawned. 'But I seem to have done nothing but sleep for the last three days.'

'Well, you needed to. And the hospital were right to keep you there that long. They were great, weren't they?'

'Yeah.' Luke yawned again. 'How about you? How do you feel?'

'Like I've been trampled on by the entire England rugby team but, apart from that, pretty good.'

'You were so brave,' said Miranda. 'Trying to catch Luke when he fell.'

'No, I wasn't,' said Roger. 'Just too stupid to get out of the way. I had no idea he weighed so much.'

Miranda laughed, but was quickly serious again.

'Roger?'

'Hm?' said Roger, sipping his beer.

'Is Luke's tree really going to die?'

'It's not my tree,' said Luke.

'I always think of it as your tree,' she said.

'So do I,' said Roger. He smiled at Luke, then turned back to Miranda. 'I'm sorry but I'm afraid I can't see it surviving. The fire people did a fantastic job to stop the blaze as quickly as they did, especially when you consider they were dealing with tyres soaked in diesel and it was a really difficult spot to get to. The trouble is, quite a bit of the bark got burned off, especially down the side where the boys stacked most of the tyres, and it's bark that protects a tree. So I just don't know if this one's going to make it or not. It might but, to be honest with you, I don't fancy its chances. I'm really sorry.'

Luke thought of the tree—his beautiful tree, his friend—and bit his lip. It seemed so terrible that it had to die. He wished someone would change the subject. Fortunately Roger did exactly that. 'Luke, I meant to ask you, has anybody spoken to you yet about what happened in the forest?'

'What? You mean journalists?'

'No, not journalists. You shouldn't be bothered by them. They're not allowed to say very much at this stage and they're certainly not allowed to mention any names as all the people involved are fourteen. I don't know whether things'll change when the case comes to court but hopefully you'll be left alone. No, I meant the police. Have they spoken to you yet?'

'Yeah, quite a bit. They came into the hospital and asked me lots of questions and stuff. Went on for ages, but it maybe just felt that way because I was so tired. And the inspector guy's phoned me here, too.'

'When was that?'

'About an hour ago.'

'What for? More questions?'

'No, he said it was just to make sure I was all right.'

'That was nice.'

'Mum reckons it's just normal police follow-up.'

'Still nice.'

'Yeah. Did they speak to you?'

'Briefly,' said Roger, 'but I'm not the main story. You are. That's why they've spent so much time with you. Anyway, did it go all right?'

Luke thought of his interview with the police—what he'd said, what he hadn't said—and chose his words just as carefully now. 'It went fine. I told them the thing with Skin and Daz had been building up for some time and just came to a head. I'd been hanging around with them for a couple of years but I was trying to break free because I realized they were having a bad influence on me. They started to pick on me and it just got nastier and nastier, and in the end they decided to give me a bad time.'

'A bad time?' Roger stared at him. 'Is that what you call it? Jason Skinner tried to kill you. You do realize that?'

'Yes, I do.'

'And you told the police that, I hope.'

'Yes, I did.'

'It wasn't a harmless bit of fun, Luke. He put tyres on the fire. He doused them with diesel. He knew what he was doing. It was attempted murder, never mind all the other stuff they did to you beforehand. That's why he's in custody. And you'll probably have to testify against him.'

'I know. I've been told.'

He thought of Mrs Little. He'd said nothing about her or The Grange or Barley to anyone, and he was still in two minds whether or not to do so. The old woman had done wrong; he knew that. But there was still so much he didn't know about her part in Barley's life. He had to speak to her first, before he could decide what to do. And what he said would also depend to a large extent on the stories Skin and the others gave.

'What's happened to Darren Fisher?' said Miranda.

'Same as Skinner,' said Roger. 'In custody, and rightly so. Both boys deserve everything they get. Torture and attempted murder—that's some package. I imagine Jason Skinner will get the heavier sentence, since he was the instigator, and he's also got more previous convictions than Fisher, I gather.'

'Far more,' said Luke.

'And Bobby Speedwell?' said Miranda.

'Not so sure what they'll do about him,' said Roger. 'Hard to gauge. He might not cop it too badly. He did run off and try to get help, after a fashion. We'll have to wait and see what the court decides.'

Again Luke thought of the old woman, closeted away with her photographs and her grief, and now, no doubt, her fear of what would happen to her. She must have heard the news; and she must be wondering what he had told the police. He pictured her sitting room with the great grand piano, now silent again after its brief flutter of life. Miranda spoke again.

'Roger?'

'Yes?'

'Can I sign your plaster now?'

'Sure, but remember—'

'I'll be gentle. Have you got a pen?'

'Sorry, no.'

'There's one here,' said Luke. He handed her the pen from the telephone pad and she started to write on Roger's plaster, one hand underneath his arm to support it as her other hand pressed down. Luke looked over her shoulder at the message that appeared.

Roger, get better soon because we need lots more sculptures from you!
Love, Miranda xxx

She handed Luke the pen. 'Your turn.'

'OK.' He took the pen, supported Roger's arm the way Miranda had done, and tried to think what to write. There were lots of things he wanted to say, but in the end only one word came out. So he wrote it three times.

Thanks, thanks, thanks.
Luke

Roger glanced down at the message. 'Any more thanks and I'll get worried you're starting to like me.'

'I wouldn't go as far as that,' said Luke.

'Oh, that's a relief.'

And they all went in to dinner.

31

Even at eleven o'clock the next morning the curtains of The Grange were still drawn. Luke stood uneasily outside the gate. He knew he should be at home practising for the concert tonight; but this had to be done. There was no avoiding it. He didn't like the drawn curtains, though. They made the house look more forbidding than ever; and why were they still closed at this time of the morning? He thought of the old woman, of her loneliness and unhappiness, and her fear, no doubt, that she would be more hated than ever for what she had done and, of course, in trouble with the police. He glanced at the curtains again, then hurried to the door and rang the bell.

There was no answer. He waited for a couple of minutes, then rang again. Still no answer. He tried a third time. Again, no response. There were no sounds from within the house. Perhaps she was away. Perhaps, fearing arrest, she had gone to ground somewhere. He wandered round to the back of the house and looked up. The study window was open and so was one of Mrs Little's bedroom windows. She appeared to be at home; but why the drawn curtains everywhere?

His unease grew. He moved closer to the sitting room and started to search the windows for a gap in the curtains. There was one, close by. It was only small but it would do. He peered through and gave a start. Mrs Little was sitting in the armchair, facing away towards the other side of the room. All he could see was the back of her head above the top of the chair. Next to her, on a small table, was a glass and a bottle of pills tipped on its side.

He felt a rush of alarm. What had she done? He tapped on the window. The figure did not move. He tapped more loudly; still the figure did not stir. He felt panic rising within him and started to bang the window as loudly as he could. 'Mrs Little!' he shouted.

No response. No movement.

He looked frantically about him. What should he do? He had to ring for help, get an ambulance. But this time he had no mobile with him. He shot another glance up at the study window. He'd done it before—he could do it again. If he climbed in, he could use Mrs Little's phone and he might just be in time. He ran over to the drainpipe, scrambled up it and clawed his way in through the window, then raced along the landing and down the stairs to the sitting room.

Only to find Mrs Little standing before him.

He stopped, breathing furiously and startled at the sight of her. Her eyes were glazed and she looked unsteady on her feet. She seemed to have aged ten years since he last saw her. And she was broken. He could see that at a glance. Yet her power to surprise him had clearly not deserted her. She looked him over with the expression of contempt he knew so well.

'No, I haven't taken an overdose,' she said drily. 'I've just got a headache.'

He stood there before her, unsure what to say. She watched him in silence for a moment, then turned back to the armchair without another word, and slowly sank into it. He walked over to the other armchair and sat down opposite her, his eyes on hers. She spoke, in a weary voice.

'The police called yesterday. I'd been expecting them.'

'I didn't tell them anything,' he said quickly. 'About Barley, I mean.'

'I know you didn't.' She looked at him steadily. 'They didn't come to see me about Barley.'

'What? I mean—pardon?'

'They didn't come to see me about Barley. They didn't even mention her name.' She leaned her head back against the top of the chair. 'They came to see me about you.'

'Me?'

'Yes.' She paused. 'I'm sorry about your accident.' She didn't sound sorry, but he said nothing and she soon went on in the same flat tone. 'They called because one of your so-called friends claimed you'd broken into my house two nights in a row to try and steal a jewellery box.'

Luke stiffened. He'd said nothing whatever to the police about The Grange and they hadn't mentioned it either, whether in the interview at the hospital or since; and the officer in charge had phoned him again only this morning to see how he was, without a word about The Grange or Mrs Little or Barley or anything. Indeed, they'd spent most of the time talking about football. Mrs Little went on.

'I told them I don't have a jewellery box. I said I'd seen the other boys watching the house in a suspicious manner on more than one occasion but that no one had broken in. I said I'm up most nights because I don't sleep well—which is true—and I'd have heard if anyone had got in, certainly two nights in a row. They asked me if I knew you and I said yes. I said you came here occasionally to play the piano for me and we'd become good friends so you were hardly likely to break into my house in the dead of night. They asked me if anything had been stolen and I said no. But of course that was a lie. You did steal something.' She looked at him hard. 'You stole an identity bracelet. And you stole knowledge of my former life that was not yours to take.'

'I know,' he said. 'I'm sorry. That was wrong.' There

was a heavy, oppressive silence. He frowned. 'Why didn't you give me away?'

'Because you didn't give me away,' said the old woman. 'Oh, I know my crime's greater than yours. Greater by far. And if the truth ever comes to light, you'll no doubt be quickly forgiven and elevated to the status of local hero, and I'll be vilified even more than I am already. And I expect I'll deserve it.'

'But some of what you said was true,' he said. 'I mean, about me coming round to play the piano.'

'I suppose.'

'And the bit about us being friends?'

'We both know that's not true.'

He bit his lip and looked away. 'What did the police say when you told them I hadn't broken in?'

'They said they never really thought you did. It was only one of the boys who mentioned The Grange and the box, and I gather his account was so garbled and inarticulate they didn't really take it that seriously. But they felt they ought to follow it up. The other two boys apparently denied all knowledge when asked.'

Luke stroked his chin. It was easy to work out who had said what. Speed would have confessed the truth in his rambling way; Skin and Daz would have denied everything, including, no doubt, the torture and the attempted murder. He would have to testify against them all when the time came and presumably push the line he had given to the police. But he was still unsure whether or not he should expose Mrs Little. She had done wrong—that was clear—yet somehow he could not see her as a criminal. However it had come about that she had taken Barley from her parents, she had obviously loved the girl desperately, and been loved in return; and she was a woman who he knew had had very little love or friendship in her life; and now that Barley was gone, she would probably have even less. He hesitated, then said: 'I'm glad you told the police we were friends.'

She sniffed. 'You'll feel differently about that when I'm gone.'

'Gone?' He gave a start. 'You don't mean—'

'No, no, no,' she said testily. 'I don't mean I'm going to top myself, though I'm sure most of the village would love it if I did. I mean I'm going back to India. I've still got one or two contacts out there who aren't yet dead.'

'Do you have to go?'

'Yes.' She looked around her. 'Every room in this place makes me think of Barley now.' Her voice softened slightly. 'All I ever wanted, apart from Bill, was a child. And when Bill died, I thought my life was over. I didn't want to marry anyone else. I knew I couldn't love anyone else. And who in their right mind could ever love me?'

'Bill did.'

'Bill was different!' she snapped. 'He never saw me as ugly, for some reason. But everyone else did. No other man's ever shown the slightest interest in me, not that I wanted interest. But I did want a child. I wanted a child so much, even though children find me repulsive, too, just like men. But Barley never saw me. She never knew what I looked like.'

Luke stared at the careworn face before him and suddenly realized that though he had once seen her as ugly and repellent, he no longer did so. He wasn't sure why. Mrs Little went on.

'I found her just over two years ago when she was eight years old. I'd come back from India a few weeks before and had moved into The Grange. But I'd driven to Hastings to go to my brother Ralph's funeral. He'd been my last surviving relative in the world, though we never got on. He was a complete waster and he'd never forgiven me for

289

the fact that our father left me so much money and him so little—knowing my brother would only gamble it away within a year. Anyway, Ralph lived on his own in Hastings and died just after I returned from India. I had a car in those days, though I've got rid of it since, so I drove to the funeral. I was on my way back, driving down a deserted lane just outside Hastings, when I saw a young girl lying in a ditch. I pulled over and went to look. It was Barley, unconscious. She had bruising down one side of her and a nasty head injury, though she was still alive. It looked like a hit and run accident.'

The old woman threw a defiant look at him. 'What I said to you the other day about my being a nurse out in India was true. I've had a lot of experience with accident victims.' She paused, still watching him, as though she needed reassurance that he believed at least some of her story. But he said nothing and, after a moment, she went on. 'I managed to resuscitate her—just—and then checked her over as best I could. She was starting to moan a little and she was moving her limbs and even wriggling around a bit. She didn't seem to have broken anything but she was obviously in a bad state. I decided to try and drive her to the nearest telephone box so I could ring for an ambulance. So I picked her up, got her in the car and we drove off down the lane.'

Her face darkened. 'It was then that the idea came to me. God knows, I knew it was wrong and I kept pushing it away. She wasn't mine. She was hurt. She was in shock. I didn't realize at the time that the head injury had blinded her. But as I drove off I just started to feel this . . . this link with her.' The old woman looked away as though she couldn't face him. 'I'd put the front passenger seat back and she was lying on that, and as I drove along, I was stroking her to try and comfort her, and she just . . . she just suddenly reached out her hand to me. She was so trusting. It was like she knew me, and I felt . . . I felt . . . I don't know what I felt.'

'So what happened?'

'I took her home with me,' she said simply. 'I know. It was wrong. It was totally wrong.' Some tears had appeared round the old woman's eyes. She wiped them away brusquely, as though they were a blemish. 'You can't know what it's like to want a child that much. It's like . . . it's like an ache. It eats away at you inside. Every child you see just makes it worse. And seeing this little girl, so loving and trusting, I . . . I just couldn't help myself. I got her home without anyone spotting her, took the identity bracelet away from her and called her Natalie, and started to nurse her. And I knew I could do that, with my training and experience. She started to get better and we developed a bond and at first it was wonderful. It was like meeting the child Bill and I could never have.'

'But she wasn't yours,' he said. 'You shouldn't have taken her.'

'I know that!' She glowered at him. 'Do you think I didn't realize what I was doing? I felt terrible guilt in the beginning, especially when the story broke and her parents went on the news and pleaded for her. That was how I learned what had happened. There'd been some mix-up between the mum and dad. He'd thought she was looking after the child and she'd thought he was, or something like that. Anyway, somehow or other Barley must have wandered off and ended up in this lane and then got knocked over and left there. For me to find.' The old woman's voice softened again. 'I was meant to find her. I was meant to find her.'

'But not to keep her!' Luke shook his head. 'It was wrong! You know it was!'

'I know, I know.' More tears appeared round Mrs Little's eyes. 'And I did think of trying to get her back to her parents, especially after their appeal on television. But the weeks went by, then the months, and I was growing so fond of her, and she was growing fond of me. We were together all the time. It was wonderful. I'd hold her and comfort her and feed her, and help her find her way round the house, and . . . I just got so close to her.' Mrs Little pulled out a handkerchief and dabbed her eyes with it. 'She was so beautiful. I didn't dare take her out anywhere, for fear of people finding out, so I kept myself to myself and discouraged people from coming to the house. That wasn't difficult. I'd been doing that for years anyway because people hate me so much. But Barley didn't hate me. She loved me. And that was enough.'

'It was still wrong,' he muttered. 'You know it was. Didn't you think about what her parents were feeling?'

'They let her go!' The old woman glared at him. 'They let her go wandering off on her own!'

'Because of a mix-up.'

'It was still their fault! I thought, they don't deserve to keep their daughter if they can't take proper care of her!' But Mrs Little's anger died as quickly as it had come. She slumped back in the chair. 'I know, I know, I know.' She wiped her eyes again. 'I should have got her back to them somehow. Especially when she started to show the first signs of real distress.'

'Real distress?'

'Yes.' The old woman took a deep breath. 'For the first few months, once her physical injuries cleared up, I was able to soothe her and calm her down. She seemed to have such a happy, trusting nature. I knew she was in a state of terrible confusion, especially not being able to see or express her thoughts very clearly, but I always managed to calm her. And the story eventually died down in the news when the police hunt yielded nothing. But then she started to have tantrums. She'd cry all night and just not stop. She didn't scream. I think if she'd done that, someone would have eventually heard from outside and guessed someone else was here with me. The screaming only started after you played the piano to her. But the tantrums were still bad enough. I tried to find a way of calming her but it was no good, and over the next year or so, things just got worse. Then, not that long ago, the man came to tune the piano.'

He looked over at the great instrument, its warm surface bathed in sunlight. Mrs Little took another deep breath. 'That's another thing I told you the other day that was true. About the effect the piano had on Barley. But you've seen that for yourself. I didn't realize how powerful it was until that day because she'd never heard the piano before the tuner came. I'll never forget how she changed. He finished the tuning and started to play, and she just froze. Her mouth dropped open. It was as if she was a different person. It was a part of her I'd never seen before. But there was a down-side because after the man had gone, she started to bang the keys of the piano as though she was trying to recapture the music. Which of course she couldn't. And that upset her even more.'

Luke went on staring at the piano. The little girl's history was becoming clear at last, just as Mrs Little's was. As for his own part in this business—well, that was becoming clear, too. 'So I was just a means to an end,' he said. He didn't try to keep the bitterness from his voice. 'Someone who could play the piano for Barley and calm her down just so you could keep her locked up here a little bit longer.'

There was a silence, then the old woman answered. 'I didn't just want you to play for Barley.'

'What do you mean?'

The old woman paused again. 'I wanted you to play for me, too.'

Their eyes met, and there was something in hers that quelled the anger in his own. She stood up, with something of an effort, and shuffled over to the cabinet by the window, then pulled out what appeared to be a tattered piece of sheet music and hobbled with it over to the piano. 'Have you never wondered,' she said, 'why I should keep a piano in the house when I can't play?'

'I asked you once and you just bit my head off and told me it was none of my business.'

She ignored this and went on. 'I can't play a note but I've had a piano ever since the end of the war: Wherever I've lived, I've kept a piano. Always a good instrument, like this one. And I've always kept it tuned. Out of respect.'

'Respect?'

'For Bill.' She put the sheet in the holder. 'He was a good pianist. Not in your league, I'm afraid—nowhere near that—but good. He used to play to me for hours and I'd sit there and just listen and dream. I'd never heard music like the pieces he played, and there was one that was always my favourite. I haven't heard it for over sixty years.' She turned suddenly towards him. 'Would you play it for me now?'

'What is it?'

'Come and see.'

He stood up and walked over to the piano, and looked down at the music in the holder. Étude, Opus 2, No. 1, by Scriabin. 'I don't know this piece,' he said, his eyes running over the notes.

'It's beautiful.' She sounded almost girlish with excitement for a moment. 'And Scriabin was only about your age when he wrote it. Did you know that? Bill told me. Imagine—composing such wonderful music when you're so young.' She looked at him suddenly with an expression that was the closest thing to affection he had ever seen from her. 'And it's right that you should play it. One brilliant young man performing the work of another.'

He looked away, too embarrassed to answer.

'Will you play it for me, then?' she said.

'If you want me to.'

She moved to the side of the piano to make room for him and he made to sit down. Then stopped. Something had caught his eye, something he'd forgotten about, something that moved him more than he could express. There before him, still etched in dust on the piano top, was the star that Barley had drawn with her finger. He stared down at it and felt a rush of emotion; and for a moment, it was almost as though Barley and not Mrs Little were standing here next to him, waiting for him to play. He closed his eyes and looked into the darkness of his brow, searching for the tiny white star against the gold and the blue; and there it was, brighter than he had ever seen it. Was it this, he wondered, that had enveloped him as he sped towards death? And did Barley see it, too, in her own inner world? He heard Mrs Little's voice.

'Are you all right? You've got your eyes closed.'

He opened them again and found himself staring at the picture of the multicoloured star on the wall. He turned and looked back at her. 'Yes, I'm all right,' he said. He studied the music in front of him for a moment, then, on an impulse, said: 'I'll play this for you. I'll play it with all my heart. But not here.'

'Where, then?'

'At the concert in the village hall tonight.'

'I'm not going to the concert.'

'But why don't you?' He looked at her eagerly. 'You'll enjoy it. I'll play it there for you. I promise.'

He saw the dismay on her face but forced himself to go on.

'I only want to play it for you there. At the concert.'

The dismay he had seen now turned to anger. 'You can do what you bloody well like,' she snarled. 'I won't be there.'

'Please come.'

'Why should I? No one in the village wants me there.'

'I want you there. We're friends. You said so yourself.'

'To the police. To get them off your back. And mine.'

'I still want you there.'

'Well, I won't be there!' she barked at him. Her face was now fierce with rage. 'You just don't think, do you? You say come to the concert as though it's as easy as breathing. Have you never asked yourself why I don't like to go out?' She lowered her voice, but it was like a muted scream. 'Have you any idea what it's like to be as ugly as I am? No, of course you haven't. How could you? You're young. You're good looking. You've got the world at your feet. You're never going to have a problem making friends, finding a partner. You don't know what it's like to see people look the other way, see the revulsion in their faces. Or have them call you names. Or make fun of you. Or just ignore you, as if you're some disease they might catch just by seeing you.'

'Bill didn't think you were a disease.'

'Bill was different!' She was shouting now. 'I told you that before! Bill was a one-off! There's never been another man like Bill and there never will be!' She broke off, scowling, then went on in a low, angry mutter. 'Why do you think I loved having Barley here so much? Because she couldn't see me. She was so . . . trusting and loving and . . . and happy. She never knew how ugly I was. If she had done, do you really think she'd have let me anywhere near her?' The old woman snorted. 'She'd have reacted the same way all children do. She'd have run a mile before she let me touch her.' Mrs Little snatched the music from the holder. 'If you won't play the music here, you won't play it anywhere. And you can clear off now!'

He found himself trembling. He couldn't believe he'd misjudged the situation so badly. 'I'm . . . I'm sorry,' he stammered. 'I only wanted to . . . to encourage you to come out. I . . . I didn't mean to upset you so much. Let me play the piece now.'

'Go away!'

'Please. I'd really like—'

'Clear off! I don't want to see you!' She turned away, her mouth twitching, her eyes dark and fixed. Luke watched, desperately trying to think of some way to make amends.

'Mrs Little?' he said. She didn't speak, didn't look at him. He tried again. 'I'm really sorry.' Again no answer. He thought for a moment, then said: 'Mrs Little? I'm . . . I'm still going to play the piece at the concert tonight. We've got all the Scriabin études at home. Dad bought the lot, so . . . ' He paused. 'I'm going to spend the afternoon practising it and I'm going to play it at the concert tonight. Whether you're there or not. But I . . . I really hope you will be.'

'I won't,' she muttered, still looking away.

'And . . . and . . . '

'Just go,' she said.

'And I'm really sorry. For what I just said. It was wrong. And . . . if you ever want me to come over and play for you again . . . any piece you like . . . I'll be really happy to do so.'

She spoke again, in a voice close to tears. 'Just go.'

He felt guilty and angry with himself. His intentions had been good enough but it had been stupid trying to force her to come to the concert. He should have known she'd never agree to it and now he'd fallen out with her completely; and he hadn't wanted that to happen. Because no matter how unusual their relationship was, and no matter how many doubts he still harboured over her actions with Barley, he had come to realize that he felt a curious bond with this woman, even a kind of protectiveness towards her. Why this should be so, considering how little she appeared to like him, he did not know. Perhaps it was that brief stolen glimpse of her former life that had done it; or the softness in her voice when she had spoken to Barley. He would probably never find out. She had drawn the curtains across her life once more and he doubted whether she would ever open them again.

One thing he was decided upon: he was going to play the Scriabin étude at the concert tonight, come what may, and tomorrow he was going to go back to The Grange, apologize to Mrs Little again, and make another attempt to persuade her to let him play the piece to her on her own piano, as she'd originally requested. He spent the afternoon practising, glad to have the house to himself with Mum over at Roger's. It was strange how comfortable he felt about that now. She'd wanted to stay with him, to make sure he was all right, but he'd insisted she go, telling her he was fine and that he wanted to be alone to practise. The latter was true; the former was not. He wasn't feeling fine at all. He was feeling vulnerable again, though he didn't understand why. Perhaps it was the business with Mrs Little that had upset him; or perhaps a touch of delayed shock. Yet he sensed it was something deeper, and the more he played, the more the feeling of vulnerability grew, as though something inside him was opening up and a part of him that had long been hidden was being exposed.

He played on and tried to lose himself in the music. At least the Scriabin étude was a beautiful piece. He hadn't heard it before but he was glad to now. There was a yearning to it, a beseeching quality, especially in the opening phrases. He played it again and again, each time a different way, and each time growing to love it more; and as the music flowed, he thought of Mrs Little listening to Bill as he played these very same notes. Perhaps she had stood by him at the piano; or sat in an armchair; or lain back on the floor, listening. He tried to picture the young couple he had seen in the photograph outside the pub: the young happy woman, the young happy man. Then the picture faded and he saw the old woman's face again, dark with her loss.

He broke off, close to the end of the piece, feeling angry with himself again for his behaviour earlier, and still vulnerable and edgy. He also felt hot. He looked towards the window. It was closed and the afternoon sun was bright upon the sill. Just beyond, the leaves of the wisteria were moving in the breeze. He stood up, walked over to the window and opened it, and stood there for a moment, watching a robin on the bird table; then, feeling somehow called back to the music, he returned to the piano, played through the final notes of the étude, and sat there in the silence. Why was he feeling so restless? It made no sense. He should be feeling happy. Everything had turned out all right. He was still a bit weak and aching and groggy after all that had happened, but he hadn't come to any serious harm; Skin and Daz and Speed weren't going to bother him any more; things were OK with Mum and everything was sorted with Roger. And Barley was safe.

Barley.

The girl who was lost and found. He wondered where she was right now; what she was doing, thinking, feeling; what sense she made of the world she could not see, with no clear memories and a mental age so far below her years. He pictured her face as it had been when he carried her through the forest. She had seemed like a sprite in his arms, as trusting as if he were a father or mother or brother. He closed his eyes and looked into his own darkness and confusion, and for a strange moment felt almost as though he, too, were blind. And maybe that's it, he thought. Maybe I am blind, in a way. Blind and confused and unable to remember clearly where I come from or to understand very much of what my life's all about. And maybe, like Barley, I've just got to trust and hope someone will pick me up and carry me part of the way.

'Where are you now, Barley?' he murmured. 'And what are you doing? Do you remember me?' He started to play 'Reverie'. 'The way you remembered this piece?' He played on, seeing her face still in memory, then he caught a sound nearby. He stopped playing and listened. For a moment there was silence, then he heard it again: it was a whisper of strings so faint he was surprised it even reached him. He strained his ears to hear the sound more clearly, then suddenly realized where it was coming from. He turned towards the window.

It was the harp, the poor old instrument that nobody ever played; yet the breeze was playing it now, through the window he had just opened, stroking the strings with invisible hands. The murmuring sounds fell over him. They were so light they seemed to caress him. He looked towards the window, as though Barley were sitting there and not the harp. 'Speak to me through music, then,' he said. 'And I'll do the same back.' And he played 'Reverie' through to the end; and in the silence that followed, heard the harp tinkling still. Then the sound died, too, as the breeze dropped. He sat at the piano and listened to the silence again. 'Lost and found, Barley,' he murmured. 'You and me both.' And he looked back at the music in the holder.

Étude, Opus 2, No. 1 by Scriabin. Strange to think that this piece had been composed by a boy about his own age. He stared at it for a moment, trying to picture that young Russian lad, now long dead, scribbling these very notes; then, to his surprise, he found himself playing again. Not this piece, nor 'Reverie', nor anything by anyone else, but the unfinished tune that had come to him before, the one he always thought of as Dad's tune. It came upon him like a fragrance and he simply followed it on the piano, wondering what would happen this time when it broke off, mid-bar, as it always did. Normally it simply started again from the beginning; but this time, as that moment approached, he sensed that it would continue. He did not know, as note followed note, how the tune would go, yet he could feel the unexpressed melody hanging from him like a pendent fruit; and suddenly it fell. The old melody ran out and the new melody ran in, hesitantly at first, then with greater strength until finally it was a river of sound that would not be stopped. He played and played, not knowing where the music was leading him or what it meant, only that it seemed both to drain and quench him at the same time. He played on and on until the music mastered him and he knew nothing else.

32

The village hall was full twenty minutes before the concert was due to start, apart from some put-up chairs Mr Harding had left at the back for late arrivals. Even Miss Grubb was there, though she was known to be completely tone deaf. But Mr Harding's concerts of pieces performed exclusively by his pupils had been part of village life for so many years now that hardly anyone seemed to want to miss them. Luke sat at the front next to Miranda, with Mum and Roger on the other side of him, and glanced round every so often to see who was there.

The young kids—who made up the bulk of the performers—filled the first four rows, together with their parents, and there was an excited twittering and twanging and tweaking of instruments. Mr Harding, looking outrageously flamboyant in a blue suit and pink bow tie, moved comfortably down the aisles at the side, chatting to all he passed. He looked relaxed and happy and was clearly determined that his last concert was going to be a good one.

There was no sign of Mrs Little.

Not that Luke had expected it, though he kept checking, so much so that Mum and Miranda eventually asked him why he was constantly turning round. He shrugged and didn't answer, but he kept on looking, surreptitiously. It was foolish, he knew. She would not come to a public gathering like this. Even the lure of the music Bill had played to her all those years ago would not be enough. She would no doubt be at home right now, planning—like Mr Harding—her departure from the village. He was going to Norfolk, she was going back to India. Both were moving on; and, in a strange way, he felt he was, too. Not leaving, like they were—on the contrary, there was nowhere else he wanted to be right now but here—but moving on nonetheless, as though he were leaving not a place but a state of mind that was no longer relevant to what he now was. Yet in spite of all this, he still felt vulnerable.

And surprised. People were being so kind to him. He had expected a certain frostiness, at least from certain members of the village, who—he knew—disapproved of the way he used to behave with Skin and the gang. But there was none. Even Miss Grubb had asked him how he was. The story of what had happened had obviously raced round the village and he found himself the target of nothing but kindness and concern. And curiosity—especially from Miranda.

'Why won't you tell me?' she said. She read aloud the last entry in the programme again. *'Luke Stanton: Personal Choice*. So what piece are you going to be playing?'

She was watching him playfully and he knew her goading expected nothing serious in return.

'You'll just have to wait,' he said.

'Oh, go on.'

'I'm not telling you.'

'I won't let on.'

'I know you won't. Because you won't know what it is.'

'I thought we were friends.'

'So did I.'

Miranda looked across at Mum. 'Mrs Stanton? What's he going to play?'

'I don't know,' said Mum. 'He won't tell me either.' She slanted her eyes at Luke. 'As long as it's not too long.

There are so many young kids here tonight and they'll only get bored if it goes on for ages.'

'How about Beethoven's "Hammerklavier" Sonata?' put in Roger. 'That only takes about an hour. If Luke plays it quickly, we could be away by midnight.'

'I'm not listening to any more of this,' said Luke.

Mr Harding was making his way up to the stage. The babble of talk died away and there was an expectant silence. Luke glanced round one final time but the old woman was not there. He frowned. It was foolish to keep looking like this. He would not do so again. He tried to put his mind on the music he was to play. Mr Harding cleared his throat.

'Good evening, ladies and gentlemen, boys and girls. I hope no one's too hot. It's a bit of a stuffy evening so we're going to leave the door at the back open. And that'll also make sure that anyone in the square who's been trying to avoid hearing the music won't be able to do so.'

There was a polite laugh from the audience.

'And if we play really loud, we might even be able to drown them out in The Toby Jug, which I've been trying to do for years.'

Another polite laugh from the audience. Mr Harding winked at Mr and Mrs Davis, who were sitting a few rows behind Miranda and Luke, and went on.

'Anyway, since this is my last concert—I can hear you all weeping at the thought, or is it just a sigh of relief passing round the hall?—I'm hoping it's going to be a good one. And I'm very confident that it will be. We've got some wonderful performers and every one of them has worked extremely hard, and I'm very proud of all of them. But you didn't come here to listen to me drivelling on so let's get straight on with the music. Please welcome, with the first piece of the evening, Naomi and Jenelle, who are going to play "Sheep May Safely Graze".'

Amid great applause, the two little girls walked nervously forward with their recorders, climbed up to the stage, and the concert started. Luke watched and listened and tried to relax, but found that he could not. It wasn't just nerves for his own performance; it was more than that. It was this restlessness again, as though something was calling him. He didn't know what. One by one the performers made their way up to the stage and played their pieces: Geraldine and Ben and Suzy and Sally and Zoe and John and Andrew and Sian and Sarah and Peter—and so it went on; and in between pieces—in spite of his resolution—he checked the hall behind him.

But Mrs Little was not there.

The evening drew on and the time approached for his piece with Miranda, after which he was to remain on stage for his solo performance: the final event of the evening. He felt Miranda fidget beside him and caught her eye. She looked pale and tense; even frightened. She leaned over suddenly and whispered into his ear. 'I won't let you down, Luke. I promise.'

'I know you won't.'

'I'm so . . . nervous.'

'You'll be fine. Just do your best.'

She pressed her lips tightly together and stared fixedly at the stage where George and Joe were performing their guitar piece. Luke reached out and gave Miranda's hand a squeeze, then let go. She looked round and flashed a smile at him; then the applause broke out again. The boys on stage bowed and high-fived each other, then made their way back to their seats. Miranda picked up her flute and turned to Luke. 'OK,' she said. 'This is it.'

She led the way up the steps to the stage. Luke walked over to the piano, sat down and waited for her to turn to him and give the signal that she was ready. To his right, the audience felt like a single body, moving restlessly this

305

way and that as it waited for them to start. He took a deep breath. He wished the people would stop fidgeting but the young kids, especially those who had been performers, were now stirred up with excitement. He sensed, too, a buzz of attention on him. Miranda turned to him and he saw the anxiety in her face. He smiled to try and reassure her. She was so obviously keen to start and get this thing over with that he was beginning to worry she might race through so quickly that she ruined it.

But his fears turned out to be groundless. The audience settled and the moment she started, he knew she was going to be fine. 'The Dance of the Blessed Spirits' turned out to be exactly that. As the notes cut through the air, he felt as though all the dancing spirits he had sensed in that magic world of light and sound were here again, moving endlessly around them. Miranda played on, not as well as she had done earlier, but better, much better. The silence at the end was the richest music he had ever heard. When the applause broke out, he found himself so moved that he stood up at the piano and clapped, too, clapping Miranda, whooping and grinning at her and whooping again; and she grinned back, her face flushed with happiness. He joined her at the front of the stage and they bowed together, the applause still thundering in their ears.

'Thanks, Luke!' she said, as they straightened up. 'Thanks, thanks, thanks!'

She gave him a smile, then made her way down the steps and back to her seat. The applause died away. He walked slowly back to the piano, sat down and propped open the music in front of him, and tried to compose himself, aware of the silence deepening around him again, and of the eyes upon him. Even the young children were still now, as though the mood of excited expectation touched them, too. And he knew the expectation was great. As the star turn, this was meant to be something special. Yet as he stared at the music in front of him, he found that all he could think of was that young woman he had seen in the photograph, that plain, unprepossessing young woman; and the young man who had loved her, and died.

He turned to the audience and spoke. 'This piece is by Scriabin. It's his Étude, Opus 2, No. 1. I'd . . . ' He looked down, then up again at the sea of faces watching him. 'I'd like to dedicate it to a friend of mine, and . . . her husband. Thank you.' He reached out his hands to play, anxious to finish with words and lose himself in the music as quickly as possible, just like Miranda; but before he could touch the keys, he caught a movement at the back of the hall. He stopped, his hands poised, and stared; and the audience, following his gaze, turned and looked, too.

Mrs Little had appeared in the doorway. The timing was so perfect he felt certain she must have been standing just outside the hall for a while, listening through the open door but out of sight of those inside. She looked awkward, embarrassed, scared, and seemed, as the eyes fixed upon her, on the point of turning and hurrying away; but Mr Harding stepped forward, a smile on his face, and motioned her to one of the put-up chairs at the back. She walked over to it amid total silence and sat down, still clearly strained and uneasy under the scrutiny of the others; then her eyes met Luke's.

He smiled at once, desperate to do something to make her feel welcome. He could sense her terror, her need for reassurance. It seemed to reach out to him like the pleading first notes of the Scriabin étude. He tried to imagine how much courage it had taken for her to come here like this, and found he could not. But there was one thing he could do to help. He started to play; and at once everything changed. The hall—with Mum and Roger and

307

Miranda and Mr Harding and Miss Grubb and all the children and parents—seemed to empty. Where before he had felt surrounded by people and even by spirits, now suddenly it was as though there was no one in the hall but himself and the frightened old woman sitting at the back. He kept his eyes on the music, the keys, the shiny wooden face of the piano, anything except her; yet his mind was on her. He sensed her sitting there, rigid, watching, listening. She was crying, too. She had started crying from the very first note. He could feel it, as though the tears were his own. He played on, as if in a dream, and the music rolled out of him, as though someone else was playing it. As the final notes died away, he looked up at last and saw her sitting there, watching him, a quiet smile on her face. Beside her stood a young airman looking down at her, a hand resting on her shoulder.

The applause was so loud it startled him. He stood up, slightly shaken by what he had seen and by the response, and made his way to the front of the stage. Miranda and Mum and Roger were on their feet, clapping. Others stood up and clapped, too. He glanced at Mrs Little and saw her clapping, the quiet smile still on her face, but he knew her mind was turned away somewhere deep inside her. The young airman had vanished from view, but Luke knew he was still beside her. The applause grew louder and louder. Luke bowed to the audience and started to make his way down the steps to the floor. Everyone seemed to be standing now and shouts of 'Encore!' resounded round the hall. Mr Harding stepped forward and took Luke by the arm, then looked round at the audience and motioned for silence. For a moment, no one took any notice and the applause and shouts continued, then gradually the clamour died away. Still holding Luke by the arm, Mr Harding spoke to the hall.

'Well, everybody, I hope you've all had a good evening. And now I'm sure you're all dying to get back to your homes and—'

Shouts of protest broke out, though they were good-natured shouts since everyone was used to Mr Harding's quirky sense of humour. He waited for a pause in the noise, then gave a look of mock-surprise. 'I'm sorry, was there anything else?'

'Encore!'

'Encore!'

'What was that?' he said. 'Did someone say "encore"?'

'Encore, you old buzzard!' shouted Bill Foley, also on his feet.

Mr Harding motioned for silence again.

'Well, I'd love to play an encore but I don't think I'm really up to it. However . . . ' He looked round at Luke. 'I wonder whether we could persuade Luke to . . . er . . . ?'

The clamour broke out again all round the hall. Luke caught Miranda's eye and saw her smiling at him. The hall fell quiet again at last and Mr Harding went on.

'Luke, it's obvious they're going to tear me to shreds if I don't oblige and much as I realize there are quite a few people here who'd probably be delighted to see that happen, I wonder whether—as a favour to a friend—you could dig around in the locker and pull out another tune for us?'

Shouts from the audience broke out again.

'Go on, Luke!'

'Another one!'

'Another one!'

He caught Miranda's eye again, and Mum's, then turned back to Mr Harding and nodded. The shouts turned to a cheer as he made his way back up to the stage and over to the piano. Mr Harding waited for him to sit down and then turned back to the audience and motioned for silence again.

'Well, everybody, we'll make Luke's encore the final piece of the evening. I'm sure he needs a rest and if he doesn't, I certainly do. But before we bring things to a close, I just want to say a big thank-you to all the usual suspects who've helped me organize this final concert— they know who they are—and, of course, most of all the performers for being so wonderful and such good fun and for playing so well. I hope you'll all write to me when I'm in Norfolk because I'm going to be very lonely living there with just my sister, who's even more ancient and out of touch with reality than I am. So please write and I promise to answer everybody. I might even learn how to use e-mail one day. Who knows? Stranger things have happened. So once again—'

But his words were interrupted by the massive form of Bill Foley bustling forward. 'I'm cutting you off for two reasons,' said the farmer briskly. 'Firstly, if I don't shut you up now, you'll ramble on for the rest of the evening and the sight of you standing there much longer— especially in that suit—is more than any sane person should have to bear. And secondly, we want to hear Luke play again.'

There was a cheer of agreement from the audience.

'And thirdly—'

'Pardon me,' said Mr Harding, 'but I thought you only had two reasons.'

'Well, I've remembered a third.' Bill Foley cleared his throat. 'Thirdly, Suzy's got something she wants to say.'

Five-year-old Suzy stepped forward, still holding her recorder in one hand. In her other was a card and a slim package. Mr Harding bent down gravely and waited for her to speak.

'We want . . . ' She bit her lip, her eyes searching the

floor. 'We want to say thank you for . . . ' She bit her lip again, then rushed through the rest of her speech. 'For doing the concert and the music and this is a present.'

And she pushed the card and package into Mr Harding's hands and turned back to her mum as quickly as she could. Mr Harding straightened up with a smile. 'Thank you so much, Suzy. I don't know what to do next.'

'Open the bloody thing!' bellowed Bill Foley. 'And get on with it so we can hear Luke!'

Laughter broke out all around, then silence quickly fell again as Mr Harding opened the envelope and read it. He looked up at the audience again. 'Thank you,' he said. 'Thank you all so much. I don't know what to say.'

'Lost for words!' said Bill Foley. 'That's got to be a first!' There was more laughter, then a lull while Mr Harding opened the package. Bill Foley's voice boomed out again. 'For those of you who don't know what we got him, it's a cheque to buy the computer he's been trying to avoid getting all these years, and a CD with the software he needs to go on the Internet and get himself an e-mail address.' He turned to Mr Harding. 'So there you go— Norfolk ain't going to be far enough away for you to escape us.'

More cheers broke out, and laughter, and clapping. Mr Harding waited for the noise to die away again, then said: 'Thank you. Thank you all so much.' And he turned once more to the stage. 'Luke, my dear boy—one final piece to send us all home.'

And without any words of introduction Luke started to play. He had been trying to think, while the talking was going on, of something he could play that even Mr Harding, with all his vast musical knowledge, had never heard before; and the choice was obvious. What else could it be but the piece that had flowed through him in the music room at home? Dad's now finished melody—music

311

that no one, not even Mr Harding, could possibly know. This time, as he played, he saw no pictures at all, only the twisting contours of the music as the notes danced through his fingers like the shifting sand-patterns on the metal discs that the old man had talked about. He played on, no longer in a hall or a village or a country or a world, but in a firmament of stars and spheres, sounds and shadows, and more beauty than he could contain.

The music ended and silence reclaimed the space; and this time remained.

No one broke it. No one moved. He sat back, breathing hard, sweat racing down his face and hands, then turned and stared out at the faces as though he were seeing them all for the first time. And the faces stared back, in silence; almost in awe. It was Suzy who broke the spell, in a whisper to her mother so loud that even Miss Grubb at the back must have heard it.

'Why aren't we clapping like we did last time?'

At which point everyone began to clap. It started slowly, then quickly built up. By the time Luke had reached the front of the stage, they were on their feet and cheering. He bowed, feeling more awkward and embarrassed than ever, then stepped down to the floor. He was enveloped at once, and not only by the children. Everyone seemed to want a piece of him. He was kissed, cuddled, shaken by the hand and slapped on the back; Sian and Zoe wanted his autograph; Bill Foley told him he wasn't as big an idiot as he'd once thought. Even Mrs Speedwell came up and congratulated him, then turned and hurried away before Luke could thank her. Mum and Roger and Miranda held back, waiting for the crowd to disperse, and gradually, to Luke's relief, it did, and they came forward, followed by Mr and Mrs Davis, and Mr Harding.

But one person stayed apart. Luke watched for the old

woman, even as the others covered him with praise. She had not left the hall but she had stood up and was looking towards the door. He wished someone would go over and talk to her but no one did. He tried to catch her eye. She mustn't go. She mustn't just leave. If she went, he'd run after her.

'You were very mysterious, Luke,' Miranda was saying. 'All that talk about a dedication and stuff.'

Luke stiffened. The old woman had turned and caught his eye. He wanted to beckon but knew he couldn't. She would feel insulted by that. But he had to do something.

'Luke?' said Miranda.

He glanced at her, then back at the old woman, pleading with his eyes.

'Luke?' said Mum.

He turned and looked at her.

'Luke? Miranda's wondering about the dedication for the Scriabin étude.'

'Loved that piece,' said Roger. 'Beautiful. Never heard it before.'

'But who was it dedicated to?' said Miranda. 'Who was the friend with the husband?'

'It was me,' said a voice behind them.

Luke turned with a start and saw Mrs Little standing there. The others turned, too, and looked at her. Mrs Little's eyes moved warily from face to face.

'Mrs Little,' said Mum. She stepped forward and held out her hand. 'I'm sorry. We've never really spoken, have we?'

'I don't think we have,' said Mrs Little, taking the hand and shaking it.

'And now I find you know Luke. Obviously . . . pretty well. It just shows how much . . . I mean, how little we . . . ' Mum turned to Luke. 'You never told me you'd even met Mrs Little.'

313

'It's only happened recently,' said Mrs Little. She glanced at Luke, then looked back at Mum. 'Jason Skinner and the other two were always hanging round The Grange. I think they were planning to break in or something, and they obviously wanted to get Luke involved. But he never did. He and I got friendly instead. He was at my house on the days he was truanting. I've got a piano that never gets played and I told him about my husband who died in the war. He was an airman who used to fly out of Biggin Hill. He got shot down over Beachy Head. But he used to play the piano to me, especially that Scriabin étude. So Luke truanted just to come round and play the piano for me. I can't tell you how much that meant to me.'

'Or me,' Luke said quickly, and their eyes met again.

'And I think,' Mrs Little said, still watching his face, 'that the other boys did what they did to Luke because they were angry with him for not helping them break into the house.'

Luke looked into her face and saw the faintest smile there. Out of the corner of his eye he saw Mr Harding watching him, too. The old man spoke. 'And what of the last piece, Luke? I don't think I know that one. Who was it by?'

Luke looked round at him and knew at a glance that the old man was fully aware of the answer; but he gave it anyway. 'It was by Stanton, Mr Harding.'

'I thought it might be.'

'Stanton?' said Roger. 'Matthew or Luke?'

'Both,' said Luke, but Mr Harding shook his head.

'I think not.' The old man glanced at Roger. 'I think you'll find it's a piece for Matthew, by Luke. Right, Luke?' And Luke smiled. Mr Harding reached out and patted him on the arm. 'And I must say the piece was an absolute dream.'

There was a loud murmur of agreement from the others.

'Thank you,' said Luke.

'And can we expect more such dreams in the future?' said Mr Harding.

Luke could already hear them singing in his head. 'Watch this space,' he said.

'I will,' said Mr Harding; then he gave a sigh. 'You know, I'm beginning to think my plans to retire to a mossy little cell in Norfolk might just be a little premature. Especially now there's a new Stanton on the loose. Ah, well . . . ' He turned to Mrs Little. 'It's so nice to meet you after all this time. I don't know why we haven't really bumped into each other before. It's probably my fault—I get so wrapped up in my own little affairs. Anyway, we must meet up before I set off for Norfolk. If you'd like that, I mean. I don't want to push it. But it would be nice to have a proper chat with you.'

'I'll be moving back to India in a few months,' she said. 'I've already put the house on the market.' Her eyes met Luke's again, then flickered back to Mr Harding's. 'But that would be nice. You'd be welcome at The Grange.' She looked round at them all. 'You all would. I'd like it if you came.'

'So would we,' said Mum. 'And Luke can play the piano for you again. I'm sure he won't mind.'

'He won't have much time for playing now,' said Mr Harding. 'He'll be too busy composing his next magnum opus.' The old man winked at Luke, then leaned across and said: 'And I meant that.'

'I know you did,' said Luke.

They all moved off towards the door, Mr Harding now deep in conversation with Mrs Little. 'I wasn't far from Biggin Hill myself during the war,' he was saying. 'I didn't do any of the brave stuff like your husband. I was based at . . . ' And the two of them went on talking as though they had known each other for years. Luke hung back,

315

trying to make sense of all that had happened, but especially of the strange feelings that were flooding his heart. He was happy—that much he knew—yet still something nagged inside him. That strange restlessness and feeling of vulnerability remained; and once again, it was as though something was calling him; something too powerful to resist. Miranda walked silently beside him and he was glad that she was there.

The others reached the door ahead of them and walked out into the night, then stopped and gathered for a moment. Back in the hall Mrs Foley and her helpers were already busy putting away the chairs and tidying up the hall. Luke and Miranda joined the others outside.

'Stars are out,' said Mr Harding, gazing up.

'Beautiful,' said Mum. 'Full moon, too.'

'Mrs Little and I are going back to have some tea at my house,' said the old man. 'Would the rest of you like to come? You're all very welcome.'

'That's very kind,' said Mum. 'But I think . . . ' She glanced at Roger. 'I think perhaps it's a bit late.' Roger smiled at her, then looked over at Mr Harding.

'Thanks all the same, Mr Harding,' he said.

'We'd love to come,' said Mr Davis, 'but I'm afraid we'll have to get back to The Toby Jug. We've got Philip looking after the bar and he's not confident at the best of times.'

'I quite understand.' Mr Harding beamed round at them all, adjusted his bow tie, then looked back at Mrs Little. 'Looks like it's just us, then.'

'It does,' she said.

And with a smile of goodnight, the two of them set off in the direction of Mr Harding's house. Mum turned to Luke, but he spoke first. 'Mum? I'm not ready to come home yet.'

'It's OK.'

'I just need to—'

'Be by yourself.' She smiled. 'It's OK. I understand. Come home when you're ready. Do you want me to take the music back for you?'

'Thanks.' He handed her the Scriabin. 'Only . . . ' He glanced at Miranda and tried to phrase the question he wanted to ask. Mrs Davis answered it for him before he could even speak.

'Miranda can stay out, too,' she said. 'She's as high as a kite anyway after her performance.' She leaned forward and kissed her daughter. 'Aren't you, sweetheart?'

Miranda smiled back at her.

'We'll see you later,' said Mrs Davis, and the others moved off, leaving Luke and Miranda alone. He waited until everyone had disappeared round the corner of the lane, then turned and looked at her.

'What is it, Luke?' she said. 'You look kind of strange. Is something not right?'

'I don't know what it is.' He frowned. 'I don't know that something's not right. It might be the opposite. It might be that . . . something's very right. I just don't know. Sorry, I'm not making much sense.' He thought for a moment. 'Miranda?'

'Yes?'

'There's somewhere I want to go. Somewhere really important. Will you come with me?'

And she nodded at once.

33

The forest was silent and still. No wind stirred the leaves. No owls called. No scampering paws or beating wings disturbed the tranquillity. It was as though everything slept all around them. They walked through the trees, neither speaking, their footsteps as soft as their thoughts. Above them, through the great unmoving canopies, they could see the night sky, creamy with stars. They walked on, close to each other, yet each deep in silence, like the forest. And as Luke walked, he found himself thinking of Barley again, and how he had carried her this way only a short while ago.

He wondered where she was now. Sleeping, no doubt, or so he hoped. She had not slept much of late; but now, perhaps, she would be happy again. Like him. And yet this other thing—this restlessness, this vulnerability, whatever it was—still stopped him from settling. It was a relief to have Miranda so close beside him. They walked on through glades brightened by the moon, both still locked in their own thoughts, and finally neared the clearing where the injured tree waited for them. Luke stopped suddenly.

'Wait.'

Miranda stopped, too, and looked at him. 'What's wrong?' she said.

He stared towards the clearing. He was sure he had seen some kind of movement close to the base of the oak. But who would be out here at this time of night?

'Luke?' she said. 'Are you all right?'

He caught another movement by the tree, and this time the distinct outline of a figure standing close to the trunk. Someone was there; he was sure of it. Or was it . . . ? He looked again. Was it just a trick of the night? Miranda clearly hadn't seen anything. He wondered whether they should turn back.

'Luke?' Miranda moved closer and he saw the fear in her face. 'Something's wrong,' she said.

'No, it's not,' he said quickly. 'Nothing's wrong. It's OK, but—look, can you just stay here for a moment?'

'I thought you wanted to go and see how the tree was.'

'I do but—'

'You want to be by yourself for a bit. Just you and the tree. It's OK. I understand.'

He looked at her gratefully. She couldn't have been more wrong—he wanted her with him more than anything else in the world right now—but at least her misjudgement gave him a reason to keep her safely out of harm's way while he checked out the tree. And he had to check out the tree; and whatever or whoever was there, too.

'I won't be long,' he said.

'It's OK. I'll wait here.'

'Will you be all right?'

'Of course I will.' She touched him on the arm. 'You'll only be about fifty yards away. Stop worrying.'

'I'll be back soon.'

'Stop worrying, Luke. It's OK. I understand.'

'I'll see you in a minute,' he said, and set off through the trees towards the clearing, his eyes fixed on the old oak, and the strange figure standing by the base. And it was a figure. He could see that clearly now, a dark figure, turned away from him, the face close to the bark of the tree, as though studying the damage done to it. Luke stopped at the edge of the clearing and watched. Still the figure did not turn but went on staring at the tree. Who was this person? He thought of calling out, while keeping his distance, just in case it was an enemy. But as he watched, he sensed that it was not. Indeed, he sensed, even as he studied the black form of this unknown person, that all his restless yearnings, all his fears, all his vulnerabilities had somehow been drawing him to this place, this moment. He walked forward, slowly, across the clearing and up to the tree, and as he drew near, the figure seemed to hear him, and turned; and he found himself gazing upon the moonlit face of his father.

It was so clear and so close and so familiar Luke felt they had never been apart. It was almost as though they'd been out for a night-time walk together and had come to this place, as they used so often to do, to see their favourite tree. Luke looked on, trembling, and Dad looked back, his eyes warm and bright and alive, a wistful smile playing round his lips. Luke moved closer, and closer, until their faces were only inches apart; and still the eyes watched him quietly, still the smile played round the mouth. 'It's OK,' Luke murmured. 'I'm going to be all right.' And in that moment the face and body before him started to fade. He stared, still trembling, at the evanescent form of his father, yet still, even as it faded and the image of the tree pushed through the space where it had been, he felt Dad's eyes watching him, and the smile playing round his lips. And then all was gone. He felt a moment of stillness, of peace, of beauty; then of shock, disbelief, panic. With a moan of despair he reached out to hold the figure that was not there; and found himself embracing the tree instead. Behind him a voice called his name. He turned, tears running down his cheeks, and saw Miranda standing there, the moon bright upon her face, just as it had been on Dad's.

'Luke,' she said softly, and she held out her arms.

320

He ran towards her and pulled her to him, and they held each other tight. She felt warm and full of love. She stroked his back, his neck, his hair. 'It's OK,' she whispered. 'It's OK, it's OK.' He was sobbing now, so violently he felt it would tear him apart, and she went on holding him, stroking him, whispering all the while; and then she was kissing him, on the neck, on the cheek, on the mouth, softly, tenderly, and he was kissing her back, kissing and crying, kissing and crying, his heart pounding like a drum; and then they stopped kissing and just held each other. He was still crying, quietly now, and he could feel tears on her cheek, too, though whether they were his or hers he did not know. He dug his face into her neck and pulled her closer, drinking in her glistening beauty. She was breathing hard and so was he, and it was all he heard in the stillness of the forest. Behind him the old oak stretched up and over them like a great wounded hand.

'Don't let go of me,' he murmured.

'I won't.' She held him tight. 'And don't let go of me either.'

He pulled her closer still, then stiffened. Sounds were reaching over him again like echoes down the dark: sounds of the forest, of Miranda and himself standing here; sounds of Barley and Mrs Little and Mum and Roger and everyone he had ever known; sounds of Dad, sounds of spirits he could not see yet sensed even now dancing around them; sounds of music he'd heard and music that was yet to come, welling up from deep within him; and beneath and around all this the flute-songs and harp-songs and bell-songs and all the buzzing melodies of creation, woven together in the deep, booming roar he now knew so well. He realized then that Mr Harding was right. These sounds were not here to harm him but to comfort him. He clutched Miranda and closed his eyes and looked through the darkness into the gold and the blue within his brow, and saw the white star open like a lotus; and the song of the firmament went on around him, within him, everywhere.

He felt Miranda's lips on his cheek and turned his head, seeking her mouth again, and they kissed, softly, then, still holding each other, drew back a little and rested foreheads together. 'You're still crying,' she said. She reached up and stroked his face. 'It's all right. You're going to be OK.'

'I know,' he said.

She went on stroking his face, then stopped suddenly and gave a sigh.

'What is it?' he said.

'It's so sad about the tree.'

'Don't worry about the tree.' He ran a hand through her hair. 'The tree's going to be OK, too.'

'Roger thinks it's going to die.'

'It's not going to die.'

'How do you know?'

He listened again to the sounds, and a picture came to him of that other girl he had held in his arms: the girl who was as light as air. And her words came back to him.

'Tree singing,' he murmured.

'What?' said Miranda.

'Tree singing.' He looked into Miranda's eyes. 'It's singing. It's waking up again. It's been hurt but it's going to mend.'

'How do you know?'

'I can hear it.'

'I can't.'

'It's like a low murmuring sound.'

He saw her watching him with the same quiet smile she had had back in the concert; the same quiet smile Mrs Little had had; the same quiet smile Dad had had just a moment ago, and no doubt still had, wherever he was now. A quiet, loving smile. And he found himself smiling back at her in just the same way. She drew him close and kissed him again; then, without a word, they took each other by the hand, turned as one, and set off through the darkling forest.

Other novels by Tim Bowler

Storm Catchers
ISBN 0 19 275200 6

Winner of the South Lanarkshire Book Award
Winner of the Stockport Libraries KS3 Award

'Tell a soul and she's dead. We'll be in touch.'

Fin is devastated by guilt when his sister, Ella, is kidnapped. He should have been there to look after her, to save her from whoever snatched her from their isolated family home in the middle of a raging storm. And he should have looked after Sam, too, his little brother, not left him to go wandering on the cliff top, playing with an imaginary friend, and trying to 'catch the storm' as it blows out to sea.

As the kidnappers make their demands, Fin's guilt is replaced by a fierce determination to find his sister, by whatever means he can, and bring the criminals to justice. But as the drama unfolds, and long-held secrets are revealed, Fin begins to realize that Ella is not the only victim and that the real villain may be closer to home than he thought.

'That rare thing—a thriller that makes you think. It's a powerful mix of suspense and subtlety.'
> *Gillian Cross*

'It's heady stuff, full of atmosphere, energy and emotional shrapnel.'
> *Guardian*

'Thrillers don't come much more suspenseful than this. *Storm Catchers* is an intelligent and compulsive read from the first page to the last.'
> *Waterstones Book Quarterly*

'Suspenseful and scary.'
> *Sunday Times*

'Bowler's latest classic is a psychological thriller that's every bit as classy as the works of Barbara Vine.'
> *Guardian*

'I didn't have a particular favourite part—I loved it all! This book keeps you on the edge of your seat the whole way through, and urges you to want to read on.'
> *Teen Titles*

River Boy
ISBN 0 19 275158 1

Winner of the Carnegie Medal
Winner of the Angus Book Award

When Jess's grandfather has a serious heart attack, surely their planned trip to his boyhood home will have to be cancelled? But Grandpa insists on going so that he can finish his final painting, 'River Boy'. As Jess helps her ailing grandfather with his work, she becomes entranced by the scene he is painting. And then she becomes aware of a strange presence in the river, the figure of a boy, asking her for help and issuing a challenge that will stretch her swimming talents to the limits. But can she take up the challenge before it is too late for Grandpa . . . and the River Boy?

'*River Boy* has all the hallmarks of a classic . . . You are not the same person at the end of this book.'
Carnegie Medal judges

'A superbly written, well-crafted story.'
School Librarian

'Haunting, poetic and written with great feeling.'
Mail on Sunday

'Beautifully written and brimming with startling imagery.'
Junior Education

Shadows
ISBN 0 19 275159 X

Winner of the Angus Book Award
Winner of the Lancashire Children's Book of the Year Award

Jamie knows what to expect if he doesn't win: his father is obsessed with the idea that Jamie will become a world squash champion, and succeed where he had not. But Jamie doesn't share his father's single-minded ambition and is desperate to escape from the verbal and physical abuse that will follow when he fails.

Then he finds the girl hiding in his shed, and in helping her to escape from her past and the danger that is pursuing her, he is able to put his own problems into perspective. He realizes that he can't run away for ever—he must come out of the shadows and face up to his father, however painful the process might be.

'Tim Bowler scores again . . . a real page turner.'
The Bookseller

'It is exciting and sensational. It is moving and caring.'
Books for Keeps

Dragon's Rock
ISBN 0 19 275219 7

Benjamin remembered leaning back and resting, and rocking to the motion of the train. And closing his eyes.

The next moment it was upon him, racing like an angry fire through the landscape of his sleep. He ran, gasping for air in the stifling heat of its breath, but it was no good. He could feel it drawing closer, roaring its fury after him. Any moment now he would have to face it and suffer for the wrong he sensed he had done it.

Sleep had become a place of fear, a place where the dragon hunted him. But now he had a chance to go back, back to Dragon's Rock and put things right. And perhaps then the dragon would leave him alone.

'Likely to appeal to confident readers who enjoy a blend of fantasy and realism.'
> *School Librarian*

'A nightmarish chiller.'
> *Times Educational Supplement*

'This book was a brilliant read'
> *Teen Titles*

Midget
ISBN 0 19 275218 9

Winner of the Belgian Boekenwelp Award
Winner of the New York Library Book of the Teen Age

Locked in himself, locked in the body he hates, Midget still keeps thinking of the dream. The dream that they told him he could never have—the boat with the sail bent on the boom, the boat plunging out through the water with Midget at the helm, away from the shore, away from the darkness and the pain.

'A masterly handling of suspense and cold trickling horror.'
> *Sunday Telegraph*

'A risky and powerful novel.'
> *Times Educational Supplement*

'A powerful, disturbing, highly original story.'
> *Junior Bookshelf*